MIDLIFE MAYHEM

SUE HAWLEY

Cover designer: James Price, The Author Market
Interior Layout: James Price, The Author Market
All rights reserved.
ISBN-13:978-0-9997678-2-5

DEDICATION

This book is dedicated to my seven grandchildren. They are precious, and they bring joy and laughter to our family. I want each of them to realize life itself is the greatest teacher, to enjoy the twists and turns of our personal journeys, and to live it to the fullest. Laughter brings us closer to heaven and while there are the occasional tears, you never know what's around the corner bringing fresh perspective for us to savor.

CONTENTS

ACKNOWLEDGMENTS

I have no idea how I managed before my publicist, Sandy Lawrence, slipped into my life. Actually, I wasn't managing! I had no idea how to promote my work or what my next steps should be as a writer. She has guided me, held my hand through the confusion and, become a treasured friend. She has taught me much concerning the world of publishing and is fearless when it's time to try something different. While I may carefully allow one toe in the waters, she joyfully dives in to learn new concepts and ideas. I wouldn't want to walk this road without her. Thank you, friend..

CHAPTER 1

The phone rang as I walked in from the backyard. I frowned, shooting a quick glance toward the woods to make sure there was no signs of trouble brewing. Wiping sweat from my face, I answered the phone before the racket drove me nuts.

"Hello?" I said, realizing my sweaty hands were caked with dirt. The dirt from my hands now smeared my face thanks to my brain being on vacation... yuck. Thankfully, this sweat was earned gardening in the summer heat rather than from my dreaded hot flashes. Those experiences were tolerable in the winter when I could step outside in subzero weather—it was a relief to know it only took a few minutes before I could *feel* the cold temperatures. Summer didn't allow for relief, merely more sweat. I'll be happy when my internal thermometer begins working correctly again ... probably sometime around the age of ninety—judging by the way my menopause experience is progressing.

A sweet voice came on the line. "Peg? This is Amy."

"Okay, what's up?" I glanced around, searching for a towel I could use for my disgusting hands. I wasn't about to ruin good kitchen towels—they are too hard to find nowadays—even expensive kitchen stores are selling cheap, thin towels. What's their problem? Drying dishes takes a sturdy fabric that actually absorbs water rather than smushing it around ... jeez.

"I didn't want you to forget our class today," she informed me. Amy is my widowed, eighty-something-year-old neighbor. She is also a retired schoolteacher and secret genius. A few months ago, she talked me into taking self-defense classes, which came in handy due to the nature of our part-time job—we were now official consultants to our local police department.

I sighed. "Let me get cleaned up, and I'll be right over."

"I knew changing the time from early morning to afternoon was a bad idea," she scolded.

Our classes were originally scheduled for eight in the morning, but ... I'm barely conscious at that point in the day, due to the fact pieces of my body wake up on their own schedules. After much arguing, Amy agreed to an afternoon time slot. Secretly, I hoped the afternoon schedule would bother her to the point of quitting, but for someone her age, she had the energy level of a plugged-in four-year-old. She was going to eventually kill me with her get-up-and-go attitude.

"Well, you need to hurry, or we will be late."

I could hear the irritation in her voice but refused to react. "Yep, just a few minutes ... I promise."

I hung up and got myself into the shower. Somehow, I managed to get ready to go in record time. I checked myself in the mirror to make sure I was presentable to the outside world. Quickly inspecting the roots of my hair, I was relieved to see no massive amounts of gray peeking through— the box hair dye I've used for decades still worked like a charm. I yanked on my blouse. While smoothing out the pesky wrinkles, I noticed a few pounds somehow managed to sneak back into my life ... jeez. At five feet, one inch, even a couple of pounds shouted their presence from the hilltops ... so unfair.

I despise the classes, and I hate the fact that they probably saved our lives on a few occasions. Amy would never quit now. Her increasing dedication made it so she severely opposed chopping our time spent at the studio. The owners, who were well-known to us, watched our bickering with obvious enjoyment. My mood did not improve on the drive over to Amy's.

I honked the car horn once, then made it to her front door before I noticed movement in the woods behind her house ... uh-oh.

Amy came stomping over to meet me. Her lips formed a thin line of disapproval—she was irritated with my negative attitude. I ignored the silent criticism as I turned and headed back to the car. Once she was firmly planted in the seat next to me, I pointed to the woods. "Extra activity out back?"

"Oh dear! Can you see them?" Anxiety flashed across her face as her naturally curly hair quivered with worry. "It can't be good if the guys are visible to you."

The 'guys' are a band of dead Indians who live in the woods between our houses. They protect both properties from bad guys. Amy can always see them for some reason, but I can only see them if my safety is at risk—it's a long story.

My stomach flipped, and I could feel sweat form on my upper lip. "I can see movement but no actual forms. Who is out back? Just the Indians?"

She peered through the windshield. "Well ... their numbers have increased from this morning but not by much. Oh dear ... I can see the soldiers too."

British soldiers, who lived a couple of hundred years ago, joined the Indians a few months back. They weren't always around, but if Amy could see them, then there was a reason our surveillance was increasing—not good at all. I still couldn't see the Brits, which was a good sign.

She gave me a worried look. "Have you been contacted?"

I shook my head. "Nope. Not a peep."

Usually when the Indians were restless, I was already aware of the reason. This was the first time I hadn't heard from the group we work with... which consists mainly of dead folks.

"Not even your dad?" Amy didn't frighten easily, but any spirit activity made her cautious. I didn't blame her one bit. My inner radar also moved into high gear.

Dad died when I was a kid, and the incident left a huge hole in my heart. Until recently, I had to live with those feelings. Once I started seeing the nonliving, Dad showed up to help me navigate my new endeavors—it was great having him back in my life. My grandmother, Nana, helped raise me. The fact that I now interacted with the spiritual realm was her doing. Since I'm not one to enjoy complexity in my life, this current way of living was not always what I considered fun. Some of our experiences were downright dangerous, almost to the point of joining my newfound friends in the afterlife.

I sighed. "No ... nothing. I'm surprised even Bob hasn't been by to check on us."

"We need to alert someone that there is something afoot," she said, her determination surfacing.

I watched over Amy like a mother hen. Her advanced years concerned me as we solved problems in our township. Bath Township is approximately twelve miles northwest of Akron, Ohio. Akron was the one-time 'Tire Capital of the World' due to the headquarters for both Goodyear Tire and Firestone Tire residing downtown. Lake Erie, the fourth largest of the Great Lakes, is thirty-nine miles north. We enjoyed our small town and worked diligently to keep it safe. I didn't want Amy hurt or overworked. She had an iron will, but she wasn't getting any younger, and neither was I.

I sat drumming my fingers on the steering wheel, trying to decide which departed soul I wanted to alert, when I heard a slight pop in the backseat.

"Hey, Peg. Hiya, Amy." Bob's bouncy voice filled the car.

"Hi, Bob," I said, glad the decision was made for me. Though not my first choice to call, he was dead, and he was here.

"Bob, are you aware Peg can see activity from the Indians?" Amy asked before I had a chance to speak.

Did I hear a bit of snark in her voice? Wow ... maybe I was having an influence on the old gal.

Watching him from my rearview mirror, I saw his face pale. How dead people pale or blush has remained a huge mystery to me since my adventures with them began. Let's face it, they have *no* blood, so how on earth is it possible?

"Gosh ... I had no idea. I was in the area and thought I'd drop by." His fear seemed to be increasing with every word.

I sighed. "Bob, maybe we should find out what's happening." I noticed he appeared more disheveled than usual, which is never a good sign.

He nodded. "I'll check in with the boss." A small pop again and he was gone. His 'boss' was a powerful spirit by the name of Logan, who lived centuries ago. He wasn't the famous Logan whose statue is somewhere in West Virginia. My Logan borrowed the name, with permission, simply because it was easier for those of us with heartbeats to pronounce. His real name must be a humdinger, but he never shared much of his personal history. He won't even pinpoint when in history he walked the earth— private sort of fellow.

Amy glanced at me. "Should we go to class or wait?"

It was not a hard decision for me. "I think we should wait. I'll call the guys and let them know why we won't be there. There's no sense in letting them worry about us."

She nodded. "You're probably right. I will miss the exercise though."

A small sense of guilt began creeping in. Bob could find us anywhere we went, so canceling class was technically cheating. I was tired from working in the garden, and I hate those darn classes! I don't think I was fooling Amy, but she refrained from chastising me. If I were her, I would have made any number of snide remarks—she has way more manners than I do. I dug through my purse for a few minutes, nabbed the cell phone, and made the call.

"What did you do for the Fourth?" I asked, deciding to fill our wait time with chitchat. Andy and I invited Amy to watch July Fourth fireworks with us from our favorite spot in Montrose—a busy intersection about a mile from our house. Twenty years ago, it was a sleepy junction with little traffic. Today, it enjoyed every fast food joint known to mankind. It was close to where the fireworks were set up, and if you arrived early enough, you got a front-row seat. The deciding factor for choosing that particular spot was the fact that there was plenty of burger places with bathrooms—four pregnancies had blown my bladder to smithereens.

She started to squirm, causing my eyes to narrow. "Not much, really. I went over to a friend's house for a nice dinner." She paused. "We did go to the fireworks. They were spectacular!" she added with a touch of glee.

I frowned. "You've never been to see the fireworks before?"

She shook her head. "Oh, no. Albert thought they were too dangerous to be near. Now that I've seen how careful they are, I think Albert was wrong."

I kept my big mouth shut, but the more I heard about her deceased husband, the more I hated the jerk. The only decent thing he ever did for her was leave her in fantastic financial shape. I suspected his assumption was that he would outlive her and have all the lovely money to himself. Having a heart attack served him right!

Another pop in the backseat. "Logan's on his way. We aren't aware of any problems in the area." Bob sounded worried, but I wouldn't react unless his boss was disturbed ... then I would sweat.

I opened the car door. "Come on, Amy ... no use sitting in the car if there's to be a meeting."

Nodding, she followed my lead, and we made our way into her house. I'd only been inside a few times, and I enjoyed the layout of her home. Built in the fifties, it was a great deal newer than the century old farmhouse Andy and I lived in for most of our married lives. She had wall-to-wall carpet, a dishwasher, and no wallpaper. I had a love-hate relationship with wallpaper. It can be beautiful, but when you get sick of it, redecorating is a prenominal pain in the butt.

Once inside, she headed toward the kitchen. "Might as well make us a cup of tea."

I sighed. "Sure ... sounds great." I was a coffee gal myself, but Amy loved tea. She drank teas of every flavor and color. I hoped she didn't reach for the green stuff—I hated it.

She puttered around her kitchen humming to herself as she prepared our refreshment. Watching her, I marveled at how young she looked recently. I wondered if consulting for the township's police department gave her a new lease on life. Our police department is on the small side, but we have less than ten thousand people living in the township, so I suppose we don't need a huge law enforcement agency.

Bob didn't follow us into the house, and I was curious where he went. He was one of the victims in the first case I worked, and while he is irritating most of the time, I have a soft spot for him ... usually. Knowing he works for Logan helps me not worry about the poor guy, but he still has to watch out for his wife, Elaine. She had been a piece of work while alive, dead… she hooked up with the bad guys on the other side. It wasn't a good situation, but Bob grew personal strength working for Logan. Elaine still unnerved him, but he was learning to either avoid her like the plague or put up a good front if he found himself in her vicinity. I was looking forward to the day he smacked the nasty sneer off her face, but maybe my goals for him were a tad too high—time will tell.

Dean Martin's voice rang out from Amy's purse, making me jump in surprise. Frowning, I looked over at her. It was obvious she was ignoring the noise, but I was intrigued to see her blushing. "Interesting ringtone. When did you get a cellphone?"

"Hmm?... A few weeks ago. So convenient, don't you think?" She worked hard to avoid my expression.

"What made you decide you needed a cellphone?" I persisted. Amy wasn't technologically stupid, but to my knowledge, she never expressed an interest in having a cellphone. So … why now?

"Oh … you know … just in case." She continued preparing the tray with our tea. She must have watched way too many British shows because she always made such a big deal out of a simple cup of tea. I throw a tea bag in a cup and pour hot water on the darn thing. Amy uses loose tea leaves, and she has a special teapot with a little strainer that catches the pesky leaves as she pours our tea. She has a beautiful tray that holds cups, saucers, the teapot, the sugar, and the cream. If you want cream at my house, you darn well better get off your butt and make your way to the fridge to grab the milk.

"Just in case? Of what … exactly?" I was pushing boundaries here, but my curiosity was certainly growing by leaps and bounds.

Placing the tea tray on the table, she sighed. She opened her mouth to answer but a pop saved her.

"I'm back! Logan is discussing the situation with his gang out back." Bob used his thumb to point to the woods.

I nodded. "Where did you go to find Logan?"

His left shoulder raised a bit. "Can't say right now … maybe later."

Bob started keeping secrets a few months back due to 'need-to-know' malarkey. I thought he was taking his job with Logan too seriously, but Andy got a kick out of Bob's enthusiasm for his new role. Not too long ago, Bob would've never kept a secret from me—he'd bounce off the walls as he told me everything and anything. Now, ever since Logan asked him to join his forces, Bob became enthralled with the idea of being a part of Deadsville's spy world. It was aggravating, and it had the potential to make my job harder; not to mention, there was a degree of danger if I was ignorant of certain facts about a case. Logan believed the less I knew, the better. I disagreed and wasn't quiet about the fact.

Amy remained silent during my questions to Bob, but she broke her silence when I was through speaking. "Bob, if we have a problem, isn't it rather unusual for Logan to be unaware of the fact?"

Logan's voice interrupted from behind me. "Peg, can you see the men?"

Sighing at the tone of his voice, I closed my eyes and turned my head toward Amy's huge kitchen window. I slowly opened one eye and snapped it shut. "Yep … but only the Indians. Amy mentioned the soldiers, but I still can't see them."

Logan remained quiet for so long my skin crawled. I opened my eyes again and cautiously looked back at him. "What's going on here?" I demanded.

His eyes slowly met mine, and he shook his head. "An unexpected turn of events."

Uh-oh. *Unexpected* was not a word I wanted to hear. If Logan was taken by surprise, the situation was grim.

"How unexpected?" I hoped he had more to offer.

Ignoring me, Logan turned to Bob. "Please alert our friends. I may need them soon."

Bob nodded. "You got it, boss." He was gone in a split-second.

"Our friends?" I asked. "Are you referring to my trio?" My life had been protected more than once by my trio of mobsters. Anthony, Santino, and Bill worked for an old mob guy by the name of Sal Spanelli. On the surface they might appear to be criminals, but they have secretly worked with Logan for years. I met Sal during the last case when his cuckoo son went off the deep end. Bob accidentally leaked the huge secret that the trio actually worked for Logan, which made my affection for them easier to emotionally handle. I did feel guilty as hell for liking them because they were in the mob, but once I knew Logan was involved, I relaxed. Our chief of police, Jack Monroe, still had mixed feelings concerning their activities. I understood his dilemma; they *were* officially working for a mobster even if their boss was helping Logan. The perplexities of the situation could make your head spin, but it made a certain amount of sense.

Logan smiled. "Yes, Peg … your trio. They may come in handy. It helps to allow them time to prepare themselves."

"Do you always 'alert' them?" This was news to me—I assumed they were ready at all times.

Reading my thoughts correctly, Logan continued, "They have responsibilities to more than just me. Their business, their job with Salvatorio, and their private lives."

"Private lives?" I was stunned. It never occurred to me the guys had private lives. They were always available when called, so I never considered they had any time for personal involvements.

"They have no serious relationships, but even casual acquaintances must be handled carefully," Logan informed me.

"Yes, they should," Amy said as she tapped her finger on her teacup, thinking. She looked at me. "Peg, maybe we should invite them to dinner one night."

I frowned. "Okay, why?"

"We take them for granted. They treat us so well, we should let them know how much we appreciate their sacrifices."

Sacrifices? I was confused but shrugged. "Sure, why not?"

She shook her head thoughtfully. "They have no wives, children, or extended families. Well, Santino does since he works for his uncle … but we need to give them a sense of family."

Oh dear, here we go. Amy had no children, but her maternal instincts had been fulfilled while she taught high school. Her retirement closed that particular door, but if she wasn't careful, she'd be mothering everyone who came through the door. I noticed she and Laura Spanelli, Sal's daughter-in-law, had grown very close over the past few months—once the case was solved. Laura needed a mother figure, and Amy needed a daughter; it worked out nicely. I worried she'd adopt our trio. I needed them to be on their toes and not wondering what was for dinner.

I looked over at Logan and stuck out my tongue when I saw his grin. He knew exactly what would happen when he brought those two lonely women together, and he probably realized Amy would be mothering everyone who came along her path … the stinker.

CHAPTER 2

I looked at Logan, determined to stay focused. "So, what's going on here?"

He shook his head. "I do not know. The lack of knowledge concerns me."

Crap … if Logan was worried, then I could officially sweat. I wanted him to be all-knowing. Facing the fact that he wasn't omniscient made me want to throw up. In the past, Logan had a handle on the heart of a matter, but this time, it appeared he didn't know squat. This was unfamiliar territory for me, and I didn't like it one bit.

"You want me to call Jack? Maybe there's some incident you think is insignificant but it's really a wreck."

He thought a moment before nodding. "I agree. Thank you."

I was digging around in my purse for my cellphone when Dean Martin began singing again. I looked pointedly at Amy. "Just answer the damn thing!"

Growing red, she reached into her tidy purse and pulled out the phone, answering it. "Yes?"

I hated to admit it, but while I was pawing through the mess in my purse, I had my ears glued to her conversation. Snooping, being nosey, or just being all-around curious whatever you want to call it—I was it.

She shot me a nervous glance. "No, I'm fine. I just have a couple of visitors."

I kept digging around even though my fingers already found my phone. It was a well-known fact my purse was home to more junk than I liked to admit. I cleaned it out every once in a while, to make room for important stuff, like my phone, wallet, and assorted bits and pieces. My interest in her phone call was driving me to stall my own call to Jack.

"Yes, it would probably be best. Thank you." Amy ended her call but didn't share any information.

I'm nosey, but not rude, so I didn't ask the question burning in my brain. Who the heck called her?

I pulled my hand out of the mess. "Found it!" I declared. Ignoring the twinkle in Logan's eyes, I punched in Jack's number and listened to the ringing.

"Hey, Jack," I said when I heard his voice.

He immediately responded. "What's wrong?"

"What makes you think something is wrong?" I snapped.

"Peg, *you're* calling me! That never happens unless mayhem is brewing."

"That's so unfair. I called last week when there wasn't mayhem happening!"

"You and Amy were working on something for me, so that call doesn't count." He was holding back a chuckle. He had me, and he knew it.

We worked a couple of minor issues for Jack over the past few weeks. Ever since he talked the trustees into hiring us as consultants, I suspected he was pulling us into any situation he could think of. They didn't argue with him about the consulting job, probably because the two, big, nasty cases we solved didn't find their way onto the front page of the newspaper. The trustees were grateful the township's good name wasn't dragged through the dirt. Jeffrey Dahmer put Bath Township on the map, so to speak, and the trustees wanted to make sure it never happened again. So far, it hadn't been too hard to accomplish. The township with the local cop who spent decades murdering people, along with our mobster issue, would have been a real newsmaker. The fact that we successfully managed both situations quietly *and* kept the stories from being splashed all over the local paper and airwaves, finally convinced them to hire us as part-time consultants. I had a tiny suspicion the mayor of Akron may have also helped them make the decision. Jack and I saved his son's butt from hot water; plus, our proof that the old politician played footsies with the mob probably helped make him an ally. Neither situation would have helped his next campaign—our help kept him in his newly carpeted office downtown.

"Fine ... I can see activity in the woods, but even Logan isn't aware of anything troubling. Do you have any helpful information?" I could almost hear him frown as he mulled over my words.

He cleared his throat. "To be honest, not much. A few break-ins around the township, one drunken brawl in Montrose, and a guy who ran a red light and hit a car turning left."

Since Montrose is our version of Times Square, the traffic can be a nightmare during certain key points of the day. Traffic picks up about midmorning and increases at an alarming rate until well after the dinner hour—it's a headache.

I scrunched my forehead. "Nothing sounds promising. Are you sure there isn't something else?"

My question was met with total silence. I glanced up at Logan, who nodded ... bingo.

Deciding I'd out wait Jack, I kept my trap shut. He was good at his job, but my silent treatment made him squirm.

He sighed. "I can't talk about it."

"Is it an ongoing investigation?" I pressed.

"In a manner of speaking," he muttered.

I drummed my fingers on the handle of my now cold cup of tea, giving him more time to contemplate things. "You know the crime, and you might know the criminal ... you just need to connect the dots?"

"You're in the ballpark, but I really can't say anything on the phone."

"Fine, we are at Amy's. Get your butt over here!" I snapped.

"Peg! I'm up to my eyeballs in work. I can't hurry over to Amy's just because you want me there," he countered.

"Jack Monroe, you may know the reason for all the activity in our backyards. I don't like it any more than you do, but we need to talk ... now."

He sighed. "Is Logan there now?"

I glanced at Logan just to make sure he didn't disappear on me. "Yep."

"Figures." He sighed again. "I'm on my way. Make sure Logan doesn't do his disappearing act, ok?"

I snorted. "I'll try." I couldn't control Logan, and Jack was well aware of the fact. I'm not sure of the hierarchy in the next world, but I'd bet money no one over there controlled Logan either.

"Boss?" Bob broke the silence, looking at Logan. "Do you want me to stay for this? I've got a meeting to attend."

Logan shook his head. "You need to be at the gathering. I will inform you later of any news discovered here."

Bob nodded, then faded away.

Another thing about death ... there are still meetings to attend, social gatherings, and work to be done. As far as I can tell, there is no rest for the weary. I don't know who was more disgusted, Jack or me. My husband, Andy, however, was fascinated by every tidbit he learned concerning the afterlife—I was depressed by it. Let's face it, in my opinion, we've been sold a bill of goods. All the talk about streets of gold, rest, and harp-playing angels ... I've never witnessed one bit of evidence any of that stuff exists.

Amy stood once Bob left. "I'll get us some fresh tea."

I didn't want any more tea, but I didn't want to hurt her feelings. In the past few weeks, I've swallowed more darn hot tea than in my entire life.

I turned toward Logan. "Do you think there's a drug ring?"

He cocked his head slightly. "Why do you believe it is drugs?"

My fingers tapped the table thoughtfully. "Makes sense. They are doing some type of undercover work, I'd bet money. Jack wants to keep it totally quiet, which is why he wouldn't talk on the phone. Drugs are the first thing to jump to mind."

Logan nodded. "Your logic is sound."

Logic? That's Amy's department. To be honest, there isn't a logical cell in my body. If Logan wanted to believe Amy's logic rubbed off on me, I wasn't going to argue with the guy.

I shrugged. "Well, it's the only thing that makes sense."

"You may be correct, Peg," Amy said, filling the teakettle.

Why the woman didn't buy an electric kettle, with all the water she heated for tea, was a mystery to me. The last time we were at the mall, I made sure she knew they existed. As much as I hate shopping, I took her to replenish her makeup supply. She never wore the stuff until recently; now, she slapped it on her face every day. Sean, my favorite makeup artist at the counter, was surprised she came back to buy more lipstick so soon. It never dawned on me that Amy would actually wear it daily. I figured she wouldn't bother. I only took her in the first place to boost her self-image, not to start a new habit. She added a few products—who would have guessed the old girl would love eyeshadow? Now, if we could calm down her wild, curly hair, she'd be set.

I shook my head and forced my wandering brain to focus. "You think? It could be anything."

"I don't know much about these things ... but I imagine a drug bust would take weeks, maybe months, to plan," she answered, still tinkering with the darn teakettle.

I stayed silent, allowing my brain to exercise a little. It wouldn't hurt to actually use a few brain cells rather than trust my gut. Gut reactions have their place, but I was coming to the conclusion that my gut could get me in a lot of trouble—must be all the junk food I love to eat.

"Well, not necessarily." My fingers were still dancing on the table, but I didn't tame them—I let the darn things have some fun every once in a while.

Amy turned to face me. "Surely there must be some type of protocol to follow ... a plan that has been put into place."

I nodded. "Sure. I'm positive there's quite a bit of drug use among the school kids in the township, but I have never known it to be serious enough to need undercover work. Jack's guys could open lockers at the high school and probably find enough to fill a pharmacy."

Amy looked at me. "Peg, honestly ..." She shook her head. "I taught high school kids for almost forty years. I was aware there was quite a bit of drug use, but it wasn't as widespread as you make it sound."

I sighed. "Amy, when our boys were in high school, I learned even parents indulged at their kids' parties. It was shocking, but we managed to keep our kids out of most of the activity. Well ... maybe not Bryan, but the other three for sure."

Her brow furrowed. "Bryan? Which one is he?"

"The second one ... brown hair, tall, popular, and a pain in my butt." Actually, Bryan was a decent kid, but those four years of his life almost put Andy and me over the edge. We worried about him and kept his butt as busy as humanly possible—he was the reason I had to start coloring my hair. I went so gray by the time he graduated, I looked twenty years older than I was ... brat. Now, he's a successful lawyer in Dallas. I'm not sure why he chose Dallas when we have perfectly good places to live around here—could be the warmer weather.

"Was he the one who broke the window in our garage?" she asked.

I shook my head. "Nope, that was Christopher. He was convinced he could throw a ball across the township if he used one of those super bouncy ones." I shook my head as memories flooded my mind. Albert almost sued us over the damn window, even though we paid for the replacement.

Amy smiled. "He was so cute. How old was he when it happened?"

I scrunched my face, trying to remember. "About ten ... I think. He kept us hopping, always dreaming up some scheme he was positive would make him rich."

Amy laughed and turned back to her tea-making process.

The doorbell rang, and with a quick glance at Logan, I knew it was Jack.

As Amy went to answer the door, I turned to Logan. "You really don't know anything?"

He shook his head. "There are many situations I am unaware of in this realm."

"Not good."

He gave a brief nod. "I agree."

Oh, boy! Logan admitting his limitations ... I wasn't happy.

Amy made small talk as they made their way back to the kitchen. Usually, she made us have tea in the dining room, but this time, we remained in her cozy kitchen. There was no wallpaper, instead a lovely shade of mauve that was popular back in the eighties. Her table was small, and unlike my own kitchen table, it was in pristine condition—no scratches, marred spots, or stains. She had a cute stool she stood on to reach her higher cabinets. The first time I spotted it, I was determined to find one of my own. I wasn't much taller than Amy, and I was tired of dragging a chair over every time I needed an item from the top shelf of a cabinet. I still hadn't taken time to buy one, but I did think about it often.

One look at Jack's face told me that I wandered into a pickle. Once built like a linebacker, he was still on the beefy side, but not as fit as he was a few months ago. The gray was gaining traction, overtaking his dark hair by leaps and bounds. These past few months aged him—dealing with dead folks added stress to my old friend.

I flashed him a smile. "What's new?"

His glare made me flinch. Ok … so maybe I stumbled on more than a pickle.

"Good afternoon, Chief," Logan said.

Hearing Logan use Jack's title made me frown. Logan usually only addressed Jack like this when he was unhappy with our chief of police for some reason—I wasn't aware of any hiccups in their relationship.

Jack glanced at him, giving a brief nod. "Logan."

Uh-oh, even Jack had a cool attitude toward my Indian.

"Jack, would you care for a cup of tea?" Amy asked, obviously picking up on the tension.

Tea? Amy was offering Jack, who is absolutely addicted to coffee, tea? Good grief.

His lips formed a thin line, but his tone remained pleasant. "No, thank you, Amy."

Nodding, she poured me a fresh cup. I eyed it suspiciously. "Amy, this isn't the nasty green stuff is it?"

"It's good for you, Peg. Drink up."

I threw my head back, looking at her ceiling. Damn … no cobwebs. Every time I dared look at my own ceiling, I spied new webs as if those sneaky spiders knew exactly when I wasn't going to remember to run the vacuum cleaner up in the corners. I came to the conclusion Amy's house was free of any type of pest—they probably didn't dare bother her.

Sighing, I looked over at Jack. "Ok, what's going on? You look miserable."

Jack studied my face for a few moments before speaking. "You really don't know?"

I frowned, slightly confused. "How would I know? We called because I can see activity out back." I jerked my thumb toward the woods the two properties shared.

Jack continued to watch me carefully. "What type of activity?"

I raised both eyebrows. "What?" I was flustered. "What do you mean? Activity."

"Indians? Or all the other guys?" he pressed.

Jack knew the more dead folks out back, the bigger the problem we faced.

"So far, just Indians. Amy noticed the soldiers have returned though."

Jack looked at the floor, and I stayed quiet. Amy looked at Logan, whose face was grim … jeez.

After a few moments, Jack looked up. "We may have a slight problem."

"How slight and what problem?" I asked.

Jack pointed at Logan. "Your friend here stirred up a hornet's nest, and I'm having trouble keeping a lid on it."

My friend? What in the heck was happening here?

Looking at Logan, I narrowed my eyes. "Logan … what's Jack talking about?"

Logan turned toward the window. Each of my dead friends have quirks I learned to decipher. If Logan turns to look out a window, he is avoiding the conversation. I had to be cautious about how I handle these situations because the dead can easily leave by fading away. I have no power to stop them, a fact they use to their advantage.

Amy intervened, which was fine. Logan respected her a great deal.

"Logan, if we are to help you, we must know details. I appreciate the fact that you have need-to-know rules, but this may be one of those times we need information you may not be fully ready to share."

Logan turned to face Amy and nodded. "Quite true."

Well … great. Amy made a statement of truth … big damn deal. I needed Logan to tell me what was irritating Jack.

I opened my mouth to make a snappy comment, but Amy shook her head. I clamped my lips together and let her continue.

"Yes. What information do you believe you could divulge at this point?"

I had to admit the gal was good. She didn't ask if he would tell us anything at all, she asked what he *could* tell us—smart thinking.

Logan smiled. "There are problems here with drugs."

Jack snorted. "I knew that without your help." Jack had kids the same age as our boys and sweated through their teen years as much as Andy and I did with our boys.

"What you may not realize is the problems you face today are not new."

Jack's frown increased. "What do you mean?"

Logan sighed. "You accuse me of 'stirring a hornet's nest', but there was no need for me to stir this particular nest; it stirs without my help. I merely warned you the drug use has recently increased in the area. I did nothing to cause this development."

"Wait a minute," I cut in. "Go back to the part where you said the drug problem isn't new. Even I know we've had issues for at least fifty years."

Logan shook his head. "No. Fifty years is not the number you should focus upon." He turned back toward the window and continued talking. "Drug use is as old as civilization itself. In ancient Mesopotamia, alcohol addiction was rampant. India, Assyria, and Egypt had opium. Ancient Greece discovered mead. The Romans ..." He paused long enough to shudder. "... received many drugs because of the trade routes."

I swear there was a tear in his eye at this point. I was a little shocked. "Wow."

Logan nodded. "The Aztecs, Mayans, and Incas used many drugs to induce spiritual hallucinations." He snorted.

My eyes widened—this was only the second time I ever heard him emit that particular noise ... sorta beneath him, in my opinion. "I know you were a spiritual man. Did you ever use drugs to help you have visions?" I knew the question could spur his anger, but I had to ask.

He shook his head. "I had no need for drugs. True spiritual visions do not need drugs; they are pure. Those fools who believed drugs helped their experiences were not pure, and they were influenced by the evil that exists on my side of life." He paused. "The same is true today."

"Evil has a door to walk through when drug use is rampant?" Amy asked.

Logan nodded. "Sadly, the use of drugs does not need to be rampant. Much depends on *who* is partaking. A supreme ruler who indulges frequently makes unwise decisions. The Romans proved the truth by their partaking; study their history." He looked sad, which surprised me a little. He noticed my expression and smiled slightly. "Peg, it does sadden me when people indulge in mind-altering elixirs. They fail to understand the mind is fully capable of providing exhilarating experiences without help." He shook his head again. "A type of mental and spiritual laziness."

"Life is so busy today." Amy sighed thoughtfully. "Maybe it is the reason some people decide to take shortcuts."

"Do not be fooled ... life has always been busy. It is no excuse!" Logan growled.

Uh-oh, another noise I seldom hear from my Indian. Maybe he needed a rest from his duties—centuries of cleaning up the world has to take a toll on a person.

"Uh, Logan?" I watched him hesitantly. "You ok?"

Sighing, he turned to me. "Peg, I have been fighting the same battles for hundreds of years. I admit there are times I find myself weary."

My eyes widened, and my mouth dropped open in shock. "Logan, I can't do this work without you."

He turned back toward the window, quietly watching the fresh leaves dance in the breeze.

Jeez Louise.

CHAPTER 3

No one dared make a noise as we sat watching Logan. His attitude was making me nervous, but I couldn't think of anything helpful to say. I looked over at Jack, who allowed both shoulders to rise and fall but shook his head—he was no help at all.

Amy finally broke the silence, not bothering to soften her words. "Logan, I believe your ego has gotten a little out of control."

Even I would never have the nerve to tell Logan he had an ego problem.

Logan's posture became ramrod straight as he listened to her words.

I tried to signal Amy not to continue, but she ignored me. "Unless I am mistaken, you are not God. Quit behaving as though you have the weight of the world on your shoulders." Amy was patting her foot on the floor as she spoke. The darn thing must have been moving about a hundred miles an hour—I'd never seen her so furious. "Your job entails very challenging work, but it is no excuse for self-indulgence." She glared at his back, but I'd bet money he had sight in the back of his head … he's sneaky.

Logan turned slowly to face Amy. His eyes glowed, moving my sweat glands into high gear. I had no idea if his many powers included death rays shooting out of his eyes. I found myself glancing around Amy's kitchen for a safe place to hide.

"I am not accustomed to being spoken to like a mere child." Ice formed around each word he spoke.

"Hmph. Well … it's time someone took you down a peg or two!" Amy snapped.

Good gravy … what's gotten into the old girl? Has she lost her mind? Was all her green tea affecting her famous logical thinking?

Logan raised an eyebrow but said nothing.

"Um … Logan, I think what Amy is trying to say …." I began, but she cut me off.

"Peg, I know exactly what I'm saying! We've been brought in to fight battles that include the spiritual realm. There is power involved that we have very little, if any, capabilities of fighting. Some of us have been injured, and some of us have been placed in dangerous, life-threatening circumstances. Not one of us asked for the job, it was thrust upon us. So, the least Logan can do is behave!"

I pursed my lips but kept them clamped tight. I knew she was referring to Laura, an innocent wife, from the last case we worked for Logan. She endured years of emotional and mental abuse from her insane husband. The dirty little secret was simple … Logan befriended her when she was a lonely child living in an orphanage. As she became an adult, he steered her life in the direction of a mob family. He did it all, so he could destroy the insanity that ran through the DNA of the family. His plan worked, but Laura was still emotionally scarred. Amy and Laura developed a tight relationship—not to mention Laura's only child, Caterina, gained a grandmother. Their relationship was strong and grew stronger each day.

"Andy was injured earlier this summer and so was Peg's mob trio," Jack said, agreeing with Amy. Jack hated my mob guys most of the time. Even I have to admit, the situation was complicated … but it worked.

"I make no apologies." Logan's voice was calm and quiet, but I knew he was angry that his judgments were being questioned.

I decided to speak on Logan's behalf—someone had to defend the guy. "Look, guys … I don't always agree with Logan. Hell … I usually never do, but he's always been there, even if it is at the absolute last second."

Logan cut his eyes to meet mine. "Peg, I do not need your help." I felt my face flush at his tone. "However, … I appreciate your response." He turned to Amy. "You may have valid points. I will not defend my decisions or my plans." He sighed. "It is not ego though. We, on both sides of the veil, have opportunities to act for good. We must be ever vigilant; the enemy must only be perfect once out of a thousand times to be effective." He shook his head. "They have an advantage, we do not."

Amy's wild curls bounced indignantly. "I disagree. We can't be perfect all the time. We do the best we can and call it a day. Evil will never win in the long run."

Logan cocked his head to one side. "How can you be so sure?"

She shrugged. "Scripture teaches us evil will lose in the end."

He paused before speaking. "Faith … you have a great deal of faith in your Christian doctrine."

She nodded vigorously. "Yes, of course."

Logan gave her a small smile. "Good. One of us needs to remain optimistic during these challenging times."

"Oh, pish posh!" Amy waved her hand dismissively at his words. "You yourself said drugs have been around for centuries! These times are no more difficult than Roman times. The world survived that ordeal!"

"True," he conceded, nodding. "However, I see increasingly negative activity on my side of the veil, which leads to more confusion on your side."

Pouring more of the nasty green tea in my cup, Amy continued, "Logan, it isn't the end of the world. Let's focus on the problem right in front of us and not dwell on issues down the road."

"It is my job to guard the future," he countered.

"Guard the future by guarding today!" she snapped.

Gosh … she certainly wasn't backing down. I frowned but kept my trap shut. I didn't start this argument, and I wasn't sticking my nose in this mess. Amy must have some sort of thorn in her side to take on Logan.

"There is much you are unaware of in the spiritual realm." Logan's reply was so quiet I had to strain to hear his words.

"Of course, there is! We …" She waved her hand to include Jack and me. "… have no experience with your side of life. However, we do have plenty of stinkers on our side that eventually find themselves in your territory. Multiply that number through the centuries, and it doesn't take a rocket scientist to realize both realms have problems."

Logan opened his mouth to speak, but she cut him off as fast as a blink. "Oh, I know … 'problems on your side make problems on our side' … we know! We do the best we can, then we hand it over to a higher power."

Logan studied her face for a moment. "Amy, I agree. Those of us who have been given positions of authority must be alert at all times. We take our responsibilities seriously, and we work with much diligence to accomplish our goals."

Amy nodded. "I can see the truth in your words, but I don't necessarily like your tactics."

Logan sighed. "I am aware of your sensitivity, especially concerning Laura."

Uh-oh … was he out of his mind? Mentioning Laura in this discussion was like adding fuel to her already boiling irritation.

Amy narrowed her eyes. "Yes … Laura … it was a rotten situation. The poor girl!"

"She accomplished what no one else would have been able to manage. It was important for her to be part of the family."

Amy's face flushed red hot, and I momentarily feared she was having a stroke. "Really? No other way? I'm sure you could have come up with a better plan."

"There were many discussions. I believe I shared information pertaining to the plan. She was the best person for the job."

"Did you ask her permission? No! You didn't! Did you warn her? Nope!" Amy started patting her foot again, as her fingers danced on the rim of the teapot. If she wasn't careful, her whole body would start shaking soon.

Jack cleared his throat. "Uh ... may I ask a question?"

Relief flowed from my head to my toes as he interrupted their contest of wills.

Logan's eyes swiveled to Jack—I figured he was just as grateful for the break in Amy's fiery conversation. "Yes?"

"Who exactly gave you this job?" Jack held up his hands. "I'm not trying to butt into your personal business, but I'm curious."

Logan turned back toward the window. I was positive he wasn't going to give Jack an answer, but he surprised me. "The spiritual realm has many levels. You have become aware of the lower regions dealing with the spirits who have made contact, such as Bob and Peg's father. However, ... I answer to the highest level in our realm." Exhaling, he continued, "You would call the entity 'God', however, the term does not encompass the entirety involved. There are no words that translate the *truth*, which is why mankind has spent centuries inventing new religions and beliefs."

Well, hell ... with one statement, Logan managed to sweep away religious teachings for the last forty thousand years.

Amy nodded. "Yes ... I understand our comprehension is quite limited, but that fact doesn't negate faith. Faith goes deeper than thinking ... it is part of our very soul."

Logan looked surprised at her statement. "Very astute observation."

Jack scoffed. "Theology is all well and good, but it has nothing to do with the problem!"

I laughed. "You brought it up."

"Sadly, Jack ... theology has everything to do with the present state of affairs," Logan said quietly.

Ah ... he used Jack's name rather than his title. The ice that recently covered their relationship must have melted a tad.

Jack cocked his head slightly. "How so? I'm trying to build a case against drug runners, and you're talking church stuff."

"Oh, Jack! This isn't churchy!" Amy sighed. "Most people don't realize going to church has little to do with their spiritual lives. Albert went to church faithfully, and he was a real stinker."

Jack shook his head. "I don't want to have this conversation right now. Let's focus on the drug issue I'm facing."

Logan nodded. "Yes, the problem needs our attention immediately." He turned to face me. "Peg ... our three friends will be arriving momentarily. I will explain my needs once everyone is comfortable." He turned back toward the window, and I knew he would remain silent until the trio appeared. The guy never was one for small talk, so the three of us sat silently staring at Logan's back.

Amy's doorbell rang a few minutes later, and I knew from Logan's posture that the gang was here. Thank goodness—the silence was giving me the creeps.

They chitchatted as they made their way to the kitchen. I snuck a glance at Jack. He was usually miserable around the mob guys, but he was working hard to overcome his feelings. They helped us more than once, and I think it irritated Jack. His beloved law enforcement wasn't enough to handle those sticky situations. As far as I was concerned, the trio's unique talents certainly came in handy.

"Hey, guys," I said as they entered the kitchen. "Nice to see you anywhere but in your classroom!" The trio owned and operated self-defense studios around the area, and Amy and I stumbled across their studio near us. They were all aware of how much I hate the classes, and they took great delight in my misery.

Santino's laugh bounced boldly throughout Amy's small kitchen. A big man with dark hair and eyes, he was the best looking of the trio. I would classify him as handsome, but the other two couldn't be considered ugly by any stretch of the imagination. Santino had a special place in my heart. "Hey, Mrs. Shaw. Are your bruises healing?"

Every self-defense class blessed me with at least one new purple splotch somewhere on my body. The guys focused more on Amy defending herself in a dicey situation, and I usually ended up being the baddy.

"Not funny," I snapped.

His grin grew wider but disappeared once he spotted Logan. "Logan." He nodded briefly at Logan.

Logan returned the nod, then silently waited as they got settled at the small table.

Amy put a cup of fresh, hot tea in front of each man. They glanced at one another, before smiling their thanks to Amy. I had them pegged as coffee guys. I wondered if they would bother with manners and drink the stuff. I noticed she didn't serve them the crappy green mess ... go figure.

Logan finally spoke, silencing everyone. "Amy has brought up a few thoughts I have determined need to be addressed before we continue." Even though his words were spoken calmly and quietly, I realized Amy's scolding deeply affected the old Indian. "As much as it bothers Peg, it is true ... I am not an all-knowing spirit. I am a human, who once having crossed the veil of earthly life, became a servant to the highest authority." He paused, frowning. "Those of us who have been given assignments to curtail the evil here on earth never lose sight of the fact that the problems begin in our realm. We have many battles that spread to include the living." He turned to Amy. "My responsibilities are vast, but I am not alone in this war. It does weigh on me at times, and I apologize that you witnessed a momentary lack of control."

Amy's eyes grew wide, welling with tears. "Oh, Logan! I was angry with you, but I do have some understanding of the enormous problems you face."

His expression became thoughtful. "Yes ... I believe you have a depth that is rare. It is one of the reasons I chose you. I have no regrets about my decision. You gave wise counsel, and I will take it into consideration."

Wise counsel? All I heard was Amy chewing his butt out. What did he hear that I didn't?

Logan turned to the men at the table. "We have discovered an increase in drug activity. I will allow Jack to explain."

Jack's startled expression told me he didn't plan to make a speech, but he took a deep breath. "We became aware of this issue when Logan ..." he nodded in Logan's direction. "... visited me a few weeks ago with information." He sighed, then continued. "This township has many well-to-do residents. Only one or two have given us problems in the past, but we usually have a handle on the situation. Drugs have been in this area for over forty years ... the problem comes and goes."

"We know all of this," I cut in. "What's new now?"

Jack's shoulders sagged. "Heroin and meth."

Amy frowned. "Those have never been a problem before?"

He shook his head. "Not to this level. We know of two meth labs smack dab in the middle of the township, and we are in the process of collecting evidence." He looked at me. "The exact reason I didn't want to say anything on the phone. We're not too sure how sophisticated the communication and monitoring systems these guys have is, and I didn't want my words snatched out of the airwaves."

The shock hit my body. "Snatched out of the airwaves? They can do that?"

Antonio spoke up. "Mrs. Shaw, technology is advancing so fast we can barely outsmart the bad guys. It gets expensive trying to stay one step ahead of the latest equipment."

I looked at my friend and realized his face was still pale from the injuries he sustained on the last case we worked on together. He almost didn't make it, and without Amy's first aid knowledge, he probably would have died on my lawn. I hoped he was physically up to working. He lost weight and still looked tired, but it obviously wasn't holding him back from this meeting.

"Technology is merely a small part of the problem. Remember, there are those, such as Peg's mother, who strive to insert evil and tear apart the good on earth. We are diligent in our endeavors to control access, but their numbers are increasing with each passing year," Logan stated.

My body sagged at his mention of my mother. She was a real pistol while alive, and dead ... she became worse. There's probably an extensive list of adjectives available to describe her—self-centered would be in the top three. Bob's wife, Elaine, hooked up with my mother, and the two of them took a lot of pleasure from creating chaos and havoc. Not to mention, they were definitely working for the evil side of Deadsville.

Jack looked over at my guys. "You fellows hear anything about drugs in the township?"

Bill looked surprised at the question, but Santino grinned. "Chief, just because we work for Uncle Sal doesn't mean we run drugs."

Salvatorio Spanelli was the head of the mob family, which was based in Youngstown. He also happened to be Santino's uncle. Over the past few decades, their power waned because Spanelli worked with Logan to clean up the situation. His goal was to make the family business legitimate, and he made huge strides. As the Spanelli family receded from criminal activity, gangs filled the void—which took everyone by surprise. Even Logan didn't foresee such a huge wrinkle in his plan.

Jack's face grew a slight shade of pink, but before he could make a retort—which could possibly ruin our meeting—I spoke up, "Santino, maybe you've heard some tidbit through the grapevine."

Antonio spoke up. "As far as we are aware, drugs around here are fading. It concerns me that the chief sees meth ... meth is bad news."

Jack calmed down upon hearing Antonio's words. "Yep. I have no idea why they picked our little township to start their business."

"That's easy," Bill said, and every eye turned to him. "It's quiet here, there's very little criminal activity." He paused. "Except for the occasional nut that falls from an old family tree."

I frowned, slightly confused. "Those weren't highly publicized."

Bill nodded. "Yep. Whoever these people are, they probably weren't aware of any big issues that would draw the eye of the law." He shrugged. "I bet they figured they'd go unnoticed." He looked at Jack. "How'd you stumble across the labs?"

Jack's face closed down, but I kicked him under the table. "Jack, I can almost bet money that before this is all over, we will need the trio's help. You can trust them."

Jack glared at me, then glanced at Logan, who nodded, prompting Jack to continue. "A couple of high school kids got caught selling at school right before the end of the school year ... we didn't think too much about it at the time. Hell ... Akron is only a stone's throw away from here, and they could have easily gotten the stuff there. They have more meth labs in basements than they can keep up with in that city." He shook his head.

"Ok, but how did you find out they didn't buy from Akron?" Bill asked.

Jack scowled. "We started questioning them, which wasn't easy let me tell you! One of their fathers is a lawyer, and he threatened to sue us if we didn't let his kid off the hook."

I could tell his blood pressure was climbing, so I asked the question everyone was thinking. "But they finally fessed up?"

"Oh, yeah, after I threatened them with being charged as an adult. They were both months away from their eighteenth birthdays. That's how we found out we had labs here."

"Why didn't you go arrest these people?" Amy asked, confused.

Jack shook his head. "Because one of the labs is on the property of Tom Newman!"

Antonio let out a long, slow whistle. Bill's mouth dropped open, and Santino grinned.

"Tom Newman? The head trustee?" I stuttered. He was not a well-liked man, but he became head trustee a few years back. When he worked full time at a regular job, he wasn't too big of a problem, but he recently retired and began to drive Jack nuts. Our trustees have normal careers, so their service to the township is in their spare time. I'm sure their lives are a balancing act, but it works. "Is he aware drugs are being cooked on his property?"

Jack shrugged. "No idea. Since it was his land, we decided to go slow and build the case carefully. I don't want any hiccups once we start making arrests."

"Gosh ..." I was at a loss for words.

My phone started screaming. I hadn't dropped it back into the bottomless pit of my purse, so I grabbed it fast. The boys thought it was funny to install different ringtones on my phone the last time they were in town. Since I had no idea how to change them, I finally had to take it to the phone store to get them returned back to normal. I was surprised to see Andy's number on the caller ID, so I answered quickly. "Hey, sweetie. What's up?"

"Where are you?" I could hear tension in his voice.

I frowned. "Over at Amy's. What's wrong?"

"Anyone there with you?" he asked.

"Yeah, tons."

"Dead or alive?" he demanded.

"Both ... Andy, what's wrong?"

He paused before continuing. "If Logan is there, tell him I can see

Indians in the woods."
My mouth fell open in shock.

CHAPTER 4

I looked up at Logan with my mouth still hanging open, but I couldn't muster words. I shouldn't have been surprised when Logan merely nodded his head—face serious and mouth pursed. I was stunned … he changed the rules yet again. He spoke answering my unasked question. "Andy now has the ability to detect those assigned to protect this land." He swept his arm indicating both Amy's and our property.

My mouth snapped shut as thoughts ran through my brain. The big question was … *why?* Logan was ready for the question.

Logan pointed to Amy. "Amy sees them all the time. She alerts us to increased activity." He pointed to me. "Peg, you only see them as the threat level increases for you." He paused, studying my face intently. "I have learned to trust Andy's steady intelligence, which led to the decision."

I narrowed my eyes. "Ok … why?"

One thing I learned about Logan was he never does anything without a darn good reason. He looked out Amy's window, toward her woods. "Considering the increased unrest on both sides of life, and after much discussion, it was decided you needed expanded security."

I raised my eyebrows. "Discussions with who?"

Logan sighed. "Peg, you are well aware I am not the only person involved in situations facing our worlds. Let it suffice to say, your name is often mentioned in our meetings."

A chill ran through my body, which wasn't comforting considering Amy didn't seem to believe in cooling her house much during the summer. Add all the hot tea to the mix, plus menopause, and I should've been sweating.

"Meetings?" My stomach clenched as I fought to keep my emotions under control.

Jack intervened. "If Andy can see Peg's gang out back, what exactly does it signify?"

"Excellent question." Logan paused before continuing. "Andy's ability now alerts us to further complications and developments."

Before I could make a snotty reply, I heard Andy's voice. Surprised, I looked down at the phone in my hand. Oh crap ... I forgot about the poor guy.

"What's Jack saying?" Andy demanded.

My eyes remained glued to Logan as I answered. "Sweetie, I think it would be a good idea if you came over to Amy's house."

"Is Logan there?" His voice was a mix of fear and anger, and I didn't blame him. Acquiring the ability to see the Indians out back must have been a shock. He was used to Bob and Logan but being able to see our protection squad in the woods was a new ability, and they were quite a sight—Indians who lived on the land over two hundred years ago, British soldiers from precolonial times, Vikings who occasionally appeared, along with the odd spirit who walked those woods in the past. The Viking's presence was the rarest of them all.

"Peg, settle down." A familiar voice came from the corner of the kitchen. My eyes drifted over to the sound, and relief washed over me as I focused on my dad leaning against the wall. I was still his little girl, and I felt safer when he was around me. He was back to looking healthy and normal, wearing the plaid shirt I gave him on the last Father's Day he was alive. He didn't possess Logan's extensive powers, but he had his own special power ... he was my dad. He was a balance to my mother's selfish personality. A true narcissist, she had been a demanding mother while alive; dead ... she was dangerous to my health.

Nodding at Dad, I turned my attention back to Andy. "Yep. Come on over. I'm sure Amy will make a fresh pot of tea for you."

"I'll be there in a second," he replied quickly.

Hitting the End button on my phone, I turned to Logan. "Well?"

Rather than answer my question, Logan turned to Jack. "How far have you investigated the situation?"

Jack narrowed his eyes. "We can't seem to discover the main source." He waved his hand, obviously irritated. "The small fish are easy ... they aren't as careful as they believe. We've been able to follow them around the township. I want the big guy who is supplying the materials."

Logan nodded. "Yes."

"We are talking drugs here, right? Only drugs … no murders?" I asked, wanting to clarify what the heck was happening.

"Yep," Jack replied tersely. I studied his face, noticing his jaw was clenched tighter than a drum.

I frowned. "Jack … what's going on?"

Jack sighed. "Somehow, a major drug dealer has moved into our township under our radar. My question for Logan is … how much information did you withhold?"

Logan's eyebrow raised, surprise clear on his face. "Chief, I believed the immediate area to be calm until quite recently. The moment I was aware of a problem I contacted you."

Jack looked away from Logan. "I can't believe you don't know who's behind this mess," he muttered.

"Jack …" Logan's voice was so quiet, I had to lean forward to hear him. "I have been reminded recently that I am not God." He smiled at Amy, whose face became beet red. "I am aware of many matters, but I am not all-knowing. I have my own investigators involved, and I'm sad to say … we are no further in our endeavors than you."

Jack looked at Logan. "You're investigating? Since when? And why didn't you tell me?"

Sighing, Logan raised a hand to quiet the questions. "First, you are angry because I do not know the culprit, now you are upset I sent my own agents to examine those involved." He shook his head. "You cannot have it both ways."

Amy placed a cup of tea in front of Jack while he was arguing with Logan, and Jack absentmindedly picked it up and took a healthy sip. Gagging and sputtering, he eyed the liquid in the cup. "What the hell is this stuff?"

Unbothered by Jack's reaction, Amy smiled kindly. "Green tea. It helps cleanse the toxins from your body. Drink it all."

Jack's look of disbelief would've been hilarious under different circumstances. Jack turned his stunned face to me.

I held up a hand. "Don't look at me. She forces this crap down my throat constantly."

"Peg! I don't force you, I encourage you!" Amy exclaimed, turning to answer the knock on her kitchen door.

Andy's worried face looked through the window in the door, and I suddenly felt protective toward my sweetie pie. I stood. "I'll get it, Amy." Opening the door, I grabbed Andy's hand and squeezed it tightly. "Come on in, Logan will explain."

"There are a ton of people milling around the woods! Can you see them?" His voice was laced with fear, and I completely understood. He was injured during our last big case, and he didn't want a repeat concussion.

"So far, only the Indians," I answered, standing on my tiptoes to give him a quick peck on his cheek. Andy is almost a foot taller than I am, which makes us look odd together—but it works for us. His blue eyes looked down at me, but no smile appeared.

Andy turned toward Logan. "Why now?"

"Andy, why don't you sit down. I'll get you a cup of tea," Amy offered, hoping to calm my poor husband. He *liked* her tea concoctions.

Andy nodded as he made his way to the table.

Logan waited while Andy got himself comfortable at Amy's small table, then he answered Andy's question. "We have become aware of the need to increase the protection for Peg and Amy. Their recent successes have brought them to the attention of unsavory elements on our side of life."

My eyes narrowed, and I began tapping my foot on the floor. "A fact you didn't anticipate?" I heard my snotty attitude reflected in my words, but I ignored the fact.

"We hoped it would go unnoticed or at the very least, considered beginners luck," Logan calmly replied—he seldom allows my rudeness to ruffle his feathers.

"Who is 'we'?" Jack asked. Oh boy … was he in for another shocker. Jack didn't like the way the afterlife worked. He wanted it to be all sweetness and lollipops. Tough luck, my old friend.

"One of the committees I serve." Logan's eyes twinkled. He was well aware of Jack's ideas and enjoyed his reactions to each new revelation of the spirit realm.

"Committees?" Jack's shock reflected in his voice. "Along with everything else, there're committees? Hells bells."

Logan's eyes were at full sparkle now, but he controlled the grin that tried to escape. "Yes, Jack. All of you are part of the discussions at each meeting."

Jack held up a hand. "I can't take anymore! Just get on with the details."

Nodding, Logan continued. "I am afraid the case involving Salvatorio and Anthony intruded upon our adversaries' territory adequately enough that they now consider these two women a threat to their endeavors."

My stomach dropped, I started sweating, and I suddenly had to pee … jeez.

"Why didn't you tell us this before?" Jack demanded. I was glad he asked the question because I didn't think my mouth or brain was up to speed.

"There was no need to raise the anxiety level of those involved." Logan looked around the table, studying each of our faces carefully.

Jack's expression was easy to read—he disagreed with Logan's opinion. Before he could express his displeasure with Logan, Dad interrupted. "One thing everyone here needs to understand is, this is a war and has always been a war. To be fair … the living are usually not privy to what is happening on our side of life, but it bleeds over into your world." He shrugged. "It's the same old story and the same old fight." He nodded at Amy. "I know Amy believes the good side will win." He threw her a quick smile. "She may be absolutely correct, but we have to continue fighting."

"How long has this 'war' been going on?" Andy asked, speaking for the first time since the conversation started.

"Since the beginning of life." Logan's eyes focused on my face as he spoke. Uh-oh … why was I getting all this attention from him? I didn't have to wait long to hear the answer. "Peg, we need you to play your part."

"Well, haven't I been?" I snapped.

He nodded slightly. "Yes. You need to continue." Sweeping his hand around the table, he continued. "We have added trusted members to your ranks." Antonio's eyebrow hit his hairline at the statement, and Logan noticed his unasked question. "Peg is a key player, just as you three were keys to the Spanelli family problem."

My lips tightened. I didn't mind being part of a team, but I sure as heck didn't want to be team captain!

"How key?" Andy's voice was full of uneasiness.

It was fun to start with, but the problems we encountered were becoming a bit more dangerous as time progressed. Solving a case that was two decades old was easy compared to dealing with more current situations. The mob investigation was dicey, but with Amy's help, it ended well. If drugs were involved this time, we could really be in hot water.

Logan's eyes swiveled to meet Andy's. "To be determined." He hesitated before continuing. "Certain facts have recently emerged that were unexpected."

New, unexpected facts? Good gravy … what was Logan hiding? My bladder began having spasms, causing me to jump up from the table and head for Amy's nearest bathroom.

Once I took care of business and was walking back to the kitchen, I heard a small sound behind me. Jeez Louise … what now? Slowly turning, my stomach dropped when I saw my spirit guide. She rarely appears—I was surprised she chose this moment to make herself known.

She smiled "Hello, Peg … nice to see you again."

"Hi." The simple word was all I could muster. I didn't particularly like her, a fact I was pretty sure she was aware of. "Here to keep me on task?" Ok, so … there was a little snottiness in my tone of voice … shoot me.

Her smile widened slightly. "I believe you have proven you are capable of succeeding all by yourself. I am here to tell you goodbye."

I frowned, slightly confused. "Goodbye? Where are you going?"

"I have been reassigned. It's obvious you no longer need me."

"Reassigned? Gosh ..." What else was I going to say—I darn well wasn't going to miss her.

"A word of caution ... Logan has many plans, and they don't always have your best interest at heart. Be careful."

My throat tightened, and my stomach twisted into a nice big, fat knot. Thanks for nothing, lady.

"What type of plans?" My voice squeaked, which was a huge embarrassment. I didn't want her to realize her words scared the crap out of me. I needed to trust Logan completely. Dad reassured me months ago I could trust the guy; now, this creepy lady was hinting that might not be the case.

Smiling her sugary sweet smile, she faded away slowly. When she was totally out of sight, I sagged against the wall. Tears formed and threatened to stream down my face.

"Peg?" Dad's voice broke the silence.

I looked up at him and let the tears flow. "Oh, Dad ... are you sure I can trust Logan? I mean, *really* trust him?"

Dad watched my face as I spoke. He reached out to touch me but didn't make contact. He didn't have the superpowers Logan did, so actual physical contact was rare. The fatherly gesture made me cry harder.

"Oh, sweetie ... don't let her get under your skin. There's so much you don't understand about our side of things."

"Such as?" I asked, sniffling.

Dad sighed. "Personality conflicts, arguments, turf wars ... not much changes when you cross over to our side. People are still people."

"Not necessarily what I want to hear. What's it got to do with her?"

"Everything. She and Logan never really got along well. She truly believes her longevity on our side should automatically give her more power over newer spirits." He shook his head. "She still doesn't understand how the spiritual aspect of our lives influence the responsibilities we are given. Logan was miles ahead of her in that category, which is why he has more power. Don't get me wrong, she is an important spirit guide and would have worked well with you but ..."

I didn't let him finish. "Logan got involved, and her position suddenly became obsolete?"

Dad grinned. "More or less. It's one of the many reasons she has been allocated to help elsewhere." He shrugged. "I'm pretty sure her parting information was merely her way of getting back at Logan for having her moved."

I cocked my head. "How sure are you?"

He raised an eyebrow. "Do you trust me?"

My eyes widened. "Of course!"

"Then relax ... Logan's a good guy. His methods may frustrate you, but he wouldn't purposely allow you to be harmed."

"That doesn't make me feel super safe. Andy and I could still get the crap beat out of us! Anthony almost killed Antonio and Andy, don't forget!"

Dad nodded as I raged. "I know … but everything turned out fine in the end."

"For Pete's sake! You sound like Logan!"

He laughed. "Simmer down." He jerked his thumb down the hall toward the kitchen. "They're waiting for you."

"Fine." I stomped back to the kitchen.

Logan's glance in my direction alerted me to the fact that he was well aware of my meeting in the hall. Hell … he probably sent Dad along to talk to me.

"So why did you have her sent away?" I demanded.

"I was not aware you required her help." He remained calm despite my indignant tone.

"She drove me nuts … but that's beside the point!"

Everyone at the table looked confused; they weren't aware of the meeting down the hall with my newly fired spiritual guide. I ignored their looks. I'd explain once I calmed down enough to where I no longer wanted to strangle Logan—too bad he was already dead.

He watched me as I fought to control my anger. I wasn't exactly sure why I was so mad, maybe because she frightened me with her warning. My attitude toward her was never super positive, so I should've been thrilled she wasn't going to be occasionally showing up in my life. Strangely, I felt some sort of loss, as if someone important was whisked away from me. Her relationship with Logan could have minimized her involvement with cases I was thrown in the middle of, but I had no way of knowing if that was true.

"She might have been helpful eventually," I blurted.

Logan smiled. "Sadly, I believe it is doubtful. She has never understood my standing in our world."

"Ok, smart guy … explain to us what exactly *is* your standing? Are you considered some sort of supreme spirit?" Boy … was I on a roll or what? Here's Logan, getting chewed out by two gals in one day—probably not one of his better encounters with Amy or me … tough beans.

His eyes narrowed by the slightest margin, and my brain screamed at my mouth to shut up. Somehow, I remembered I made the decision to listen more to my logical side rather than my gut. Not surprisingly, both my brain *and* my gut were in agreement … I needed to shut up—too bad my mouth wasn't listening. "I mean, really … why do you have so much power in your realm? Are you blackmailing someone?"

At this point, everyone at the table sucked in air at the same time. Hearing this enabled my mouth to finally catch up with both my brain and gut—if only it all came together one sentence earlier.

"Would you rather cope alone?" Ice formed around each word, noticeable even to me.

I may be an idiot at times, but I'm not entirely stupid. I didn't want to back down though. "Not what I said at all. Honestly, Logan, you've put all of us in some rather dicey situations recently. Amy isn't a spring chicken, you know. Andy and I aren't too far behind her. These guys ..." I waved my hand at the mob trio. "... have two bosses. One alive and one dead. Good gravy ... have you ever considered our positions?"

"You have all risen to each occasion admirably. There have been no lasting consequences," he replied calmly.

I gave him an incredulous look. "Really? I've had nightmares about Owen and Anthony. Andy recovered from the conk on his head, but let's face it ... it's made him warier. Look at how freaked out he is seeing the gang out in the woods."

Logan nodded patiently. "Yes, I have noticed. However, Amy is doing quite well."

I tossed my head back, looking at the ceiling for an answer. I sighed, bringing my head back to its normal position. "Amy doesn't count; she's thriving on this crap." I threw Amy a small smile, which she returned.

He became thoughtful, which made me itchy. Was Logan's silence a good thing or not? "She warned you about me, I assume. You have always trusted me, Peg. I am not your enemy."

"I hope to high heaven you are telling me the truth!" I snapped.

He smiled slightly. "An excellent arena to place your hopes."

Jeez Louise.

CHAPTER 5

Dad intervened at this point, and everyone in the kitchen was grateful for the interruption. "Let's stay on the task at hand. This problem with drugs in the township needs to be handled as quickly as possible." He looked straight into my eyes. "Peg, we can discuss your concerns later."

I nodded and stayed quiet. I knew a parental command when I heard one.

Logan nodded as his next statement turned the conversation back to the current problem—I was relieved since I was pretty sure I stepped over about a gazillion boundaries with my outburst. "Santino, would you please contact your uncle and inform him we may need his involvement?"

Santino, reaching for his phone, nodded. "Yep, on it."

Logan turned to Antonio. "I would appreciate it if you called your friends, the ones who have their ears to the ground concerning local crime."

Antonio nodded and remained quiet as he began dialing on his own phone.

"Bill?" Logan turned to the last of my mob trio. "Have you seen evidence of increased drug traffic in the township?"

Bill shook his head. "Sir, if they've been moving drugs here, it hasn't been advertised through the usual sources. I'll check it out though."

Logan nodded before turning to Dad. "Dave, have you seen Nell recently?"

Dad frowned. "Not in the past few weeks. I'll nose around and get back to you."

"Thank you." Logan turned to face Andy. "Andy, I apologize that your injury a few months ago so greatly affected you. Anthony gaining access to your house and those inside it was not anticipated. We concluded that we provided more than enough protection." He paused for a few seconds. "I cannot ensure your safety, merely provide the best protection available." He nodded to my favorite trio. "I do not exaggerate the fact, in my opinion, these men are an elite ensemble with much training. I would not have chosen them otherwise."

Andy studied his face a moment before speaking. "I believe you. I understand there are no guarantees." He paused to get his thoughts organized. "Peg and I realize the work you do is important." Grabbing my hand, he continued. "A couple of these investigations have turned ugly, and it takes some getting used to." He was squeezing my hand so hard, I had to grit my teeth to keep from groaning. The last thing I needed was for him to accidentally break my fingers.

"Would you rather I release Peg from our work?" Logan's expression was blank as he watched Andy. I couldn't decide if he was serious or not.

My stomach clenched hearing his words. In a flash, I realized I didn't want to quit working with Logan. I never considered it an option, but hearing him question Andy made me realize quitting was not on my agenda … jeez … who knew?

Andy turned toward me, then looked back at Logan. You could've heard a pin drop in Amy's kitchen. Every one of us was holding our breath, waiting for Andy to answer.

I opened my mouth to explain how I felt to my sweet husband, but he shook his head, ready to answer Logan. "No. That's a coward's way out of a messy situation." Sighing, he leaned back in his chair. His grip on my hand loosened enough that the blood was able to flow back to my fingertips, making them tingle. He dipped his head, looking at his lap. "Kids grown, house paid for, and retirement within reach … we had plans for traveling, visiting the boys, and seeing the country." His eyes closed for a moment, then he turned to face Logan. "Life throws curve balls sometimes … this was a doozy. I never expected either of us to be involved in activities so …" He paused, searching for the right word. "… unorthodox."

Logan turned to me. "Peg?"

I shook my head, not willing to chance my voice cracking with emotion. The tension in the room evaporated almost immediately, and everyone began breathing easier. Amy walked over to the table and poured fresh tea. I think she had to find something to do with her hands to ease her own tension.

Logan nodded once. "It is important for everyone here to realize how much we, on the other side of life, appreciate your willingness to join us in this fight. Our efforts would face far more challenges if not for your aid." He paused, so lost in his own thoughts I began to wonder if he remembered we were in the same room with him. He spoke so quietly, we had to lean forward to hear him. "I was once ... a very long time ago, in the same predicament you find yourselves facing." He hesitated again as his own memories overtook him. The rest of us exchanged looks of surprise hearing Logan's revelation. He never talked about his life. Heck ... as far as I knew, absolutely no one knew a damn thing about the man except that he was extremely powerful.

"So, you were just like us?" Jack asked, surprised.

A small smile appeared on Logan's face as he turned back to the table. "Yes, but many years have passed. I also had to decide if I was capable of aiding the spirit world. I had many responsibilities to my people. My spiritual awakenings prepared me, to some degree, to accept the existence of visiting spirits." His eyes got a faraway look again, alerting us that he was reliving memories.

Antonio cleared his throat. "Sir, we are completely committed. There have been numerous discussions between the three of us over the past few years debating whether our work was wise." Giving Logan a tight smile, he continued. "You have to admit ... it gets unhealthy. Spirits can be a real pain in the ass."

Gosh ... I never knew Antonio could smile—I learn something new every day.

Logan threw his head back, laughing. Once he got himself under control, he spoke. "Yes, Antonio, you are correct."

"Logan, do you think Peg and I should buy guns?" Amy asked.

Santino had his chair tilted, perched on two legs, but hearing Amy's question made his chair slam back on all four. My boys were never allowed to abuse chairs that way; I would've skinned them alive.

"Hell no!" he snapped. "The last thing we need is two, little old ladies packing."

Old ladies? He could forget an invitation to dinner if I was reading Amy's expression correctly. Her eyes became beady, narrowed, and smoldering. "I'll have you know, young man, with the correct training, both Peg and I would be able to handle a firearm."

I had no idea why the idea of using guns smacked into Amy's brain, but I thought she was loony. There was no way I was admitting that fact to Santino, after he called us old ladies. He was nuttier than Amy to even mention our age. Hadn't his mother explained to him that you *never, ever* mention a gal's age?

I shook my head, watching Amy's face flush with color. Santino stepped in a pile of goo, and he could wiggle out of it all by himself.

Antonio looked down at the table, and I suspected he was hiding a grin. Not famous for his sense of humor, he probably didn't want any of us to know his mouth could form a smile twice in the same day. Wow ... his lips curving twice in less than ten minutes!

Bill shook his head, but even he was keeping his mouth firmly closed. Dad tried saving Santino from his own stupidity, waving frantically, but Amy dug in and wasn't backing down. "Who do you think you are telling us we can't take gun training? This is a free country, and if I want a gun, I'll damn well buy one!"

Jeez Louise ... this was unfolding to become a banner day for Amy. First, she tells Logan off. Now, Santino is getting an ear full. What was going on with her?

Santino foolishly decided to hunker down equally to match Amy's stubbornness. "You have no business handling firearms! You could get hurt!"

Her foot, already patting a hundred miles an hour, stomped against the linoleum floor of her kitchen. "That settles it!" She abruptly turned toward me. "Peg, tomorrow we are going to the gun store across town. I'm picking up the biggest gun I can lift."

My eyes widened. "Don't drag me into this snit fit! I never said I wanted a gun. Let's face it, I can barely stand going to self-defense training. Do you think I'm excited about gun training?"

Amy waved her hand dismissively. "Pfftt, any fool can learn to use a gun! You point and pull the trigger."

"Oh, God," Santino moaned. "That is exactly why you shouldn't have a firearm!"

Amy whirled around, facing Jack. "Well ... what do you think?"

Jack jumped in his seat, surprised at being pulled into the fray. "Um ... let me think about it for a few minutes."

"Oh, for Pete's sake! This isn't the end of the world!" Amy stomped over to her purse, pulled out her phone, and after hitting a couple of buttons, waited for whoever she was calling to answer. Her foot was back to tapping the floor with sonic speed, and her body was quivering with irritation.

Jeez Louise ... what was going on with the old gal?

"Sal? Do you have a gun I can practice with?" she asked the person on the other end of the line.

Sal? As in Salvatorio Spanelli? She had his number on speed dial? Since when?

I looked over at Logan, shocked to see his eyes twinkling. The stinker knew something I didn't—no surprise there. He is always a gazillion steps ahead of me.

Santino's mouth fell open, and even Antonio looked stunned. Bill shook his head but had no expression of surprise.

"Yes … uh-huh … ok. Sounds good. Thank you so much. No … I still have a house full. I'll call you later." She finally ended the call and looked Santino square in the eye. "I don't need your permission to do anything! Do you understand me?"

Santino's face flushed red, but he simply nodded. Wisely, he finally decided to keep his thoughts to himself. It was about time!

Boy … all those years of Albert telling her how to live formed a pressure cooker. When Amy blew, she really blew big. It was nice to know I wasn't the only one in the room stunned by her reactions today. The lone person who wasn't stunned seemed to be Logan, but his reaction didn't surprise me at all. He brought her into our little family for his own reasons, and I finally understood he foresaw much more with Amy than I had.

"Santino, please remember Amy had the capability to not only disarm Anthony, but to subdue him. With Peg's help, of course." Logan said.

Yeah … he had a point. Amy's fast thinking and quick reflexes got us out of a real pickle. Without her, Andy and I would've been toast.

Nodding, Santino remained silent. Logan's words might not have been a reprimand, but they held a certain amount of chastisement.

Andy squeezed my hand, catching my attention. When I looked over at him, he winked. Ah … my sweetie was back to his normal, fun-loving self, if only for the moment.

I returned the squeeze and grinned. There was no way I was interested in owning a gun. I was comfortable being a spectator as I watched the circus at the table.

Antonio coughed politely, and I knew he wanted to return the conversation to the issues. "Amy, we can talk to you later about gun ownership … ok? Let's get back to work."

Everyone nodded, Amy included. She calmed down enough, so the color in her face returned to normal. Thank goodness … too much more of her temper and I would've bolted, leaving the guys to deal with her.

Antonio continued when no one protested. "Logan has given us our assignments. I suggest each of us get busy and find any bit of information available." He looked around the table. "We all in agreement here?"

Again, everyone nodded.

"What about me? Anything I should be doing?" Jack piped up.

"Jack, you are already doing what you can. Keep investigating and building your case. However, I would ask that you do not move in the direction of arresting anyone unless you contact either Antonio or Bill," Logan replied, then held up his hand as Jack began to protest. "I am not obstructing justice. Rather, it may prove prudent to pool our information, so we can gather as much intelligence concerning those involved with the recent surge in drug trafficking."

Jack slammed his mouth shut upon hearing Logan's reasoning. He instinctively knew the mob guys might dig up gossip that he had no capability of finding by himself. Everyone in the criminal community knew my trio worked for the mob, so they might be more willing to talk shop with the guys. Let's face facts … they'd never open up to Jack, but they might love to brag to Bill or Antonio. Since Santino was the boss's nephew, someone shady could decide it was unwise to boast in front of him about their activities—could be crossing a line of some sort with old man Spanelli. He still had quite a reputation in certain circles, and the fact that he worked with the good guys was definitely not common knowledge.

"What about us?" Amy asked. The foot tapping ceased, but she still had a tad bit of fire left in her eyes.

Logan smiled. "Please return to your normal daily activities until you are contacted by one of us. There are those in the spirit world aware of sudden changes concerning your daily schedule. As it is, canceling your self-defense class has no doubt aroused their interest."

Amy sighed, turning to me. "I knew changing those classes to the afternoon was a bad idea."

I shrugged. "Oh well … we can't make every decision based on the fact that the bad, dead people are keeping tabs on us." I looked at my watch. "Gosh … look at the time. We need to scoot, or it's scrambled eggs for dinner again."

Amy shook her head at me, disgusted.

"I'll meet you there," Dad said as Andy and I turned to leave.

I nodded but wondered what in the world he needed to talk to us about.

Once outside, Andy turned to me. "What's with Amy?"

"Who knows! Maybe after all those years with Albert bossing her around she wasn't about to start allowing someone else to do the same." I stood on my tiptoes to give him a peck on the cheek. "See you at home." I continued walking toward my car, but I slowed down when I realized someone was in the passenger seat. Logan … jeez Louise … what did he want now?

I sighed as I got in the car. I ignored his presence until I pulled away from Amy's. "Ok, what?"

"Thank you for helping us these past few months."

"No problem. But you didn't wait in my car to tell me thanks. What's up?" I pressed.

"Are you steadfast in your commitment to continue working?" His tone was easy, but I detected a tiny bit of anxiety in his voice.

My eyebrow rose. "Sure. Why?"

"I am concerned Andy is wavering. I am not surprised by his reaction. Not only was he injured, but he loves you and wants no harm to come your way."

"I don't think you need to worry. Getting conked on the head was a shocker for him. Up until that point, it was fun. Well … maybe not the Owen situation, but mostly fun." I paused, thinking about Andy for a moment. "Look … he is fascinated by each piece of information he learns about your side. He loves that my dad is around, he gets a kick out of Bob, and he's always had a soft spot for Nana when she was alive, but Anthony trying to knock a hole in his head took some of the fun and smashed it to smithereens."

"Yes, his emotions are sensible. What we do is not fun, it is work."

"Andy didn't really see it the same way. He goes to the office, comes home, and listens to me gripe about Bob and you. He thought after Owen was shot, I would never be in danger again."

Out of the corner of my eye, I saw Logan nod. "Would you be more comfortable if I ceased utilizing you?"

I parked the car, then turned to face the old Indian. "Actually, no. I realize *not* knowing what is happening would make me crazy. I would be much more frightened understanding the nastiness here was hidden from view. At least being involved keeps me in the loop. I don't have to wonder what's going on in my own neighborhood."

He sat quietly, thinking over my words. I wasn't about to inform him that I was having a blast. I still hated self-defense classes, Bob still aggravated me to pieces, and I was still scared spitless about a few things, but … all in all, it was *fun*. I would admit it only to myself—that tiny fact was no one's business but my own.

"Promise me if at any time you need to remove yourself, you will inform me."

I looked him square in the eyes. "I promise."

He returned the look, and after a few moments he nodded. He must have believed me because he smiled and began fading.

I plopped back against the headrest, feeling the strain of our short conversation. Gosh … Logan was worried about me, and Andy too. I felt tears sprout and a few escaped even though I quickly blinked my eyes … damn hormones.

I sighed, deciding I needed to get inside. I didn't need Andy having a meltdown because I took a few extra minutes to talk with Logan.

"Do you believe me now?" Dad asked.

I almost had a heart attack hearing his voice. "Jeez, Dad! You scared me!"

He gave a quick grin. "Sorry, twinkle toes. I told you Logan cared about your safety."

"Yeah … I know. Sometimes it sure feels as though he puts his assignments before our safety. I figured he felt we will be joining him sooner or later, so what's the big deal if we get killed in action." A healthy pout started.

Dad laughed. "He probably does feel that way occasionally. I know from working with him, though … he would rather keep you alive."

"Why? So, he has his trusted group here on earth doing his bidding?" I shook my head. "Jeez."

"Peg … Logan has to be extremely careful choosing allies in this war. I was surprised he was willing to work with you, to be honest."

Shocked by his words, I looked at him. "Me? Why would Logan not trust me?"

Dad sighed. "Your mother."

I slumped back against the car seat. Mom. Did Logan really wonder if I would work on Mom's side? I never considered it to be an option, and I never considered that her influence in my life would have made Logan hesitate to trust me. Let's face it … she was a pill, and the fact that she was working with the bad guys over in Deadsville must have given Logan serious pause.

"Ok … I guess he had a good reason not to trust me. I hope he trusts me now!"

Dad smiled but didn't respond.

Silence settled comfortably in the car. After a few minutes, Dad broke it. "Andy's at the window. Maybe you should go in so he quits worrying."

I glanced at the house and saw Andy's face peering through the curtain. Waving, I was rewarded with his famous smile. "He's fine. I'm home, so he isn't worried."

"You sure he's going to be fine?"

I hesitated a moment before answering. "Pretty sure. He was so worried about me, especially after Owen tried to slice and dice me into the next life. It never dawned on him Anthony would conk him instead."

Dad smiled. "He's a nice guy. If I haven't told you before … I approve of your choice."

Fresh tears threatened again. "Good to know." I paused. "Dad … how much of a problem is Mom becoming?"

Dad turned his face toward the house. "Bigger every day. Logan tries to keep tabs on her, but she is gaining skills that are not in our favor."

"He asked you to find out where she is … did you?"

"Somewhat." He paused, which made my throat tighten. "She is involved with an unsavory group on our side. Not necessarily the worst bunch available to her, but a group where she can feel important."

I was thoughtful for a minute. "Is Elaine with her?"

He nodded. "Two peas in a pod. Thankfully, Elaine has fewer abilities than your mother." He cocked his head. "I honestly believe Elaine is more selfish than your mother, and I didn't think it was possible."

"So, what's the plan?"

He shook his head. "Not my problem. Logan will decide what to do with any information I give him."

"At least Logan is keeping apprised of her shenanigans."

"He does what he can, but she is a complication."

I sighed. "Yep, always has been I suppose."

"Go take care of your husband. He is still at the window." Dad hesitated. "Watch over him, sweetie."

"He protects me!" I protested.

His eyes softened as he continued to watch me. "He loves you, but the fact that he can't always keep you from harm is a worry for him."

"How about we protect each other?" I conceded.

As Dad faded, he smiled.

CHAPTER 6

Dinner accomplished, and dishes done, Andy and I snuggled on the living room couch. Between digging in the garden and the big meeting at Amy's, I was pooped.

Andy cleared his throat. "You never made it to your self-defense class."

It wasn't a question, so I didn't answer.

"How many classes have you missed since changing the time to afternoons?"

Crap … that *was* a question, one I didn't want to answer.

"A few." I was silently hoping he wouldn't push the issue … he did.

"What's a few?" He was a persistent little stinker.

I shrugged. "I don't keep count."

"You would have never allowed the boys to skip music lessons."

I sat up. "That was different. Those lessons were to help build their character!"

"Yes, and this is more important. Your lessons are to give you the skills to stay alive."

Well, hell … he had me there. I could try pouting to get him off my back, but I knew him well enough to know it wouldn't work.

"Fine. I'll be more diligent." I could hear a teensy bit of whine in my voice, but I ignored the childish sound.

Andy chuckled. "Don't think I won't be paying attention. Remember, I have Amy on my side in this matter."

Jeez Louise … Amy. She was a pit bull if there ever was one.

I sighed. "I promise to be better. I get tired of being slammed on the floor though."

He smiled. "Then don't let yourself … fight back!"

"But she's a little old lady! I don't want to hurt her."

He threw his head back, laughing so hard I wondered if he was having some sort of emotional breakdown. "Sweetie … I don't think you need to worry about hurting Amy. She's a tough cookie. I'm more concerned she'll make mincemeat of you!"

I narrowed my eyes, irritation building at his words. I stood, deciding I had enough. "I'm going to bed." Stomping down the hall to the bedroom, I heard a faint pop. I sighed—now what?

"Peg? I don't mean to bother you, but we have a problem," Nana said.

I turned at a snail's pace to face her. Her voice was strange, sounding as though she had a cold. Could they get sick over there? If so, how on earth was it possible?

When I finally saw her, I was shocked. I leaned against the wall for support. "What happened to you, Nana? You look horrible!"

"Your mother's gang is hunting me. I need Logan, but I can't find him." Her voice was weak, worrying me.

I was way out of my depth, and I knew it.

"Bob!" I yelled, then I heard Andy running toward me.

"Peg? What is going on?" He jerked to a stop once his eyes landed on Nana. He normally couldn't see her, but I was so worried about Nana, I didn't pay much attention to his ability.

"Uh-oh. What do we do?" I heard the panic in his voice, and I was glad I wasn't the only one who was alarmed at this development.

Pushing myself off the wall, I stood straight. "No idea, but maybe Bob can help."

I felt, rather than heard, Bob appear. His mouth was open to ask what I wanted when he spotted Nana.

"I'll get Logan … he's in a meeting." Bob was gone in a flash. I was grateful my instincts were correct, and he knew where Logan was at the moment.

I looked at my grandmother feeling helpless. I basically knew what to do with a live person if they were hurt, but I had no idea what procedures to follow with the dead—having her sit down was probably not an option.

Within seconds Logan was standing next to her, supporting her body. "I'm here. Relax. I will take you to safety." Without another word or even a glance at us, Logan and Nana were gone.

I looked at Andy but kept my mouth shut once I saw how pale he was.

Noticing his hands shaking, I grabbed him, pulling him into a hug. "Logan knows what to do." Well ... I hoped he did.

Bob reappeared out of breath. How could the guy be breathless when he's dead? Not for the first time, I was confused by the fact that dead people still respond as if they were alive—the situations get confusing.

"Ok, here's what is happening. Nell and her group are on a rampage." He looked directly into my eyes. "She's basically after you, Peg. Your grandmother held her off but at a big cost."

Tears filled my eyes. "How much of a cost?"

Bob's eyes jerked away from my own. "Not sure."

My stomach knotted. "How bad is she?"

"Pretty bad." His eyes were still averted—not good.

"Bob!" The tone of my voice forced him to look at me. "What are we talking about? Is she ok? Where is Mom now? Can Logan fix this?" The questions were pouring out of me so rapidly that even I was losing track, and my mind felt as though it was exploding.

Logan appeared in the hall next to us in record time. "She is safe. I have trusted people caring for her."

"You got back fast." I took a slow breath. "Tell me exactly what happened?"

"I sent Dave to make inquiries. Your mother becoming physically violent is a warning that the evil believes it has a stronger foothold here. I will contact Jack. Please rest tonight. I fear tomorrow will bring more trouble. I will return in the morning." He left so fast, I didn't have a chance to respond to his news.

I turned toward Bob. "Ok, buster ... what the hell is going on? What did Logan mean by a stronger foothold?"

"Don't get mad at me! I haven't done anything!" he protested. "I do what I'm told, well ... most of the time. Gosh, Peg ... I had no idea your mom was this vicious! It's pretty bad when you attack your own mother!"

I sighed. "She's been verbally attacking her for years." Shaking my head, I continued. "It never occurred to me she would physically harm Nana. I agree, it's bad when you have no guilt about hurting your own mother." Realization dawned on me when I heard my own words. Under the circumstances, *I* would take immense pleasure in hurting my mother. She harmed someone I loved very much for her own selfish motives. For a split-second ... I despised her.

"What's caused this increased activity with Mom's friends?" I asked.

Bob cocked his head to one side. "I think it's drugs. Something to do with the fact that drugs are a gateway for evil to boost their influence on your side of things." He paused as he thought about it. "At the last meeting, the bigwigs were discussing how to decrease the flow of dangerous narcotics."

"Who exactly are these bigwigs?" I was hoping to get as much information as possible.

He shook his head emphatically. "No way am I giving you info. Logan would skin me alive!"

I could only push Bob so far, then he came to a complete halt. If I insisted, he would either fade or stand there mute. He was more afraid of Logan than he was of me, so I changed tactics. "Fine. What other information did you manage to hear at the meeting?"

Scrunching his face in thought, he was quiet for a moment. "It isn't only here in the Akron area. They are worried about the entire country. It's a big mess in my opinion. The authorities here thought they had the whole drug issue under control a few years back, but for some reason, it's reappeared." He shook his head. "No one knows exactly why, but they do know they dropped the ball along the way."

I leaned back against the wall, thinking. Andy stopped shaking, but he grabbed my hand and squeezed. I looked up at him, thankful his color was back to normal.

I shifted my eyes back to Bob. "Ok, Bob ... can you do me a favor?"

Bob nodded. "Sure, what's up?"

"I need you to stay here and watch over us, so we can get a decent night's sleep. If I have to keep one eye open all night, watching out for my mom, I'll be a mess tomorrow."

Bob straightened his shoulders and smiled. "Sure thing, Peg. No problem." I heard the pride in his voice—he must have taken my request as a sign I trusted him. Well ... he was right. I did trust him, and I appreciated that he was willing to stand guard through the night.

I turned toward the bedroom. "Let me know if you hear any news of Nana ... will you?"

He nodded vigorously. "Absolutely!"

Andy and I made our way to bed, and I wondered how I would sleep knowing my mother had officially gone nuts.

It turned out we slept like babies, which in my book meant lousy. My boys slept horribly until they were almost two years old, and it was pretty much how our night was—up every couple of hours, checking the clock, jumping at each creak of our century old farmhouse. It's amazing how noisy an old house can be, but more striking is the fact that on a normal night, I never hear any of it—it wasn't a normal night.

Finally, at six in the morning, I decided I had enough and pulled myself out of bed. Dressing quietly, so I didn't wake Andy, I slipped down the hall. At least I could have my morning elixir of strong coffee coursing through my veins before whatever meeting Logan planned. I entered the kitchen to find Bob faithfully standing watch; he was surprised to see me.

"I hoped you would sleep a little longer." His sweet statement brought tears to my eyes, but I turned away, so he couldn't spot them.

I sighed. "A person can toss and turn only so much before they have to get up and move around."

He nodded. "Yep, I remember. Oh … Logan came by to tell me Nana is improving, and she'll be fine in a few days."

Well, the news did it … I burst into tears, and poor Bob couldn't do a thing but stand there.

"Gosh, Peg … I thought it would make you feel better."

I grabbed for a tissue. "It does, but I think the strain got to me. I'm fine," I answered, blowing my nose.

He looked uncomfortable, so I worked hard to pull myself together. There was no sense making him miserable after he was kind enough to guard us all night. "Did Logan say anything else?"

"Yep. He wants a meeting at Amy's. I don't know why, but that's the deal."

I wasn't surprised at all. "What time?"

"Eight." He watched me cautiously, knowing I didn't like to get moving too fast in the morning—I didn't mind today. The meeting sounded too important, and now wasn't the time for a snit fit.

I nodded. "I'd better wake Andy; his morning routine is important to him."

Bob snorted. "Like yours isn't?"

I raised an eyebrow but kept my snarky attitude under control.

He blushed. "There's going to be more people at this meeting than yesterday. I know Jack is planning to attend, along with your trio, and a few other guys."

I felt better knowing Logan was calling in the big guns after last night's incident. I had no idea what the plan was, but it was a comfort knowing there *was* a plan. Logan wouldn't call a meeting otherwise—at least I hoped that was the case.

After my needed amount of caffeine and Andy's morning ritual, we headed to Amy's. Bob tagged along with us even though he could pop over quicker by himself. I figured he wanted to keep an eye on us until he safely delivered us to Logan.

When we pulled into Amy's driveway, I was surprised to see it was filled with cars. The most obvious of them all was Sal Spanelli's SUV. As a mob guy, he might have insight on things the rest of us overlooked. Tucked behind Amy's garage, I spied a limo; which meant only one thing—the mayor was here. He was the last person on earth I wanted to see, but hey … you never know, he might actually have valuable information. Miracles happen, right?

Andy parked the car next to Antonio's, then he looked over at me. "You ok?"

"Yep, it's a full house. Sal, the trio, and even the mayor." I paused. "Here comes Jack." I was watching him maneuver his way around the mess of cars.

Once out of his car, Jack stood in Amy's driveway, hands on his hips, glaring first at Sal's car, then over at the mayor's limo. He shook his head, disgust written all over his face. I understood his feelings ... the last thing we needed was for an elected official to be within a hundred miles of the Spanelli mob. Here he was, probably sitting at Amy's kitchen table sipping green tea with Sal. Stomping over to where Andy and I were standing, he jerked his thumb in the direction of the cars. "Have they lost their minds?" he demanded between clenched teeth. "Do either of them possess one ounce of common sense?"

I held up my hands. "Sal is smart as hell and may have vital information given his connections. As for the mayor, well ... I'll behave and keep my mouth shut."

Shaking his head, he started up the walkway. The front door opened, and Amy smiled. "You're the last ones to arrive. Come on in and have a snack."

I shuddered, knowing her snack had tea stuck in there somewhere. I would've thought the woman figured out by now that most of us were coffee drinkers.

I looked around for Bob, then realized he probably joined the group inside. "Come on, let's see what the game plan is this time around." I left Andy to walk with Jack—I figured he needed some guy time.

Stepping across Amy's threshold, I was met with a surprise. The aroma of fresh coffee enveloped me ... I was in heaven. Looking over at my friend in surprise, she chuckled. "Sal brought his coffee maker."

I nodded, looking forward to tasting Sal's coffee—it smelled fantastic.

Jack and Andy came up behind me.

"Thank God, something I can actually drink," Jack muttered, once the aroma of fresh coffee hit him.

Amy winked at me, then stood further aside to allow us to enter. As Jack passed her, she smiled sweetly. "Tea is better for your health, Chief."

His jaw hardened, but he nodded and kept his feet moving in the direction of the kitchen. He liked Amy, so he didn't want to be excessively rude.

As we entered the kitchen, I nodded to all the men gathered. I looked at each face, surprised Logan wasn't among them.

"He'll be here soon. He's allowing us time to settle," Antonio said after seeing my expression.

I smiled, nodding ... made sense to me.

Sal spotted us and grabbed three more coffee cups from the cupboard. I raised an eyebrow at the fact he was playing host because Amy usually had everything ready. She took pride in her hostessing skills, and she usually made sure everything was in tip-top shape for company. I hoped these meetings weren't becoming too taxing for her.

Somehow, Amy managed to squeeze enough chairs into her kitchen for everyone. I found an empty seat and plopped down. Andy followed suit, but Jack leaned against the wall. He could be stubborn about becoming too cozy with the mob guys. Plus, he was still uncomfortable around Antonio ever since the incident with Owen.

The mayor placed his seat away from the vicinity of the mob crew. I guess he hoped if any paparazzi happened along it might not look as though he was in a meeting with them … go figure. I had to hand it to him though, he did acknowledge me with a nod. It's more than I expected—we have a like-hate relationship … he likes me, and I hate him. It works for me.

Bob was standing alone in the corner, so I figured he was gathering any information he could for his boss, Logan. Not to say there was much talking at this point. We all seemed to be keeping to ourselves; which was fine by me—eight in the morning was not a time for chitchat in my book.

There was a loud pop and the air suddenly changed drastically, becoming heavy with emotion, accompanied by a strange dampness. A high-pitched shrieking noise pierced the center of my brain. Everyone jumped in their seats, obviously hearing the same noise I was. Antonio reached for his gun, Santino pulled a knife from his back, Amy grabbed hold of Sal's arm, and I almost peed my pants. Our eyes collectively searched for the source of the gawd-awful noise. We spotted Elaine, tied with some type of glowing rope from neck to toe, and screeching like a banshee. Her normally perfect hair stood on end, and her face was filthy. I never saw her in this condition before and couldn't understand why she was allowing herself to appear to us in such a state.

"I'll kill that son of a bitch! Where is he?" she demanded.

Not one sound came from our group as we stared at her. Our mouths dropped open in shock as she continued her demands. Ignoring those of us alive, she honed in on poor Bob. "You worthless man! Where is he?"

Bob's mouth, like ours, dropped open. He stared at her, filled with horror that his evil wife was suddenly dropped into our midst. This had to be Logan's doing, but it was obvious Bob had no clue she was part of the proceedings.

He closed his mouth, regaining some of his composure. "What happened to your hair?"

It took a lot of self-control not to burst out laughing at his question. Elaine shows up tied up with some mystery rope, screaming to high heavens, and he wants to know what was up with her hair? Hilarious.

She glared at him. "Forget my hair, you dolt! Where is that bastard

Logan? I'll tear him from limb to limb!"

Bob shook his head, clearly wanting nothing to do with her. "No idea."

"It's not a surprise considering what a loser you are! Seen any good movies lately?" she sneered.

Bob blushed bright red. I kept his secret—he spent a great deal of time and effort watching the *Harry Potter* movies … in order, no less.

Logan appeared, responding before Bob could. "I appreciate that Bob stays in tune with the present recreations of society. The fact that he will devote his time staying alert to current trends is quite helpful." So, he knew about Bob's little covert entertainment. It wasn't surprising to me, but considering Bob's face was now scarlet, I knew he was shocked Logan stumbled across the information. Bob had a lot to learn concerning Logan's habit of knowing as much as possible about those working for him.

Elaine glared at Logan. "Let me go!" she spat at him. "Right this minute!"

"I do not believe it is a wise course of action." He smiled, then he glanced at the assembly around the kitchen table. "She was quite difficult to capture." From her appearance, I would guess his words were vastly understated. She must have put up quite a fight by the looks of her.

She released a wail; a sound I never would have believed possible coming from a human, not even a dead one, until that moment. My ears vibrated, and my brain hurt. Gosh ... I thought only kids throwing temper tantrums had that particular pitch.

With a wave of his hand, the mystery rope binding Elaine covered her mouth, and the noise abruptly ceased—it was heaven. Once the noise was silenced, we turned to Logan hoping to learn the reason for her presence.

After assuring himself she was indeed bound securely, he turned to us. "She has answers about Nell, and I want them."

I frowned, never having seen Logan in this mode. I wasn't sure I liked this side of him.

As if he read my mind, he looked at me. "Peg, it could change the course of the war we are fighting."

Great.

CHAPTER 7

Changing the course of the war between good and evil was a great idea, but wars are nasty buggers. The rules change and not necessarily for the better. Logan had Elaine magically tied up, and he hinted he was willing to torture the woman. I hated her, but I'm really not one for violence—it was way too early in the day for those antics.

Logan raised an eyebrow at my obvious distaste for his plans. "Peg, I believe you are under a false assumption. Gaining information using negative means is not my intention." He turned to Elaine. "You will provide the necessary knowledge." The tone of his voice could curdle milk. I definitely wouldn't want to be Elaine.

Struggling with her restraints, she could only glare at Logan in response.

He smiled. "Elaine, please calm down. The harder you struggle, the tighter the ropes become. I believe it is referred to as a Chinese finger trap. However, mine is substantially stronger."

She immediately stopped fighting the ropes, but her glare stayed put.

Logan turned to Sal. "Salvatorio, please direct the questioning."

Sal nodded and walked closer to Elaine. She swiveled her eyes to watch his advance. Once she recognized him, her eyes became huge. Ah ... so she knew exactly who Sal was. So what surprised her? The fact that he worked for Logan or the fact that he was going to be the one interrogating her?

"I know your family from the old days, and even they don't like you," he said to her.

I frowned. Her family? From the old days? What was Sal talking about? I glanced at Andy, but he shrugged. We were both clueless.

I turned to face Antonio, but he refused to meet my eyes. This was interesting. Elaine was a bigger player than I imagined. I thought Bob could be the key to this puzzle, but when I looked over at him, his mouth had dropped open in shock. It was plain as day that whatever Sal was referring to was news to Bob.

Elaine's face, what I could see of it between the ropes, went white. She couldn't take her eyes off Sal, almost as if he hypnotized her somehow. Whatever power he held, it was mighty strong.

Sal continued after a minute or two. "I will have Logan remove the ropes on one condition ... are you listening?"

She nodded.

"You will tell us what we need to know. If you start bellowing again, he ..." Sal pointed to Logan. "... will banish you. Understood?"

I had no idea what banishing meant, but Elaine sure did. She almost fainted but managed to nod again.

Sal turned to Logan giving him a slight nod. Logan flicked his finger, and the ropes covering her mouth vanished.

I could see Elaine gritting her teeth but not from anger this time—she was scared spitless.

Sal nodded. "Much better. Now, where are the drugs coming from?"

"South," Elaine whispered.

"South is a lot of territory. Please be more specific."

Her eyes closed. "South America."

"Ah, thank you. Which family?" Sal's voice was cool as a cucumber.

She hesitated, weighing her options. "Mendoza." she said, deciding Sal and Logan were more of a threat to her than giving up the information.

Nodding, Sal turned to Logan. "I thought they were the suppliers, but I couldn't be sure."

Jack cleared his throat. "Big drug family?"

"One of the biggest, but they're stupid. They flood the market, believing cheap drugs will cause more addicts." Disgust was clearly written on Sal's face.

I was slightly confused. "But doesn't it happen?"

Sal shrugged. "Sure ... for a brief period of time, but then you have dead druggies. The Mendoza family is greedy, which gets them into trouble with the cartels of South America and Mexico. They have been running one step ahead of the major players for decades. One of these days, they are going to run out of luck. I'm surprised it hasn't happened already." He turned and headed back to his original spot next to Amy.

Logan stepped forward. "Elaine, thank you for your help." In the blink of an eye, she was gone.

Andy spoke up at this point. "Logan, where did you send her?"

"She is safe, Andy, but she will not be interfering for the near future. I cannot hold her forever; she has not caused enough problems for the committee to deal with her permanently."

"You mean to tell me there is a legal system over there?" Jack sputtered.

Logan smiled. "Yes, Jack. I believe we discussed this previously. It is similar to yours. It is my understanding the idea for the system you work with actually came from our side of life."

Jack snorted. "I wouldn't be surprised."

Logan nodded. "It is an excellent system."

"Well, you have a point," Jack conceded.

I snuck a quick look at Bob, and I was relieved to see he recovered from the shock of being in the same vicinity as Elaine. He avoided her like the plague, and Logan plopped her into the middle of our meeting … jeez.

"Peg?" Logan's soft voice caught my attention. "Who do you detect in the woods?"

Uh-oh ... those damn woods. I took a deep breath as I turned my head. My shoulders sagged at the sight in front of me. "Everyone except the Vikings."

Logan nodded. "As I thought. Dave, were you able to find Nell?"

I looked up, surprised. When did Dad arrive?

"Yes, and it's not good. After she finished with her mother, she retreated to their usual location. She is still hunkered down there trying to find Elaine," Dad finished with a small smile.

"Wait a doggone minute!" I cut in. "I have a question."

Logan raised an eyebrow but nodded for me to continue.

I turned to Sal. "You told Elaine you know her family. Who exactly *is* Elaine?"

After a quick questioning glance at Logan, who nodded, he turned back to me. "Her uncle was part of another family I did business with back in the old days. They were beginning to go legit about the same time I did but for different reasons."

"What reasons?" I was determined to get complete answers for a change.

Sal shrugged. "The old man's kids were tired of the racket, and I don't blame them." He shook his head at the memories. "I was looking for a way out myself when Logan showed up."

"I married into a mob family?" Bob's faint voice came from the corner. "A real mob family?"

I looked at Bob surprised. "Bob, you never knew?" I figured even Bob should've been able to figure that one out for himself.

He shrugged. "We never saw much of her side; she never liked them."

Sal laughed. "I think the truth was more along the lines of the family hated her and her mother."

"Bob, do you mean to tell me you never had even an inkling of suspicion?" I was still not quite trusting him on this point.

"Never! Do I look like someone who would knowingly marry a mobster's niece?" he demanded, then turned red when he remembered we had a real live mobster in our midst.

"True, but what about the remark you made a few months back about how cemeteries hold family secrets?" I was a persistent gal when I wanted answers.

He waved a hand dismissively. "Oh, that. For crying out loud ... all cemeteries contain enough secrets to fill a canyon. Just about everybody takes some type of secret to the grave." He had a point.

"I still don't understand why I was asked to come to this meeting," our friend, the mayor, said peevishly.

I forgot the twerp was here. I ignored him, but Logan turned toward him. "Mayor, it is nice to meet you finally."

The color drained from Mayor Hayes's face when he heard Logan's voice with no body attached to the sound.

Ha! I thought. Wait till he allows you to see him, then you'll really feel the impact. Hadn't he been able to hear Logan this entire time? If not, didn't he realize there were pieces and parts of conversation he was missing? It didn't make sense at all.

"If you had been paying attention, you would realize this meeting is quite important for your city. Drugs are actively moving through your community in large volumes," Logan informed him. "Were you unaware of this fact?"

No elected official wants to admit to either being unaware of dangerous activities occurring in their realm or worse, ignoring the lawless enterprises for their own personal, and usually, selfish reasons. The little creep squirmed in his seat.

"Who are you exactly?" His eyes darted around, trying to locate the source of the voice instead of answering Logan's question. Arrogance was dripping from his words as thick as molasses. Jeez ... what an idiot.

You could've heard a pin drop as Logan studied the mayor. What the mayor didn't know was he entertained Logan in his office a while back, during the Owen case.

"If I remember correctly, when you were visited by Mrs. Shaw in your office a few months ago, papers flew off your desk," Logan said. Yep ... exactly what happened, and the mayor almost had a heart attack.

The mayor's eyes grew huge, his face paled further. "It was you?"

Logan gave a brief nod. "Correct."

We watched as the seasoned politician gathered his thoughts. It was clear he was deciding how to handle his current dilemma. Stupidly, he settled for arrogant posturing, which was never going to break the ice with Logan. "I refuse to discuss important matters with someone, or some *thing* I can't see. Why don't you make yourself visible to me?" He swept his arm around the room. "It is obvious these people can see you." He actually sat back in his chair, pouting.

I wanted to smack the arrogance right out of him.

Antonio, his head bent and eyes on Amy's table, shook his head hearing the mayor's words. Even he couldn't believe the stupidity of the man, and in his line of work, he must deal with a lot of stupid. Criminals are seldom masterminds, and I would bet big money that Antonio dealt with more criminals than even Jack.

Logan's smile was tight, and I knew it was a signal he wasn't happy with Akron's mayor. In a flash, Logan's entire appearance changed and everyone, including the mayor, sucked in air. I hate politics, and I have always been happy that townships, like ours, only have a board of trustees rather than a full-blown political entity.

Logan always appeared in his native clothes, which was already impressive. However, he must have wanted to make a statement about himself when appearing to the mayor. He stood ramrod straight, eyes boring into the mayor's. His long, dark hair streaked with gray had feathers tucked into a braid I never noticed before. Beads covered his breastplate, almost glowing with color. The design on his leggings was true workmanship and included an array of animal depictions. It was clear someone possessing extraordinary talent made them. It was also obvious Logan was aware of the splendor of his appearance.

I snuck a peek at Mayor Hayes, and I was satisfied to see the irritating man awed by the spectacle he faced. Whatever Logan hoped to achieve, he certainly accomplished his goal. The mayor's mouth hung open. Unable to hide the shock of actually seeing Logan, he looked as if he saw a ghost. Well … that was exactly what he *was* seeing.

Logan spoke, filling the silence. "You currently have the ability to see me, but do not assume the privilege is permanent. Please answer my question."

"What question?" the mayor stuttered.

Logan's eyes narrowed. "Do you have information concerning drug movement in your city?" Logan's steely voice made my stomach knot. If the mayor was smart, he would answer the question immediately.

The political aspect of the query was not lost on the mayor. He squirmed for a moment. "The council was considering actions that could be taken to solve the problem."

Logan's expression was priceless. Already straight as a pin, he pulled himself taller. "I believe you are maneuvering yourself to place any blame on your council. Your answer informs me that you and your council were fully aware of the influx of drugs into this area. Sadly, you refuse to use your power to abolish the problem."

The mayor opened his mouth to rebut Logan's analysis but was faced with the Indian's upturned hand, an obvious gesture to quiet any comment. No one in the kitchen was brave enough to speak, but I was stupid enough to do so. "Uh, Logan … do you really think the mayor could stop the drug traffic?"

Logan turned to me. "Peg, any action intended to curb the movement of crime would force our enemies to form other plans. Action would give us a window of opportunity that would be beneficial."

I nodded. "Yep … but this country has been battling the drug problem for over forty years. We aren't one step closer now than we were back in the sixties, which was before drugs were mainstream."

Logan was not thrilled with my comments, but he slowly nodded agreement. Looking around at the entire ensemble in Amy's kitchen, he continued. "Winning any war cannot be measured easily during the battles. Sometimes, the small skirmishes turn the tide. Every community must fight consistently, it is how wars are won."

Jack spoke up. "Logan, your view is different from ours, but we do the best we can. Those of us living in the township are fortunate that it is a small area, but we aren't ignorant enough to believe our own kids can't get sucked down a hole. It's every parent's greatest fear. How do you propose we move forward now?"

Jack's question was legitimate, and Logan treated it seriously. His face softened. "Jack, I share your fears. Evil penetrates every weakness a society allows. It has been this way for centuries." Shaking his head, he continued. "We must continue to battle even though our judgment informs us we are losing." He smiled at Amy. "You are convinced good will eventually overthrow evil. I concur, but I must warn each of you … the battles will weary us, but we persevere in spite of our emotions, or …" He cut his eyes to the mayor. "… our personal endeavors."

At least the mayor had the good grace to blush at Logan's obvious slam on his character.

Logan turned to Sal. "Salvatorio, I believe you may be of great aid to us during this dilemma. You are aware of the significance of the Mendoza family's involvement, and you have dealt with them previously. Your connections are vital to our mission."

Sal nodded but remained silent. When Logan is issuing orders, any sane person keeps their mouth shut tight.

Logan continued. "I will need the assistance of your men once again. I thank you for allowing them time to help."

Santino grinned at his uncle but also kept his trap shut. Antonio watched Logan, waiting for his own orders.

Logan surprised me when his next comments were not directed at Antonio, but Bill. "Bill, your presence at the conclusion of this gathering would be appreciated." Bill's face reflected his surprise at the summons, but before he could respond, Logan turned to the mayor. "Further contact is necessary; however, at this time, is not appropriate. There will be an emissary assigned to you, but in the meantime, please contact the chief with any pertinent information."

Mayor Hayes gave Logan a slight nod, probably hoping no one saw how much the regal Indian scared him.

Amy—bless her heart—started filling everyone's coffee cups and placed a plate of fresh cookies on the table. I didn't notice the aroma every cookie on the planet radiated as it was cooking, but once I saw the darn things, I could smell the warm oatmeal in the air. Jeez … when did she sneak those suckers in the oven? Jack dove in the moment the plate hit the table, and I had to hide my grin. The man loved sweets and wasn't shy about it one bit.

Andy snagged a cookie, then smiled at me. I was glad to see his smile; he'd been on edge lately, and I knew the meeting wasn't helping much. At least an oatmeal cookie consoled him.

"Jack?" Logan broke the silence that had momentarily taken over. "Do you have a time frame tomorrow when we can meet privately?"

Jack looked up from his stack of cookies, startled. I was well aware Logan rarely asked anyone for a timed meeting; he usually showed up whenever it suited him. The fact that he was actually giving Jack a say in the matter surprised even me.

Swallowing a mouthful, Jack nodded. "Eight in the morning sound good to you?"

Logan nodded. "Yes, it will suffice."

Wow … Logan must have been trying to improve his relationship with Jack to check what would work for our chief of police. I hid a grin, then sneaked a peek at Amy. She was hiding her own smile. Maybe her ass chewing of Logan worked—he needed to realize he doesn't own us. Amy might have helped him understand we weren't chess pieces to be moved as he pleased. Hey, it's a possibility. If Logan was willing to concede that my mob trio has other obligations that didn't include him, there's a chance he might have the capability of seeing us in the same light—miracles do happen once in a while.

"Peg, considering your mother's endeavors to reach you have increased to the point of harming those on our side, I am adding special guards for you and Andy." Logan paused, giving me time to react.

"Listen, extra guards aren't going to keep Mom from me. She's always able to reach me, so what are a few extra chaperones going to be able to accomplish? Jeez Louise, Logan … living people can't fight the dead!"

He allowed me to blow, and when he was positive I finished, he continued. "Have you seen your mother recently?"

I frowned, thinking. Wow … when did I see her last?

"Exactly. I have surrounded you with protection. Your mother has not been able to break through the barrier." He sighed. "The attack on your grandmother was caused by the fact that Nell cannot gain access to you."

My mouth dropped open as tears formed. Poor Nana took a beating because Mom couldn't get to me? I wanted to throw up. My eyes found Dad. "Did you know?"

His eyes never left mine. "Yes, which is why we've been trying to keep tabs on her."

I took Andy's hand in mine, then turned back to Logan. "What do we do now?"

"I made arrangements for increased security. They are from my side of the veil and have powers that will protect you both in ways Antonio and the other men cannot. However, they …" He gestured to my trio. "… will still be utilized for physical threats."

Capable of little more than nodding, I slumped against Andy's chest. I think this was one of those curveballs Andy mentioned yesterday … jeez.

CHAPTER 8

After everyone was given their orders, the meeting finally broke up. The mayor skedaddled out of Amy's house as fast as his chunky legs could carry him. My trio went to perform their duties, and Jack followed closely behind them. I knew the fact that the drug lab was located on the head trustee's land was a major headache for Jack, but we didn't make time to discuss his problems concerning Tom Newman's property. Even Logan left quickly with Bob close on his heels. I felt for Bob. Discovering his wife of twenty plus years was connected to a mob family must have been a real stunner.

Sal, Andy, and I remained seated at Amy's kitchen table. I was thankful the cup in front of me was filled with steaming coffee rather than Amy's tea concoction. I took a sip, savoring the flavor of Sal's coffee—thank God for Sal's portable coffee pot.

Sal watched as I enjoyed the cup of coffee. "Glad you like it."

"It's fantastic! What brand is this stuff?"

He shook his head, smiling. "Not a brand. I have it specially blended in Hawaii. You can't find it in the stores."

I sighed. "Just my luck."

Sal laughed. "I'll make sure you have a supply."

"Wow … thanks." I hoped he knew my gratitude was genuine. The coffee was great, and I knew his act of kindness came from his heart. He may be a reforming mob guy, but he is also a big sweetie pie.

"What did you think of our meeting?" Amy asked.

Andy looked down at his hands, which were clenched into balls. Obviously, he was still concerned for our welfare, but I was surprised to see how anxious he was after his answer to Logan's question. Was he regretting his commitment to our old Indian?

I nudged him with my elbow. "You ok?"

He looked over at me, trying to give me his usual grin, but it fell short. "Your mother is a problem. I worry about her."

"Logan said he has extra ghostly protection for us. It makes me feel better." I knew Sal had something to add when he cleared his throat. I cocked my head as I looked at him. "Sal … you've worked with Logan much longer than we have. What's your take on this situation?"

He glanced at Amy, then turned toward us. "Look, guys … it is my opinion, professional and personal, that all three of you should take further steps to safeguard yourselves."

I nodded. "Ok. Any ideas? We can't necessarily have safety procedures against dead folks."

"Well … maybe *that* group of enemies needs to be handled by Logan, but don't underestimate the drug people. They are damn dangerous too. Take my word for it, they won't stop to think … they'll shoot and scoot." He shrugged. "I've watched them for years in other family networks."

"You never moved drugs in your line of work?" The question bordered on rude, but hey … I didn't mention the mob, only the drug trafficking.

He shook his head. "Nope. Never wanted to be involved. After living with people who should have been on *prescribed* medication, the last thing I wanted in my life was drugs making people act nuts."

Well … he had a point. His wife and son should've been on prescription medication. It wouldn't have changed the fact that they had mental and emotional issues, but it might have helped control their instabilities to some degree. I had to hand it to the old mobster, he had a decent head on his shoulders.

Andy's brow furrowed. "Sal, what kind of steps do you mean?"

Sal shot another glance at Amy. "You all need to be armed." I snorted, but Sal held up a hand. "Peg, please hear me out."

I threw my hands up in surrender. "Fine."

"The living people are our problem. Logan's dealing with the dead, and as far as I'm concerned, he can have them. Drug movers are in a different league than normal, uh … criminals." His hands waved around. He was trying to distance himself from the world of crime. A little hard for a crime boss to accomplish, but hey … he was in the middle of reforming his entire enterprise. "I don't worry about the users. Instead, I focus on those handling the bulk of the business side of things." He hesitated. "Let's just say they have issues."

"Issues?" Andy sighed. "More people with problems."

Sal scrunched his mouth as he debated whether or not to explain his concerns to Andy. "Andy, you've never dealt with criminals until recently, correct?"

Andy shifted nervously in his chair. "Yeah ... we've always lived a steady life. Don't get speeding tickets, don't run red lights, don't ..."

Sal interrupted him. "I get the picture. Pretty much what I thought." He studied Andy for a moment longer. "Logan has pulled you into situations out of your depth. From what I can gather, you've both done quite well under the circumstances." He hesitated. "You did good with my Anthony, and he wasn't easy."

I squirmed around in my chair. Anthony was a touchy subject with Andy and me. He conked Andy on the head, Amy disarmed the kook, and I kicked him in the ... um ... groin. It was actually Sal who finally brought the entire episode to a close by subduing his own son, but it was dicey.

I looked at Amy and Sal. "It wasn't Logan's fault. Nana started the mess and called Logan for help."

Sal nodded. "I heard the story. Who do you think asked your grandmother to enlist you?"

My jaw dropped along with my stomach. Jeez ... I'd been played! I placed my head on the table and groaned.

Sal chuckled. "Peg, he's very picky about who he uses, so don't feel bad."

"I'm beginning to realize he is *using* us! I don't like being taken for a fool!" I snapped.

"Peg! Grow up!" Amy admonished. "I would rather live out my days being *used* than being ignorant of the truth."

"Truth? Half the time, Logan doesn't play by any rules I know of!" I wasn't backing down. The words my spirit guide had spoken were stuck in my brain. Dad trusted Logan, but doubt was driving me crazy.

Sal nodded. "He plays by his own rules. I don't always agree with him, but circumstances tend to work out ... eventually."

I shook my head. "I don't want to end up dead ... or worse."

"I've worked with Logan for a long time. Never once has he been wrong with his actual plan. He knows what the stakes are, and he plays the cards in front of him. The biggest problem I have with him is that he has to stay forty steps ahead of the bad guys, which means I walk around in the dark most of the time. It's necessary for him to think in those terms. I learned to trust Logan, which wasn't easy. I grew up in a business stressing distrust of all your business partners." Sal shook his head. "I've learned so much from him."

Amy offered her hand, and the old mobster grabbed and squeezed gently.

A thought popped into my brain, and I felt my eyes narrowing. "Amy? Anything you want to share?" My voice was tight. I didn't need more complications, but I had a sneaking suspicion there was a big fat problem standing in front of me.

Her face flushed, and Sal looked at the floor. Jeez! I was right.

Andy glanced at me, frowning. "What are you talking about?"

"Sal and Amy sitting in a tree." I started to sing the old, childhood rhyme.

Andy's startled glance shot between me and the new couple. "You two are … um … dating?"

Amy's face flushed a deeper shade of red, but Sal held on to her hand stubbornly. "Depends on your definition of dating."

I looked at him skeptically. "Really? She has you on speed dial on her new, fancy phone, which I'm guessing you bought her. Plus, you are quite comfortable in her kitchen. I've been here countless times, and I still don't know where she hides the coffee cups!"

Sal scowled. "She needed a cellphone! I'm worried about her safety."

I nodded. "I understand the cellphone, but what I don't get is you two deciding to date."

"You think I'm too old to date?" Amy demanded as her natural curls danced with anger.

Since it was exactly what I thought, I changed tactics due to her tone of voice. "Amy, we don't need complex romantic issues. I want to know your mind is on our work!"

Disgust with my attitude oozed from every pore of her body. "You sound like Logan."

I knew she didn't intend for her statement to be a compliment. I didn't want Logan's attitude toward our mission to seep mysteriously into my soul. Someone had to balance the old Indian, which wouldn't happen if we all began thinking the same way he did.

I sighed. "What you do on your own time is your business, but please don't allow your personal feelings to erode our partnership."

"I won't." Her words were clipped. I could feel the ice forming as I watched her face. Maybe I should've kept my nosey trap shut.

I held up a hand in defeat. "Fine." I turned toward Sal. "What's with Elaine being a mob kid?"

He grinned. "I feel bad for Bob. I had no idea the guy wasn't aware of her background."

"Yeah, he was shocked, it was plain as day. How could he not know that bit of news?"

Sal shook his head. "No idea. It's pretty obvious he didn't meet the bulk of her family."

"Will this new twist cause us problems?" Andy asked. I wasn't the only one in the room to hear the worry in his voice.

Amy and Sal exchanged a glance before Sal continued. "Nah, I wouldn't give it a second thought. Her family doesn't like her, so even those on Logan's side of the fence won't come to her rescue."

"Did Logan tell you that?" I asked. "How can he be so sure? The rules over in Deadsville work differently. They may decide blood is thicker than dislike."

"I guess the scuttlebutt over there is the same as here. Logan isn't concerned." Sal seemed to know an awful lot about the other side.

"Do you hear dead people?" My eyes became slits as I continued to watch him.

Sal threw his head back, laughing. "I hear pretty much the same bunch you hear. A few extras ... but only once in a while."

"What extras?" I pressed.

"You can hear your grandmother, right?"

I nodded.

He shrugged. "Well, a couple of my ancestors come through once in a blue moon."

"Like who?" I really wanted to know. I didn't care if I was being nosey.

He paused, looking at the floor.

Amy squeezed his hand. "Tell them, Sal."

Sal's eyes met mine. "My real parents have tried a couple of times."

Sal was secretly adopted as an infant. His adoptive mother couldn't have kids, but the family continuity was needed for the business side of life. His mob parents arranged for his 'birth' to happen while they were on a year-long world tour, so they could come home with their new, little boy. No one questioned the occasion, accepting the deception as truth. Logan took advantage of the new gene pool in the Spanelli bloodline. New genes meant the possibility of weakening the mental health issues that ran through the family. His now deceased wife, Bella, was also a Spanelli. That meant she had the insanity heritage herself. Their son, Anthony, was as nutty as a fruitcake. He almost finished Amy and me for good.

"What do you mean, 'tried'?" I had a heavy suspicion that I knew the answer.

He gave a tight smile. "Logan."

Yep ... I knew it.

He sighed. "To be fair, he has a point. No one over there is aware of my birth circumstances. It has been well guarded."

I waved a hand. "Yeah, yeah, yeah ... I get tired of Logan's logic."

"I have to agree with Logan," Andy said.

I turned toward him. "What?"

Andy shook his head. "Peg, the best way to protect Sal is to keep his secret safe. I'm sure Logan explained that once Sal is ... well ... you know ... dead ..." He threw Sal an apologetic smile. "... he'll have plenty of time to visit with his birth parents."

Sal nodded. "Exactly what Logan told me."

Amy gave him a quick hug, standing on her tiptoes to achieve her goal. Sal was as tall as Andy, and Amy was shorter than me. Now I knew what we looked like to others—Mutt and Jeff to the max.

Watching the affection between Sal and Amy was a bit uncomfortable, but I was happy she found someone who knew how to treat her. His devotion to her was obvious. If their mutual admiration got any stronger, Andy and I would be forced to leave out of embarrassment.

"Now that Elaine has been stowed away in solitary confinement, we need to focus on evading my mom." I was trying to get the conversation back on topic—I had enough of Sal and Amy's love fest.

Sal turned his attention to me. "Do you have any idea what type of security Logan has surrounding you?"

"Nope. Not a clue." I shook my head, nervously biting my lower lip. I sure hoped whatever he had in place was strong enough. Mom was becoming way too powerful in my opinion. A few months back, she had the capability of blocking Bob from reaching me. The block only lasted a brief time, but it was unnerving. I didn't need her developing more powers and forcing Logan to invent maneuvers merely to keep me safe from her shenanigans.

"How does the mayor fit into this mess?" I asked. "Anyone know what's going on with him?"

My kitchen companions grew silent as we mulled over my question. After a few minutes of listening to our own breathing, Andy shook his head. "No idea ... other than maybe Logan believes the mayor knows more than he is admitting."

Sal slowly nodded. "I agree with Andy, but the guy is savvy to his city's criminal element."

I snorted. "You think? He's a slimeball, and I don't trust him."

Sal's mouth twitched with humor. "I've known him for quite a few years."

My eyes became tiny slits. "Are you the one responsible for making sure he stays in office?"

He held up a hand. "I wouldn't exactly use those words, but I do have some influence. Not much, mind you, but some."

"Why in the world would you want someone like him in office?" I demanded. "He wastes tax money, he didn't encourage his son to turn himself in when he witnessed a murder, and he's rude!" My hands were flying around during my rant, much to the amusement of my audience. Ok ... so I get a little worked up sometimes.

"How do you 'influence' the elections?" The deep frown on Andy's face clued me in to the fact that this tidbit upset him more than I would have thought possible.

Shrugging, Sal continued. "You make sure the other guy is worthless. It's easy to encourage minor politicians to run for office, throwing millions of dollars into a campaign. It's an ego trip for a lot of people even when they lose by a mile. I need Mayor Hayes to stay in his current position for business reasons."

My eyebrows raised in surprise. "Business reasons? What type of business?"

"When I decided to go legit, it was important to have certain ... um ... friends in high places. I was able to snag building contracts, permits, and all the rest. I made damn sure the work done was high quality and paid good salaries to those doing the labor." He shrugged. "Basically, it boiled down to gentlemen agreements. I don't apologize for my actions because walking away from the old existence was too important. I want to be proud of what I hand over to Caterina. She will be trained correctly, and the business will be a hundred percent legit by the time she's grown."

A sudden revelation smacked me right in the face. "You were never going to hand your empire over to Anthony, were you?"

His head moved back and forth slowly, and a sadness settled over the old man's face. "No." He sighed. "It was obvious, once Anthony returned to the Youngstown area, that Bella's influence was ruining him. I watched, horrified at the thought of Anthony running the family business." He looked me square in the eye. "It wasn't only Bella who was desperate for a heir. I knew the best solution was to bypass Anthony and count on the next generation. When it proved to be impossible, I jumped at Logan's idea to father another child."

Caterina was Sal's legal granddaughter, but biologically, she was his daughter. Turned out, Anthony couldn't father children, which complicated their lives. Anthony was convinced it was his wife, Laura, who was at fault, so he sent her all over the country to see specialists. Every doctor told her the same thing ... it was Anthony, not her, who couldn't produce a heir. By that time, Anthony and Bella were too far gone mentally to believe the doctors. Logan finally stepped in and encouraged Sal to donate the necessary biological ingredients for Laura to become pregnant. The plan worked, and Anthony's ego never allowed him to question whether or not the daughter born to them was his. Common sense should've kicked in at some point. Let's face it ... if he hadn't been able to impregnate his wife for years before Catarina was born and he wasn't able to after she was born, why didn't he connect the dots? Anthony must have one huge ego to swallow the scam hook, line, and sinker.

"Ok ... no argument from me on Caterina's parentage." I held my hand up to let him know I wasn't against their decision; honestly, it wasn't any of my business. "Anthony would've taken the family back to the old ways, and everyone agreed he wasn't a desirable choice for ruling the business. We have a problem now that doesn't involve you, so how on earth will we dig out the truth?"

"Old associates come in handy." Sal smiled.

I nodded as I thought about the drug problems in the area. Nothing new… other than the fact that today's drugs can be made in a basement, attic, or garage—so different from the sixties and much more troublesome. As my fingers drummed on the table, I realized everyone was staring at me. "What?"

Andy grinned at our hosts. "Whether you realize it or not, her brain is dreaming up something interesting."

"My brain doesn't 'dream' up anything!" I snapped.

Andy threw his head back, laughing. It was good to see the strain gone from his face, even if it was at my expense.

CHAPTER 9

The next morning, I was jarred awake by a shrieking sound. I was in a deep sleep, so it took a few seconds for me to recognize the noise. Some moron was actually calling me. While my hand was searching for the offending item, I peered in the general direction of the clock. Realizing it was seven-thirty in the morning, I decided I would kill whoever was stupid enough to think this was an acceptable time to ring me.

"Peg?" Hearing Amy's voice, I plopped back into my comfy pillows. Groaning, I remembered we agreed to return to our old schedule concerning those blasted self-defense classes.

"What?" My nasty tone of voice had no effect at all.

I heard her sigh, but I ignored the sound. Maybe she would go away if I kept my mouth shut—no such luck.

"I knew you would try to wiggle out of our plans. You're still in bed, aren't you?" she demanded.

Boy, she could really be pushy sometimes. I nestled further into my pillows. "Sorta."

"Well, you aren't getting out of our class. Time to get moving, young lady!" she snapped.

Wow, what was the cause of her temper? I made a face, knowing full well I was the reason.

"You have forty-five minutes until we need to leave. Plenty of time for your coffee, so you need to start moving. I expect you to be on time." The line went dead, and I was left staring dumbfounded at the phone. Her bossiness was becoming a little out of control in my opinion.

Slamming the phone down, I knew my stubborn streak would kick in if I wasn't careful. After yesterday's meeting, I was aware those classes were more important than I cared to admit. Sighing, I swung my legs out from underneath the covers, allowing them to dangle over the edge of the bed for a moment before I got my butt in gear.

Andy stuck his head out from the bathroom. "Did I hear the phone?"

I looked over at him absently. "Hmm?"

He burst into laughter. "Amy?"

I took a deep breath. "Yep. Just my luck I get stuck with a partner who loves the early morning," I grumbled, finally plopping my feet on the floor.

Since Andy was occupying our bathroom, I headed for the spare toilet. Once done with the morning necessities, I headed longingly for my coffee. As I popped a pod into the coffee machine, I looked around, hoping none of my dead friends decided to grace my morning with their presence. I smiled happily, I was alone to enjoy my first cup of coffee. Silence is golden … too bad it didn't last long.

"Hey, Peg." The whisper came from the corner.

Sighing, I turned to face the voice.

Bob stepped out of the shadows, his face filled with concern. I was so used to his bouncy personality, I was a bit alarmed at his demeanor.

"Bob, what's wrong?" My irritation at the interruption of my morning ritual evaporated when I saw the expression on his face.

"The situation with Elaine is really bothering me. Logan won't tell me where he has her hidden, and I'm worried about her." He paused. "I know she is working for our enemies, but I *was* married to her. It sorta feels like I'm abandoning her, ya know?"

I wasn't sorry one bit that Elaine was hidden away, but I did feel bad for Bob since he was struggling with the situation.

"Bob, Logan knows what he's doing. Maybe it's best for Elaine ... keeps her out of trouble and away from the bad side. It might help her in the long run."

His face cleared as he listened to me. "You really think there's a chance she'll change?"

No way, no how, but I wasn't about to burst his bubble. Let Logan handle Bob's emotions—I'm not qualified.

I hesitated. "Time will tell." I didn't want to outright lie to the guy, but it wouldn't help our current investigation if Bob was busy worrying about Elaine. I needed him to stay focused.

Satisfied with my analysis of his wife's situation, he nodded. He glanced at my coffee cup. "Sorry about showing up before you filled your caffeine needs."

I wasn't about to jump down his throat when the poor guy needed someone to talk to. "No problem, Bob. I understand but try not to worry. Ok?"

He nodded. "You're right. Logan knows what he's doing. I trust him."

Maybe, maybe not. Logan did things his own way ... not necessarily the right way, but I kept those thoughts to myself.

"See ya later, gator." Bob disappeared as he spoke.

I looked down at my coffee cup. I knew my elixir was no longer hot, so I hauled my butt over to the sink and dumped the lukewarm brew down the drain. I decided I'd start from scratch and brew a fresh cup. Standing in front of the coffee maker while hot coffee streamed into my waiting cup, my thoughts drifted to the drug case. The Mendoza family scared me. Drugs weren't up my alley, but I was sure Jack was aware of the problems caused by the influx. Shaking my head, I was disgusted at the thought of another case getting ugly fast.

The shrill of the phone made me jump. Glancing at the clock, my stomach knotted. Who now? I'd never be able to drink my needed amount of coffee, get dressed, and get out the door to meet Amy on time if people kept interrupting my morning.

I grabbed the phone. "Yes?" Not necessarily the best way to answer a phone, but tough beans.

Adam's voice came on the line. "Hey, Mom." Adam is our oldest son. He calls periodically to catch up on any news he thinks his three younger brothers might be privy to that he, somehow, missed.

"Hey, babe. A little early you know."

He laughed. "Mom, I'm on my way to work and wanted to let you know we're coming to town in a few weeks."

My radar zoomed in on one word. "We?"

I could feel his grin through the miles of phone line. "Yep. I want you and Dad to meet someone. She's pretty special."

My stomach dropped as I leaned against the wall. "How special?" I felt a teensy bit of sweat forming.

"Pretty special ... special enough that I'm bringing her to meet you two."

It was way too early in the morning to be hearing about a potential future daughter-in-law. Adam was picky about girls, and I decided a long time ago he'd probably be the last of the boys to marry—he was proving my theory wrong.

I pulled myself together. "Ok, when are you planning on getting here?"

"We're trying to nail down a time frame. I'll get back to you with the details." He paused. "You ok, Mom?"

"Sure, why wouldn't I be?" Hell no! I wasn't ok! I'm in the middle of a drug cartel case, and Adam decides to bring a special someone home to meet the parents.

"Gotta get going, the traffic is picking up. Tell Dad, ok?"

"Yep, I will." I agreed. "Love ya."

"Love ya back," he said, then he hung up.

Slowly sitting down, I instinctively reached for my coffee cup. I could hear Andy coming toward the kitchen. I made up my mind, I would be happy about this new development.

As Andy made it to the kitchen doorway, he stopped. "What's wrong?"

I burst into tears. "Adam's bringing home a girl to meet us!" So much for happiness.

He took the few steps to reach me, then pulled me into a bear hug. "It had to happen sooner or later."

I sniffed. "I know, but now? My life is crazy, and he wants to introduce us to his girl. He's never brought a girlfriend home before."

He patted my back lovingly. "Peg, it's fine. It's about time for him to settle down. I'm sure we'll like her."

"Maybe."

He looked up at the clock. "What time are you meeting Amy?"

I grabbed a tissue to blow my running nose. "Damnation! I haven't even been able to drink a full cup of coffee."

Andy grinned. "You better get a move on, or Amy will lecture you forever. Drink a cup on the way to your class."

Sighing, I started toward the bedroom to get dressed. "Then I'll have to pee the entire session."

Andy chuckled as I walked away, but I refused to acknowledge his obvious enjoyment of my lack of coffee … the rat!

Once dressed, I made my way back to the kitchen. Andy greeted me with a travel mug full of steaming coffee. I grinned as I accepted it. "Thanks."

I searched my purse for car keys, which always seemed to find a spectacular hiding place.

He cleared his throat. "Sweetie … try actually fighting back today. Don't let Amy's age hold you back."

"I'll try, but it goes against my principles. Ah! I found the little suckers!" I declared victory, holding up the prize, my keys. "I'm on my way." I headed for the car, my mind preoccupied with Adam and his girlfriend. Why didn't he mention this girl before now? I scanned my memory, wondering if I somehow missed stray remarks he might have made during one of our conversations. Shaking my head, I decided he never said one word about her. What was she like? What was her profession? How did they meet? What did she look like? The questions tumbled over each other as I fought to have a sense of peace concerning the mystery woman in my son's life.

A familiar voice broke the silence. "You'll like her."

My eyes watered. "How can you be so damn sure, Dad?"

He laughed. "I've checked her out, and it's a good match ... trust me."

My eyes narrowed. "How long have you known about her? I don't even know her name! Why didn't you tell me?"

Grinning, he shook his head. "The only information I'm giving you is that you'll approve. I'm not spoiling Adam's surprise. He'll answer your questions when they get here."

I sighed, my frustration growing by the minute. "It's not fair!"

He shook his head again. "I need you focused, which is the only reason I am willing to tell you anything at all."

"Fine, but you better be correct in your estimation. What makes you think I'll approve of her?"

His grin widened. "Won't work."

I sighed. "What won't work?"

"Trying to dig information out of me. I'm not saying another word about Adam's girl."

I guess I inherited stubbornness from Dad because he sure was being pigheaded about handing out information.

I crammed the key into the ignition and started the car. If I didn't get my butt in gear, Amy would be furious.

As I drove up to her house, I was a little surprised to see her outside waiting for me.

She stomped over to the car. "We'd better not be late."

My grip on the steering wheel tightened, but I managed to smile. "We'll be on time, promise."

Once Amy was buckled, I headed to our class. The silence in the car was thick with tension. I couldn't decide if the cause was Amy's anger at me or my own feelings about Adam. I decided to break the silence or class would be a misery. "Bob came by this morning. He's worried about Elaine."

"He needs to trust Logan. Elaine will be fine," Amy stated in her very matter-of-fact tone. Wow ... she must be furious with me. She wasn't concerned about Bob ... not even a little.

"Pretty much what I told him." I was hoping she would calm down.

We drove a few more minutes in silence. I was used to Amy's chatter on the way to class—the quiet was unnerving.

As we sat at the red light, waiting to turn onto Market Street where the self-defense studio was located, I glanced at her. "Amy, the silent treatment isn't like you. If you have something to say, damn well say it!"

She took a deep breath. Oh boy ... she was going to unload on me, I felt it coming. "Peg, I know you dislike these classes, but they have already saved our lives once and they probably will again. You need to take our situation seriously. It isn't like you to be so childish!"

Well, hell … she had me there.

"I do hate the classes. I am tired of being slammed to the floor. Let me point out that *you* tend to be the only one of us actually learning self-defense. I end up learning how to treat bruises," I snapped.

"It's your own fault. Don't think I haven't realized you use kid gloves with me. Why do you think I'm so hard on you? I'm hoping you'll fight back!"

A honk from the car behind me alerted me the light turned green. I turned into the studio parking lot and maneuvered the car into a spot.

Once I killed the engine, I faced Amy. "You're over eighty. I can't make myself push back; it goes against everything Nana taught me about respecting my elders." I shrugged. "If I hurt you, I'd never forgive myself."

"Oh, for Pete's sake! If you hurt me, I'll learn how to dodge an attacker better. The only reason I got the better of Anthony was because he didn't see me as a threat! Anyone else may have been able to defend themselves."

My mouth dropped open … it was a good point. "Ok, I promise I'll try to fight back … not sure how successful I'll be though."

"Hmph. I'm not breakable you know."

Well … yeah … she actually *was* breakable, but I decided to keep that opinion to myself.

When we got inside the studio, I was surprised to see Antonio. He wasn't usually at this particular location; he usually ran one of their many other classes. Seeing the look on my face, he allowed himself a small smile. "Hello, Mrs. Shaw, Mrs. Branch … how are you ladies today?"

"Please explain to Peg that she needs to defend herself against my actions. She is having a hard time fighting me," Amy explained.

I rolled my eyes.

Antonio's eyes grew wide, but he remained professional as always. "Yes, ma'am, I will talk with her. Class will be starting in five minutes."

I looked at Amy. "See, told you we wouldn't be late."

Amy stalked off to get ready for the class without saying a word to me. I looked at Antonio and shrugged.

"Mrs. Shaw, you really should be defending yourself. Mrs. Branch will not be prepared to truly defend herself otherwise." He held up a hand as I opened my mouth. "I know she's older than you are, but neither one of you are here to take etiquette lessons. You are here to learn how to stay alive in a bad situation."

Damn … he was right, and I knew it. I nodded but kept my mouth firmly shut.

He leaned closer to me, lowering his voice. "This case has mean people attached to it. You won't be facing an unbalanced, arrogant, spoiled brat like Anthony. These are hardened criminals who won't think twice about killing you."

Sweat started to form on my upper lip as I listened to Antonio. I nodded again. "It's hard … I'm afraid of hurting her."

He shook his head. "Better for her to be hurt *here* than find herself in a situation that she is unprepared to defend herself against out *there*." He nodded toward the street. "Here, I can make sure she has help." He cocked his head. "Were you aware she practices at home every day?"

My eyes widened in shock. "You're kidding!"

"No, ma'am. She is serious about the training; you aren't."

Jeez ... he was nailing my butt to the wall. "I hear you."

Antonio nodded. "Time for class."

As we proceeded through the training, I sadly realized I spent more time learning how to fall than learning the self-defense moves. As we progressed through the hour-long class, Antonio instructed me how to bar most of Amy's tactics. By the end of the hour, we were both sweating and out of breath.

Amy nodded at me. "See, Peg? I'm not as breakable as you thought."

"Maybe, maybe not."

"When you block me, I have to trust my instincts will lead me to another move. I'm amazed how fast my reactions have become and how hard it is to truly defend myself when someone won't let up. It was great!"

I saw the wisdom in her words and nodded. "Yes, but you are pretty good at this stuff."

She smiled. "I realized from the start I was at a disadvantage."

My eyebrows scrunched together. "What disadvantage?"

"My age, sweetie. Plus, I'm short. I need the training."

I laughed. "I'm no spring chicken, and I'm only an inch taller than you."

"The important thing to remember is that whoever we will be defending ourselves against won't be as old as either of us. They'll be younger, fitter, and very determined. Anthony was a piece of cake in comparison to whoever we may be working against in the future." She paused. "I'm a little worried about this case. Everything I've read about the drug families leads me to believe we may be in over our heads."

Wiping the sweat from my neck with the towels provided, I nodded. "I know, it scares me. I'm sure it's the reason Logan already started calling in the pros." I jerked my head in Antonio's direction.

"Even Sal is concerned for us. Which is exactly why I want a gun," Amy said.

Jeez Louise … guns again.

I began digging in my purse for my keys. "Amy, I'm not so sure guns are a good idea." How can the darn things hide so successfully?

She sighed. "I realize we would need training, but it's worth knowing we have extra firepower."

Good grief ... isn't that why Logan uses my trio? They should be plenty of firepower.

"Remember last time it came down to us. Your friends were overwhelmed by Anthony," Amy said as if reading my mind.

I sighed. She would remember that one little fact.

CHAPTER 10

After depositing Amy at her front door, I made my way home. Once I showered, I decided a bit of research was in order. Amy wasn't the only one of us who knew how to use a computer.

I sat down at the table with a bowl of fresh salad. Since my jeans tightened a bit around the waist recently, I had to face the fact that salads would be on the menu for the next week or two—fine by me. I loved them, and I already noticed a difference. Pulling my computer in front of me, I typed 'gun training' into the search engine. Shocked by how many websites popped up, I quickly scanned the list to find the nearest class. I groaned when I realized it would involve driving across the valley into a neighboring city. I perked up once I saw the place was only two streets away from my favorite bakery. I decided it would definitely be worth the trip.

I wrote down the phone number to the place as I munched on fresh lettuce laced with garlic salt and lime juice—one of my favorite salad dressings. It had no fat or carbs, so it was a win-win meal. My jaw stopped moving when I spotted the prices. If we planned to go once or twice, it wouldn't be a problem. I had to be honest with myself, efficiency would not occur in one or two sessions. Much like the self-defense classes, it would take hours of practice and many lessons … jeez.

The phone rang as I was mulling over the problem.

Amy's voice came on the line. "I've been looking into gun ranges. They're a bit pricey in my opinion."

I nodded. "Yep … just noticed it myself. I'm on one of the websites."

"Oh, good girl! You've taken my suggestion seriously." I could hear the pride in her voice as if I was one of her students.

I sighed. "Still doesn't solve the problem of the prices."

Amy had no financial worries, but I couldn't spend freely. Andy and I lived on a budget.

"I talked to Sal, and he's willing to give us basic lessons. Plus, since he's living at Anthony's house, there's plenty of room to set up a firing range for us to practice."

After Anthony was committed to an asylum for the criminally insane, Sal moved into his house. I eventually figured out it was actually Sal who owned the property and the house where Laura lived. He decided that with Bella dead and Anthony safely incarcerated, he could have a normal grandparent relationship with Caterina, and he could help Laura better if he lived near them. So far, the arrangement worked just fine.

True to his word, Logan protected the little girl emotionally, and he spoke with her while she was in a coma after her father ran her down with his car. Anthony wanted a son to inherit the family business from him, so he decided his daughter was a disposable complication that was in the way. Caterina heard Logan's voice throughout the ordeal and trusted him completely. She came out of the situation reasonably well, and she was relieved to be with her mother.

"Can we shoot guns in the township?" I asked. I couldn't keep up with the changing rules in our community. Once a farming area, guns would fire periodically at coyotes who found their way into chicken coops, or at deer who ate through a crop. Not too many farmers were left in the township, but many gardens still needed protection from critters roaming at night, looking for an easy snack. Occasional shots could still be heard during the summer months, but the amount was decreasing with time.

Amy shrugged. "Jack should know."

"Yep … I'll ask him when I see him next." I had no wish to speed up the entire gun toting process, and I thought slowing down Amy's gung-ho attitude was in order.

"Hmm … you aren't stonewalling, are you?" she asked, suspicious of my dodge. How the old gal could zero in so precisely was unnerving. Must be all the psychology courses she took eons ago in college.

"Absolutely not! I just don't want to become a headache for Jack since we do *work* for the police department."

"Oh, dear. I didn't consider our work with Jack." She sighed. "We need to check and make sure this isn't going to cause a problem."

Bingo! Amy was basically a law-abiding citizen. Given her emotional need to be a model citizen, I was able to kick this particular can down the road a little. The last thing we needed was for her to get a concealed carry permit—what a nightmare. I could imagine her hauling some huge handgun around, ready for action. I shuddered at the mere thought of Amy owning a gun. I would talk to Sal. Surely he understood the need to tame her ... just a tad. I just hoped love didn't blind him completely, concerning her safety anyway. Amy would be a hell of a lot safer unarmed, but that thought was merely my opinion.

I nodded, agreeing. "Yep, I totally agree. I'll get right on it and let you know what information I find."

Silence greeted my statement. After a few more seconds, I heard her sigh. "Fine. Let me know."

"Absolutely. Jack will know the rules and regulations, so we don't step over any lines."

"Yes. Don't forget we have another class in a couple of days." Amy hung up before I could acknowledge her remark, which was fine by me. The conversation made me itchy. The quicker she gave up her obsession with guns, the happier I would be. I was positive everyone else involved would agree.

I heard a pop. Turning to see a stranger standing in my kitchen, I began to sweat, and I wasn't sure how to handle the situation. I decided to go with manners and see where it got me. "May I help you? I think you might be in the wrong place."

The man standing in front of me was studying my face as if he needed to memorize every pore. He had a greasy appearance as though bathing and general cleanliness were not part of his education. He was of average height with dark hair and eyes. His eyes never left my face. My skin began to crawl, and the hairs stood on the back of my neck—this probably wasn't good.

"Are you Peg?" he asked, finally speaking.

"Why do you ask?" I decided evasive action was called for, so I refused to hand over information I might later regret.

His eyes narrowed. "I asked you a question."

"Yes, you did." I had no idea who this yo-yo was, so no outgoing information was my plan of action.

His eyes left my face and began to wander around the kitchen. He seemed to be looking for something in particular, but I sure as hell wasn't about to ask what he wanted. As he scoured the room, his face became puzzled. I found myself following his lead, and my own eyes began to wander.

Finally, he faced me again. "I was told I would be in the correct place if the wallpaper was peeling. Where is it?" He was clearly frustrated.

My favorite Bath police officer, Dougal MacMillian, was freshly hired on the force. He offered to fix the wallpaper for the price of cake and coffee. It was a done deal, and I was glad he accomplished the job a few weeks ago.

I shrugged. "As you can see, there is no peeling wallpaper."

He frowned again, obviously confused. "Are you Peg? Nell's Peg?"

"What do you want?" The mention of my mother's name was a big, fat red flag, so I wasn't about to spill any beans if I could help it.

"Answer the questions!" he demanded.

I refused. "Who are *you*?"

I could see his anger growing by the minute, but I held my ground. "You must leave!" Why didn't I think of this earlier ... before my sweat glands went into overdrive?

The fury on his face was the last thing I saw before he faded into oblivion. Once I was positive he was gone, I leaned against the wall for support. My knees wouldn't hold me, so I slid slowly down the wall until my butt touched the floor. I glanced down at my hands, and I wasn't surprised to see them shaking wildly.

"Bob!" I called. Even I could hear the panic in my voice.

A small pop and there he stood. One look is all it took. "I'll be right back."

I must've looked pretty bad for Bob to assess the situation in a split-second. I opened my mouth to argue, but he skedaddled too fast. He was back before tears started to flow, and he wasn't alone.

"Oh, Dad!" The tears began to fall freely down my face.

Squatting next to me, he waited patiently until I pulled myself together. I struggled to haul my body off the floor, then I headed for the tissue box. Once my nose was taken care of, I took a deep breath. "Ok ... some guy showed up. He was creepy ... asking if I was Peg ... Nell's Peg."

Bob frowned. "Uh-oh ... this can't be good."

Dad stood, shaking his head. "Your mother can't reach you, so she sent someone else. I'm not sure if Logan anticipated this situation." He turned and looked out the window—I knew what would come next.

"I'm looking," I snapped before he had a chance to ask.

I closed my eyes, turned my head, and opened one eye. Yep ... the whole gang was out back walking around anxiously.

I sighed. "They're all there ... every last one of them."

"Vikings?" Dad's expression remained neutral as he watched me.

"Yep ... more than usual."

Dad turned to Bob, who nodded at the silent command, then Bob was gone in a flash.

I held up my hands. "You sent for Logan." It wasn't a question.

"He needs to be informed." Dad's calm expression remained in place.

I nodded. "I agree."

"You might want to warn Amy," he added.

Reaching for the phone, I felt my heart begin to pound. I hoped the guy didn't already head over to Amy's place.

By the fourth ring, I began to pace. I let it ring at least twenty more times but no luck.

I glanced at Dad. "Maybe she's not home."

"Possible, but once Bob returns, I'll head over to check on her."

We waited for Logan and Bob silently. I was too scared to talk, and Dad was deep in thought, which didn't make me feel all warm and fuzzy.

After an eternity, the room was suddenly full of people. Logan gave orders the moment they hit the kitchen, and his small army of men began spreading out to every room in the house.

Logan turned toward me. "Peg, remain calm. I will return momentarily."

He quickly faded, but I instinctively knew where he went. Looking out at the woods, I spotted him as he spoke with the dead gang out back. He pointed to the four corners of the property, and with his arm movement, he included Amy's property as well. Once he was satisfied his orders were understood, he reappeared in my kitchen. "I have increased your protection to include the interior of the house. Please call Amy and inform her."

I shook my head. "I just called, no answer … I'm worried."

Logan turned toward Dad, who nodded and was gone instantly.

Logan studied me a moment. "Describe the man who was here."

I gave him the description. He nodded as he listened. "Yes, I am aware of this man. He works for the Mendoza family on our side of life."

I came to the same conclusion all by myself, but I kept my mouth shut because I didn't want to ruin the flow of his thoughts. He continued to gaze out the window as he watched his orders being followed. I joined him at the window. I was surprised at the number of people who were carrying out Logan's commands.

Frowning, I turned to him. "Logan ... um ... are there more than usual?"

He nodded. "Before Bob came to me, one of my men informed me of your visitor. It is wise to increase their numbers." He nodded at the activity in my backyard. "When the enemy uses reinforcements, I also increase those who protect." He shrugged. "Basic battle plans."

I continued to watch the scene outside. "You weren't kidding when you said this is war."

"No, I was not."

Jeez … what would Andy say when he got home? This was not a good situation.

Logan spoke as if he read my thoughts, a habit that always pissed me off. "I have been in contact with Andy. He understands the new development increases the level of danger." He paused. "Andy assured me he remains resolute concerning his decision to remain in the fight."

A random thought hit my brain. "What is the guy's name that scared the living daylights out of me?"

"His name is of no importance. His appearance is our utmost concern. Nell is enlisting the help of the Mendoza family." He sighed. "We now have positive proof the information Elaine gave us is true. We are fortunate to have the assurance that we are planning correctly."

My temper started to rise. "We are fortunate? Really? Some creepy guy shows up, and you decide we are fortunate?"

I had to hand it to Logan. By now, he was used to my angry outbursts and handled them easily. When I say 'handled' I mean he ignores them, giving me time to emotionally explode before I become rational again.

Once he was convinced I was finished talking, he turned to me. "Peg, I understand it was uncomfortable to have this man in your house. You handled yourself exactly as I would have led you to, if I had been here. I am pleased with your command of the situation."

I snorted. "Really? How nice of you." The snark in my tone didn't irritate him. Sometimes Logan's self-assured attitude got on my nerves.

"Did you offer any information?"

I shook my head firmly. "Nope."

He nodded. "He asked questions. How did you handle those?"

I shrugged. "I asked my own questions."

He smiled. "Yes. You probably confused him greatly. He was expecting a compliant person, which you most certainly are not."

I let the comment slide, mainly because he was right. I wasn't necessarily an easy person to deal with once the fuse to my anger was lit. Add in the fact that I was scared spitless, and you have the recipe for a major pissing contest. I had to admit, I was afraid of providing information my mother could use. I'm not sure I actually used cunning as much as fear. Either way, it worked, so I could rest easy.

Glancing at the clock, I was surprised to see how late it was getting— time to start dinner.

I headed for the refrigerator to pull out leftovers. I was glad I wasn't responsible for feeding the entire crew of protectors who now roamed the property. Dead people don't eat, sleep, or need to use the bathroom.

"Do you think the creep will show up again?" I asked Logan as I bent down to get the skillet I kept in the lower cabinet. I heard a loud snap. Glass shattered, and air rushed past me, followed by a thud. I began to stand trying to see what the commotion was.

"Peg, keep down," Logan warned. "There is someone in the woods shooting a gun, and I believe it is aimed at you."

Well ... hells bells.

Dad suddenly showed up. "I heard a gun. Peg, are you ok?"

"Yep, but Logan won't let me stand." I made a command decision because if I kept squatting my knees would never forgive me. I turned, sat on my butt, and leaned against the cabinet door. I looked up at Dad. "Did you find Amy?"

He shook his head, clearly concerned.

"Have you tried contacting Salvatorio?" Logan asked as he continued observing his orders being followed to a T in my backyard.

"Crap … never thought Amy might be with Sal. I'm not moving from this spot for my phone though."

Dad smiled. "Since he lives at Anthony's house, I'm sure I can find them … give me a few minutes." He was gone before I had a chance to say another word to him.

I looked over at Logan. "Logan, should I call Jack?"

"Excellent idea, though I surmise he is aware of the gunshot by now."

I decided it was time to make a move, so I crawled over to grab my cellphone out of my purse. I punched in Jack's phone number.

He answered on the second ring. "What?" he barked.

I frowned. "Why are you yelling at me? Someone tried to shoot me if you're interested."

Silence.

Finally, Jack sighed. "I hope this is a joke, but somehow I don't think it is."

"I now have a bullet hole in my kitchen cabinet." I inspected the damage and wondered if insurance would pay for the repair.

A few seconds of silence passed before Jack spoke again. "Did you get hurt?"

"No, but Logan won't let me off the floor. I think the shooter is still sitting in the woods, probably waiting until I stand up."

"Holy hell. Ok … I'm on my way, and I'm sending a cruiser out to inspect the hill. Sit tight until I get there. I'll come around to the kitchen door."

"Sounds like a plan." I hesitated a moment. "How long do you think it will take you?"

"About two minutes." His voice was gruff indicating his discontent with the situation. "I'm in the car already. Did you call Andy?"

"Didn't have to. Logan went by his office and had a chat with him."

Jack hesitated. "Logan went to Andy's office? … Wow."

"Yeah … I was surprised myself."

"I'm pulling out of the station parking lot now, so keep down until we clear the area," Jack ordered.

"You got it," I assured him, then hung up the cellphone.

I looked over at Logan, who continued observing his army of dead folks out back. I had no idea what he thought of our present situation, and he didn't seem to be in a mood to share any information … what a pickle.

CHAPTER 11

I wasn't surprised when Jack showed up at the kitchen door in record time. I kept my head down as I crawled to the door and unlocked it. My head must have risen higher than I realized because I felt another puff of air as a fresh bullet whizzed past my ear. Another hole in my cabinet ... damn.

Logan turned to face me. I was sure he was wondering if I joined him on his side of the veil. He nodded and turned back to survey his troops once he was satisfied that I still had a heartbeat.

Jack crouched down on my level as he opened the door. He crawled toward the refrigerator, making me wonder if he decided pie sounded good—might take the tension out of the situation.

Jack looked at me. "Hells bells, Peg. What is going on around here?"

"Your guess is as good as mine. My first hunch would be the Mendoza family." A shiver ran up my spine. "How'd they know we are interested in them?"

Jack's eyes grew wide. "We better not have another snitch in the department!"

"Owen wasn't a snitch," I reminded him, referring to our first case together. "He was trying to stop our investigation."

"True ... but he leaked information."

I nodded. "Yep, trying to block our efforts ... not the same thing at all."

We were sitting on the floor, leaned against the cabinet, when his cellphone rang. As he answered, I inspected the newest hole in my woodwork. My heart was pounding in my chest, but I was surprised at how well I was handling bullets zipping around my kitchen. Logan was still parked at the window. As he moved slightly to his left, I spotted my now demolished window where the bullets made entry into what I consider my sanctuary—my kitchen. One more shot, and I'd have more glass all over the floor. I studied the angle of trajectory and realized the bullets passed straight through Logan's form ... wow.

"Well ..." Jack interrupted my thoughts. "... they missed whoever was shooting at you by about one minute. They are scouring the area, looking for clues. To be honest, if the guy was a professional, he wouldn't leave a trace, but it's worth the effort."

"Can I stand now?" I asked.

Jack stood, then helped me get to my feet. We walked over to the cracked window.

Jack let out a whistle. "Wow ... high-power rifle."

I frowned. "How do you know?"

"The hill where the shooter was positioned is a decent distance. Plus, it's far enough away I'd venture to guess he's a damn good shot."

My emotions finally caught up with the facts surrounding the situation. Hands shaking, I went numb from head to foot. Uh-oh ... not good, especially when stars started floating in front of my face.

I started a slow slump to the floor when Jack's arms shot out, catching me.

"Damn, Peg. I thought you were handling this too calmly. I should've known you'd fall apart eventually."

"Place her carefully on the floor. I will handle the situation." Logan sounded so far off, I wondered if he was still in the room or talking from a mile away.

Moments later, I felt a familiar sensation. Some part of my brain realized Logan was at work calming my body, mind, and heart. Logan only made physical contact a few times, but when he is in healing mode, it is pure heaven—no aches, pains, or other signs of age. It's fabulous but, sadly, it only lasts a few minutes.

It didn't take long, and I was in better shape. I looked up at Logan. "Thanks ... I appreciate your help."

He nodded. "We need you at your best. Frayed nerves would slow our work."

Jeez ... he only helped because he needed me?

Jack's eyes narrowed. "Do you know who was on the hill?"

Logan grimaced and shook his head. "Jack, I would inform you if I was aware of the culprit. I wish no harm to Peg or the rest of you. Your involvement is extremely important."

A snotty remark was making its way to the surface when I heard a soft pop. Looking around, I spotted Dad. "Amy's safe. She is with Sal, and I told her to stay put."

Logan nodded. "It is the safest place for her now that there is a sharpshooter moving around the area."

"I agree," Jack added.

I looked at him with slight surprise. "Since when are you a fan of the mob?"

His face grew red, but he held his position. "Peg, we have a mess on our hands. Sal may be a mobster, but he does have resources available to him. Amy is safer with Sal than at home alone."

I agreed with Jack, but I was still surprised by his attitude. I was glad he finally realized our mob guys weren't so bad after all.

"Peg, I am expanding your protection. Extra guards will now be stationed around a much wider perimeter," Logan informed me quietly. While he didn't seem worried, he certainly wasn't happy. He looked over at Jack. "How far does a bullet travel?"

"Doesn't really matter. There is no direct line of sight to the house much more than a quarter of a mile." He pointed out the window. "Peg has mostly woods surrounding the property. There is only a small clearing to the north, and even that wouldn't amount to much."

"Well, it doesn't make me feel much better!" I retorted hotly. "Someone sure as hell fired two shots into my house today."

Jack looked at Logan. "I'm not happy those shots came from the woods. It would be easier if the guy picked the only clear line of fire. He must be damn good to attempt a direct hit through a wooded area." He paused. "It would be wise to have your friends roaming around the spots with a clear view of the kitchen. Peg is in this room more than any other area of her house."

Logan nodded as he listened to Jack. "Thank you. I believe it would be wise."

Jack agreed. "The more of your invisible friends we have milling around, the better chance we have of nabbing the guy."

"Please remember we do not have the ultimate advantage. The Mendoza family has many people on my side of life," Logan informed Jack.

Jack frowned. "So, if they have their dead guys out and about your dead guards could be spotted."

"Yes, it is a possibility. I think we should assume the enemy is present." Logan paused, then looked at me. "Which is why I believe the family is aware of Peg."

"Well, that's just peachy," I snapped. "We had the advantage having access to ghosts, now you're telling me the Mendoza family has their dead family members watching ... not good."

My cellphone rang before anyone could comment on my observation. "Hello?" I answered.

"Peg? This is Amy."

I breathed a sigh of relief. "You ok? Do you need anything?"

"Oh, no, dear. Sal has taken care of everything. I wanted you to know I'll be staying here for a few days. Sal thinks it's safer."

I took a deep breath. "Tell Sal it's a good plan, and I'm glad he can watch out for you."

While I agreed with Sal's plan, I am very protective of Amy, so the thought of her staying at his house for days was a bit unsettling. Did I turn into a prude? As I glanced over at the window, I caught the smile on Logan's face. He knew Amy's romance with Sal caught me by surprise. I knew he got a great deal of enjoyment from watching me struggle with the relationship.

Once I hung up with Amy, I looked at Jack. "Do you think Tom Newman has any idea drugs are being processed on his property?"

Jack shook his head. "I may not like the man, but even I admit he's probably clueless. I don't see him getting involved with drug cartels; he just isn't the type."

Logan cocked his head. "You believe a man's guilt or innocence can be determined by his *type*? People are very capable of shielding activity they want hidden from society."

Jack thought a moment. "I've known this guy for a long time. He's a stickler for rules and regulations, and he's a straight shooter. He happens to be a pain in the ass, but that doesn't equal being involved with drugs."

"Your logic is sound. I assume you are confirming he is innocent." It wasn't a question, but Logan was skating pretty close to telling Jack how to do his job—not a good idea.

Jack's jaw tightened, but he held his temper. "Yep ... it's not sensible to ignore the possibility no matter how ridiculous. To make a compelling case against the Mendoza family, I need to eliminate every other prospect." He paused, thinking. "You have to hand it to these guys, they picked the one stretch of land I would never suspect."

"How'd you figure it out?" I asked.

"Undercover work eventually led us to his place. There's an old shed at the back of Newman's property that I bet no one has thought about for years. My guy snooped around and found their stash and operation." He shook his head. "We aren't dealing with total idiots."

Dad cut in when Jack finished speaking. "Logan, do you want to put a couple of our guys at this shack?"

Logan's eyes returned to the wooded area at the back of our property. The three of us stayed silent, allowing him time to decide. Finally, he shook his head. "I do not believe it is wise."

Jack's mouth dropped open. "What? I think it's a great idea. Your guys are invisible to almost everyone. It could point us in the right direction."

Logan turned to face Jack. "In other circumstances, I would agree with your suggestion. However, if the Mendoza family is responsible for the drugs here, they will be using their own family members on my side to guard their enterprise. I do not wish the extent of our involvement to be known; it could compromise the leverage we have built."

Dad's brow furrowed thoughtfully. "You think they already know?"

Logan nodded. "I believe they may suspect. Peg has become well-known to the other side of life. I would keep her association with us shielded if possible." He smiled at me. "She has been quite successful dealing with her assignments, which has caught the attention of many."

My face grew warm, and I knew it was turning shades of red. Praise from Logan was rare and it warmed my heart.

Logan turned to Dad. "Dave, you know how to find me."

Dad nodded, then Logan faded.

"Damn … I really thought he'd have one of his guys …" Jack hooked his thumb toward the woods. "… spy on Newman's property. It took me by surprise when he refused."

Dad was quick to defend Logan. "He has good reason."

I nodded in agreement. "Yep, if the bad guys have a dead squad of their own, they'd spot Logan's guys in a split-second."

Jack sighed. "I know. I guess I count on Logan's help more than I realize."

"Are you sure not talking to Tom Newman about the shed is the best way to handle the situation?" I asked.

Jack nodded. "I need to know who is using the damn shed before I confront him. If it's his grandson, who I strongly suspect is the culprit, I need facts. Suspicion won't be enough, and it might make him unwilling to work with us. I need him to be cooperative."

I frowned. "How involved do you think his grandson is with the drug trade? Tom's not going to be very happy with the kid."

Jack hesitated before answering. "I'm not sure he's the main person we are after, but he certainly is connected to someone who knows the drug business. There is a strong suspicion he's selling the stuff at school, but until I have absolute proof, I'm not telling Tom anything. Once school is back in session, we'll watch him closely."

I thought about what he was saying for a moment. "I see your point. If Tom thought you were picking on his grandson as some sort of retaliation against him, he would fight you tooth and nail."

Jack nodded. "Exactly … that's why I'm keeping quiet. Let's see where our investigation leads." He looked at the refrigerator. "Any pie?"

Laughing, I turned to go to the fridge but stopped in my tracks. I was face to face with my earlier intruder. My throat tightened, and my heart pounded so hard inside my chest, I thought it would burst through.

Thankfully, Dad took control of the situation. "Come on, fella. I have someone who wants to talk with you." Dad grabbed my uninvited guest. They both faded quickly, leaving Jack and I standing in the middle of the kitchen with our mouths hanging open.

Jack found his voice first. "Was he the guy you saw earlier?"

I nodded. "Yep … creepy … isn't he?"

Jack sighed. "Worse than that … I recognize him."

"What?" The knots in my stomach became tighter.

"Yeah, he's some lowlife from New York."

I frowned. "How do you know?"

"When I was researching the Mendoza family's drug business, his picture was in the file as a known associate. I didn't pay much attention to him since he's from New York. I figured he'd never show up here."

"Did you know he's dead? Let's face it … living people don't pop up in my kitchen," I snapped.

Jack shook his head. "Nope. The file listed him as alive and well. There's still a warrant out for his arrest."

"Are you going to call someone and let them know he's no longer in the land of the living?"

Jack's eyebrows raised. "And when they ask me how I know I tell them his ghost showed up here? That's not going to sound too reasonable."

I sighed. "Yeah … I see your point. So, what can you do with this new information?"

"Call Sal. I bet dollars to donuts he will know more about the guy than any file I could read. Do you have his number?"

I grabbed my cellphone and scrolled through my contact list until I found Sal's number. Once I relayed the information to Jack, I decided to sneak a peek out back. My protectors were spread throughout the property. If I squinted hard enough, I could spot them prowling through the woods. They were limited to the amount of help they could actually give me. Notifying Logan or Bob was the most they were able to accomplish, but it was usually enough. Standing there watching the activity, I wondered if our mystery New Yorker could see all the help I had from Deadsville. Logan blocked them from my mother's view a while back. I decided I would ask the next time I saw him. I'd feel better if he did hide their presence from any spirit nosing around my property. We might have found our snitch. If my visitor *had* seen them and reported back to his boss, it would explain why I had a sniper taking shots at me.

I turned back to Jack once I heard him end his call with Sal. "Well?"

"Yep, he knows of the guy. Goes by the name of Joseph O'Malley.

Worked for a seedier crowd but not any one mob family."

"Irish mob?" I asked.

"No idea. Sal thinks he worked mainly for himself, but he's bad news dead or alive. Sal wasn't happy he's involved."

"I'm wondering if he's our blabbermouth who told the bad guys you've discovered their drug enterprise."

Jack's eyes widened. "So, the crooks have access to ghosts as much as we do?" He shook his head. "I have to admit, I never thought criminals would have the same type of help."

I frowned. "Anthony had help … his mother, and Owen heard voices."

"Yeah, but they were squirrelly. I just didn't think it was coordinated in the same fashion as Logan formed. Let's be honest … Logan is one organized individual." He sighed. "I have heartburn thinking about gangsters tapping into the spirit world. Way too many possibilities for complications. My life is squirrelly enough now." He rubbed his stomach. "I never got my pie."

I shook my head and headed for the refrigerator. "You better watch the calories … your waistline is expanding."

"Yeah, I know. Over the past few months, Lori's been hinting about diets for both of us." Lori was Jack's wife of thirty plus years and a real sweetheart. She put up with his long hours and frustrations concerning township politics with obvious grace. She's a better woman than I am … politics irritate me.

I grabbed a fork and napkin, then glanced at him. "Coffee to go along with this pie?"

"Sure." Jack nodded. "No sugar though."

I laughed. "Enough sugar in the pie?"

"Yep." He smiled.

As he was getting settled at the table, the air changed.

"Well, your unwanted visitor is contained." Dad was looking at the pie in front of Jack, he grinned but kept his thoughts to himself.

"Exactly where did you take him?" Jack asked, ignoring Dad's grin.

Dad shook his head. "That's privileged information. The less you know, the better off you are."

I raised an eyebrow at his comment. "Somewhere we wouldn't approve of, or more along the lines of 'loose lips sink ships'?"

"Logan's worst fear is that invisible eyes and ears are watching you. He has great power, but even he has limitations. Evil has many resources, and Logan wants you and Andy as safe as possible. The less said aloud, the better."

Sweat formed on my upper lip, and my stomach clenched. "Jeez, Dad."

He watched me carefully. "I know it puts more stress on you, but those are the facts. You need to be aware how dangerous this work is becoming."

"Unhealthier than it is already?" I snorted. "I didn't think it was possible."

He stood quietly studying me, his expression was so serious sweat began to trickle down my back. "Twinkle toes, the more successful our work, the harder evil fights us. It's been the main battle through the centuries, and it isn't going to change anytime soon."

I leaned against the wall, hoping to hide the shakes that were suddenly taking over—his words were not good news.

Jack swallowed a mouthful of pie. "Peg, focus on this case. It's not our job to worry about the big picture … leave that shit to Logan. One case at a time … otherwise, we'll be overwhelmed."

I couldn't believe my ears. Jack was usually furious with situations we found ourselves in the middle of, and he blamed Logan's master plan. When did he decide to trust Logan's ideas? Jeez.

CHAPTER 12

Once Andy got home, he immediately inspected the damage the bullets caused. The window was easy—a simple call to our local glass guy to replace it. Our township isn't swamped with businesses, but the few we have are excellent. The Glass Solutions resided in our bordering township, but thankfully, it was only four miles from the house. Andy set up an appointment for the next morning. In the meantime, he cut up old cardboard boxes, and taped them carefully over the cracked window to keep the weather and insects out.

The cabinets would prove to be more of a challenge. They were the original woodwork, and a repair job wouldn't be easy.

"I don't know, sweetie. We might have to tear them out and install new ones." Seeing my face, he rushed on. "Or we could dig out the bullets and try to fill the holes."

Tears formed, but I fought to maintain control. I loved the old woodwork throughout the house. The solid oak and the century-old stain, golden with time and life, would be impossible to match with new wood.

"It won't match. We'll never be able to find stain with the richness of color this old wood has."

He nodded. "I'm fine with patching."

"Could we just leave the bullets in there?"

Confusion creased his face. "What? You're kidding … right?"

I peered at the damage again. "Nope. Sorta adds a bit of character to the old place. If we dig the bullets out, the holes will be bigger. Anything we use to fill the holes will have to be stained, then we'll be back to the original problem of not being able to match the existing color."

He sighed. "You're serious. Damn it, Peg … I don't want two bullets stuck in the cabinets forever."

"Not forever … just for now. If we rush to a decision, we'll regret it," I warned.

He studied my face, then sighed. "You have a point, but only until this case is over, then we fix the damage."

I nodded. No sense in arguing about holes—we had much bigger problems.

We finished dinner, and after cleaning the kitchen, Andy decided it was time to discuss the day's events. "Ok … bring me up to date. Logan only told me there were shots fired at you."

I filled him in on the status of the case and left nothing out. I watched his face as I informed him that the bad characters in Deadsville have their own network of informers.

His frown deepened once he heard that Logan was concerned. "I guess we need to stop believing Logan is all powerful. He has his limitations, which is a little unnerving."

"Yep, fact is … Logan is basically a dead human, just more powerful than the average ghost. The way he and Dad talk about evil is creepy." I shuddered.

"Once I stop and think about stuff, I realize good and bad have always existed." He turned to me. "We aren't used to facing evil the way your dad and Logan have to deal with it. The whole situation is still damn new to us."

I nodded. "Just about the time I think I've figured out the rules in Deadsville, I find out the rules have changed, or my ideas were wrong to begin with." Andy was quiet for so long, I began to squirm. "You ok?"

"What? Oh … sure." He turned to me again. "Peg … a few months ago, we thought we had a nice, quiet life. Now, we have more excitement than we know what to do with, and it isn't slowing down. It makes you start wondering."

I frowned. "Wondering what?"

"Our true purpose here and once we're dead. What is life actually all about?"

Oh, jeez … I wasn't in the mood for philosophy tonight.

Logan's voice broke the silence. "An excellent question."

I didn't bother turning around. "Do you have the answer to that question?"

He chuckled. "No one has the complete answer. I would encourage everyone to strive to leave earth better than when you entered."

"Ha! Impossible. When in the course of human history has that happened?" I snapped.

"Sadly, not often."

"Logan?" Andy cut in. "Is our purpose here truly worth the trouble?"

Logan moved closer to the window. His tall, magnificent stature seemed to glow in the setting sun. I had to admit, even though I was used to his appearance, he was an impressive figure, who made my heart race a bit. His long, thick, dark hair had one small side braid that fell past his shoulder. There were no ornaments in his hair today, unlike past appearances when his intention was to impress. I decided this must be his casual look. There was no need for formal attire when it was just Andy and me.

"Life holds many mysteries and does become difficult at times." He paused, then continued. "It is my opinion, based on my own experiences, our lives make a difference. Each person has the opportunity to influence the world through positive avenues. Our lives are intertwined with each individual we encounter." He sighed. "However, human nature, at times, displays itself very poorly. Wars, brutality, greed, and selfishness scar the soul."

Andy listened to Logan's words intently. The sadness that covered my sweetie's face broke my heart. A few weeks ago, Andy was a patient, fun-loving man; tonight ... he seemed disheartened.

Andy shook his head slowly. "Sometimes these situations are overwhelming, and I wonder if it's worth the bother."

Logan turned to him. "Andy, life *can* be overwhelming. However, I promise the work you are willing to perform with Peg, Amy, Jack, and the others will count in the long run. You must know there is much more than you are able to realize while you are on this side of life's veil. Trust me, your efforts are not worthless, quite the opposite."

Andy looked at Logan for what seemed an eternity, then slowly nodded his head. "I'll try to remember your words."

Logan acknowledged Andy's nod with one of his own, then faced the window again.

I snuck a peek out back, but the only movement I detected was the leaves on the trees swaying slightly in the breeze. "Is the danger over? I can't see any of the guys out back."

"The immediate situation is under control. The man who shot at you has not been found, but I feel confident we will eventually discover him." Logan spoke without bothering to turn to me.

A slight pop and Bob was in the kitchen. "Boss ... the fella Dave captured is secure. So far ... we can't make him tell us anything."

Logan, his eyes glued to the backyard, nodded but kept quiet.

Bob turned to us. "Hey, guys ... how are you doing?"

I shrugged. "Better now that no one is taking pot shots at me."

"Gee whiz, you've got two holes in your cabinets! Did you know that?" He was peering at the fresh marks in my beloved oak.

Irritation started to rise, but I relaxed when Andy chuckled. "Yep, we know. What have you been up to?"

Bob slid his eyes to Logan, then back to Andy. "Not much ... you know, working." He began rubbing his hands together, and I realized he was being careful because of Logan's presence.

"I'll tell you later," he mouthed silently.

Andy grinned, nodding.

"Well, I'm off," he said, a bit too loud.

His volume was obviously for Logan's benefit. Hadn't he realized by now that Logan was probably well aware of his intentions to tell us any juicy news? Jeez.

I gave him a slight wave with my fingers, and after another small pop, he was gone. Never one to be comfortable around Logan, Bob seemed more antsy than usual. I'd bet dollars to donuts he had information he couldn't wait to tell us, but he knew Logan's firm rule concerning 'need to know' information. If I didn't need to know, I didn't have access to the information. Logan's attitude caused more than one argument between us, and I anticipated many more in the future.

"Peg?" Logan broke the silence. "Please refrain from leaving the house before checking in with either Santino or Antonio. They have their associates available for twenty-four-hour escort service, should you need to have an excursion."

I burst out laughing at his use of the term *escort service*. He frowned at my laughter, so I felt an explanation was in order. "Escort services usually refer to um ... well ... prostitutes."

It was obvious he was well aware of who prostitutes were, and I could've sworn he turned red.

He gave a brief nod. "Thank you for updating my terminology. I was unaware of the definition. However, I believe you understand my intentions."

"Yep, I do. Why do I need an escort?"

His eyes drifted to the fresh bullet holes in my cabinets, then back to me. "I trust once you have thought through your circumstances, you will arrive at the same conclusion I have."

"Jeez ... next thing I know you'll be agreeing with Amy about the damn guns," I snapped. His silence made me uncomfortable. I raised an eyebrow. "Really? You actually agree?"

"You should consider the option. If you decide a gun is in your best interest, I insist both of you take extensive training. Firearms are quite dangerous in inexperienced hands."

I sighed. "Exactly why we shouldn't be playing around with guns! What is wrong with you today?"

"There is a difference between 'playing' with guns and using them as an advantage," he corrected.

"We don't know squat about guns! We could kill ourselves!" My hands flew around my head as I exploded.

"With the proper training, which includes practice, a gun could mean the difference between you getting hurt or not." He remained patient despite my outburst.

I looked over at Andy for some backup but was shocked at his response.

"He may have a point, Peg. We've never had people shooting at us before. If you learn to handle a gun, it would sorta even the playing field."

I threw my hands up in disgust. "For Pete's sake, Andy. I don't know the first thing about the damn things."

Andy remained quiet, then shook his head. "Just think about it."

I saw the tension on his face and knew he was worried about our safety.

I sighed. "Fine … but thinking about it is all I'm willing to do at this point."

Logan turned to Andy. "I believe it would also be beneficial for you to join the ladies in their training."

Andy's mouth dropped open. "What? I don't have time for training. I still have a job … remember?"

Logan nodded. "I have not forgotten. However, I believe the time has come for those working with me to advance their abilities. Santino, Antonio, and Bill cannot guard you to the extent that may become necessary."

I narrowed my eyes. "What the hell does that mean?"

Logan's eyes wandered back to the window, well … the part not covered with cardboard. "Trouble is increasing, so we must be as prepared as possible. I have the ability and resources to work effectively on my side of the veil, but my living army needs expanding. Until that point, those who work with me should be at a higher level of competency."

Well, hell … his words weren't comforting one bit.

"You have an army?" Andy was awed at the thought.

Logan smiled. His eyes remained on the wooded area out back. "Of sorts. Many others aid my efforts, but defensive action have become of real importance." He turned to face us. "While I appreciate your involvement, a few more living people would be welcome. I am very careful about those I choose to join our endeavors, which causes the actual number of those helping to be rather on the low side." He shrugged. "The plan has been sufficient until recently."

"What has changed?" I asked. "I pretty much figured the bad guys have always been working hard to screw up life."

Logan shook his head. "We are entering a new era, one that has been prophesied for millennia. There will be much confusion and unrest. Our job is to minimize the damage while being victorious in the coming years."

My mind flashed back to Nana's quick explanation of 'preparing' the world for the next phase. I looked at Logan. "Nana said something about preparing the world. Preparing in what way?"

A small smile formed on Logan's lips. "Yes, your Nana has a rudimentary understanding of the war we are currently experiencing. However, she is correct in her basic analysis ... there is a new beginning in the future. No one knows quite when or how, only of the plan for this world to advance."

"This world?" Andy sounded intrigued. "There are other worlds?" Oh jeez ... Andy and his alien theories.

Logan's face became guarded. "An intriguing question."

Damn, those words would inspire Andy to dig for more information. Aliens were one of his few obsessions, and he was completely convinced of their existence. I didn't need Logan to feed those ideas just because he needed our help.

Andy's face lit up, all his fear gone now that his pet theory was possibly about to be proven. "So, there *are* other populated worlds out there." He was pointing to the sky as he spoke excitedly. "I knew it!"

Logan shook his head. "I do not believe those were my words."

Ha! He could try to get Andy off this subject, but it would be a challenge.

I cleared my throat and looked at Logan. "Back to the more important topic ... are you telling us to buy guns?"

He seemed relieved I changed the subject of our conversation. "I would encourage you to make inquiries and examine the possibility."

"I wouldn't know where to start," I said, exasperated.

He studied my face a moment. "I would advise you to use the resources available to you."

"What resources?" My temper was rising again.

Andy chuckled. "Peg, we have mob guys in and out of this house constantly. *They* are our resources."

I sighed. "I never thought about them. My trio is here to guard me not to teach me to shoot anyone. Besides, Santino thinks it's a really bad idea!"

Logan shook his head. "Your 'mob guys' are not only responsible for keeping you safe, they *do* have other responsibilities too. However, they are not to whom I was referring. Salvatorio would be an excellent choice for schooling all of you. He was trained by the very best, and he would be my first choice."

After I lifted my jaw off the floor, I stared at Logan. "Sal? But he's ..." I left the statement unspoken. I almost called Sal too old, which would have been a mistake. Amy was quite a few years older, and she could outperform me in every aspect of self-defense. I didn't necessarily take Amy seriously when she mentioned Sal earlier.

Logan smiled slightly. "Yes?"

I shook my head. "Never mind."

Andy grinned. He knew exactly what I was about to blurt out, and he also knew it was best left unspoken. Sal might be in his mid to late seventies, but the old boy still had clout physically. He subdued his own son after Amy and I surprised Anthony with a few self-defense moves. I knew Sal had elite training when he was younger and stayed in shape better than average men of any age group.

"If I am not mistaken, Salvatorio has already begun teaching Amy basic gun safety. He plans on constructing a practice range on the property for anyone needing to sharpen their skills," Logan continued.

Jeez Louise … Logan was, once again, a thousand steps ahead of me.

The phone ringing brought an end to the crazy talk about guns. One look at the caller ID informed me our oldest son was calling. I looked over at Andy. "Adam."

I grabbed the phone and heard Adam's voice. "Hey, Mom. Following up on our earlier conversation. How's next Friday sound for a weekend visit?"

"Let me check with your dad." I sighed as I put my hand over the receiver and turned to Andy. "He wants to bring his girl next week. I don't think it's a good idea, considering the stickiness of this case."

"True, but what excuse will you use to put Adam off for a while?" Andy asked.

"I have no idea!" I snapped.

"I believe it would be in our best interests to allow your son and his friend to visit." Logan's eyes remained glued to the woods as he spoke.

I shook my head. "No way! I don't want him in danger."

Logan turned to face me. "Peg, a family weekend would illustrate a level of normalcy here. The mere fact you are comfortable with your son's presence could throw the enemy off of your trail. Do you believe your mother would consider your involvement to be as deep as it truly is if you were allowing your children to appear?"

My anger grew. "You think I'd put my children in danger just so we could trick Mom? No way, buster!"

His eyes glowed as they bore into my own. "I have no intentions of putting your son in danger, but his visit would be quite advantageous for our side. The enemy would naturally assume you have little influence or care concerning their enterprise."

I shook my head. "No."

"Please consider the bigger scenario," he pressed.

"No."

"Peg, he has a point." Andy sounded hesitant but continued. "If Adam and his girl were here, even Nell wouldn't believe you'd involve them in a mess. Plus, we could have the weekend off from all the possible risks of this case."

My mouth dropped open. "You'd risk Adam's life?"

Andy shook his head. "The way I see it, if we don't push evil back, Adam's future is in jeopardy. What we do has a direct impact on his life, not just ours."

I couldn't believe my ears. I took a deep breath, trying to control the emotions running through my body—fear and anger being the top two on the list.

"Peg, I understand how frightened you are of physical harm to your son. I am more concerned these situations may become larger than they are now. Andy is correct in his analysis of Adam's future."

As the tears welled in my eyes, I nodded. I stuck the phone back to my ear. "Dad thinks that would be perfect."

"Great! We'll see you then," Adam said excitedly. "Love ya, Mom."

"Love ya, back." I hoped he didn't hear the catch in my voice.

CHAPTER 13

The next morning, I stood in the doorway of Adam's bedroom, surveying the room. I shook my head as a sigh escaped my lips.

"What's wrong?" Andy asked, fresh from his shower. He looked down at the cup of coffee I was holding, then his eyes returned to my face. "I'm impressed. You haven't even finished your coffee."

"It's my third cup," I informed him. "It's almost empty."

His grin reached his eyes, but he wisely changed subject. "What's up? Are you thinking of redoing this room?"

My eyes were glued to the bunk beds we never bothered to change. "I'm pretty sure Adam and his girl aren't going to enjoy bunk beds, but I hate getting rid of them."

It didn't occur to me to redecorate in all the years these rooms stood empty. I wasn't one to welcome change, and my throat constricted with the thought of the boys' childhood rooms being turned into accommodations for guests. Even after the emergency slumber party we had on the last venture with Logan and his pals, it didn't enter my mind to update the rooms.

Andy leaned against the doorframe. "Ah, that explains your expression."

"What expression? I'm fine."

He snorted. "You won't even redo the kitchen, so now we have two bullets living in the cabinets."

"It's a good thing we didn't already change the kitchen!" I retorted hotly. "You'd be furious if we spent thousands just to find ourselves facing another expense."

Laughing, Andy gave me a quick hug, then turned and headed for the kitchen to eat his breakfast.

Someone chuckled behind me. "Well, at least you're finally considering changing something around here."

Turning, I saw Nana's smile and returned it with one of my own. It was good to see her looking healthy.

"How are you feeling? I was worried." I scanned her body quickly. She was torn up pretty badly the last time I saw her, so it was surprising how well she looked now.

"Logan fixed me up pretty good. He has me on the back burner for a while, but I wanted to see you."

I frowned. "Anything wrong?"

"Oh, heavens no! I'm just bored. When Logan decides to sideline a person, he really means it. I have no idea what's going on with anything. I'm not even allowed to go to my club meetings, and those are a hoot." She pouted.

Club meetings were another surprise I encountered as I learned about the afterlife—social clubs, committees, and the afterlife hierarchy—just to name a few items that were a shock. Heaven didn't turn out to be quite what I expected. Actually, the entire structure of the afterlife left me dumbfounded. Andy loved it, but I was having trouble with the revelations.

"Getting back to this room," she said. "It's so outdated."

"I know. I'm terrible about any type of remodeling." I paused as tears formed. "Damn it, Nana, it's their childhood I'm throwing away!"

"Oh, baloney! Their childhood is here." She pointed to her heart. "No one can remodel your memories or emotions of the boys' years living in this house ... those live forever."

She was right. I nodded but didn't trust my voice to comment.

"Sweetie pie, I remember every bit of your childhood. You bring those memories right along with you." She pointed inside the bedroom. "This stuff is only a physical reminder, and boy ... does it need an overhaul."

"I know, but other than the beds, what should I do?"

Together, we poured over wallpaper samples, paint examples, and carpet pieces for each room of this house. I wasn't sure I wanted to plunge into a major project without her support.

"Well ... I wouldn't do wallpaper in here. A little old-fashioned if you ask me, but a fresh coat of paint and new furniture would probably do it." She peered at the carpet, examining it for any stains. "Somehow, the boys managed to keep the carpet pretty clean."

I laughed. "No way! I had it professionally steamed once they were out of the house. The amount of filth was appalling."

Nodding, she continued her scrutiny of the room. "I'd also replace the curtains. You don't have enough time to whip them up on the sewing machine, so I'd buy something inexpensive for now." She approached the window and sighed. "I did love these curtains when we made them. On second thought, maybe you could keep them for now."

I was slightly surprised she knew I was on a time limit, due to Adam's impending visit. "You know Adam is visiting?"

"Of course, ... your dad told me the last time he checked up on me." She barely spared me a glance, her mind was completely focused on the new project. "Ya know ... a nice sage green would be perfect! Not too dark though, with a cream-colored bedspread. I wonder if you can find some with little pink flowers?" She looked over at me. "How much time can you spare for shopping?"

"Shopping! I don't have that kind of time. Adam will be here next Friday." Panic settled into my body. Jeez ... a major overhaul of a room takes more time than I had.

"Hmm, well ... we have to think outside of the box." She paused, then her face brightened. "What about that computer of yours? Can we look at stuff on it? Sure would save time from running around to stores."

I looked at her in admiration. Dead as a doornail and she was still saving my butt in the redecorating arena. "Great idea, let's get moving," I declared.

She rubbed her hands together gleefully. "Just like old times."

Her comment brought tears to my eyes, but I reminded myself that she *was* here helping me—I wasn't facing the job alone.

Andy finished his breakfast and was busy brewing a cup of coffee for himself when we entered the kitchen. His eyebrows hiked up a bit when he saw us. "Hi, Nana. Are you feeling better than the last time we saw you?"

She waved an impatient hand. "Oh, for Pete's sake, yes. Everyone has been making such a big deal about it. I'm fine."

Andy and I looked at one another, then back at Nana. "Nana, you were in bad shape. I don't think we were overreacting," he said gently.

Her bottom lip quivered for a split-second, but she shook it off. "Well ... I'm fine now. Nell couldn't beat me down when we were living, and she sure as heck isn't about to win now that we're dead!"

I closed my eyes, the frustration growing. "Nana, Mom is dangerous. Don't pretend she isn't."

"I know, I know. That temper of hers will be her undoing ... you mark my words. Logan has taken care of my protection, and I'm safe. Nell will try again, but she won't win." She stomped her foot. I realized the amount of determination it must have taken for her to protect me from my mother while I was growing up. New tears threatened, but I followed her example and shook them off.

Andy shook his head but remained silent.

Her face brightened. "Let's get that computer of yours turned on so we can shop!" Her feisty attitude was contagious.

I grinned, sat down at the table, and grabbed my computer.

Andy joined us at the table as we began searching for beds, curtains, and quilts for the overhaul.

"What colors were you planning on?" Andy asked.

"A light sage green," Nana answered, as she focused on the screen in front of us.

He nodded. "Not a bad color."

There was a slight pop, and I turned to see Bob.

He smiled. "What're you guys up to?" Spotting Nana, he frowned slightly. "Logan won't be happy that you aren't in your safe place."

She waved her hand dismissively. "I'm busy helping Peg redecorate one of the bedrooms. We have plenty of protection here." She pointed to the woods. "I know Logan increased the protection around both properties, so I'm as safe here as I would be..." She stopped.

I looked at her, concerned. "What?"

"We aren't allowed to disclose exactly where the safe place is in our realm ... almost let it slip."

I was slightly surprised. "There are secret areas over there?" Well ... this information was new.

"Logan will kill you," Bob declared.

"Ha! I'm already dead, you moron," she snapped.

Andy smiled. "Bob, were you visiting, or did you have a reason to come by?"

"Crap! I'm here to deliver a message from Logan." He looked at me. "You are to stay put until Santino arrives."

My eyebrows raised. "Santino is coming here?"

"Yep, Logan wants you to have a living bodyguard until we figure out the drug issue." His attention was now on the computer. "I like that bedspread ... nice colors."

We all turned our focus to the screen. I had to admit, Bob's taste matched mine pretty well.

I smiled. "You may have found the perfect color scheme to match the sage green we are painting the walls."

Nana nodded. "Not bad, Bob. It even has those little pink flowers I like."

One look at Bob's face was all I needed to realize the guy was one hundred percent fascinated with the idea of redecorating a bedroom. He was so engrossed in the images on the computer screen that he failed to hear the arrival of his boss, Logan.

"I was unaware you decided to visit Peg." Logan's eyes were glued to Nana. "I do not believe it is wise to be away from the secure area I have supplied for you."

Nana, bless her heart, never missed a beat. "Tough beans, Logan. I was bored to tears. Peg needs my help with the bedroom, and we have *always* worked together on this house. I even helped with the den, though I still disapprove of the furniture. I do like the big screen TV." She grinned at Andy, who grinned right back at her.

Logan sighed. It had been a rough week for my old Indian where women were concerned. First, Amy chewed his butt out, then I lost my temper with him. Now, Nana was joining the ranks of women *pissed at Logan.* Maybe we should start a club ... the *PAL* club.

I looked at Logan. "Are you tracking Nana, or is there something new I should be worried about?" I remembered how worried he was about the Mendoza family, and I tried to convey a kinder attitude. I was not sure if I succeeded, but he answered immediately.

"Securing Mr. O'Malley created commotion within the Mendoza ranks. They are concerned since he does not have the ability to report news to their leadership. In my opinion, Jack now has proof the information supplied was not from his own office."

"That's great! I know Jack worries about leaks ever since he realized Owen was leaking information like a sieve to various parties protecting the mayor." Struck by a realization, I looked at Logan, stunned. "Jack is a lot like you. He's not happy when information is spilled, even accidentally."

Bob's face turned beet red. He spilled an entire pot of beans during the Spanelli case concerning my mob trio working for Logan, so he wasn't comfortable with our conversation. Logan dealt with the mishap gracefully and pulled Bob into the ranks. Bob reported directly to Logan now, and he was proud of the fact.

Logan nodded, but he remained quiet as he stared at the computer screen, fascinated. "You have the ability to buy items on the machine?"

"Yeah, I do it all the time. I hate shopping, but I can sit in my own kitchen and buy almost anything I need."

His eyes remained on the screen. "Interesting." Finally, he was able to tear his eyes away from the computer. "Jack may need your help in the next few days. Mr. Newman needs to be informed of the illegal activity on his property."

I frowned. "I can't help break the news to the stinker. He'll be upset, and my presence won't help."

"Jack needs support from a friend. The situation could become ..." He paused, searching for the right word.

"Sticky?" I supplied.

He nodded. "That word will suffice."

I sighed. "Ok … let me know when and where."

Logan continued to stand there, and I wondered what was on his mind.

I gave him a questioning look. "You ok? Is there anything else?"

He hesitated. "I realize you are unhappy with the idea of firearm training. However, I would appreciate it if you would seriously consider my recommendation."

I slumped in my chair. Jeez Louise … it was too early in the morning for gun talk.

"I agree." Andy cut in, then he turned to Logan. "When should she start?"

Logan shook his head. "Andy, I recommended training for you also."

"I know, and I'm all for it … but let's face the facts." He shot a quick glance at the clock. "I've got to head to the office and don't really have time."

Logan cocked his head. "You have enough time to allow Sal to instruct you on basic usage. As time proceeds, your training could increase to the point you are proficient."

Hell … Logan wasn't letting up on either of us.

"Fine!" I snapped. I had a sneaking suspicion Logan already had the training completely organized. "When do I start?"

"Sal will be expecting you in an hour."

My eyes widened in shock. "An hour! I can't be ready in an hour!"

Glancing at my coffee cup, he smiled. "You have had your required three cups of coffee. An hour should be plenty of time to prepare."

I groaned. "But I have to shop for paint colors, curtains, and a bedspread. Adam will be here in the next week."

"Oh, don't worry, sweetie," Nana said. "I'll take care of it for you."

"Nana, that won't work. You … well … let's face it, you can't actually *shop, shop* you know." Hell … she was dead. What was she thinking?

She waved a dismissive hand. "No, but I can zip around looking for the perfect paint color. I can make better time than you can with the curtains, and Bob found the bedspread. So, go … learn to shoot."

My head dropped in defeat. Andy laughed, and I shot him a dirty look, which brought his laughter down to a grin.

Logan looked at Nana. "I do not want you in danger."

"I'll take Bob with me. He can be my guard." Nana smiled, happy with her idea.

Logan considered her remark. Finally, he slowly nodded. "Yes, it may be a reasonable compromise." He turned to Bob. "If you believe at any time there is an issue, contact me."

Bob nodded. "Will do, boss." His face glowed with excitement at the prospect of my redecorating project.

I shook my head but kept quiet. Bob was a great guy in many ways. He might even have skills but playing protector of my grandmother was probably not one of them.

"I'll go get ready." I resigned myself to the fact that Logan would never allow me to wriggle out of his plans for me.

"You must wait for Santino. He will be here soon," he called, as I stomped back to my bedroom to get dressed.

I heard Andy answer the doorbell and knew Santino had arrived. Zipping my jeans, I happily noted there was no snugness. Ignoring the pie in the refrigerator finally paid off, and those pesky five pounds must be gone, thankfully.

A quick trip to the potty, teeth brushed, the mascara wand quickly applied to my eyelashes, and I was ready to go. My hair was at an impossible stage, so I merely ran my fingers through it, hoping the mess would sort itself out. Amy had unmanageable curls, and I had stubbornly straight hair that required a great cut to look decent. It had been awhile since my last haircut. Life had gotten complicated, so salon appointments didn't enter my mind.

Entering the kitchen, I noticed a new face among the gang gathered. His haircut reminded me of the late 1940s, and his suit looked like it came right out of an old Humphrey Bogart movie. The fedora he held was taking a beating as he used it to punctuate his words. He was talking with Logan, arms wildly gesturing to the den. Logan listened patiently, then nodded. Logan turned to me. "Peg, Andy, this is Henry. He is guarding your den and is concerned. He believes the window should be covered at all times."

"Sure, not a problem." I smiled. "Hi, Henry. It's nice to meet you."

"Henry was a private investigator during his lifetime. His skills should match any situation," Logan informed us.

Andy had his car keys in his hand, ready to leave for work. "Hi, Henry. Thanks for watching over us."

Henry nodded. "Ya'll really need to keep the drapes pulled in the den. I realize you two don't use the room often, but no sense in taking any chances." His southern accent startled me. I'm not sure what I expected, but a southerner was not on my radar.

I turned to Logan and noticed the twinkle in his eyes. He always enjoyed my reactions. "Henry lived in Atlanta, Georgia. He was quite successful in his chosen profession."

"Obviously, or you wouldn't have him in your little army." I turned back to Henry. "I agree about the drapes. I'll pull those closed before I leave." I started for the den and noticed Henry was on my heels.

Once the drapes were securely closed, Henry relaxed. "Thanks. You'd be amazed how far binoculars work, and open drapes invite snoopers."

"This window faces a wooded area," I protested.

He nodded. "All the more reason to protect yourselves. People can hide in those woods quite easily. Can't have that happening."

"Yes, but have you noticed the guards in the woods?"

His brow furrowed. "You mean those Indians?"

I nodded.

"Do you talk with them daily? Do they contact you if they notice someone prowling around?"

Slowly, I shook my head. "No, Logan talks with them."

"Yep, just as I thought. Look ... I like Logan, but I also know how the guy operates. He's closed-mouthed as hell, and it probably never occurred to you to walk out back and have a conversation with those guys yourself, has it?"

I shook my head again. "Nope. Never crossed my mind. I figured Logan ..." My voice trailed off.

He sighed. "Look, lady ..."

I interrupted him. "Peg."

"Fine. Look, Peg ... you've got to take control of these situations. I've been around a while, maybe not as long as other folks, but long enough to know these dead guys can intimidate people."

I had to smile. Henry was one of those dead folks, but he seemed unaware of the fact. He, at least, was not willing to be considered one of them.

He noticed my smile and put a hand up. "Ok, ok ... I'm dead too. I know, but I still think 'living ... you know what I mean?"

Strangely, I knew exactly what he meant. "Yeah, I get it. You mean take control."

"I heard ya'll talking about gun training for you and your husband. My advice is to take any training you have very seriously. It could mean the difference between life and death." His expression was stern yet kind.

"You really mean that, don't you? Even though I've never held a gun in my life?"

"Yes, ma'am. I can't stress the point enough. If you are prepared, it could save your life." His eyes bored into mine. "Do you understand?"

I nodded. "Yep, learn to shoot a gun." A glimmer of intuition struck home. "Did you have someone special in your life who ... um ... died because they couldn't defend themselves?"

He looked at the floor, not moving. After a few moments of silence, he faced me. "Yes, ma'am. My baby sister refused to learn, even though we were raised on a farm. We shot rattlesnakes every day on that farm, but she refused to learn. One day, while taking a walk through the corn fields, a big granddaddy rattler reared up and struck. If she carried a revolver with her, like the rest of us, she wouldn't have died. There was nothing we could do for her, and it was a bad way to go." He shook his head. "My daddy warned her all her life, but she was a stubborn cuss. Smart as a whip with a heart of gold, but she didn't have a lick of common sense."

"You really believe a gun would have saved her life?"

He shrugged. "Would have given her a fighting chance. She, more than likely, startled the old guy, but if she spied him, a gun would have made the difference."

I thought about the story of his sister for a moment. "You've given me some food for thought. I appreciate you sharing such a painful memory."

He nodded but didn't say a word. As I turned to go, he spoke up again. "Don't forget about the damn drapes … keep 'em closed."

Jeez.

CHAPTER 14

I headed back to the kitchen and informed Santino I was ready for a trip to his uncle's house. He obviously knew about the training Logan set up because disapproval covered every inch of his face. He kept his mouth shut though, and we headed for Sal's.

My stomach turned as we drove up to the house where Anthony used to live. Poor Sal committed his son to a mental illness hospital. He knew a judge who owed him a favor, and somehow, Anthony ended up stuck in the place for the rest of his life. I didn't ask a lot of questions because I didn't want to know the answers—some stuff is better left alone.

I was startled when Santino pulled out a set of keys instead of ringing the doorbell. He unlocked the door, then stood to the side to allow me to enter first. Manners count, and I appreciated his thoughtfulness. The entire drive over to Sal's, I wondered if Anthony's expensive paintings would still be hanging in the foyer. I wasn't surprised that every single painting was gone. Since they were originals, I assumed he either sold them or had them moved to a different part of the house.

"We're in the kitchen." Sal's voice boomed through the hallway.

As Santino and I entered the kitchen, I was amused by the sight in front of me. Amy was in full makeup, and her naturally curly hair was somewhat controlled. Her short frame stood on a stool, reaching high in a cabinet for a bowl. Sal was at the kitchen sink washing fresh green beans. He seemed at home in the kitchen, and I wondered if he was a good cook. There was an air of companionship as they worked together.

"We've been down at the farmer's market. You should see the produce! Amazing," Sal said as he shook the colander, the draining water spraying over the counter as he did.

I smiled. "I had no idea you were a fresh vegetable kind of guy."

"Oh yeah. We're going to tear up the tennis court and put a garden in for next year. I can't wait to start. Why Anthony wanted a tennis court is beyond me … the kid never held a racket in his life." He shook his head.

I didn't offer my own thoughts on the matter. Anthony was nuts, and he wanted everyone to know how rich he was. A tennis court screamed money. Too bad the money was actually Sal's, a fact I was convinced irritated Anthony.

"Need help, Amy?" I asked as I watched her struggle with a set of stacked bowls.

"No, but Santino could give me a hand." She handed him the bowls. Once the items were safely in his hands, she steadied herself and stepped down off the stool onto firm ground. She smiled up at Santino. "Thanks. They were heavier than I expected."

The smile he gave her didn't quite reach his eyes. I knew he wasn't happy about the firearm training, but Logan insisted, so Santino kept his opinions to himself. I felt a little sorry for him since I happened to agree that guns could cause more problems for us in the long run.

Once Sal finished with the colander full of beans, he turned. "You ready to learn about guns?"

I shrugged. "Not really, but Logan thinks I should."

Sal laughed, shaking his head. "You'll be fine. I'm happy with Amy's training so far. Give me a few minutes, and we'll go out back." He headed out of the kitchen, then paused. "Peg, I wouldn't have brought this subject up with you two if I didn't think it was important."

I looked over at Santino, his lips were clamped tighter than a drum. It was obvious he and his uncle didn't see eye to eye where firearms were concerned.

My eyes swiveled back to Sal, and I nodded. "I know. Logan wants Andy to train also. Is that going to be a problem?"

Sal shook his head. "Not at all. I have plenty of time to make sure all of you can handle at least one firearm. Let's see how it goes." He turned and scooted down the hall.

Amy glanced at me. "Peg, it's not as hard as I thought it would be."

I watched as she transferred the beans from the colander to a bowl. "You guys seem busy. Other than beans and guns, what else have you been doing?" It was a rude question, but it popped out of my mouth before my brain turned on.

Her hands, full of beans, stopped moving for a second, then continued working. Her face grew beet red, but she bravely answered my question. "Oh, this and that. You know how the day can slip by without really accomplishing much."

I had to hand it to her, her answer was a pretty good dodge, so I decided to change the subject. "When is Sal ripping out the tennis court? I think it's a good idea."

"The crew is supposed to be here next week, weather permitting. We've already taken down the net so I could practice. Sal decided it was the best place since the area is in the middle of the property."

I nodded. "Makes sense."

"Yep. We've also been busy making a few changes to this house." She shook her head. "You'd be surprised how much money Anthony spent on useless items. Those paintings alone were worth millions."

"I noticed they no longer hang in the foyer. What did Sal do with them?"

"Oh … he sold the lot. The amount of money he made was shocking. They weren't copies, and Anthony bought a few of them illegally. Something about World War II." She paused, then whispered, "I think a couple of the paintings were from the Nazi plunder of Europe during the war." She shook her head. "Made me a little sick to my stomach. I had no idea items from the war were still floating around the world."

I nodded. "Yeah, I remember reading an article a few years ago about items still unaccounted for from the war."

She sighed. "So sad."

"What is Sal doing with the illegal paintings?"

"He's talking to his lawyers. He wants to return them to their original owners or at least their family members."

My eyebrows raised in surprise. "Wow … impressive. He could just sell them on the black market."

Amy shook her head. "He is serious about his business being above board."

Santino was leaning against the counter, listening to our conversation. "Anthony bought those paintings to prove to his father he was smarter."

I looked over at him. "How do you know?"

Santino shrugged. "He told me. Anthony saw them as an investment, and he didn't care where they came from." He shook his head. "The guy was convinced he could take the family business back to the golden years."

I was thoughtful for a minute. "I remember he thought Sal was weak."

My remark made Santino snort in disgust. "Sal is one of the strongest men I know, and I'm including Antonio, Bill, and myself. He may not be young anymore, but I wouldn't want to find myself in a fight with him. I'm pretty sure he could knock me on my ass."

"Wow … high praise." I looked over at Amy, and I was surprised to see her face glowing with pride as she listened to Santino. I realized her feelings for Sal were quite deep, and there was a good possibility she found someone to truly love for the first time in her life. The old mobster certainly treated her like a queen, which was the opposite of her late husband. I sighed, deciding I should reevaluate my attitude toward their relationship. Damn … I hated when I was wrong.

Sal entered the kitchen. "You ladies ready to rock and roll?"

We nodded, then he and Amy walked outside hand in hand.

I looked over at Santino, surprised by the smile on his face. "You approve of them dating?"

He laughed. "I'm not sure 'dating' is the correct term, but they both deserve to be happy. Aunt Bella was crazy, and from what I gather, Amy's husband was no prize catch either."

"You really love the old guy, don't you?"

He nodded. "Absolutely. He's been good to me my whole life."

I smiled. "Good to know." I watched Sal and Amy turn the corner around the house, headed for the tennis court, and sighed. "I guess we better get out there, or Amy will have a fit."

Santino gave me a short nod but no smile. He wasn't any happier than I was about the lessons about to take place.

The air was warm but not hot. One pleasant thing about northeastern Ohio was that, most summers, we had cool fronts coming in from Canada. As we approached the aging lovers, I noticed a table was set up at some point. Once close enough to see it properly, I realized there were guns of all sizes laid out in a straight line.

"Wow." I looked up at Sal. "I had no idea there were so many different types of guns."

He nodded. "I want to establish the best fit for both of you. Amy tried most of the samples I have, but you need to handle each one."

"Ok … what do I do first?"

"First, we find out what *won't* work for you. Take this .45 caliber and let's see how you handle it," Sal instructed.

He handed me the gun, and my hand dropped a good inch from the weight.

"Gosh … it's pretty heavy." I tried to bring the gun level.

"Yep." He nodded. "It's got a pretty good kick, but you need to try it."

"Ok." I looked at the gun and wondered how anyone could aim and shoot something so damn heavy.

Sal cleared his throat. "First of all, … a little gun safety so no one ends up injured. Never, ever point a gun at someone unless you are willing to shoot them. Not even if you're positive it's unloaded. Accidents happen, and there's no sense in feeling guilty for the rest of your life because you didn't follow a simple rule."

I nodded.

"Next ... never, ever put your finger on the trigger unless you are prepared to shoot the person you happen to be aiming at. Rest your forefinger along the frame of the gun. It forces you to make a conscious decision and keeps any nervous habits from compressing the trigger."

He looked down at me, ensuring I was paying attention. He didn't need to bother, I was scared spitless, so I was absorbing every word falling out of his mouth. I snuck a quick peek at Amy, but her eyes were glued to Sal's face.

"Ok ... now face the target."

I turned and saw a bullseye about a mile away. Jeez Louise ... there was no way I could hit the darn thing. "Sal, how many miles is the target from us?"

His belly laugh filled the air. "Come on, Peg. It isn't that far. The average tennis court is seventy-eight feet long. Some private courts are shorter but leave it to Anthony to make sure his court was regulation size."

I shook my head in disbelief. "I will never be able to hit it, Sal. I can barely see it."

"Don't worry, that target is mine. Santino will set up one closer for you and Amy." He turned, giving Santino a silent order, which was immediately carried out.

We watched as Santino set up our target where the net used to hang. It was better, but not by much, in my opinion.

Once Santino returned to the table, Sal looked at me. "Ok ... stance is important. Stand up straight, and line your feet up with your shoulders."

"I am standing straight!" I snapped as I moved my feet apart. I was short, but he didn't have to rub it in so much.

Sal ignored my tone. "Comfortable?"

I gave a brief nod. "Reasonably."

"Good. Now bring the gun up, lock your arms at the elbow." His hands guided my arms, then he checked my elbows to confirm they were indeed locked. "Finger alongside the frame, look down the sight." He pointed to the piece of metal containing a notch. "See the target?"

"Yep," I answered, busy concentrating on the task at hand.

"Slide your trigger finger down from the frame onto the trigger, take a breath, and squeeze the trigger."

I took the ordered breath and squeezed. The blast reverberated through the air, my hands shot up to the sky like a rocket. My body pulled back, and I would have landed on my butt, but thankfully, Santino was prepared and caught me.

"For God's sake, Sal!" I yelled, waiting for my ears to stop ringing.

Grinning, Sal retrieved the gun from my hands. I looked down and wasn't surprised to see both hands shaking uncontrollably.

"Don't worry, the shakes will wear off pretty fast. I wanted you to see the force of these weapons ... they aren't toys."

Santino flashed a quick grin at me. "We all learned the same way. If Uncle Sal teaches you to shoot, you damn well learn to respect the firearm."

My mouth dropped open. "He taught you to shoot?"

"Yep. I was about twelve, and no one was behind me to break the fall. I landed on my backside ... had bruises for weeks."

Sal was back at the table. He grabbed a pair of ear muffs and handed them to me, his grin still in place. "Put these on for the rest of the training."

"Great, my ears hurt, and *now* you give me protection?" I snapped.

"You need to be prepared for the sound. Guns are loud and not anything like in the movies."

I grabbed the ear muffs and slammed them onto my head. My shoulders were killing me, and I'd bet good money most of the muscles in my back were pulled. I'd be lucky to lift anything heavier than a feather when training was complete.

"Now ... study the guns on the table, and tell me what looks good to you," he instructed.

I shook my head. "I don't know the first thing about picking out a gun."

"Let your instincts take over," he encouraged.

I let my eyes wander over the table—long barrels, short barrels, and stuff I'd never seen before. "Why are some long and others short?"

"Good question." Sal nodded in approval. "Long barrels have less kick and more accuracy. Short barrels are good for close range, and they fit in your purse." He grinned.

I ignored the grin but listened to his words. Finally, my eyes glued themselves to a small, shiny gun.

As I reached out for it, Sal murmured his approval. "Nice. A PPK. German made. Small enough for you to handle but big enough for your needs. Let's try it out." He showed me how to load the clip and pull the slide back for a bullet to enter the chamber. "We need to alter your grip. Last time it was lousy."

I scowled. "You never said anything about my grip!"

He shrugged. "Ya never know. Some people have a natural knack. I wanted to see if you're one of them."

I sighed. "I'm not ... huh?"

He laughed. "Don't lose heart."

He positioned my hands on the gun, moving my fingers to line up exactly how he wanted them. I made sure my forefinger was resting on the frame, so I wouldn't accidentally shoot myself.

Sal pointed to the target. "Let 'er rip."

I adjusted my stance, brought the firearm up, locked my elbows, then pulled the trigger. The kickback wasn't nearly as bad as my first try. I didn't hit the target, but I didn't land on my butt either.

Sal nodded. "Much better."

"I didn't hit the target," I unnecessarily informed him.

He smiled. "You shut your eyes. It's pretty hard to hit anything useful if your eyes are closed."

My mouth dropped open. "What?"

"It's a newbie mistake. Don't worry, we'll work on it." He signaled to Santino, and once again the target was moved closer to us.

"I don't believe you two will ever need to shoot long distance. Logan wants this training as protection only. I figure maybe ten to twenty feet is perfect. Anything more than that distance, and you'll have other options; such as ... hiding, running, or calling for help."

I sighed. "Hopefully all this work will be for nothing."

Once Santino joined us, Sal continued with the lesson. "For right now, work on keeping your hands steady while your arms are locked. It's not hard, but if you have to aim at a bad guy for too long, you'll get tired. Getting tired means shaking arms, then next to go is your aim."

Amy and I stood in our stances, arms locked for what seemed like hours. Sadly, it was really only about three minutes. In spite of the breeze blowing across our faces, sweat was forming in irritating places.

"Ok, ladies ... we need to work on your stamina. Every day, we'll increase the amount of time until your arms are strong enough to hold your aim for at least ten minutes."

I glared at Sal, but Amy smiled up at him ... jeez. She may not have questions for him, but I did. "Why ten minutes as opposed to five?"

"Any longer and I'm pretty sure you'd be dead. The real professionals don't stand around for long having conversations. Mendoza's men are well trained, so ten minutes is probably too long, but I'll rest easier knowing both of you could hold out until the cavalry arrives. I timed myself from every part of the township, and ten minutes at high speed is about right."

Santino nodded, and I gave him a raised eyebrow before he spoke "He's right. The guys and I already ran the same test, but Uncle Sal wanted to be sure."

I looked down at the gun in my hand. "Don't we have to have permits or something to have these?"

Sal nodded. "Couldn't hurt, along with classes. I want both of you to have a concealed weapons license. I've already set it up here at the house."

"What? Here?" I looked at my surroundings. "Aren't there special places designated for those classes?"

Sal shrugged. "Sure, but I have a friend that owes me a favor. He's an instructor in Akron, but he is willing to come out to the house."

I closed my eyes. I didn't want to know what type of favor the guy owed Sal. Some information isn't worth knowing … jeez.

CHAPTER 15

The training finally ended after what seemed like hours. As the four of us trooped back to the kitchen for much-needed coffee, I glanced at the clock hanging above the sink. My heart sank when I realized we were only practicing for forty-five minutes. My head swam with too much information—safety, stance, aim, grip, and safety again. Between Sal and Santino, we had enough instruction to last a lifetime.

I sank into a cushioned chair at the table as I waited for Sal's famous Hawaiian coffee to be served. Sal drank it exclusively, but it was too pricey for my budget.

"I made a blackberry pie last night," Amy said. "Want a piece?"

My mouth watered at the thought of one of her pies. Amy's pies and cakes were better than my favorite bakery. I pulled at the waist of my jeans, happily noticing there was room for a piece of heaven. "Yep, make it a skinny piece though."

She smiled. "You want those jeans to continue fitting, don't you?"

I shrugged. "Pretty much."

Sal placed the anticipated cup of coffee in front of me, grinning. "Drink all you want."

I nodded, reaching for the coffee. "Thanks, Sal."

Santino leaned against the counter, coffee cup in hand, watching the three of us.

I looked over at him. "Come sit down and relax."

He shook his head. "No time. As soon as I finish this coffee, I have to head to the office. Antonio took my classes this morning, but he'll be relieving me in a few minutes. He'll be with you until after lunch, then Bill will take over until evening."

"I thought Logan only wanted me escorted not guarded."

Santino shrugged. "I follow orders, and those were the orders."

I frowned. "When did he change his mind?"

Santino was unaffected by my annoyance. "No idea."

"He wants you guarded all the time now." Bob's voice came from the doorway.

"How long have you been here?" I was irritated that I didn't feel his arrival. He was becoming entirely too adept at using his stealth mode these days.

He snorted. "Long enough to notice neither of you ladies are very good with a gun."

Out of the corner of my eye, I saw Santino trying to control his grin as he listened to Bob's analysis of our practice session. I opened my mouth to speak, but Amy beat me to the punch.

"I didn't know you were an expert on firearms, Bob." Sugar dripped from every word, and I hoped Bob realized she was being catty.

Bob's face reddened. "Well, I wouldn't necessarily use the term *expert*."

"What term would you use?" Amy persisted, sugar continuing to drench each word.

I smiled slightly. "You've never fired a gun in your life, have you?"

He looked at the floor. "Depends on what you mean."

I frowned. "Did you pull the trigger and a bullet came out of a gun?"

His face brightened. "Yep."

My eyes became slits as I studied him. He was maneuvering for some reason, using evading tactics. I drummed my fingers on Sal's kitchen table, watching his discomfort as my stare continued. I was completely focused on his face.

His eyes began wandering around the room. "Nice kitchen, Sal. Nice view from the window over the sink."

Yep ... he was trying to change the subject.

Sal nodded. "Thanks, Bob."

"What type of gun did you shoot?" I fully intended to drag the information out of him.

He flitted his eyes to me for a split-second, then returned to scanning the room. His face was beet red, and it was obvious he wasn't happy with my question.

"It wasn't even a real gun! Right?" I demanded.

"It was sorta real," he countered. My eyebrow rose an inch, and Bob sighed. "Fine. It was at one of those fairs ... you know what I mean. They travel around and have rides and games. There was a shooting gallery, and I shot a moving target ... it wasn't easy."

I looked at him a moment before speaking. "Bob, those aren't real guns."

"I know they aren't *real,* but I did shoot a gun! Sort of."

I shook my head. "So, you decided that shooting a toy gun at a carnival allows you to pass judgment on our ..." I gestured to Amy "... abilities? Are you serious?"

Bob tried to stay defiant, but he gave up after a few seconds. Looking down at the floor, he remained quiet. I felt remorse for my belittling attitude toward him, but since I'm stubborn, I fought the desire to apologize. The last thing I needed was Bob grading my lack of abilities with firearms.

I turned to Sal. "Did you redecorate the entire house when you moved in?"

Sal looked around the kitchen. "I had every room repainted. Anthony's color scheme was too erratic for my taste. I like the tones to flow easily throughout a house. More peaceful than the 'every room has a theme' idea Anthony liked. Bella and Anthony both leaned more toward vibrant colors ... I like subdued." He shrugged. "Their personalities matched their decorating tastes—loud, strong, and irritating."

I nodded. "I never realized how much you can learn about a person merely by the way they furnish their homes. It's quite amazing, the amount of information all of us advertise by the way our houses appear."

He cocked his head. "You sound like Amy. She tells me it's possible to read a person's emotional status by the color scheme they choose to live with ... sorta like radar."

I glanced over at Amy, whose smile was a mile wide as she listened to Sal. "Yes, it is rare for people to have the ability to hide their true selves in every way. We give out so much information even with the smallest decision ... the type of cars we drive, the clothes we wear, right down to the shoes we buy."

I gave her a questioning look. "Shoes?"

"Oh, yes." She looked down at my shoes. "You always wear comfortable shoes ... never glitzy or expensive. I knew right away you were a down-to-earth person, not one worried about impressing others."

I wasn't sure if her comment was a compliment or not, so I kept my mouth shut. I needed to face the fact that she could be saying I was either lazy or a self-assured individual. I was pretty sure I didn't want to know the answer.

"Have you been able to discover any new info about the drug problem in the township?" I figured it was better to change the subject than allow Amy to dissect my entire personality.

Sal shook his head. "Antonio has poked around as much as he dared, but he came up empty-handed. Not good, in my opinion. We should be alerted to any new traffic, if only as a way of keeping the peace between families."

I frowned. "What do you mean?"

He spread his arms out. "This isn't necessarily my area of operation. I do have business concerns here, but not *family* business."

I nodded. "Ok … so other mob guys don't have to ask permission to operate?"

"Good way of explaining the situation. Usually though, when a family is living in an area, there is a protocol followed. No one has contacted me or, to my knowledge, Anthony when he was living here. I've looked through his files and found no mention of drug activity."

I sat quietly and thought about Sal's lack of gossip. "Do you think Anthony is sane enough to ask him?"

Sal turned to look out the window. "I think Anthony fell off the sanity cliff years ago. It's a waste of time to ask him anything."

I agreed, but I had to ask—you never know. I looked at Santino. "You hear anything useful?"

He shook his head, pushing off the counter as Antonio entered the kitchen. They nodded at one another, then Santino waved as he walked out of the kitchen. Wow … not even a goodbye.

Antonio looked at me. "Whenever you're ready."

I drained my coffee cup and stood up. "Thanks for everything, Sal."

Sal grinned. "See ya tomorrow morning."

Groaning, I nodded and waved at Amy. "Later."

She grinned at me. "I know you hate the mornings, but now you have the rest of your day."

I smiled. "True. I need to work on Adam's old bedroom."

"See? It's a great schedule!" Amy's grin became wider.

I shook my head but didn't reply. Antonio and I started out to his car. Santino insisted I ride with him, so my car was still at home. I wasn't sure I liked being chauffeured around, and I hoped it wouldn't be necessary for long.

As I reached for the car door, a voice spoke. "You cannot go back to the house."

My heart started racing. I noticed Antonio's head snap around to search for the source of the words. At least I wasn't the only one that heard the warning.

Frozen in place by fear, my eyes glued to Antonio's shocked face, I nodded. "Ok." It was the only word I could force through my lips.

Finally, I turned to face the owner of the voice. Standing next to me was one of the Indians from my woods. My mouth dropped open. I was stunned by the fact that one of my faithful guards, not only left my property, but was actually talking to me.

Turning to Antonio, I noticed the concern on his face. I understood his reaction … if one of my Indians was here, whatever was happening at the house must be serious.

I returned my attention back to the Indian. "What's wrong?"

"Three men are prowling through the house. We tried reaching Logan, but normal channels of communication are blocked. The man with the hat in your house told us to find you." His eyes never left mine, and it was obvious he was nervous being away from his assigned post.

"Call the chief," Antonio instructed, pulling out his cellphone to make calls of his own.

I nodded, then dug through my purse for my own phone. I was relieved when I was able to locate it in record time. As I waited for Jack to answer, I studied the Indian stood next to me. He wasn't as tall as Logan, who I decided was well over six foot. His long, black hair had no gray in it, and his face was unlined with the wrinkles of age. He was probably in his late twenties. I was surprised to find myself wondering what his life had been like. Was he married? Did he have kids? This was the first time I ever stopped to think about the fact that the men in my woods had been real people with real lives. Shame surged through me as I realized I never once stopped to think of those men as anything other than my guards, and I hated when I could see them since it was a warning of my level of danger.

Jack's voice came through the phone. "What now?"

"A couple of guys are in my house," I said simply.

"Shit … are you there?"

"Nope … I'm at Sal's."

"How do you know about the guys in your house?" Jack asked, confusion clear in his voice.

"I was warned …" I started to explain, but Jack interrupted.

"Tell me later. Right now, I'm heading over to your place with a couple of patrolmen. Stay put." He hung up before I had a chance to reply.

I looked over at Antonio, but he was on his phone barking orders. I caught his eye, and he pointed to the house. I got the message and headed back inside.

"I'm back!" I called out, hopefully warning the love couple before I walked into an embarrassing scene.

Sal came barging out of the kitchen, worry stamped all over his face. "What's going on? Where's Antonio?"

"Out in the driveway on his phone."

Sal stopped dead in his tracks, mouth open, staring past me.

I turned, surprised to see my Indian followed me into the house. I glanced back at Sal. "He's one of the guys from our woods. He was the one who warned me that we have a couple of prowlers at the house."

"Oh, dear." Amy joined us. She noticed the Indian—it was a bit hard not to. She looked at me. "Have they ever left the woods before?"

I shook my head. "Not to my knowledge." I turned to face the Indian. "Have any of you ever followed me around?"

He shook his head. "We stay in the woods to protect the land ... and you."

I pointed to Amy. "Her also ... right?"

After a moment's hesitation, he nodded. I frowned. Why the hesitation? Did they resent having to watch over both of us? It was clear from his expression he was nervous about the questions. I decided to leave it for the moment and ask Logan later.

Amy broke the silence. "I'm surprised he came looking for you. Why didn't they call Logan?"

"They tried ... something about normal channels being blocked." As I spoke, the words sank in, and my brain actually kicked into gear. Normal channels blocked? This couldn't be good.

Amy didn't look happy. "Uh-oh."

Sal's face looked grim. He turned and headed back to the kitchen. A few seconds later, I heard him on his phone. I couldn't make out his words, but his tone of voice was fierce. Someone's butt was on the receiving end of a butt chewing.

Antonio joined our gathering a few moments later, his face matched Sal's. I decided I needed another cup of coffee.

Amy had other ideas. "A strong cup of tea is in order."

As she made her way back to the kitchen, I looked over at Antonio. He shook his head and sighed. "That woman and her tea ... she'll kill us all."

I laughed, but it was nice to know I wasn't the only one who hated Amy's tea concoctions. We joined Sal and Amy in the kitchen, both of us dreading the tea we knew Amy was brewing.

Sal looked at me. "Do you know who is in your house?"

"No idea ... just two guys." I turned to see if my Indian joined us. I wasn't surprised to see him standing, quietly, about five feet away from me. "You have any idea?"

He frowned as he thought about my question. "The man with the hat ..." he began.

I interrupted. "Henry?"

He looked at me, nodding. "He mumbled about 'Mendoza' ... but I do not know what the word means."

Sal whistled but didn't comment.

I looked at Antonio. "Were you able to find out any news about the drug activity?"

Antonio's face closed down immediately. Logan gave him the assignment, and he wasn't about to divulge any information to me.

Sal snorted. "Well? Logan isn't here, and we need facts."

I could see the conflict on his face, but I didn't care in the least. There were two guys milling around my house. At this rate, we'd need steel bars on the windows and doors … jeez.

After a few more moments of internal struggle, Antonio nodded. "Not much, to be honest." He was fighting an internal war over such lousy information? For Pete's sake. "I do have feelers out to a couple of trustworthy people, though. I'm waiting to hear from them."

Sal nodded as he listened to Antonio.

My phone rang, and the caller ID informed me Jack was checking in.

"Well … the house was empty by the time we got here," he said when I answered.

I sighed. "How big of a mess did they leave?"

Silence greeted my question. Uh-oh … not good. "That bad, huh?"

He remained silent for a moment longer. "Let's just say, you're going to need a little help getting it back in order."

My head dropped in despair. While I'm not Suzy homemaker, I'm not a slob either. If Jack determined the house was a mess, then I probably faced a minor disaster.

I sighed heavily. "I better alert Andy, so he doesn't have a heart attack when he walks in."

"I already made the call. Figured if he heard it from me first, he'd know you were safe."

I decided I needed to get home to see the mess for myself. "If the coast is clear I'm coming home. Might as well start the cleaning process."

Jack hesitated. "Um … take your time. My guys are taking fingerprints now, and it might be better for you to wait a bit."

I frowned. "Fingerprints? If these two were pros, they wouldn't leave prints!"

I saw Sal nodding his head, but I couldn't decide if he agreed with me or the fact that Jack's men were taking the prints.

Jack sighed. "Maybe not … but we might get lucky."

I shook my head but didn't argue.

He was undeterred by my silence. "Give us about an hour before you make it back here. We should be finished by then."

"Ok, I'll see you then," I said, then I hung up. I looked at Sal. "Do you think these guys were pros?"

He thought a moment before speaking. "The Mendoza boys are stupid, but I'm not sure how stupid. Jack's idea of prints may pay off, but don't count on it." Sal glanced over at my Indian. "Do you think your friends would talk with me? I have a few questions."

The Indian nodded. "We are instructed to cooperate with any associate of Logan's."

Good to know ... we could all converse with my protectors. The trick would be to actually *obtain real information*—dead people had a different set of rules than those of us with heartbeats. They aren't allowed to outright lie, but they have a tendency to skirt around the topic of inquiry. Sal's interview should be entertaining.

CHAPTER 16

After we all piled into various vehicles for the trip to my house, I felt a sudden grip of fear. My gut twisted, a headache decided to become part of my misery, and sweat formed on my upper lip.

Antonio spotted my distress. "Remember, you weren't home when the bad guys showed up. Anything they ruined can be replaced … you can't be."

His words brought tears to my eyes. His statement surprised me, I think it was the nicest thing he ever said to me. I blinked my eyes furiously, trying to keep the tears from gaining any traction, and soon, I had them under control. I still didn't trust my voice, so I nodded but kept my lips tightly pressed together.

I spoke when I was sure I could without my voice quivering. "I thought the house was guarded."

Antonio shook his head. "Nope. *You* were guarded. The house was left for the dead fellows to keep watch over, and they did an excellent job of apprising us of the situation. We could've walked in on the intruders, which is never good."

I nodded, then I turned to look in the back seat. Sure enough, my Indian protector was sitting there. In a different set of circumstances, I would've enjoyed the expression on his face as he watched the scenery swish by outside the car window. He was both amazed and scared spitless at the speed the car was traveling. Antonio seemed to believe we should arrive before Sal and Amy did, and he was making the effort to ensure it happened. The gravel in my driveway took a beating as Antonio came to a halt, but he seemed satisfied we were the first to arrive.

I took in the scene before me, deciding the police department was having a slow day. Every police cruiser was parked along the side of the drive, in the yard, and one was even pulled around the side of the house. My yard would never be the same—it looked like an invasion.

Sighing, I opened the car door, then I turned to tell our backseat guest he could get out, but he was already gone. I guess he decided it was time to return to the tribe and probably never leave again. I couldn't blame him. Antonio turned out to be a speed demon, and my stomach was still trying to decide what action to take. I hoped it would agree to stay put—the idea of puking at that moment was not enticing.

As I entered the front door, I heard voices from every corner of the house. Yep ... the entire police force was roaming around the place. Jack was barking orders from his favorite spot in the kitchen. I smelled fresh coffee—they obviously made themselves at home.

Antonio sprinted around the back of the house to begin talks with the Indians. I decided I better get in the kitchen before Jack finished off the pie in the fridge. If I could smell coffee, then I knew pie was involved in the mix.

Jack sat at the kitchen table with my computer in front of him. His fingers were zipping along the keyboard. Sure enough, I spotted an empty plate next to him with telltale signs of pie once having occupied the now empty space. I looked around the kitchen in horror. Every canister was on the floor ... empty. Flour, sugar, salt, and what I assumed was baking soda, covered the floor and counters. I was amazed they didn't bother to break anything.

Jack noticed my glance and nodded. "Yeah ... it's a mess. I wonder why they didn't smash everything along with the mess they made."

I shrugged as I continued staring at the mess, horrified. It would take me hours to clean the kitchen.

"Don't worry. Andy and I decided to call in a cleaning crew. They should be here in an hour or so." Jack drained his coffee mug after he spoke.

I looked at him, then at the pie plate.

He grinned. "I didn't have lunch, and I knew you wouldn't mind. Finished it off though."

I nodded, deciding I'd have to buy pies by the crate at this rate.

Amy walked in and moaned at the scene before her eyes. "Oh, dear ... I suppose we better get busy."

"Nope, a cleaning crew is coming." My eyes wandered to the window. Sure enough, Sal was busy talking with the Indians while Antonio talked with the Brits. My yard was chock-full of people—dead and alive.

I heard familiar voices coming from Adam's old room. Frowning, I walked back and found Nana and Bob in a full-blown argument.

Henry was standing between them trying to make peace. When he saw me, a look of relief flooded his face.

I frowned. "What's going on?"

Nana pointed an angry finger at Bob. "This nitwit thinks we should change the curtains along with everything else."

"They won't match the new color scheme and will clash with the bedspread!" Bob told her through gritted teeth.

Henry looked at me, shook his head, then headed back to the den—I didn't blame him.

Knowing Jack was the only one on the force aware of our unusual friends, I made the decision to close the door before I stepped into the fight. I looked at Bob. "Ok, what about the curtains?"

"I told you … they won't match." He pouted.

I turned to Nana. "Is he right?"

She turned scarlet, set her mouth, but didn't answer.

Ah … so Bob was right. I walked over to the window, fingering the soft material. "I remember when you made these." I smiled at Nana. "We worried the material wouldn't hold up to the boys horsing around." I ran my hand up the entire length of the material, memories flooding my mind. I turned and stared at Nana. "You made these curtains when the boys were little. Is that the reason you don't want to replace them?"

Bob's mouth dropped open as Nana stared back at me.

"You didn't tell me you made these!" Bob scolded. "If you said something, I wouldn't have argued. We could find a different bedspread." He walked over to the curtains, studying the pattern.

Nana stayed quiet, but she kept an eagle eye on his movements.

"It would need to be a solid color, but the question remains … which color should we pull from?" He bent over to get a closer look.

Nana joined him, so I decided their war was on hold for the moment. I had better things to do, so I turned to leave.

I hesitated before going. "Did either of you notice my house has been ransacked?"

"Oh, yeah." Bob nodded, his attention still fully on the colors of the curtains. "We were in here, and we did hear the commotion. I knew the guys out back would take care of it, so I didn't worry. My job is to stick to Nana."

I shook my head at their obvious disinterest. Neither of them turned to continue the conversation, so I made my way back to the kitchen.

Amy was busy putting the glass canisters back on the counter, muttering under her breath. I couldn't catch the words, but her tone alerted me that she was not a happy camper.

Jack was on the phone, taking notes as he listened. "Thanks," he muttered and hung up, then he turned to me. "We hope the guys out back can give us a description. My guys are finished and packing up their equipment. The cleaning crew is on the way, so you'll have your house back in order soon."

I plopped into a chair and nodded. I snuck a peek out back, and I wasn't surprised to see Logan joined the convention.

I glanced at Jack. "Did your men notice Sal and Antonio talking to air?"

He shook his head. "Nope. I kept their butts too busy."

Sal turned and headed toward the house. Antonio was still discussing the situation with Logan. I watched the old mobster, his stride full of purpose and determination.

Entering the kitchen, he nodded at Jack, then squeezed Amy's hand as he walked past her. He looked at me. "Peg, it was Mendoza's men. Your friends out back gave me a description of the main guy, and I was able to determine who's behind this mess." His arm swept to encompass the kitchen and points beyond.

I sighed. "I figured it out for myself."

He gave a short nod. "It's an outrage, and I will make those idiots pay!"

"Wait just a damn minute," Jack interrupted. "You can't go all New York mob on me here!"

Sal turned to Jack. "I'm not planning on it. There are many ways to make the Mendozas miserable."

My head pounded, and my stomach twisted. "Hang on a sec ... why make this mess? Were they looking for something in particular?"

Sal glanced around the kitchen, then snorted. "In the sugar?"

I shrugged. "Maybe they thought it would be a good hiding place."

He shook his head. "They were trying to scare you."

"Well, it worked!" I snapped. "I'm tired of people being able to get into my house so easily. This is ridiculous."

Jack nodded. "Yep ... about time you installed a burglar alarm."

"I do not believe an alarm will solve the problem." Logan finally joined the conversation.

I whirled around to face him. "I thought everything was under control! Guards, safety, and security measures!"

As usual, Logan allowed me to rant. He spoke when he was certain I was finished. "You were guarded. My men sent a messenger to warn you of the intrusion. The police arrived and have been busy. You were never in danger."

"Easy for you to say!" I countered. "You're already dead!"

He eyed me for a moment, then turned to Sal. "I ask you to rein in your anger. While understandable, anger will hinder our efforts. Inquiries are to be made by our people. Your contacts will be valuable, but they will serve our needs better if questions appear to be out of curiosity rather than revenge."

Sal looked like he wanted to argue, then hesitated, thinking through Logan's request. A smile appeared on the old guy's face. "You want them to believe I'm not involved! Right?"

Logan nodded. "Precisely. You happen to live here, and your interest is merely professional. Nothing more."

Sal studied the Indian's face and gave him a quick nod. "Ok … we'll play it your way. I don't want anything happening to either of these gals."

"Neither do I," Logan agreed. "Their health is in our best interest."

"Good to know my safety only interests you for your plans." There was a touch of meanness to the statement, but I figured I earned the right.

"You are aware of my affection for you," Logan chided.

Affection? News to me, but I hate to admit his words brought tears to my eyes.

"What about the Newman property?" Jack cut in. "Talk to him or wait?"

You could've knocked me over with a feather at Jack's questions. He was usually nasty about Logan's ideas, but here he was asking for guidance—my world was upside down.

Logan turned to Jack. "I would appreciate it if you could wait a few more days. I believe, by then, we will have much-needed information, and your conference with Mr. Newman will be more informative. If it helps you, I have concluded that he is not aware of the illegal activity taking place on his land."

Jack nodded. "Yeah … I couldn't make myself believe the old coot would be involved."

Antonio slid into the kitchen silently as Logan spoke. We all turned to him.

"Our friends out back were quite helpful. Not only did they provide Sal with a good description, but we know which direction they approached the house." He paused before continuing. "They came from the same area the gunshots originated. I'm sending a few of my operatives up there to scout around."

Logan nodded but remained silent, which Antonio took as a sign to continue. "Also, I'm keeping men here twenty-four seven until we solve this dilemma. Discreetly though … I don't want to alert anyone that Mrs. Shaw has considerable protection." He turned to Sal. "You want guards at Amy's?"

Sal shook his head. "She's staying with me for a while. My property is secure." He faced me. "Peg, I'm also going to have security cameras installed." Logan started to speak, but Sal held up a hand. "Trust me, no one will be able to see them. My crew is great at hiding the cameras, and they will be disguised as a painting crew. It gives us an advantage if someone comes snooping around again. Cameras, along with Antonio's men, will ensure the capture of any more intruders."

Logan was thoughtful for a moment, then nodded his agreement.

"Who owns the property on the hill?" Sal asked, pointing to the spot where the shots were fired.

I hesitated. "I'm not sure." I turned to Jack. "Well?"

He shrugged. "I'll find out." He reached for my computer. The entire room remained silent, watching Jack's fingers fly over the keyboard. After a few minutes, he shook his head. "Well, I'll be damned." His eyes were glued to the screen. "Old man McAllen owned the property. The place started out with over twenty acres, but he sold bits and pieces off through the years. At this point, there are nine acres left of the original chunk."

I frowned. "I thought the family lived on Bath Road."

He chuckled. "Yep. Some of the old-timers around here bought land as they could afford it. During the Depression, land was sold cheap. More than one family bought hunks throughout the township and hung on to them for years. I know, from stories floating around years ago, there were many times land sold for the price of the taxes owed." He shook his head. "Damn shame. This place was filled with farms, and the Depression hit every family hard. They may have been able to eat off their land, but when it came time to pay taxes, there wasn't any cash, so they had to sell."

"Does the McAllen family still own the property?" I asked. "He died years ago."

Jack pointed to the computer screen. "According to the tax records, his son owns the land now. I know for a fact the guy moved somewhere down south years ago. He must be in his seventies by now."

"There's never been a house on it but wasn't there a barn at one time?" I tried to picture the property through the years, but my memory must have been going downhill with the rest of my body. For the life of me, I couldn't remember if I ever saw buildings on the land.

Jack scrunched his face, thinking. "The tax records show a small barn, but that must have been decades ago. Probably rotted and collapsed by now."

I nodded. "Makes sense … could've been a big shed where some farmer stored equipment."

"Nine acres of woods is a dandy spot to spy from." Henry's voice came from the doorway. We didn't notice that Henry joined our merry party until he spoke. I wasn't surprised—listening to Nana and Bob argue was of no interest to him.

I watched him carefully. "I appreciate you sending someone to warn me about the intruders."

"You're welcome, ma'am. Your friends out back ..." He jerked his thumb in the direction of the woods. "... and I talked a few seconds about the intruders. One went to warn you while I took notes." He reached into the inside pocket of his tailored coat and pulled out a small notebook.

Watching him thumb through the pages, I frowned. "Where did you get the notebook? And since when do dead people take notes?"

Henry looked up from his notes and shrugged. "When I died I had the notebook in my pocket. I've always been able to use it." He frowned. "Funny thing though, I never run out of ink or paper." He shook his head slowly. "Still can't figure it out."

His revelation would be another tidbit for Andy to enjoy.

I looked at Logan for answers, but the old Indian ignored my eyes, instead he turned his attention to Henry. "Can you expand on the knowledge we have been given so far?"

Henry nodded. "Yep. There were three men ... one older, the other two young ... I'd say late teens."

Jack snorted. "That explains the mess ... teenagers."

Henry nodded again. "The older fella told them to tear the place apart. I'm sorry to say, they took a great deal of joy out of their orders." He looked around the kitchen. "They sure had a good time in here."

The doorbell rang, and Sal shook his head at me. "No way ... you're not answering the door. I'll get it. I don't want you taking any chances."

His plan sounded pretty good to me.

Jack stood, deposited his plate and coffee cup in the sink. "I'm heading back to the office. We'll send the fingerprints downtown and see what pops."

I nodded, still shaken by the state of the house. I pulled out my phone to call Andy—maybe a hotel would be a good idea for the night.

Jack saw my face and hesitated. "Peg, the crew we called is used to crime scenes. This one is a piece of cake for them ... no blood or guts to scrub away. They'll have your house in tip-top shape in short order."

Tears threatened, but I fought them. There was no sense falling apart with a house full of guests.

Sal returned with four people, loaded with cleaning gear, following close behind.

"Your cleaners are here," he announced.

Three men and one woman nodded at me, then the lead guy turned to Jack. "Whole house?"

Jack nodded. "Yep ... shouldn't take long, there are no biohazards. The kitchen's the worst."

"Sounds good," the guy agreed.

They took the mess in stride and without a word to me, spread out and began organizing their equipment for the job. I noticed Amy's sharp eyes judging their skills. After a few minutes, she gave a short nod to me and smiled. She obviously decided they met her standards.

Jack looked at me. "Peg, your house will be back to normal quickly, so relax." Easy for him to say.

My cellphone rang. Still in my hand, the sound of the phone startled me. I looked down and groaned when I saw the caller ID ... Mayor Hayes.

CHAPTER 17

I hesitated a moment, then decided answering the blaring phone was easier than ignoring the noise.

"Hello." I realized my teeth were gritted. I really didn't like the guy, but I knew Logan wanted information from him.

"Mrs. Shaw … Peg?" Mayor Hayes seemed hesitant.

"Yep."

"Um … ok." I clearly made the man uncomfortable—nice to know someone had the ability. "Is that Logan fella around? I don't know how to contact him, and I may have some news for him."

Logan fella? Jeez … I snuck a quick glance at Logan and was satisfied to see a small frown appear on his face. "Yes, but I'm pretty sure he can't hold the phone to talk. You want me to put you on speaker?"

"Hell, no! I don't think we should be discussing the situation on the phone anyway," he replied nervously.

I sighed. "What do you suggest … a meeting?"

Silence greeted the question. I was getting the distinct sense the last thing the mayor wanted was to meet with Logan again—the last time was no picnic for the guy.

My impatience was growing by the second, but Logan interrupted. "Peg, tell the mayor he can meet either you or Andy at a location where he is comfortable. His message will be relayed."

I nodded. "Logan wants you to meet either Andy or me. You name the place and time."

More silence. Finally, he made up his mind. "Why don't I just visit you at your house?"

Oh, for Pete's sake. What made the idiot think I wanted him at my home?

Logan nodded. "Satisfactory."

I sighed hearing Logan's one word … crap. "Fine. When?" I didn't bother to hide my irritation.

"Tonight? I'll be finished here soon, so I could make it out to your place by six." His voice sounded a lot more confident knowing the person he was passing information to has a heartbeat—the dead obviously made him itchy. I couldn't blame him. The dead play by different rules, and Logan scared the crap out of the man.

I glanced at the clock, then looked around the room. I silently hoped the cleaners would be finished by six, but if they weren't … tough beans. It wasn't my fault intruders tore my house to pieces.

"Ok, I'll be here, and Andy should be home by then. Don't expect dinner," I informed His Highness.

"I shouldn't be there very long."

"Fine. See ya at six." I hung up—no sense in dragging out the goodbyes.

I turned to face Logan. "You're planning on attending the meeting … aren't you?"

Logan smiled but remained quiet—figures.

Sal looked at me. "While you were talking with Bennet, Antonio and I lined up the men to guard the house. They know to remain hidden."

Bennet? Sal was pretty chummy with the mayor. I knew they were more than acquaintances, but I didn't venture into the territory of the relationship between the two men. Sometimes, it's better not to know certain things, and Sal's friendship with the mayor fell into that category.

Logan broke the silence, looking at Sal. "It is imperative that your men are not spotted by anyone watching the house."

"Not a problem," Sal said confidently. "They won't actually be on the property. I figured it was best to spread them around. One guy will be in the woods, so you might want to warn your folks out there."

Logan nodded. "Yes, I will explain the situation to them. It would be helpful if they knew how many of your men will be here and to see their faces. Could you arrange for the men to meet in the woods for instructions?"

Henry cleared his throat. "I'll help. It's always nice to know who the good guys are and who the criminals are."

I grinned at Henry, and he shot me a grin of his own. I liked Henry, and it was a comfort knowing he was prowling around the house.

Jack stood. "I'm outta here. Call me if you need anything."

I nodded and stood aside to allow his growing belly to pass me—he really needed to watch his pie intake.

Sal looked at me. "Do you want us to stick around until the cleaning crew gets out of here?"

I surveyed the team in question, deciding they were trustworthy. I shook my head. "I'll be fine."

"Antonio will be outside, waiting for our men to show up. Once he briefs them, he'll be gone." Sal looked around the kitchen. "They are making damn fast progress. I'll bet money they'll be gone before Antonio."

The guy cleaning the kitchen spoke up. "Believe me, this is an easy job. We usually have a ton of gore to deal with, so we're happy … another hour should do it."

Sal smiled. "See? I told you they were making good time."

I watched as he and Amy strolled out to Sal's car, arm in arm. They really were a cute couple, but their relationship still bothered me for some reason.

The guy in my kitchen waited until everyone vacated the house, then he turned to me. "Lady, I don't mean to butt into your business, but did you know you have dead people milling around the house?"

My heart almost stopped upon hearing his words, but I took a deep breath. And here I thought we were being quiet enough, so no one would notice our conversation. "What makes you think so?"

He shook his head. "I've been doing this job for thirty years, and I've been seeing the poor dead folks most of those years. No idea why … but there it is." He pointed at Henry. "That fellow over there looks like he just walked off a Hollywood movie set from the forties. Some Indian guy was here earlier, and there are about a dozen other Indians in the woods."

I plopped down in my chair at the kitchen table and sighed. "What's your advice?"

He leaned against the counter, still holding the nozzle for the Shop-Vac as he thought about my question. His wavy gray hair still had black strands scattered throughout, and his round face frowned slightly as he considered his answer. He wore a pair of coveralls that reminded me of something a car mechanic would wear fifty years ago.

"Depends on why they're here. I usually see the murdered folks while I'm cleaning up the scene of the crime. I guess you have to decide if you want them around or not."

I nodded, but I couldn't think of an answer. I heard voices coming down the hall and realized Bob and Nana were still in deep discussion about Adam's bedroom decor.

Bob spoke first. "We'll ask Peg. I bet she'll agree with me."

My new friend turned and gave me a shocked look. "So, you know all of these people?"

Bob stopped in his tracks when he saw the guy leaning against my counter. He turned to me. "Sorry, Peg. I had no idea you still had company."

"He can see you," I informed Bob.

Bob's face turned ashen. Nana stepped around him. "I'm Peg's grandmother. What's your name?"

Jeez Louise ... Nana didn't bat an eyelash.

He smiled slightly. "Floyd, ma'am. Nice to meet you."

Nana looked around the kitchen. "Wow ... you've fixed this place up real nice. It sure was a mess earlier."

"The rest of the crew are in the back rooms. Whoever tore the house apart wasn't necessarily looking for anything." He viewed his handywork. "It's more like they had pure destruction on their minds." He shook his head.

"Yeah, I think a couple of them were teenagers," I piped up.

Floyd sighed. "Figures."

Bob was studying my new friend with interest. "You look a little familiar."

Floyd looked at Bob for a long moment. "Were you murdered a while back?"

Bob nodded. "Yeah, both my wife and I."

Floyd continued to study Bob. "I remember both of you. I have to say ... your wife was damn mad."

Bob turned a light shade of red but didn't bother to disagree. I'd bet money anyone who could hear Elaine, knew how furious she was with the fact that she was murdered. Hell ... she was still mad.

I was curious about Floyd, so I decided to ask some questions. "How many people know you can see the victims?"

Floyd gave me a surprised look. "Seriously? They'd lock me up in the loony bin ... plus I'd lose my job."

"You mentioned them to me," I pointed out.

"Yeah, but I noticed everyone seemed comfortable with them. I figured you guys were all aware to some degree. It even sounded as though you work together somehow." He cocked his head, once again deep in thought. "Gosh ... you *do* work with these dead folks, don't you? Do you solve the murders?" Curiosity was seeping out of every one of his pores.

Jeez ... I was in the middle of a huge decision when Bob took over the conversation.

"Oh, yeah! She solved the murder of my wife and me. After years of police work, Peg figured it out pretty fast once she got on the case." Bob's voice was full of pride.

I closed my eyes and rubbed my temples, hoping to ease the headache forming before it became a monster. Logan was going to really kill the idiot this time. "Bob, I don't think we are supposed to pass information along to everybody."

He waved a hand at me. "It's ok. Floyd here knows we're around. Who's he gonna tell?" Turning back to Floyd, he continued. "She even works with cops and the mayor. It's a really important job."

I decided right then if Logan didn't kill Bob, I would. "Bob! Enough info!" My teeth were so clenched I wondered if my jaw would crack.

Floyd ignored my attempt to silence Bob. "Who's the big Indian fella?"

Bob paled at the mention of Logan. "Uh ... that's sorta my boss." He gave me a quick glance, then looked back at our cleaner. "Floyd, you can't mention this stuff to anyone ... not even your family. If it got around town, Peg could be in real danger." I was glad the moron finally realized he was handing out privileged information to a complete stranger.

Floyd nodded. "Yeah ... I can see the wisdom there. If the bad guys knew you could talk to the victims, it could get dicey."

I sighed. "Don't they tell you about it while you're cleaning the crime scene?"

"Well ... I have rules. I never make eye contact, and I don't answer any questions." He shrugged. "I just listen to their stories. I guess they need to tell someone. You'd be surprised how many details they remember."

Bob frowned. "I don't remember talking to you when you were at our house."

Floyd nodded. "Your wife was doing all the talking, but you were trying to calm her down. I didn't think either of you noticed me much."

Nana remained quiet after she introduced herself. I looked over at her. She was busy studying Floyd, but she didn't look upset that he could see her. "Does everyone on the cleaning crew see us?" Her fascination was openly apparent.

"No idea. I've never told anyone until now." He glanced at the back of the house. "You could go ask."

Nana nodded. "Good idea ... be right back." She faded quickly.

I rubbed my forehead. My headache hadn't turned into a full-blown bomb, but it could at any moment. I looked up at the clock on the wall, dismayed to see it was time to start dinner. I gave the kitchen a hasty survey and was rewarded with spic and span perfection. The old appliances, which needed to be replaced long ago, were given a face-lift. My heart soared. We didn't need to overhaul the kitchen after all.

I turned back to Floyd. "How did you accomplish this? I was here and never noticed you working, and the kitchen looks great!"

His face glowed with pride. "I have to admit no blood and guts was nice. Sorta gave me an extra boost of energy."

Before I could reply, Nana popped back in the room. "Not sure," she reported. "They seemed to react to my voice, but none of them would look at me."

Floyd nodded. "Standard procedure for me, but I'm not telling them I can see you guys … so don't ask."

I shrugged. "Does it really matter?"

"Well …" Bob's face scrunched up in deep analysis. "We should probably be more careful what we say around people from now on. I mean they could be working for the bad guys."

Now he decided caution was necessary? Jeez.

Floyd agreed. "You probably shouldn't have told me, but your secret is safe … I won't say a word." His eyes swiveled my direction. "Ma'am, you know that Sal fella?"

I nodded.

"Are you aware he's in the mob? I had to clean up a couple of his son's messes."

My stomach tightened into a big, fat knot. "What do you mean by 'messes'?" I was damn positive I didn't want to know the answer, but I asked anyway.

"Well … you learn a lot when the dead folks don't know you can hear them. A couple of crime scenes in Akron were nasty murders. At those places, the dead guys were furious with Anthony Spanelli for killing them."

Uh-oh … this was the first I heard of Anthony murdering anyone. I wondered if Sal knew. My head began to throb, and I knew it wasn't going to stop anytime soon.

"Who were the victims?" Nana asked. At least one of us could think straight enough to pull info from Floyd.

Floyd shook his head. "Not sure, but they talked about some guy named Mendoza." He shrugged. "I don't usually remember names, but the name sorta stuck out … ya know what I mean?"

Yeah … the name was enough to make me want to puke.

"Bob, get Logan. Right now." My voice must have had a certain pitch because Bob didn't waste time fading.

Nana nodded her approval. "He may already know, but I wouldn't bet on it."

"Why not?" I was trying to keep my stomach from making a command decision to puke.

She snorted. "We can't know everything."

"Logan had his eye on Anthony for years. If he knew he murdered people, why didn't he inform us?" My anger was rising.

Nana shrugged but offered no explanation.

Bob popped back. "Logan is on his way."

I nodded but remained focused on keeping my stomach contents safely where they belonged.

The air changed significantly, and I knew my Indian arrived.

Floyd sucked in air at the sight standing before him. "Wow."

I looked up to see Logan in all his glory. Did he decide to intimidate Floyd the same way he did the mayor?

"I was in a council meeting," Logan explained.

Council meeting? Was formal attire mandatory?

Logan looked at Floyd. "Floyd, I presume. Thank you for cleaning Peg's kitchen so thoroughly."

Floyd's mouth opened to respond, but not a peep made it out—I knew how he felt.

Logan continued. "I understand you are able to hear those of us who reside on the other side of the veil."

Floyd nodded, but his vocal chords still hadn't started working again.

Logan searched Floyd's face, and after a moment, he nodded to himself. He was obviously satisfied with what he saw in Floyd. "Would you feel more comfortable sitting? Maybe some of Peg's pie would help."

I sighed. "Jack finished it earlier."

"Ah. Maybe something to drink would help," Logan concluded.

I was positive there wasn't enough booze in the house to help Floyd, but I figured coffee would be an excellent choice.

Standing, I made my way to the coffee maker. "Sit down, Floyd. Give yourself a few minutes to catch your breath."

He sat as I recommended.

As the coffee brewed in Floyd's cup, Logan turned to Bob. "I believe you and Peg's grandmother need to finish your work in the bedroom."

Bob knew an order when he heard one, and with a quick glance at Nana, they both faded. I didn't blame them for getting out of the kitchen as fast as possible. Logan wasn't in the mood for their bickering.

I placed the steaming cup of coffee in front of Floyd. "Sugar or milk?"

He shook his head. "No, thank you." Well, at least his voice was back.

Logan moved to the window, and I had a sneaking suspicion he was doing his best to help Floyd relax. "So, I understand you overheard a conversation at a crime scene you were cleaning," Logan said softly.

After a moment's hesitation, Floyd nodded. "Yes, sir."

"They mentioned the name of Mendoza?" Logan pressed, trying to encourage Floyd to talk.

"Yes, sir. I don't know why, but the name stuck in my head."

Logan turned to Floyd and studied his face long enough that poor Floyd began squirming in the chair.

He looked at me and received my shrug. Glancing at Logan, my stomach clenched again. I'd seen the expression on his face before, and I knew what was coming next. Groaning, my head plopped into my hands.

"Floyd, would you be interested in joining our efforts to combat evil?" Logan's tone was so quiet, even I had to strain to hear the words—I was expecting his statement the second I spotted the expression on his face.

Floyd's mouth dropped open, and it took a beat before he could muster an answer. "Gosh, sir ... I don't know. Sounds a little out of my league. What type of work are we talking about here?"

I had to admit ... it was a good question. I lifted my head, curious to hear Logan's response.

"I have a few trusted associates who work alongside my efforts to battle evil influences present in the world."

Floyd looked back at me, eyebrow raised.

"It has its moments." I sure as heck wasn't giving him any more information. He needed to make up his mind without my influence one way or the other.

Floyd turned his attention back to Logan. "What would I need to do?"

"Do the job you do now, but if you hear anything of interest you call either Bob or Peg."

Floyd slowly nodded his head. "Sounds easy. Sure, I'll help you. I'm not sure what you expect, but if I hear something interesting, I'll let you know."

Logan smiled. "Excellent."

A hesitant look crossed Floyd's face. "How do I call Bob? Is there a special phone or something?"

I couldn't help it, I snorted right before I burst out laughing.

Logan flashed me a warning glance. "Peg will give you a way to contact her. For Bob, you merely call his name, and he'll come to you."

Or show up whenever the mood strikes or because he's bored ... I decided not to mention that.

"For now, tell me more concerning the Mendoza situation," Logan pressed.

Oh, for Pete's sake!

CHAPTER 18

I fixed dinner while Logan extracted a ton of information out of poor Floyd. The rest of his crew finished their work and left long before Logan's and Floyd's discussion was over. Floyd began sweating from the amount of brain power Logan demanded from him. I considered warning him that he might be getting himself into more than he bargained for, but I kept my trap shut.

Keeping my eye on the clock, I was relieved when I heard Andy come through the door. I was thankful he made it home before the mayor showed up to announce whatever nugget he had to share. Andy was quite surprised to find Floyd sitting at our kitchen table deep in conversation with Logan. He gave me a questioning look, but I just shrugged—I could fill him in later.

"Thank you for all you shared with me," Logan told Floyd.

Floyd nodded but didn't seem too thrilled about their session. He looked pooped, and I didn't blame him.

Logan looked at us, acknowledging Andy's presence. "Nice to see you, Andy." He turned away from us, preparing to depart. "I will leave you to enjoy your evening with the mayor." I swear he was grinning, but I couldn't tell for sure. He faded quickly to avoid any comment I might make.

Andy's eyebrows knit in confusion. "The mayor?"

My eyes swiveled to Floyd, then back to Andy. I shook my head slightly, warning him I wasn't about to divulge news in front of our newest member. I trusted the guy, but I'm not stupid.

Floyd cut in before Andy could say anything more. "Not to be rude, but I'm heading out. For some reason I'm exhausted."

I smiled. "I don't blame you. Here's my number." I handed him a piece of paper with my name and cellphone number. "Call if you think you have something important."

Floyd pocketed the paper. "Should I call you or Bob?"

"Either one. Bob shows up pretty fast, but I always have my phone on me."

He gave me a quick nod, then began gathering his supplies. "Well … it's been a hell of a day. Thanks for the coffee."

I watched him carefully. "You ok?"

"Ma'am, I'm fine … but the day sure took a turn I didn't see coming." He shrugged. "I'll be in touch."

Andy and I watched him walk down the gravel driveway and climb into his truck.

"Gosh … I feel bad for him. All he was trying to do was warn me that we had a bunch of dead folks milling around. Next thing he knows, Logan's enlisting him to work."

Andy grinned. "His life will never be the same."

I punched him in the arm playfully. "The mayor will be here soon."

Andy began to help me put the finishing touches on our salads. "So, your least favorite person is coming for a visit … what's that about?"

I shook my head. "No idea. He sure didn't want to talk about it over the phone."

Andy took a deep breath as he leaned against the counter. "Doesn't sound good."

"Nope … but with His Highness, you never know what he considers serious."

Andy opened his mouth to scold me for my attitude, but the doorbell rang cutting him off. We looked at one another, then shook our heads. The mayor was early—not by much—but earlier than I would've liked. So much for getting dinner out of the way before the big meeting.

Andy was headed for the door when Henry poked his head around the corner. "Mrs. Shaw, the guy at the door came in a big limo. Do you know who it is?"

I smiled. "Should be the mayor of Akron. We knew he was coming, but thanks for the warning."

Henry let out a low whistle. "You run in high up circles, eh?"

I snorted. "The mayor isn't what I consider high up … more along the lines of a low life."

Henry grinned, then turned and made his way back to the den. It was comforting to have him roaming the house. I liked knowing someone was always watching. I peered out the window, but I couldn't determine if Sal's extra men were out there or not. He promised they wouldn't be seen, so maybe they were in the woods. Maybe after the mayor left, I would ask Henry to pop out back and check things out.

The sound of voices coming toward the kitchen caught my attention, so I decided I should keep my manners in order. There was a chance, if I was nicer, the mayor would be more cooperative in the future—you never know.

I smiled politely as they entered the kitchen. "Coffee?"

Mayor Hayes seemed astonished at my offer, and I couldn't blame him. I was seldom cordial, so he had the right to be a little surprised.

"No ... thank you. I'll make this as brief as possible." He looked around the room. "Any of the spirit people here?"

I shook my head. "Nope ... just us."

He relaxed a bit. "Here's the scoop. My sources informed me that the Mendoza family is definitely working northeast Ohio. Once Sal left the Youngstown area, they took control of the gangs and started moving drugs through both Ohio and Pennsylvania. So far, they've steered clear of New York. I guess they decided the mob there was too strong to fight."

The mob was strong in Youngstown for years. Once Sal decided to go legit, gangs started filling the void. It became obvious those gangs played by a separate set of rules than the old mobsters, and the violence increased significantly. Sal once told me the gangs had no honor, but maybe they just had a type of honor that didn't match Sal's. I wasn't a good judge of honor among thieves since I have never been involved in their lifestyles.

"Well ... at least we know for sure it is the Mendoza family. Sal was right, after all," Andy said thoughtfully.

I frowned slightly. "Anything else?" Did the idiot come all this way to tell me such a small bit of info? My good attitude was waning fast.

The mayor hesitated, and I could see the indecision in his eyes ... uh-oh. "Um ... are you sure those dead people aren't around?"

My frown deepened. "Yep." I hoped Nana and Bob would stay put in Adam's room. I doubted the mayor acquired the ability to see or hear the dead, but I didn't need the distraction.

"I don't want you to get the idea that I'm unwilling to help, but these are not people any of us want to tangle with anytime soon. They are brutal." He shuddered, and I realized how frightened he was of the Mendoza family.

His uneasiness made my stomach flip around too much. My eyes became slits as I studied his face. "What aren't you telling me?"

He turned to Andy. "You can understand, Mr. Shaw. Weren't you injured a while back? Anthony is peanuts compared to this group." A hysterical tone coated his voice, which didn't help at all.

I tapped my foot with nervous energy. "Did you know Anthony murdered a couple of people?"

His eyes grew huge. "How did you find out?"

My mouth dropped open. "You knew! Does Sal know about this?"

"God, no! I kept it under wraps." Sweat was forming on his forehead.

I had the sudden urge to smack him upside his head. My teeth clenched as I fought to maintain my composure. "You sent me to Anthony knowing he was a murderer? For God's sake, he was your accountant!" My hands formed into fists, but Andy grabbed my arm before I could throw a punch.

The mayor took a step back. "I never knew how out of control he was until the last few months ... before Caterina was hurt."

"So, you knew it was Anthony who ran her over? His own daughter?" I yelled.

The air changed, and Bob appeared. "Uh-oh ... Logan's gonna have a conniption."

My eyes cut to Bob, then back to the mayor. "You left us in the dark for the entire investigation. He came close to killing us!" I was so mad I could've killed the idiot.

"He wouldn't have!" Mayor Hayes countered.

"You jackass! He almost killed Amy and me. He knocked Andy out, and he came damn close to killing Antonio." I threw my hands in the air, disgusted. "All to save your damn career."

"I beg your pardon. It wasn't about my career!" he stuttered.

"Ok, what was your reasoning? I can't wait to hear the bullshit."

"Peg," Andy cautioned. "Simmer down."

Ignoring my husband, I glared at the mayor. "Well?"

"Look ... Anthony somehow found out about Alex's problem ... uh ... you know ... back in high school."

My eyes narrowed. "You mean the inconvenient fact that he witnessed Owen killing Bob and Elaine? Or the fact that you destroyed evidence to save your career?"

The mayor's face turned red, but he soldiered on, much to my disgust. "Look, Peg ... uh ... Mrs. Shaw. Anthony only wanted to know how much the police knew. I didn't know until later that he was responsible for Caterina's injuries."

"What exactly *did* you know? And when?" I demanded, stamping my foot.

"Honestly, I wasn't aware of all the details."

I took a step forward, as he continued.

He held his hands up in front of him. "Ok, listen ... I knew he was involved with those men's deaths, but I wasn't exactly sure *how* involved. I finally realized he was crazy, but by then you had the information yourself.

It probably wasn't hard to judge his mental state once you and the chief had a couple of conversations with him." The mayor shuddered. "Anthony wasn't a bad sort when I first met him. In my business, you have dealings with all types of people."

"Your business? You mean representing the citizens of Akron? Or your underhanded deals with unsavory folks?" My blood pressure was sky high, but I was on a roll.

"Logan's gonna kill him," Bob whispered from the corner.

Hearing Bob's voice calmed my anger. He was right … let Logan deal with the idiot.

I shot Bob a look. "Get him."

Bob nodded and was gone in a flash.

I returned my gaze to the mayor, who was searching the room for evidence of dead visitors. "I don't know who is more dangerous to deal with, you or the criminals."

The air changed, and the expression on Mayor Hayes's face indicated he sensed a difference in the room. His body stiffened, and his eyes darted around like pinballs.

There was a sigh from near the window. The mayor whirled around to see Logan standing there, dressed to the nines. Well … what I suppose was high fashion for his time on earth. Eagle feathers stuck through his braids, which fell over his shoulders. His breastplate was different from the last meeting he had with the mayor—gold threads were woven throughout the entire covering. He also wore silver bracelets on each arm and on one ankle. The guy was shining so much, my eyes stung. His leggings reached his thighs, but there were no designs on them. Instead, they looked brand-new as if he only wore them on special occasions. I figured he was mad enough, this might *be* one of those special occasions. Maybe he was going to kill the idiot standing in my kitchen. Who knows what Logan is capable of doing?

"While I was aware of your arrogance, you have surpassed even my assessment of your character." Logan was staring out the window as he spoke—not a good sign.

The mayor's mouth opened and shut a few times until he decided to keep it closed. His face was pale as sweat formed on his upper lip. His hands were shaking a little, but I didn't feel sorry for him … not one bit.

Andy grabbed my hand, and I felt his discomfort. Let's face it, Logan, on a normal day, was a sight to see. When he was angry, he was spectacular. I was thankful his anger wasn't directed at me.

"While I am quite disappointed, I am not startled by the revelations you have shared today." He turned to face the mayor. "You have made numerous unwise decisions during your career. Anthony is merely one lapse of judgment in a lengthy list. Your selfish actions placed associates of mine in harm's way, and I fear it will happen again."

"I never meant for anyone to get hurt!" the mayor protested.

Logan studied the man standing in front of him. "While your words may be true, to a point, your motives were self-seeking."

"Anthony was blackmailing me!"

"Ah. New information." Logan's gaze returned to the woods. "You were aware Anthony was dangerous, yet you allowed Mrs. Shaw to believe he was harmless. Your actions warrant review."

The mayor's political savvy kicked in upon hearing Logan's words. "I'm sure you are mistaken. While I may have made unwise decisions, you can't prove intent." His old arrogance was taking center stage—what a moron.

Logan stiffened at the mayor's tone. He turned slowly to face him, his face grim. "There will be consequences. You seem unable to sense when you are stepping over boundaries. I fear this has become a dangerous habit you have acquired."

Logan's eyes never left the mayor's face. I was relieved when the mayor finally backed down.

Pulling out a kitchen chair, he sat down at the table. "Look … Anthony was a pain in the ass. He threatened to have Alex exposed to scandal. You know it wasn't only my job on the line. Alex has been through enough. I honestly didn't think Anthony would go as far as he did." The mayor sounded defeated as he remained unable to meet Logan's fierce gaze.

Logan studied the man for a moment. "Any further revelations you should apprise us of at this time?"

The mayor shook his head. "None I'm aware of. I'm not holding anything back … I promise."

Whoop-de-do! No way did I believe the jackass. I opened my mouth to make a snarky remark. Andy squeezed my hand before I could speak, warning me to allow Logan to handle the mess. I slammed my mouth shut, but I wasn't happy about it.

Logan broke the tense silence after a few moments. "What do you know about the Mendoza family and their drug trade?"

"I know they're dangerous as hell. I know they've been moving drugs throughout this area for a few months. They must be flying under law enforcement's radar because I had to tap into resources I don't normally contact." His face grew red. I suppose he probably has tons of shady characters in his circle of friends—no surprise there.

Andy cut in when Logan didn't respond. "Were you able to use your contacts in the police department?"

The mayor frowned. "I'm not comfortable asking a lot of questions in the department."

My eyebrows rose. "Really? Why not?"

"Gut feeling. I've been around long enough to smell some rot there. I was shocked to find out, at our last meeting, that drugs were being funneled through the area. I know you believe I merely turned a blind eye, but not this time. I figured the Mendoza family needs some type of cover to accomplish their business."

I cocked my head. "Explain."

He pursed his lips, thinking through his answer. "Ok … look at it this way. If you were running a highly illegal operation, how long do you think it would take local law enforcement to recognize a new enterprise managing a highly profitable business in the area? A month? A year?"

I shrugged. "Depends on the business. You'd think an influx of drugs would be noticeable, though."

"Exactly. Why haven't I been notified of the increased activity? I receive a police blotter every damn day, and there's not one word of the increased activity. Everything on paper is the normal rate of crime. No mention of new drugs or even more of the usual stuff every city has to cope with … pot, cocaine, etc. My fear is that the department is aware, which means payoffs."

"You did not mention this earlier," Logan said thoughtfully.

The mayor took a deep breath. "I have no proof … just instinct."

"This is not a courtroom." Logan nodded in my direction. "Instinct has led us well before. I would have accepted your analysis."

The mayor was getting nervous again. "Well … I had no way of knowing! I thought you wanted facts."

Logan studied him again. "My concern is that your main motive was to cover any activity that could possibly mar your reputation."

The mayor's face turned beet red, but he held his ground. "Believe me, increased drug deaths in the community does nothing good for my campaign!"

"Oh crap." I was speaking more to myself than to anyone in the room. All eyes swiveled my direction.

Logan's eyebrows raised. "Yes?"

"I know Sal usually funds whoever campaigns against the mayor, just to keep his friend in office. What if the next election cycle, someone new plans on running?" I turned to the mayor. "This could be a setup to boot your butt out of office."

Andy whistled. "You may have hit the jackpot, babe. If a dark horse candidate runs and proves the mayor can't control the crime rate, he'd have a good campaign. Someone big could be behind this."

"I hope it isn't a Mendoza family member. We don't need any more criminals running for office." I wasn't necessarily referring to my least favorite mayor, but even I had to admit, my words had a little too much bite to them.

The mayor opened his mouth to argue, but Logan raised his hand for silence. "While these are interesting theories, there is no proof. I will deploy people to investigate." He turned to the mayor. "You were wise not to involve the police in your inquiries. If they are part of the current problem, allow them to believe you are still ignorant of the fact." He faced me. "At this point, please keep our conversation to yourselves. I do not want *anyone* outside of this room to be aware of our discussion."

"Not even Jack and Sal?" I was shocked.

Logan nodded. "Precisely. Until we solve this possible dilemma. Neither man is known for inaction if they deem the situation warrants their own particular type of reaction. We need more facts."

I suddenly had an idea of what Logan was hoping to accomplish. "You're trying to keep them safe?"

Logan nodded. "They are important assets, and I do try to protect my resources." He gave me a small smile.

Sighing, I nodded. "Yeah, Jack is a hot head, and Sal has way too much firepower at his fingertips. Ok … I'll keep my mouth shut." Andy nodded his agreement.

Logan turned to the mayor, his eyebrow raised.

The mayor nodded. "I wasn't about to tell either one of them."

"You can count on me too, boss!" Bob declared from his position in the corner.

Jeez … maybe.

CHAPTER 19

It was a relief when our guests, dead and alive, finally left for the evening. I promised Bob and Nana that they had permission to show up early the next morning to conclude their decorating ideas—those two were beginning to grate on my nerves. I appreciated their help as far as the boys' old bedroom was concerned, but I was stuck doing the actual work—painting, buying, and coordinating.

The next morning came bright and early. My third cup of coffee wasn't quite finished, when I heard my duo discussing bedspreads. I was surprised they didn't come to an agreement yesterday. Maybe they were putting the finishing touches on their suggestions and would be ready to show me the outcome—one could only hope.

Thankfully, I was able to finish my required amount of caffeine before I heard angry voices approaching. Uh-oh … someone wasn't happy.

Bob spoke first. "We've discussed the … um … situation."

"Hmph!" Nana snorted.

I gave them a questioning look. "Is there a problem?"

Bob glanced at Nana, then looked back at me. "Your grandmother seems to think we need to overhaul the entire room. I tried explaining to her that you're pretty busy with this case, but she's convinced you and Andy can get the whole room done before Adam arrives with his girlfriend."

I sat back in my chair, stunned. Bob was the one making sense, not to mention taking up for me. Obviously, my own grandmother wouldn't listen to reason.

I grabbed the calendar, which lived in the mess on my table, and began counting the days until Adam's visit … ten days. Panic set in, which wouldn't solve anything.

Andy came around the corner for his breakfast but hesitated when he spotted Bob and Nana standing by me. Glancing quickly at my coffee cup, he raised an eyebrow.

I sighed. "I'm good … all three cups safely tucked away."

Nodding, he continued to the counter to brew his own cup of coffee.

"Bob doesn't think we can overhaul the bedroom in time for Adam's visit. Nana is convinced it's possible," I explained, watching him putter as he fixed his cereal.

He took a sip of coffee while he considered what I said. "I've been thinking about the room. Do you think your new friend Floyd knows someone who could help?"

I cocked my head, thinking. "Maybe. I didn't bother to ask for his phone number, though." I shrugged. "Guess it never dawned on me that I'd be the one needing his help."

Nana looked around the room. "I'll say this for the guy, he knows how to clean. His friends did a bang-up job throughout the whole house. The place hasn't been this spotless in years."

Jeez.

"I could go ask him." Bob rubbed his hands together as he continued. "You know … this could be a great solution to a lot of your problems. Floyd probably knows a ton of people who could fix this place up in record time."

Fix this place up? What was Bob talking about? 'This place' was fine.

My eyes became slits. "What exactly do you mean?"

Bob looked surprised by my tone. "Well … you have to admit you haven't really done much for a long time. The kitchen needs updating, the bathrooms could use an overhaul, and both of the spare bedrooms need work."

Andy laughed, and Nana grinned; however, I saw nothing funny about Bob's comments.

"I happen to like it the way it is," I snapped.

"Gosh, Peg … I had no idea you actually *liked* the way the house is. I figured you were too busy to change anything." Bob's honesty was brutal, and I was fuming.

Andy cut off any retort I could make. "Peg, Bob has a point, but we'll have to deal with a major redo later. For now, Floyd may be able to help with Adam's and Bryan's old room. You are too busy with Logan and Jack to paint or shop."

I gave my husband a curt nod but remained silent.

Andy looked at Bob. "Bob, see if Floyd has time to help or knows someone reliable. I appreciate your help."

Bob glowed with pride hearing Andy's words. He was like a little kid sometimes.

"Don't scare him!" I called to his fading figure.

"I won't," he replied.

I looked at Nana. "Why are you two fighting? This was supposed to be an easy, quick fix."

"We did finally agree about the curtains, and that the bunk beds have to go. Plus, the carpet needs to be replaced, but it can wait for a bit."

"Ok, so what's wrong?" I pressed.

"He wants you to buy a queen size bed. I don't think it will fit."

I sighed. "You're kidding! All it takes is a measuring tape to solve the problem."

Andy laughed, opened a drawer, and dug around until he found the measuring tape. "Come on, we'll settle this right now." He grinned.

Thirty minutes later, we measured the room, checked the dimensions of different size beds online, and settled on a queen bed for the room.

I smiled. "Bob was right. You owe him an apology."

"Huh, I don't see you ever apologizing to him," she snapped.

Well hell … she had me there. Andy's grin stretched across his face like the Grand Canyon. I ignored him and looked at her. "Bob can be a pain, but he tries hard to please."

Nana looked out the window.

"Where is Bob?" Dad asked from the corner.

I turned and smiled. "Hey, Dad."

He didn't return the smile. "Where's Bob?"

I frowned. "He had an errand." Thankfully, I remembered Logan's warning about Floyd—no one was to know about him.

"For Logan?" Dad asked, surprised.

"Nope. We're changing the boys' bedroom, and he needs to check on a few things."

Dad shook his head, looking over at Nana. "He should be here to guard your grandmother."

My stomach churned. Crap … we were so caught up in the bedroom we forgot Bob had a job to do. "He should be back soon."

"I'll stay until he returns." Dad's quiet tone was unsettling.

Andy looked at us slightly confused. "What's going on?" I heard the concern in his voice.

Dad sighed. "We've lost Nell. We have no idea how she evaded surveillance, but we no longer have eyes on her."

"Elaine?" I was dreading his answer.

"She's still locked up."

Relief surged through my body.

Andy seemed relieved too. "Does Logan have any ideas about who on the Mendoza side has contact with spirits?"

Dad shifted his gaze to Andy. "He's working on it."

Boy, oh boy … we sure weren't getting much conversation out of Dad today.

"Is there more bad news?" I continued to pester him with questions because I knew he was reluctant to tell me anything.

Dad's eyes were back on me. "You should be hearing from Jack soon. The Newman boy is in the hospital."

"What happened?" I was stunned by the revelation.

"Looks like he decided he was playing around with fire. The Mendoza family didn't take too well to his sudden sense of remorse and decided to teach him a lesson."

I frowned slightly. "Does his grandfather know?"

"To my knowledge, he hasn't explained anything to his grandfather. He's at the hospital. He called Jack screaming."

I plopped my head in my hands and sighed. "This is getting serious."

Andy sighed too. "It always was serious. We're a little late to this game, but it's been going on for some time."

The doorbell rang, and I looked at Andy. "It's too early for this crap."

He nodded and headed for the door.

Dad looked at me. "It's Jack."

Yep … I figured.

Jack walked into the kitchen. "We've got to get a hold of Logan." He looked around the room. "Wow … it looks a hell of a lot better than the last time I saw it. They cleaned it up nicely."

"Coffee?" Andy offered.

"Sounds good." Jack saw Dad and nodded. "Did you bring them up to speed?"

Dad nodded. "Yep."

I watched Jack carefully. "Any witnesses?"

He shook his head. "None who would talk to us." Jack made himself comfortable at the kitchen table.

"Is the Newman boy going to be all right?" I had a lot of questions, so as long as he was willing to answer them, I was going to ask.

Jack nodded as he sipped his steaming hot coffee. "Yeah, but he got beat up pretty bad. No broken bones, though … he's lucky."

"Not sure luck had anything to do with it," I said thoughtfully. "Probably a warning. Next time … bones crack."

"Yeah, probably." Jack agreed. "His grandfather is furious. The kid hasn't explained what happened, so Tom believes it was random."

"Are you going to tell him?"

He shook his head. "Nope. Not until Logan gives me the go ahead."

A pop in the air informed us Bob returned. "We're good to go! Floyd has tons of friends who do painting, wallpapering, carpeting, you name it," Bob said excitedly. "At this rate, we can redo the entire house in no time!"

I quickly cut in. "Uh … Bob … we have company."

Bob looked around the kitchen. "Oh … hi, guys. How's it going?"

Jack frowned slightly. "Who's Floyd?"

Bob's face turned snow white, and his lips clamped together. Logan would blow a gasket if one more ounce of information fell out of Bob's mouth.

"A fellow Bob met recently. He's alive, but Bob accidentally discovered the man can see and hear him. We've got to get the bedroom changed before Adam and his girl arrive." Andy's words came out smooth as silk.

Bob looked relieved at Andy's explanation, all the truth, just not all the facts.

Jack nodded. "Let me know if he's any good. Our house could use some help."

Andy smiled. "Sure will."

"I received word the Newman boy was injured." Logan's voice came out of nowhere.

When did he arrive? Jeez … I was still in my pajamas.

Logan looked around the room before continuing. "The Mendoza family has begun to panic. They have very little information from our side and are becoming desperate. It may be the reason they injured the boy."

Jack shook his head. "I disagree. The kid probably decided he was in too deep and tried to retreat."

Logan listened to Jack, nodding slightly. "It is possible. I will keep your theory in mind."

Logan turned to Dad. "Have you located Nell?"

"Not yet. I thought I'd drop in here to make sure she wasn't causing mischief." Dad didn't want Bob in trouble with Logan any more than we did.

Logan glanced around the room. "Everything seems to be in order. Discovering Nell is important." He didn't need to elaborate, everyone in the room knew it was an order for Dad to get moving.

Dad nodded, gave me a small smile, then faded.

Jack drained his coffee cup and stood. "I'm headed for the hospital. Hopefully, the Newman kid is awake and willing to talk."

Logan gave him a brief nod. "I will arrive at your office later."

Jack nodded. "Yep, see you then." Andy walked him to the door.

I turned to Logan. "You want the Mendoza family to panic, don't you?"

He thought a moment before answering. "People who are desperate tend to make mistakes. If Jack is correct, I believe it would be wise to aid that endeavor, so panic may occur."

"I understand your theory, but panic also makes people stupid. Stupid people do stupid things. They could come after me … which would not be a good thing." I figured Logan needed to be reminded that I wasn't willing to put myself in harm's way just so he could have an advantage over the bad guys.

He remained calm despite my protest. "A mistake could work in our favor."

Either he misunderstood what I was trying to tell him or he was ignoring my statement. Probably ignoring … since he was damn good at it.

I decided to change the topic of conversation to the boy. "Do you think the kid needs a guard at the hospital?"

"I believe whatever message they were trying to send to the boy by harming him was received, and they are satisfied. Unless circumstances change, I do not consider a guard necessary at this time."

I nodded. He made sense. "What's our next step?"

He gave my question a few moments of thought before answering. "While we are quite busy on our side of the veil, I would prefer everyone on this side continue as usual. It is better if the Mendoza family is not alerted by unusual activity."

I hesitated. "Could be iffy, with cameras being installed and extra men in the woods."

"I trust Sal's men to be discreet; remember … they will appear to be painting. Considering the state of your trim, it is conceivable you hired men to paint."

My mouth dropped open. Did the outside need as much work done as the inside? Jeez.

Not noticing my expression, he continued. "Antonio's men are all well trained and will not be spotted."

I considered what he said for a moment, then a thought popped in my head. "Do they have the ability to see you guys? You know … dead people."

Logan shook his head. "Not to my knowledge."

"Um … do the guys who live in the woods know about Antonio's men?" I asked. "No sense in upsetting them."

"Yes, I have spoken with them. They have been instructed that whomever Antonio brings to the woods are allies."

I nodded approval. "Good idea to have Antonio with them when they arrive."

He didn't bother to reply to my comment, but his eyes did wander over to the wood line. Maybe he decided to check on the situation. He must have been satisfied because he nodded briefly to himself, then turned back to me. "It would be advisable for you to continue your training with Sal. The Mendoza family is known to be dangerous. I would feel better if you became proficient with Sal's weapons."

Jeez … another gun advocate.

"Fine. What about self-defense classes?" I hoped he would allow those to ebb away, but I was disappointed with his answer.

"Yes, those also … both are very important." He smiled slightly. "I know you do not enjoy either, but sadly, they are necessary."

I sighed. "I know, and truthfully, I agree. Amy loves all the training. I don't know what's gotten into her."

Logan's smile widened. "Yes, she has embraced her new life with gusto. I enjoy observing her enthusiasm."

I shook my head. "I wish I knew where she got all the energy."

He was thoughtful for a moment. "I believe it has to do with her basic attitude."

"Attitude?" My eyes narrowed. Was Logan inferring my attitude sucked?

"Yes." The simple word was the only answer he gave me.

Since he could read me so well, I knew better than to argue. Let's face it… my attitude toward both types of training was in the toilet. Basic laziness … I guess.

I decided it was time to change the subject. "Time to get out of my pjs and into real clothes. My day started out busy and probably wouldn't slow down anytime soon."

Smiling, he faded.

I headed back to my room to get dressed, hoping I faced nothing new today. I already had enough excitement to fill my day. I paused as I approached the boys' bedroom. Glancing in, I took stock of the condition. Yep … it was in need of an overhaul for sure. I shook my head, wondering how Andy and I allowed rooms to become so outdated. Leaning against the doorframe, I had to admit to myself the problem wasn't Andy … it was me. I hated to let go of the past. Seeing the bunk beds made me feel safe—my boys could still be boys in my mind as long as nothing changed. Adam bringing home a girl would force me to accept that they were grown men … crap.

I made my way to my own bedroom, then I changed into jeans, a pullover blouse, and loafers. As I brushed my teeth, I checked the mirror for signs of gray hairs sneaking through the hair dye. Nope … which was good news—those suckers can creep up on a gal. A quick brush of mascara, fingers run through my hair, and I was ready for the day.

I made my way back to the kitchen, and just as I entered, the phone started ringing. I grabbed it on the first ring and was surprised to hear Floyd's voice. "Mrs. Shaw? Floyd here. Bob told me you needed my help. I can get started as soon as you're ready."

"Great." I smiled. "You should probably come by and look at the room that needs the overhaul. Let me know what works for you."

He hesitated. "I'm free now, if you have time."

"Yep. I'll be expecting you."

"I have to warn you, though, if I get called out for a crime scene I have no choice but to go."

Hmm … I didn't take his real job into account. "We'll make it work."

"Sounds good. I'll be there in a jiffy," he said, then hung up.

I looked around for Bob and Nana. Where could they have gone? I had my answer a few moments later.

A pop in the air alerted me to visitors, and thankfully, it was exactly who I needed.

"Peg, we found the perfect comforter! You'll love it," Nana declared.

Bob's smile was huge, and he nodded as Nana spoke. "Perfect!"

"Good. Floyd's on his way over here to look at the bedroom. Once he sees it, he may have a few ideas," I told them.

They exchanged glances, then looked back at me. "Ideas?" Bob asked, concerned.

"What kind of ideas?" Nana pressed.

I frowned at the barrage of questions. "You know … stuff. Will he have time to paint, if so, how long will it take? Should we go ahead and change the carpet? Just ideas." What was wrong with these two?

Hearing my words, Nana flipped her hand easily. "Oh … those ideas. Not a problem." She looked over at Bob.

I narrowed my eyes. "What's going on?"

Bob shrugged. "We've spent so much time agonizing over decisions, we didn't want some guy butting in and ruining our plans."

"Plans? Do I have a say in your plans?" I asked, teeth gritted.

"You'll love it!" Nana was obviously excited.

"Well, well, well … I've finally found you! I should have known to look here first!" The thin, reedy voice came from behind me.

I knew who it was before I even turned. Bob's pale face told me everything I needed to know. I slowly turned. "Hi, Mom. What do you want?" I sounded calm, but I wanted to puke, and my head began pounding.

Bob started to fade, but Mom's hand shot out and grabbed his arm. "Oh no you don't, buster!" She was keeping him from getting help … oh crap.

CHAPTER 20

The doorbell rang just as Mom's grip on Bob tightened. "Don't even think about it." She looked directly at me. "No way … you're not sending for someone to rescue you."

I couldn't answer the door anyway—I was paralyzed with fear.

The doorbell rang a second time, but Mom shook her head. She glanced out the window, searching the woods for signs of my Indians. Her smug look told me Logan still had them shielded from her eyes—thank God.

I shivered from head to toe as Mom shook her head in disgust. "I thought you were made of tougher stuff. Look at you … quivering all over."

I decided it was a good idea to sit, so I plopped down in a chair before my legs decided to fold.

Mom turned to Nana. "Well, Mother dear … I've been searching for you high and low for days now. I finally shook the tail that ass Logan had following me around. Who does he think he is, thinking he can control my actions?"

Out of the corner of my eye, I saw Floyd at the back door. He saw Mom's hold on Bob, nodded to me, then moved out of view.

Mom noticed my glance and whirled around. Finding no one in her line of vision, she laughed. "Don't try that old trick on me! I know for a fact no one was there, and it was probably some salesman at the door."

I frowned. Salesman? Didn't she realize people seldom sell door-to-door nowadays? Good thing her views were still stuck back a few decades, or she'd investigate.

She turned her attention back to Nana. "So … what have you been up to?"

Nana's face was pale, but she managed to hold her ground. "Nell, you have no business being here. There'll be hell to pay if Logan finds you."

"Ha! The old Indian has his best years behind him!" She laughed again.

I knew the best way to protect Nana was to divert Mom's attention away from her. "So, you work for the Mendoza family now?" My voice was a bit shaky, but it could've been worse. I could've puked the second my mouth opened.

"Work for the Mendozas?" She scoffed. "I don't *work* for anyone."

"Fine. So, you are helping them?" I persisted. I needed to keep her focused on anything other than Nana.

She paused, then nodded her head. "You could say I'm aiding them. I've never met bigger idiots, but they have access to business dealings that enhance our efforts here. It would be more apt to say *they* are helping *us*."

My stomach flipped, but I fought the feeling and nodded. "Figures. You never were one to play by the rules."

I spotted Floyd creeping toward the woods. I sent up a silent prayer of thanks. Obviously, Floyd could see the Indians and knew they could get Logan.

"Rules? Rules are for fools. To really live, you have to step out of the boundaries and go your own way. That's my motto!" she declared.

I sighed. "Yeah, so nothing's changed with you since the last time we met."

She frowned, appearing slightly confused. "Why would you think I would change? I'm happy with who I am."

"You're happy you injured your own mother?" I snapped.

Mom shrugged. "She was in my way. I've been trying to reach you to convince you to work with me."

My mouth dropped open. "In your way? You harm your mother because she was *in your way*?" My anger was building, probably to counteract the immense fear.

"Oh settle down … little miss goody-two shoes. It's not a big deal." She looked at Nana. "See? She's fine. Logan probably did his magic shit and presto, good as new."

My eyes became slits. "Really? Presto? She was a mess when she showed up here!"

She flipped her hand, dismissing my analysis of the situation. "She always was one to overplay her hand. I could've done far worse."

I opened my mouth to make a nasty remark but was interrupted.

"Ah, Nell. So nice to finally catch up with you." Logan's voice came from the corner.

Mom's face turned to stone, and her entire body went rigid with fury as she turned to face the voice. "Logan, you have no authority over me."

Logan studied her for a moment, then shook his head. "You have never understood the rules of our realm." With a quick movement of his hand, Mom was surrounded by glowing light. Her hold on Bob was immediately broken, and in a flash, she was gone.

Nana gasped, then leaned against Bob. Bob's face was still white, but he held on to Nana and didn't look as though he would be letting go anytime soon.

Tears broke free, and it took a moment for me to figure out why my face was sopping wet.

Henry appeared, his anxious face quickly surveying the scene in my kitchen. Relief swept over his features. Where was he hiding?

"That was close." He took a handkerchief out of his back pocket and wiped his face.

"Yes," Logan agreed. "Nell will be held for the time being, but I must warn each of you. We will not have enough evidence to hold her for long. Hopefully, we will be able to keep her safe until the Mendoza family is dealt with properly."

I scowled at his words. "Evidence? You need evidence? Didn't she provide enough admitting the Mendoza family are her pawns?"

"We have a strong justice system. However, there must be sufficient evidence to prove a person's guilt. I do not believe there is enough at this point."

I sighed, feeling a little defeated. "How long can you hold her?"

He thought a moment. "I believe long enough. Her own statement will cause much discussion, which will possibly prolong her captivity."

"So … you think this case will be wrapped up soon?" I was sure he didn't miss my hopeful tone.

His eyes wandered to the window … uh-oh. Avoiding my question was not what I wanted.

"You will hear from me." Logan faded before I could protest.

My mouth opened to shout at him, but a knock at the back door cut me off.

Floyd stood there, his face full of concern. "Was your Indian guy in time?" he asked as I opened the door.

I nodded as I moved aside so he could enter. "Yep. Thanks."

"Oh, I didn't do much. By the time I got to the woods, your friend here already sounded the alarm." Floyd pointed to Henry.

I looked at Henry.

Henry shrugged. "I heard your mother and knew there was trouble. I skedaddled for Logan, and he came lickety-split."

I smiled. "Thank you."

He returned my smile with one of his own. "It's my job … it's why I'm here."

I nodded, turning back to Floyd. "I'm glad you reacted so quickly too."

"She had a hold of Bob, which alarmed me. I didn't know they have the ability to do such physical stuff … sorta scared me."

"I had no idea Mom could grab someone," I thought about what occurred wondering how it was possible. She moved so quickly to get her hand on Bob. Her actions shocked me. My fear was pretty strong. If Mom could grab Bob, did she also have the power to make contact with me? I shuddered at the thought.

I shook off the feeling. "Floyd, come on back and see what you think." I was determined to carry on as though nothing happened. I was hoping that focusing on the bedroom would take our minds off Mom's visit.

We trooped down the hall and after a few minutes discussion, Floyd smiled. "This should be pretty quick. I would advise painting now and maybe even a new carpet." He inspected the old carpet closer. "When did you have this put in?"

I frowned, trying to remember.

"Right after Adam was born," Nana answered for me. "We were still working on the nursery when Peg came home from the hospital."

Floyd looked at me. "So, how long ago?"

"Wow … well … over twenty-five years." I joined him, inspecting stains, fraying, and general wear and tear. "It's seen better days."

He looked at me hesitantly. "Do you have time to go to the carpet store downtown? They've got a wide selection, and their prices are fair."

"We'll do it!" Bob chimed in. "Nana and I have plenty of time, especially since Nell's out of the picture."

Nana nodded. "I have the perfect color in mind."

Jeez … good thing those two were still on speaking terms.

Floyd pulled his gaze from Bob and Nana and looked to me. "Call me when you buy the paint. It will be better if I did the painting first, then the carpet, and after that, we can finish up." He waved goodbye, leaving us to handle the details.

The phone rang, and Jack's name popped up when I glanced at the caller ID … now what? I barely had the chance to put the phone to my ear before I heard his voice.

"Logan just left. What the hell!" He didn't even give me a chance to say hello.

"What are you talking about?" I pretended ignorance just in case we weren't on the same page.

"First, your mother shows up. Then, Logan restrains her for the dead version of court. Next, the Mendoza family is freaking out because they don't have access to the Newman property anymore."

I snorted. "They beat the crap out of the kid, what'd they expect?"

Jack sighed. "Remember … they aren't the smartest crooks out there, but they are dangerous."

I looked out the window and spotted Antonio with a group of men I'd never seen before—must be the guards. I felt better the instant I laid eyes on the group. It was nice to know there were guards with heartbeats. I appreciated the dead ones, but living guys made my heart sing. At least they could shoot back if bullets started flying around again.

"Has the Newman kid given any helpful information?" I asked, my eyes still on the woods.

"Nothing concrete. He's very evasive … especially with Tom hovering over him."

I thought about it for a moment. "Maybe you should wait until Tom isn't at the hospital. He might be more honest."

Jack snorted. "Tom is practically living at the damn hospital with his grandson. I don't blame him … he's worried sick about the kid, but it doesn't make my job any easier."

I heard a ruckus and opened the back door. Ladders, paint cans, and a couple of guys in jeans and T-shirts stared back at me.

"Are you Mrs. Shaw?" one of them asked.

I nodded. "Yep … and you are?"

"Sal sent us."

I figured they were Sal's guys here to install the cameras, but I learned the hard way to ask rather than give any information accidentally. "How long do you think your work will take?"

He surveyed the back of the house, including the yard and the wooded area. "A few hours, not more … maybe less."

"Sounds good. Let me know if you need anything." I closed the door but continued watching them through the window.

He started setting up the ladder. Sal told us they would appear to be painters and to the casual observer, they did. If anyone watched them for a period of time, I was afraid it would be obvious they weren't painting. They must have known what they were doing, and I trusted Sal.

Jack's voice pulled me from my thoughts. "Who were you talking to?"

I sighed. "The fake painters."

Momentary silence met my comment. "Sometimes I wish my life was back to normal."

I laughed. "Normal has left the building. Don't think we'll ever see it again, at least not what we consider normal."

"Don't remind me," he said dryly.

"You still doing undercover work on this mess?"

"Careful what you say on the phone," he cautioned.

"Crap … forgot … sorry."

Jack cleared his throat. "I'll bring you up to date next time we meet."

"Yep. Anything else you need to discuss?"

He was silent for a moment. "I did tell Tom Newman about the drug issue on his property. I thought the guy was going to have a heart attack on the spot. He gave permission to post a few guys on the property."

My eyebrows raised in surprise. "Wow … I'm surprised he gave you access."

"Yeah, so now that your mom is in heaven prison, do you think I could borrow Bob?"

My mouth dropped open. Borrow Bob? "Um … I never thought about Bob lending out his services. Maybe we should check with Logan."

"Shit." He hesitated. "Suppose I should go through the chain of command. Bob does work for him."

"True. I was thinking more along the lines Logan might have some of his guys there already." I was quiet a moment as I thought back to our previous conversations with Logan. "He didn't seem to think it was a good idea a few days ago, but once the Newman kid was beat up, he might have changed his mind."

Silence again. I gave him time to digest the information.

He finally spoke after a few minutes. "He didn't mention any of his men posted at the property."

"Logan forgets to tell us a lot of stuff." It wasn't my job to defend Logan's decisions.

Jack snorted. "I'm not sure 'forgets' is the correct term, more along the lines of 'decides' not to share vital information until the last possible moment."

I had to laugh. Jack hit the nail squarely on the head. Logan certainly played his cards close to his chest, and sometimes he didn't bother to play them at all.

"I'll run the request to borrow Bob past Logan." Jack hesitated. "Do I just call his name?"

"Yeah, I guess so. He usually appears when I need him. Give it a try and see what happens." It worked for me, so it should work for Jack … shouldn't it?

More silence. "Jesus, I wish I didn't have to deal with Logan."

I laughed. "He's not as bad as you think."

"Easy for you to say … Logan likes you."

"Ha! Logan *tolerates* me, which isn't the same as *liking* me. Bob likes me. Logan suffers through my rants."

"You're nuts. Logan does like you. You're entertaining to him." I could hear the amusement in his voice. "Maybe you remind him of someone from his own life."

Now it was my turn to be silent. Jack's words stunned me. It never occurred to me before that my personality might awaken old memories from his past. Maybe there was someone he cared about whom I resembled, at least in temperament.

Jack laughed. "You seriously never considered that you may remind him of someone special from his life?"

"The thought never entered my mind."

"I wouldn't ask him anything if I were you. He's pretty damn careful not to drop many clues concerning his life on earth."

"True." I contemplated Jack's insight. My imagination was running wild. Did he love the person? Was she important in some other way? Who was she? Curiosity would drive me nuts. I knew better than to bring up the subject with Logan, but I made a vow to keep a sharp lookout for clues he might drop. I sighed, deciding there was no way in hell the old Indian would slip up and tell us something juicy ... damn.

"Peg?" Jack's voice pulled me from my thoughts again.

"Hmm?"

"I just had an idea ... would you be willing to drop by the hospital and talk to Tom Newman's grandson?"

Jack's question startled me back to reality. "What? He'll never talk to me."

"Newman's parking his car next to mine as we speak. I'm positive he's on his way to grill me about the drug activity on his property. If he's here with me, he's not at the hospital," Jack said quickly.

I closed my eyes. I was smart enough to know when a reasonable idea surfaced, but it didn't mean I had to like it. "Fine. What do you want me to ask the kid?"

"Who he's working with. If other kids from the high school are involved. Give me a second to think."

I was busy scribbling down the questions to ask, and I was thankful when Jack paused to mull over what he needed— it gave me time to catch up.

"Ok ... was he aware the Mendoza family was behind the drug running? Where is the base operation? That should start the ball rolling. Go with the flow and see where the kid's answers take you."

I shook my head in disbelief. "Jeez, Jack ... he's never going to spill so much information. The Mendoza family will kill him. He knows telling too much will be trouble for him."

"I'm counting on the fact that the beating he took scared the living daylights out of him. He may realize having police protection sounds damn good about now." Just by hearing his tone, I knew his jaw was set firm, and he wasn't in the mood for a snotty teenager to stonewall him.

"I'll do my best. What if I took reinforcements?" I could always use a little help.

"Who'd you have in mind?"

"Dad," I answered.

"Good choice. If anything goes south for some reason, your dad will call for help."

I hesitated. "I was actually thinking more along the lines if some dead guy working for the Mendoza family happens to be hanging around, Dad can spot him."

"Wow … never thought of that angle … excellent plan."

I sighed. "Slowly, but surely, I'm learning to anticipate trouble."

Jack let out a half-hearted laugh. "Let me know what you find out from the kid … Tom's at my office door."

Hanging up, I looked at the clock. Thankfully, I had enough time to hit the local paint store and make it to the hospital before dinner needed to be started. These cases consumed me, but Andy didn't deserve starvation.

A pop in the air warned me I had a visitor. I was relieved to see Bob standing in the kitchen. "Where are you headed?"

I frowned. "Why?"

He shrugged. "Thought I'd ride along."

I cocked my head to one side. "What's going on?"

He tried to look innocent but failed. "Nothing … I just decided to keep you company."

I rolled my eyes. "Oh, for Pete's sake! Did you and Nana have another argument?"

He looked surprised at my question. "Argument? No, she had a meeting to attend."

"Did Logan send you?" My stomach lurched at the thought.

"Um … well … maybe."

"Why?" Yep, it might be time to start a slight panic.

Bob sighed. "Look, Peg … he doesn't want you alone."

"Henry's here." I pointed to the den as I spoke.

Bob nodded. "Yep, and Henry reported that you'll be leaving soon. You aren't supposed to go anywhere without an escort."

"Henry has a big mouth," I retorted.

"He's doing his job. The guys are all busy, so Logan sent me."

My eyes narrowed as I continued to watch him. "I was going to ask Dad to come along."

Bob shook his head. "He's in the same meeting as your grandmother."

I frowned. "What sort of meeting?"

He shrugged. "I don't ask those questions."

"Why aren't you involved in these meetings? You work for Logan." I didn't understand why he wasn't curious about these 'meetings' like I was.

Bob turned red. "Guess I'm not high enough on the ladder to get invited."

Jeez ... I didn't mean to embarrass Bob. Well ... if Dad couldn't go to the hospital with me, Bob was better than nothing. I needed someone who could see dead people—just in case.

"Fine ... come on, I have paint to buy. The faster Floyd starts painting, the faster that damn room gets done."

Bob bounced along beside me as we headed out the door.

CHAPTER 21

Bob's input at the paint store was enough to make me want to kill him. I was surprised he and Nana didn't turn each other into toads as they planned the makeover for the boys' old bedroom. They were both enough to drive a sane person over the edge.

I finally selected the shade of sage-green paint I wanted. Bob was in seventh heaven with my choice, and I was grateful to have the first part of the project decided. I was on a tight schedule, but I was determined not to rush through the decision-making process. The paint I chose was going to be on those walls for a very long time—I wasn't going through this hell again anytime soon.

Back in the car, heading to the hospital, I glanced at Bob. "I'm worried the Mendoza's dead folks will be at the hospital. If you see anyone from your side, let me know. If you think they are a serious threat, call Logan. Got it?"

He gave a quick nod. "Yep … no problem. I know the drill."

I pulled into the parking deck and was thankful Newman's grandkid was at the children's hospital. I knew my way around there much better than Akron's other two hospitals. Both had so many additions added on throughout the years, it took a map and a good sense of direction to find anything—you could get lost for hours if you weren't careful. I should know … it happened to me more than once.

Since Jack forgot to give me the room number for Newman's grandson, I stopped at the reception desk. I stood in front of the gal at the information desk, suddenly realizing I had no idea what the kid's name was. I was dumbstruck … Jack didn't tell me, and I didn't think to ask … jeez.

Bob must have realized my dilemma because he leaned closer to me. "Thomas Newman," he whispered.

I turned to him with a raised eyebrow, slightly surprised he possessed the information I needed.

He shrugged, then smiled. "You pick up knowledge here and there. You'd be amazed what can be learned by paying attention."

Really? Bob just realized this?

With a smile, I told the girl the kid's name. She typed it into her computer, and bingo … his room number appeared.

"Three forty-seven; take the blue elevators." She pulled a pad of paper toward her and wrote it down for me.

Nodding, I took the paper from her. I was glad there wasn't a problem getting the room number. When Jack and I needed to visit Sal's granddaughter, we encountered a mess. This time it was a breeze, which surprised me because the kid had the crap beat out of him.

I made my way to the color-coded elevators and pushed the button.

Bob remained quiet while we waited. It was a little shocking—he usually talks nonstop.

Finally, the doors opened, and I stepped in.

When the doors closed, Bob finally spoke. "So far, no dead guys hanging around."

Ah … so he was busy scouting the area, which explained his silence. I was glad he took my request seriously. I figured he would forget. Bob was really coming along in some ways.

Once on the third floor, I wound my way around curving hallways, medical carts, and nurses scurrying to and from patients' rooms. I finally spotted the kid's room and stopped to ask a nurse how the patient was doing.

"Fine," she said without bothering to look up from the chart she was writing in.

I watched her, surprised by her curt tone. My silence must've irritated her because she glanced up. "Are you family or a friend?"

I shook my head. "Consultant for the Bath Police Department."

She frowned slightly. "ID?"

I sighed and began digging through my purse.

"Gosh … doesn't she trust you?" Bob asked.

Ignoring him, I dug until I found the ID Jack gave both Amy and me a few weeks back. I laughed at the time, thinking I would never use it.

After studying the ID, she nodded and handed it back to me. "He's a spoiled brat, but his condition is improving. His parents left to get something to eat, and his grandfather isn't here either. Be glad ... he's a pain in the ass."

Yep ... definitely the correct room. "Can the kid have visitors?"

"Oh, sure. His injuries weren't life-threatening, but he sure took a beating." She shook her head. "I don't know what's going on, but I'd bet a paycheck the little turd got involved with the wrong people."

"What makes you think so?" I made sure my tone was a combination of surprise and curiosity—I didn't want to give anything away.

"I've seen a lot over the years. This kid was beaten by a pro. No real long-term damage, just enough to send a message." She paused. "I used to be an ER nurse over at General Hospital. I saw a lot of these types of injuries there."

"I appreciate your input. Do you think he'll give me any information?" I was a little fuzzy about the law, and I realized it may not be entirely legal to question the kid without his parents present. I decided I'd worry about that detail later.

She thought a moment. "Don't count on it. He's arrogant. If he knows you're working with the police, he'll more than likely clam up ... they always do."

"Thanks for the warning." Somehow, I wasn't surprised he was arrogant. Maybe it's genetic because his grandfather certainly fit the bill.

"Good luck," she said before she walked off to tend to her next patient.

I looked at Bob. "See anything?" I whispered so no one would think I was a crazy lady talking to myself.

"Nope ... all clear."

"Good. Let's get this over with." I pushed open the solid wood door and walked in to the blare of the TV set.

Thomas didn't even glance over to see who entered his room. He probably thought I was another nurse.

His face was swollen, both eyes blackened, and from what I could see, bruises covered his upper torso. His sandy-colored hair was as straight as mine. His build surprised me. The kid needed to shed a few pounds, not to mention take a class in general hygiene—he stank to high heaven.

"Thomas?"

"Yeah, what?" His tone of voice told me a few manners lessons could be added to the list.

"Thomas Newman?" I asked again.

"What do you want, lady?"

I narrowed my eyes as I walked over to the bed. "My name is Mrs. Shaw. I'm here to ask you a few questions."

"I'm not answering anything. Ask my parents."

I stood there wondering if anyone would notice if I added a few bruises to the ones he was already sporting. Instead, I decided to try Amy's way of handling jerks. "Thomas, I'm trying to keep you safe. Answering my questions could help." I tried to keep my voice kind, even though I wanted to smack the kid upside the head.

He turned the TV volume up a couple of notches, which finished off my nice-guy approach. I reached out and grabbed the remote and hit the power button.

"Hey! I'm watching TV!" he protested.

"Tough beans, kid. If you want to stay alive, you need to answer a few questions."

He looked at me. "Who are you?"

"I work for the Bath Police."

"Huh, I didn't know they have old ladies working for them. Maybe that's why they're so crappy." The sneer on his face begged to be knocked off.

"Peg! Simmer down," Bob warned—he must've noticed my hands balling into fists.

I took a deep breath. "Do you really believe the people who beat you up are your friends?" I shook my head. "They only want you because of your grandfather's property."

Bingo! His face paled, and he couldn't meet my eyes. "You know about the cabin on Grandpa's land?"

"Yep. That's not all we know. How long do you think Mendoza's men will tolerate you?"

His eyes grew huge at the mention of the Mendoza family. "Shit," he muttered as he grabbed the remote and turned the TV back on.

I marched over to the TV and ripped the cord out of the electrical socket—the noise died immediately.

"Plug it back in!" Thomas demanded.

I shook my head firmly. "Nope. Listen, Thomas, your grandfather is talking with the chief of police right now. How do you think he's going to handle the news that you and your friends are running drugs on his property?"

The arrogance returned to his face. "Shows what you know ... Grandpa will never let the police get to me."

My phone alerted me that I had a new text message. I swear the noise was the only thing that saved the kid from my anger.

I grabbed the phone from my purse in record time and read the text, then I looked back at Thomas. "Your grandfather is pressing charges against you." I hate to admit it, but I enjoyed the look of disbelief on the brat's face.

"He'd never do that! I was named after him!"

I shrugged. "Dealing drugs is serious … it's a felony."

"I'm underage!" he countered.

"When will you be eighteen?"

"Not until next month." He finally answered a question and rather quickly I might add.

"Sucks to be you, kiddo. You can be charged as an adult." I turned to leave.

"Wait! You're only trying to scare me … right?"

I turned back to face him. "Thomas, heroin and meth are dangerous drugs. There's a reason they are illegal. You're close enough to eighteen that you will be charged as an adult. I'd play ball with Chief Monroe if I were you."

"But those guys told me I couldn't get into trouble," he whined.

My anger was building again. "Really? You got involved in the drug trade and thought you'd get off scot-free if you were caught because of your age? Or because of your connections?"

He looked away.

"They used you … plain and simple. Your arrogance, along with inexperience, made you decide you were important. Big guy on campus? Baloney. Now, you'll be a felon … good job."

His eyes filled with tears, but I didn't believe his act for a second.

I scoffed. "Nice try. I raised four boys, so don't bother with the drama. I'm not your grandfather."

His face hardened. "They'll kill you."

I narrowed my eyes. "Is that a threat?" Hell … they already tried, but I kept that information to myself.

His face was filled with defiance, and I decided I had enough of him. I turned and marched out the door. I was so mad that my breath came in angry bursts and sweat formed between my boobs … damn!

The nurse looked at me. "No luck, huh? I didn't think the brat would give you any help."

I shook my head. "I have little patience for his personality type."

She laughed. "I hear you. What he doesn't understand is the people who beat the living hell out of him are capable of killing him next time."

I nodded. "Yep."

Shaking her head, she walked off. I stood there to gather my wits.

Bob shook his head sadly. "Gee-whiz, the poor kid doesn't understand the severity of the situation."

I remained quiet—too many people in the hall for me to comment to thin air.

I still had my phone in my hand, so I decided to call Jack.

"I'm busy," he answered before I said a word.

"The kid won't talk. I lost my temper."

My words were met with silence. Finally, he spoke. "No surprise there. I've sent an officer down to the hospital. Hang around until he gets there … will you?"

I frowned. "Sure … but why?"

I heard Jack talking with someone in his office, but the voices were too muffled to catch actual words.

"You still there?" he asked a few moments later.

"Yep. What's going on?"

"Tom Newman would like to speak with you."

My head dropped, then I leaned against the wall. "Fine."

"Mrs. Shaw?" Newman's shrill voice came on the line.

"Yep."

"I would consider it a favor if you stayed until the officer arrived. I realize how serious the situation is, but I also want my grandson guarded. The chief explained how dangerous these drug folks are, and the boy needs protection."

A light bulb went off. "Are you pressing charges because your grandson is involved in an illegal practice or because he'll get police protection?"

My question was met with total silence. I knew it! The jerk was pressing charges, so the kid could have a policeman at his hospital room door. I suspected as soon as the heat was off, the charges would be dropped. What Newman didn't understand was that he could drop the charges, but the police wouldn't. This case could easily involve the feds at some point, so Newman could dance around the system all he wanted—it wouldn't help in the long run.

I sighed. "Look, Mr. Newman, your grandson got tangled into a big, fat knot this time. Not only will the charges be severe but the group he works with will be after him now." I softened my tone a bit. There was no sense in making the idiot any more stubborn than he was naturally. "Thomas took a beating, but next time, they may not care if he survives. Thomas is going into his senior year, and I would like to think he will graduate next spring. I'm afraid the only way to ensure his future is bright is for you and him, to listen to Chief Monroe."

Newman was quiet as he listened to me. Finally, he sighed. "Please stay with him until an officer arrives. I will consider your advice."

Before I could answer Jack came back on the line. "Do you mind staying?"

"Fine, but I hope the old coot listens to reason."

Jack scoffed. "He never has in the past."

I laughed. "Well … let's hope he can be reasoned with this time. How about the kid's parents? Have you talked to them yet?"

Jack hesitated. "We'll finish this conversation later."

Ah … Jack didn't want to say anything else in front of the grandfather. I should've thought of his position before asking any questions. "Call me later."

"Yep," he agreed.

I threw my phone back into the abyss, then looked around the hall for a chair. No way was I standing around, for God knows how long, waiting for an officer to arrive. There weren't any in sight. I guess chairs in the hallway would get in the way of gurneys, along with various other mobile, medical devices.

Determined to get off my feet, I slid my butt along the wall until it hit the floor. I leaned my head back against the wall, then silently contemplated the facts we knew. Thomas was in up to his neck. Newman could be charged with an accessory because the drugs were being distributed from his property. My knowledge of law came mostly from TV shows, so I was a little hazy on the particulars. The Mendoza family is not a group of people I personally wanted to piss off, but I was sure the kid didn't have a handle on the reality of the danger he was currently in. He took a beating, but I saw no evidence his injuries taught him any lasting lessons.

"Hey, Mrs. Shaw." The voice came from above me.

Looking up, I saw the smile of our newest Bath police officer, Dougal MacMillian.

I returned his smile. "Hi, Dougal. How've you been?"

I struggled to get to my feet, so he stuck out his hand to help. "Pretty good." He jerked his thumb at the door to Thomas's room. "How's the kid?"

I fought the urge to roll my eyes. "Much like his grandfather … arrogant and stupid. Not a good combo."

Grinning, Dougal pulled me until I was standing upright.

I sighed. "Do you have to interview him?"

He shook his head. "Nope. My orders are to guard the door, and I'm not to let anyone I don't know in."

"Well … since you're here, I'm off. I didn't plug the TV back in when I left, so don't be surprised if he starts yelling soon."

Dougal raised an eyebrow and nodded. "I have no intention on entering the room. He can yell all he wants to."

Laughing, I waved goodbye as I walked toward the elevators.

"He's such a nice guy." Bob was right next to me.

I jumped a tad. "Jeez … Bob. I'd forgotten you were here."

He frowned slightly. "There's no way I could leave you alone if there is any chance bad guys could show up."

Guilt washed over me. Bob drove me crazy most of the time, but he has a heart as big as an ocean.

I smiled warmly. "Thanks."

"No problem." He was silent for a moment. "Peg … I want you to be more careful than usual. I have a bad feeling about this case. It's one thing to deal with crazies in our own township, but now we're importing nuts … it's not good."

Bob had a point. Our earlier, big cases were with people living in Bath. Now, we are dealing with outsiders and limited information. As far as we know, the Mendoza family doesn't know anyone in Bath. So … how did they get so chummy with Thomas Newman? I reached the street by the time my brain came up with that thought.

Summer arrived with a blast of humidity tagging along, which didn't suit me at all. As much as I hated winter, I wasn't a huge fan of sticky, summer air either. The parking deck was situated across the street from the hospital. I had to watch out for traffic, but as soon as I saw an opening, I stepped out to cross the road. I heard a crack, then felt myself spin before hitting the pavement.

"Uh-oh," Bob's worried voice broke the silence. "Hang on, Peg … I'll get Logan."

"Bob, if you leave me I'll kill you. Do you understand me?" I was trying not to panic, and if he left I was sure I would.

"I've got to get help." Bob sounded like he was starting to panic himself.

"Yell for someone, but don't you dare leave. Look around and see if you spot anyone." I was gritting my teeth. The pain started making itself known, but I was determined to find out who the hell was shooting at me.

"Lady? You ok?" The voice came from someone standing over me.

"Do I look ok?" I snapped. Blood seeped onto the pavement, and I fought the urge to puke.

I could hear the flurry of activity surrounding me, but my focus remained on finding the son of a bitch who shot me. I didn't dare talk to Bob with so many people around—there was no sense in some doctor thinking I was delusional.

"Hey, Twinkle Toes. You're going to be fine. It's just a flesh wound." Dad's soothing tone brought me a small amount of relief.

I burst into tears hearing his voice.

"Shhh … it's ok. I let Andy know, so he should be here soon."

I didn't dare respond, but I nodded so Dad would know I heard him. I was glad he told Andy, but this incident certainly wasn't going to make Andy any happier about my job. He was already uneasy since our last big case. Now, I was bleeding all over an Akron street … not good.

An unfamiliar voice caught my attention. "I'm going to turn you over." I turned my head to spot the owner, and I wasn't surprised the guy was wearing a white coat. I nodded, giving him permission.

Once turned over, I studied the doctor's face for signs of concern or fear—there weren't any apparent, which was good news.

I frowned slightly. "You're a little young, aren't you?"

The man was tall, well over six foot. His dark hair was cropped short, but what stood out was his Paul Newman blue eyes. Even though he was handsome as hell, the last thing I needed was some intern assessing my injury.

He grinned. "Lady, I'm almost forty, but thanks for the compliment."

"Forty!" He didn't look a day over twenty-five—so damn unfair.

He poked and prodded until I wanted to smack him. Finally, he spoke. "It's a flesh wound, but you're bleeding a lot. Let's get you inside, and I'll take a better look."

I nodded, then they lifted me onto a gurney, and rolled me back inside the hospital. Dad never left my side, but I couldn't see Bob.

Seeing my eyes searching Dad spoke. "He went to inform Logan."

Ah … I was burning to ask if Bob saw the shooter, but I knew better than to chance it.

My cellphone started blaring, but the doctor shook his head. "Let's get a look at you before you start answering phone calls."

"At least let me see who it is," I protested.

He eyed me a moment, then gave me a quick nod. "Don't answer … you don't need to be talking right now."

"Fine." I peeked at the caller ID and was surprised to see Jack's number.

"It's my boss." I was hoping the doctor would relent.

He didn't, instead he remained firm. "He'll call back."

Once my blouse was off, I realized the bullet put a hole in the material—it was ruined. Damn … one of my favorites.

I looked at the doctor. "When was the last time you worked on an adult?"

He grinned again. "Med school."

"Great," I muttered.

He laughed. "Mrs. Shaw, for this type of injury there's no reason to send you over to General. I can take care of you. Plus, it happened on hospital property, so the least we can do is fix you up."

"It's not your fault someone shot me." I narrowed my eyes. "How'd you know my name?"

He glanced at me. "I was one of Caterina Spanelli's doctors."

Ah … he must've seen me visiting Caterina once she came out of her coma. Andy and I went almost every day until the doctors felt she was strong enough to go home. Amy practically lived at the hospital until Catarina was released.

"She's doing great now."

His eyes remained on my face. "Yep … I've kept in touch."

My eyes grew huge. "How in touch?"

He grinned. "Enough."

Oh boy … could he and Laura be dating? I tucked the information away and promised myself to ask Amy next time I saw her. Why didn't she tell me Laura might have a man in her life?

"You're not an ER doctor."

He shook his head. "Nope, a neurologist. I was on my way to a lunch date when I saw you hit the ground."

I thought a moment. "Lunch date?"

He nodded. "Yep."

"Won't your date be wondering why you aren't there?" I hoped the question sounded innocent, but his grin told me I didn't pull it off.

"I sent word I wouldn't make the date."

I winced as he continued cleaning the hole in my shoulder. "Don't you give people painkillers while you're working?"

He shook his head but didn't speak until the nurse left the room. "No need … I'm almost finished. I didn't think you'd want to be out of it to the point of talking to people no one else can see." My mouth dropped open, and he laughed. "I know quite a bit about you, but I realize no one told you anything about me."

"Do you know the Spanelli family well?"

He nodded. "Yep. I've known Sal for years, but I only recently met Laura."

"Sal? How?" I was getting more confused.

"Sal paid for my medical school, and he had me relocate to the Akron area."

"Who are you? You know me, but I don't even know your name."

He smiled. "Eric Spanelli."

Jeez Louise … another Spanelli.

CHAPTER 22

"God, not another one!" The words were out of my mouth before my brain had a chance to stop them.

Eric threw his head back, laughing. "I'm not from the crazy side of the family. My great-grandparents came over to this country decades ago, so there's been a lot of intermarrying. Sal is my dad's distant cousin, and they've just always stayed in touch. When I wanted to go to medical school, Sal offered to pay all expenses." He shook his head. "It really shocked me, but I sure appreciated it."

I raised my eyebrows. "Is your dad in the mob?"

He shook his head. "Nope. Most members of the family aren't even aware there is a mob connection. The only reason we know is because my dad and Sal are close." He studied his handiwork on my shoulder. "You're going to be sore for a few days, but it was a clean shot. You'll have a nifty scar but not much more."

I waved my hand to dismiss his medical comment. "So ... you and Santino are cousins?"

"Yep, but distant. The family tree is quite confusing."

"So how much *do* you know?" I was suddenly even more curious about him.

"I know Logan kept Caterina in a coma longer than she medically needed to be in one. I know you work for the Bath Police, and Logan is involved."

"So … you know Logan?" I was a little shocked.

"Gosh, no. I can't see any of the dead folks milling around like Sal and Laura can. I also know Caterina knows Logan, but I'm pretty sure not too many people are aware of the fact."

"Logan will blow a gasket if you tell anyone else," I warned.

Eric grinned. "I don't think it will help me professionally to share certain information."

"True." A thought suddenly hit me. "Were you involved with Anthony in any way?"

Eric looked at me a few seconds before answering. "I suppose it won't hurt to tell you … I used my contacts at the Cleveland Clinic to help get him committed. It isn't easy nowadays to commit someone like Anthony."

I frowned. "Why not? He's nuts!"

Eric shook his head. "On the surface he appears normal. Anthony is extremely capable of fooling people. It takes someone with the ability to strip away the veneer Anthony created throughout the years. Once that's gone, it's pretty obvious he has serious issues."

"He's somewhere secure … right?" The last thing I wanted to hear was that he wasn't.

"Yes. We made sure he'll stay locked up for the rest of his life. It's sad, really. I remember Anthony from our college days. He was a nice kid and well-liked." Eric sighed. "But the insanity reared its ugly head, and he turned into a real mess."

"You know anything about our newest case?" I was intrigued by the thought that Eric might have insight into the Mendoza family.

"I'm aware it's sticky. Other than that, no … I don't know much."

I tapped my finger on my chin, thinking. How could I use Eric in our current case? He had connections, but I wasn't sure if those connections could help bring down the Mendoza family. After a few moments, I made a decision. "Do you know anything about the Mendoza gang?"

Eric frowned, then shook his head. "Nope … I don't think so."

Crap … well it was worth a shot.

Eric continued when I remained silent. "The only Mendoza family I know of are those drug nuts from South America."

Bingo! "What do you know about them?"

"They've been driving Sal crazy for years." He looked at me, his face full of concern. "Mrs. Shaw, don't get involved with those people. They are ruthless."

"Driving Sal crazy how?"

He shrugged. "From what I can remember, from overhearing conversations, the Mendoza family never thinks through their actions.

Quick money is all they want. Sal always said they never understood consequences."

I nodded. Pretty much lined up with everything Sal already shared with us … damn.

Eric looked at me a minute. "You've already tangled with them … haven't you?" He pointed to my now bandaged shoulder. "They shot you … didn't they?"

I held up a hand. "To be honest, I have no idea who shot me. I wouldn't be surprised if one of them was responsible, but I have no proof."

He shook his head. "Be careful."

Nodding, I cocked my head as I heard a familiar voice from the ER waiting room. I looked at Eric and smiled. "My husband is here."

He returned my smile as he stood. "I'll go fetch him for you. I'll also have your paperwork done by the time you make your way to the desk. Keep the wound clean and call me in a few days to let me know how it's healing." He handed me a piece of paper with his office phone number written on it. "Leave a message with my front desk gal, and she'll make sure I get it … good luck."

It wasn't long before my husband's pale, worried face appeared in the doorway. I felt a pang of guilt when I realized how frightened he was, so I tried to reassure him. "I'm fine. Did you meet my doctor?" I made sure my voice sounded perky, but even to me, it sounded phony.

He pulled me into a bear hug. "Oh, Peg!"

I winced from pain. "I really am fine … I promise. It's just a flesh wound. At least we don't have new slugs in the cabinets."

He didn't seem to think my little joke was amusing. He squeezed me tighter. I gritted my teeth as my shoulder screamed, but I didn't want Andy to know his emotions were almost making me pee my pants.

"The doctor is Sal's cousin. Interesting … don't you think?" I was babbling, but I didn't care. I needed Andy to be the strong one and not fall apart.

He finally drew back from the hug. "Yeah, he introduced himself as we were walking back to the room."

"Andy, whoever is shooting at me isn't a good shot. He missed at the house, and he missed again today."

"He hit you!"

I nodded. "Yep, in the *shoulder*."

"They don't want to kill you." Dad spoke from the corner, startling me a little.

"Dad, I forgot you were here."

He smiled. "Sweetie, they are trying to scare you."

"I'm scared shitless!" Andy cut in.

I scowled slightly. "Well, I'm not. I'm pissed."

"Peg …" Andy's tone was full of worry.

I cut him off. "Andy, I'm tired of getting shot at, and I'm tired of this case. The quicker we solve it, which I hope involves putting Newman's grandson in jail, the quicker things can go back to normal."

Andy shook his head as he ran his hands through his hair. Gosh … I never noticed the new gray hairs. When had those stinkers shown up?

My phone blared again, but this time I answered it.

"Are you ok? Did you really get shot? Who shot you?" Jack's questions came so fast my head ached.

"Slow down, Jack. I'm fine, and I have no idea who shot me. I sent Bob to find out, but I haven't heard back from him." I frowned. Where was Bob?

"You sent Bob? Are you nuts?" Jack barked.

"Bob was with me when it happened, and once Dad showed up …" I flashed Dad a quick smile. "… I figured Bob could scout around and find the culprit."

My statement was met with silence. "Bob?"

"Yep."

Jack sighed. "What did he find?"

"No idea … he hasn't come back. Maybe he's with Logan."

Dad shook his head. "Let me check, but I don't think so. Last I knew, Logan had a full schedule of meetings."

The dead and their meetings … I was starting to believe we are busier in the afterlife than we are in this life—not something to look forward to, in my opinion.

"Any luck with Tom Newman?" I was hoping Jack obtained some new piece of information.

"I don't know what you said to the man, but he was a lot more reasonable after he talked to you."

I shrugged even though he couldn't see it. "I basically told him it would be nice if his grandson lived to see his graduation."

"Holy smokes … you hit hard." Jack chuckled.

I sighed. "This case is becoming a pain … literally." My shoulder was beginning to more than ache—it hurt like hell. "We need to wrap it up, so we can enjoy Adam's visit."

"Not sure that's going to be possible," Jack sighed. "We aren't any closer to catching the culprits, but I still have someone roaming the woods trying to spot anyone watching your house. So far … no luck."

"Any new evidence?" I knew better than to get my hopes up.

"Nope."

"My doctor is a Spanelli," I informed Jack.

My revelation was met with silence. "Is he nuts?"

I laughed. "I don't think so. He's tight with Sal and respects him. He told me his side of the family was never involved with the mob, which is good news."

"Maybe." Jack sighed tiredly. "I never heard the name Spanelli until a few months ago, and now they're popping up all over the place."

A nurse came into the room with a stack of papers. "I have to sign my release papers. I'll call you back later."

"Go straight home, and I'll meet you there," he said, then hung up before I had a chance to comment. I wanted to go home to peace and quiet, not a meeting with Jack.

I signed a gazillion papers to gain freedom from a children's hospital, but it was worth it as we stepped outside into fresh air. I took a deep breath, then was rewarded with a shot of pain ripping through my shoulder. I winced but didn't want Andy to know there was pain involved—the less he knew, the better.

Andy broke the silence as we walked to the parking deck. "You don't have to hide the pain, I'm not ignorant." He sounded irritated, scared, and defeated.

I glanced at him. "It's not too bad. Doctor Spanelli said it would only hurt for a couple of days."

Andy sighed. "Peg, last time was bad enough … but getting shot? I don't know how much more of this we can handle."

My stomach knotted listening to him. The sad part is, I didn't know what to say to him. I grabbed his hand and squeezed.

"Hey, Peg! Guess what? I don't think it was one of the Mendoza's crew that shot you!" Bob appeared out of nowhere.

Andy and I both jumped at the sound of his voice.

"Where have you been?" I demanded.

"Everywhere! It took me longer than I expected, but I'm pretty sure those crazies aren't responsible for your injury." The pride in his voice was overbearing … jeez.

I glanced around. "Let's get to the car. People are beginning to stare." I made my way into the parking deck. Where in the hell did I park the car?

"You parked in aisle C next to the fire extinguisher," Bob said happily.

"How'd you know I couldn't remember?" The last thing I needed was Bob having the ability to read my mind. Logan and Dad were bad enough, but Bob joining in was not my idea of comfort.

"Easy … you never remember." His reply was a little too chipper for my taste.

I wanted to wring his neck for his upbeat demeanor, but instead, I nodded and headed for the correct aisle.

Once inside the car, I turned to Bob. "Ok, buster … spill the beans. Who shot me?"

He put one hand up. "Hang on a minute. I didn't shoot you, so don't take your anger out on me."

I raised an eyebrow. Bob arguing back was the last thing I needed. "Who. Shot. Me?"

"Ok, simmer down. I think it was a friend of the kid."

I frowned. "What kid? You mean Tom Newman's grandson?"

"Yep. I heard him up in Thomas's hospital room bragging about taking you down." Pride filled Bob's face.

I was so dumbfounded I couldn't think of a thing to say.

Andy frowned slightly. "What made you suspect Thomas?"

"Well … we've all been so hellbent on the Mendoza family, I figured Logan had enough of his guys spying on them. How could they get by with shooting anyone? I thought it through and let me tell you, it wasn't easy."

I hated to admit it, but Bob's logic made sense. Amy must be rubbing off on all of us.

Andy nodded. "I see your point … but what led you to Thomas?"

"I didn't like the kid from the get-go. He was rude to Peg."

"Rudeness doesn't equal lethal action," I pointed out.

Bob waved a dismissive hand. "You'd be surprised how much you can decipher from a person's nastiness. Thomas was too sure of himself, and it wasn't all based on his grandfather's position in the township."

Hmmm … Bob was more observant than I ever gave him credit for. Thinking back to my conversation with Thomas, I could see how Bob had drawn his conclusions.

I finally nodded. "I agree with you. There *was* a satisfied air about the kid. Jack is going to meet us at the house, and I want you to be there."

Bob's chest puffed out like a blowfish. "I'll meet you guys there." Bob faded, leaving us alone.

Andy blew air out of his mouth. "Whew … if Newman's grandson is more involved than we expected, this is not going to be pretty."

"Wait until Jack hears Bob's theory. He'll blow a gasket."

Andy drove home, and I enjoyed the quiet ride. Both of us were lost in our own thoughts, but it was a comfortable silence rather than a tension-filled one. As we drove up the driveway, I saw Jack leaning against his car. Bob was nowhere in sight.

I climbed out of the car. "You beat us home."

Jack's face was filled with anger at the sight of the sling on my arm. "I only have to wear it for a day or two. It just supports my arm, so I don't use the shoulder."

"This has gone too far! I want Logan in on this meeting!" he snapped.

"He's on his way." Bob seemed to appear out of nowhere.

"How long have you been here?" His abilities were increasing even more than I realized.

Bob shrugged. "Since I left you. I didn't want to bother the chief, so I stayed quiet."

Jeez.

"Let's get inside. I could use a cup of coffee." I headed for the front door.

Once inside, with a cup of steaming hot brew in front of me, I looked at Bob. "Bob, go ahead and fill Jack in while we wait on Logan."

Bob nodded and began explaining his findings to Jack.

By the end of Bob's speech, Jack had his head in his hands. He moaned. "Could this get any worse? Newman is going to have a heart attack. Damn!"

"We have no proof, though. Telling a judge that a dead man heard the kid bragging isn't going to sound so good," I reminded Jack. "We need something definitive."

"I wouldn't tell Mr. Newman anything at this point," Andy added. "Is there any way we can draw the kid out, so he tips his hand?"

Jack shook his head. "I'm not saying a word. If the Newman kid is involved more than we suspected, this will get nasty fast."

"Yes, I believe we are reaching a crucial point in our investigation," Logan said, making his presence known.

For Pete's sake! When did Logan get here?

Jack sighed. "Yep. A big fat mess."

"I must admit, when Bob explained his findings, I was astonished. I considered Mr. Newman's grandson a minor figure in this situation." Logan shook his head, his long hair swaying with the movement.

"If we aren't careful we will land in a pickle," I said.

Logan raised an eyebrow but remained silent.

"We will be in trouble," I clarified for him.

"Ah." He nodded understanding.

Andy remained quiet throughout our discussion. He took a deep breath, speaking up. "Logan, Tom Newman could cause problems for all of us. As head trustee of the township, he could sway other members of the board of trustees to question Jack's abilities, which includes Peg and Amy. We have to handle this dilemma with care."

Logan nodded. "I understand your concerns. I will personally handle Mr. Newman."

Uh-oh.

Jack moaned. "Logan, the last thing I need is for you to appear to Newman and kill him from the shock."

Logan smiled. "Jack, there are many ways at my disposal to cope with someone such as Mr. Newman. I do not need to 'appear' to him."

Jack sighed. "Fine … he's your problem. Mine is to find the punk who is shooting people." He pointed a finger in my direction. "Peg may not be his only target."

My hand flew to my mouth. "Amy."

Jack nodded. "And anyone else who gets in the way of their little drug enterprise … including the Bath and Akron Police Departments."

"Should we call the feds? I mean, this could be a major situation." Andy was starting to sound nervous again.

"Oh, hell … the last people we need milling around mucking up an investigation are the feds. I remember them from the Dahmer case. They basically pushed us to the side as if we were small potatoes." Jack's face scrunched at the memory.

Jeffrey Dahmer was Bath's sad claim to fame. The famous killer of the nineties lived on Bath Road. Visiting folks still ask which house he lived in, so they can drive by the property … creepy.

Logan broke the silence that fell over the room. "They would be my last choice. I have no ill feelings toward the federal agents. However, they tend to be difficult to work with from my standpoint."

My eyebrow rose. "You've dealt with them before?"

"On occasion." He didn't elaborate, and I didn't waste my breath trying to pry information out of the old Indian—he could be damn stubborn.

"What's the next step?" Andy asked.

"Badger that snotty kid?" Bob's hopeful tone made me smile a little. Boy … he really didn't like the brat.

Jack shook his head. "Nope. I'm going after his buddies from high school."

"Thomas thought he was sitting pretty until he learned his grandfather was pressing charges," I added.

Jack snorted. "Newman is only pressing charges to safeguard his grandson." He paused. "I'll tell you, though … he was shook up to hear the boy was involved with a major drug ring. However, the kid is his grandson, and he wants to protect him as much as possible."

I scoffed. "He's probably already scouting around for a good criminal lawyer."

Jack nodded. "Yep, more than likely. When we searched the house on the Newman property, we found more drugs than a pharmaceutical company. You should have seen the place!"

Logan turned his gaze to Jack. "You searched the property?"

Uh-oh … I recognized Logan's tone of voice. The expression on Jack's face told me that I wasn't the only one who realized Logan was silently smoldering.

Jack held up a defensive hand. "I had one of your kind check it out to ensure there weren't any of Mendoza's dead partners roaming around the place."

Logan's face hardened. "One of my kind?"

Jack's face reddened. "Yeah … you know … um … dead."

"Which one of 'my kind' did you have check the property?" Ice formed with each word Logan spoke.

Jack looked to me for help, but I kept my mouth firmly closed.

"Bob," Jack finally said.

Crap … I'd bet dollars to donuts neither one of them bothered to ask Logan before they put their plan of action into motion … jeez.

"Bob." Logan's expression didn't change one bit during the short exchange, but his tone of voice spoke volumes. Bob was in a sinkhole with Logan, and there wasn't a thing I could do to help him.

Jack quickly jumped to Bob's defense. "He did an excellent job! He has become quite accomplished, which must be your influence." Jack trying to butter Logan up was never going to work, but there was no stopping him once he started talking. "Oh, yeah … he started at the edges of the property and worked his way in, quite impressive. You would've been proud of him."

I shook my head, but I kept my mouth shut. There was no way I was about to stick my foot into these turbulent waters.

"Plus, he was able to somehow detect there *had been* folks from your side on the property at some point." Jack sat back, satisfied he made his case for using Bob and going against Logan's request to check first before acting.

Logan raised an eyebrow. "Bob was able to detect a spirit's earlier presence on the property?" Logan turned to face Bob, only to realize he was gone. The stinker skedaddled the moment Jack mentioned his involvement on the Newman property.

CHAPTER 23

Logan scanned the room, searching for Bob—no luck. I didn't blame Bob one bit for leaving as soon as the conversation took a turn in his direction. I was determined not to get dragged into a pissing contest concerning who had control over the investigation. Jack and Logan, both, had reasonable claim to control the investigation, but only up to a point. Logan needed to realize Jack *was* chief of police while Logan was … well … dead.

Jack finally spoke up. "Logan, remember … I have a board of trustees who expect me to follow official procedures. I was already pushing boundaries by not searching the cabin earlier. There were officers on the force wondering why I wasn't making the inspection of the cabin top priority. I still have undercover men on the job, waiting for me to issue further orders." He shrugged. "I do the best I can to accommodate your wishes, but in the end … I answer to living people before I answer to you." Jack kept his tone of voice even, merely giving facts to someone who might not understand the ramifications Jack could face if he was suspected of hedging on the investigation. The last thing we needed was for someone to wonder if Jack worked for the Mendoza family.

Logan listened to Jack's speech with respect. He nodded as Jack finished. "I do understand your position. However, I would have appreciated contact concerning the matter."

Jack sighed. "I made a spur of the moment decision."

Spur of the moment? Baloney. I had a sneaking suspicion Jack decided days ago to use Bob as his personal spy. Hell … he asked to *borrow* Bob as if the guy was a lawn mower. I watched Logan's face, deciding he came to the same conclusion, but he wisely kept his deductions to himself.

"Other than drugs, what did you find at the cabin?" I was curious, and it was time to move on from their battle of wills.

Jack turned to me, happy to finally be on firmer ground. "It wasn't only a warehouse but also a manufacturing plant." He looked around the table. "You know anything about heroin?"

Andy and I looked at each other, then back at Jack. "Nope."

Jack nodded. "Exactly what I thought. A quick lesson is needed, so you understand what we found. Heroin is made from opium poppies. Ninety-seven percent of the world's supply is from Afghanistan. A university in Canada developed a strain of morphine that can be made in a lab, so no need to involve Afghanistan, which obviously has problems right now. I'm sure the supply lines are interrupted by the war. The university discovered a formula using only yeast and sugar. When fermented correctly, the end product imitates the chemical compounds found in the opium poppies. Sadly … it isn't a complicated process."

I was slightly confused. "What does morphine have to do with heroin?" Chemistry was never my strong suit, and drugs were never a part of my life.

Jack stared at me for a moment. "You are really naïve … aren't you?"

My irritation grew. "How am I supposed to know about this crap? I spent years keeping my boys *away* from drugs!"

He nodded. "Point taken. To continue, Russia has a nasty form made from lighter fluid, paint thinner, and codeine tablets. It's actually worse than heroin, but it has thankfully stayed in Russia for the most part. We've only had a couple of cases of the stuff being made here." Jack looked at us. "Are you following me so far?"

"Yep. I'm not a total moron," I snapped … jeez.

"Peg," Andy chided. "Give the guy a break."

I remained quiet, but I did concede a small nod.

"Then there is the plain old homemade stuff—salt, flour, baby powder or laundry detergent, plus bits of cocaine—you have that and you're in business. The stuff from Canada found its way out of the university setting and is being manufactured at an alarming rate … no surprise there really. Some graduate student probably decided that selling the formula for a huge amount of money was worth the risk." Finished with his lesson on heroin, Jack sat back in his chair.

I tapped the table with my finger, thinking. "If I understand you correctly, you're saying Newman's cabin is manufacturing the formula from

Canada. Why not the homemade stuff? It sounds easier."

Jack shook his head. "The homemade heroin may be easier to make, and harder for law enforcement to spot, but the Canadian formula is in demand."

I glanced up at Logan. "We have fake Canadian heroin, a South American drug cartel, and local drug dealers … right?"

"I was unaware of the Russian method." Logan was either irritated by the fact that somebody in Russia cornered the market on lighter fluid and paint thinner, or the more worrisome issue was his ignorance that a newer, more lethal, type of heroin was floating around out in the world.

"The Russian angle isn't our problem. The Canadian formula is hot on the streets right now, and it's exactly what is being made on Newman's property."

Logan turned to gaze out of my brand-new window. I was amazed at how quickly Andy got the glass company in Richfield to come out to the house. They were amazed the old glass didn't shatter with the first bullet.

"Um … I hate to bother you folks, but I overheard your conversation." Henry was standing in the doorway, looking slightly nervous.

Andy smiled. "Hi, Henry. It's nice to see you. Please join us."

Henry nodded, stepping further into the room. "Still fighting heroin after all these years?" He shook his head. "Figured it'd be long gone from the scene by now."

I frowned. "What do you mean?"

"Mrs. Shaw, drugs have been a nuisance for a long time … I'm sure Logan has explained that." He nodded his head in Logan's direction. "Before laws were passed, doctors prescribed cocaine and heroin as cure-alls. People got addicted to cocaine as a cure for morphine addiction … it was a right mess. I thought people would progress beyond drugs by now, but I guess it was wishful thinking on my part."

I looked at Henry, my head crammed with questions. I finally settled on one I hoped wouldn't hit too close to the mark. "Did you know someone addicted to heroin?"

Henry's tear-filled eyes met mine. A quick nod was all I thought he was able to give me. "Yes, ma'am … a great-aunt." He grew quiet, lost in his memories.

We sat stone still, watching the pain on his face. Even Logan's expression was filled with sadness. Had Logan known the woman? I would bet money it was information Logan would never share.

Finally, Henry continued. "Her husband was unfaithful and gave her syphilis. It's a very painful condition. Back in those days, the doctors prescribed morphine. She became dependent on the drug, so the next step was cocaine to help with her addiction to morphine." He shook his head. "I know it sounds horrible but remember, modern medicine will probably sound terrible to people in another hundred years."

"What happened to her?" I was fighting the urge to cry myself.

"She died ... but I never believed it was from the drugs. She had a broken heart."

Tears sprang to my eyes, but I fought them from spilling down my cheeks.

"I'm so sorry," Andy said.

Henry shook his head. "Don't be. We have a right good time over here now. It would be different if I never met up with her again. She and my sister were the first people to greet me when I got to ..." he hesitated, shooting a quick glance at Logan.

"When you got where?" I pressed.

"Sorry ... can't say."

Logan took over the conversation. "Peg, we have to keep some secrets from you. Otherwise, what do you have to look forward to?" Eyes twinkling, he smiled.

Damn ... we almost had another nugget of information to add to our growing list concerning Deadsville. One look at Andy and I knew his mind registered that a chunk of knowledge slipped through our fingers. He glanced at me and winked.

Jack turned his attention to Henry. "Anything else we need to know?"

"Nope. It's been pretty quiet around here." He pointed to the woods. "Your friends out back were agitated a couple of times, but when I went out to ask what was wrong, they clammed up. I decided they would tell Logan and came back to the house."

My stomach knotted. "Agitated? How much?"

Henry shrugged. "Enough that I went out to check."

I looked over at Logan, who was gazing out the window. My level of annoyance was on the rise, but I tried to keep it out of my voice. I didn't quite succeed. "Logan ... what were the guys upset about? Don't bother with some long-winded explanation that doesn't answer the question."

Jack snorted at my remark. He knew how evasive Logan could be, and he usually was when asked a direct question. Logan liked the *big picture* speech, and he used it as cover for anything he wasn't in the mood to explain.

Logan turned and faced me. "A few of Mendoza's men from my side were roaming around two separate times today. No one was home, so they left." He turned back to his study of nature.

My heart pounded. "Why couldn't Henry see them?" I was pointing a finger at Henry as I spoke.

"Henry's position is inside the house. By the time he noticed the men guarding the woods, they were gone."

I looked at Henry, who nodded. "I didn't see anyone. Doesn't mean they weren't there, just means I wasn't able to see them."

I learned while dealing with dead folks, words they use have meaning … lots of meaning. Henry's phrase *wasn't able to see them* had my sweat glands working overtime.

"Is it possible they were still around? Invisible to even you?" I was determined to obtain the full story. It wasn't always easy, especially when Logan was involved.

Henry shifted his stance, and I didn't miss his quick glance at Logan. "It's sorta complicated."

I shook my head. "Sorry, but 'sorta complicated' isn't an answer." I dug my heels in and wasn't about to back off now.

Jack's mouth dropped open. "Don't tell me Henry might not be able to see other dead people!"

My eyes swiveled to Jack. "Remember when Mom couldn't see my protectors in the woods? She thought Logan removed them, but actually, they were just invisible to Mom. The dead can't always see other dead people. I have no idea how Logan accomplishes the feat, but it *is* possible."

I turned my attention back to Henry. "Someone from your side *could* have been out there … right?"

Henry's stance changed again. "Maybe."

I really liked Henry, and I knew I was making him nervous, especially with Logan in the room, but I needed an answer. I threw my hands in the air. "You people are driving me nuts!"

Without turning, Logan spoke. "Peg, we are not required to answer your questions simply because you want an answer. You must remember, not having access to information does not mean I am being unreasonable. Your protection is of the utmost importance, and I would provide any data you required to stay safe. Easing your curiosity is not the same thing."

"I beg to differ! If the Mendoza family has dead people watching the house, I have a right to know!"

"What exactly would you do with the knowledge?" Logan countered.

Well hell … he had me there.

I looked back toward Henry only to find he cleared out of Dodge—I didn't blame him. Logan and I could get into huge arguments. I usually lost, but I fought anyway.

Jack cut in, trying to ease the tension. "Any pie?"

I shot him a dirty look, but I knew he was uncomfortable with the tone the discussion had taken. I sighed and went to the fridge to drag out the last of the pie one-handed—the sling was becoming a nuisance already. Jack was eating me out of house and home … well really only out of pie, but I was buying the suckers constantly. This was the second peach pie in a short period of time that Jack plowed through.

Andy smiled at me. "Any chance you could cut the piece in two?"

I nodded. "Yep."

Andy got up and made coffee for himself and Jack. Logan remained quiet, now watching the proceedings. I ignored him, which seemed to suit his mood.

Once Jack and Andy were happily sipping coffee and munching their pie, I turned my attention back to Logan. "What's next?"

"Excellent question." Logan turned to Jack. "When are you interviewing Thomas Newman?"

Jack swallowed his mouthful of pie before answering. "When do you want me to?"

Ah … Jack decided to play nice since he pissed off Logan earlier—good move.

Logan looked at the pie plate. "When you are finished would suffice."

Jack's coffee cup stopped half-way to his mouth. "Now?"

Logan nodded. "Please finish your pie first; there is no hurry."

Jack looked at me, and I shrugged. Once Logan decides to take a step, it's usually a huge stride.

Jack jabbed the last piece of pie with his fork, crammed it into his mouth, and drank the rest of his coffee. He looked at Logan as he stood. "Are you riding along or meeting me there?"

Logan thought a moment. "I would enjoy talking on the way to the hospital."

Jack nodded, then thanked me for the pie. "Let's roll."

After they left, Andy looked at me. "What made Logan decide to talk to the kid now?"

I shrugged. "Who knows? There was no reason to ask since he stonewalls most of the time."

Andy grinned.

The phone rang, and the caller ID alerted me our son, Adam, was calling.

"Hey, sweetie, what's up?" I made sure to keep my tone as chipper as possible.

"Hi, Mom. Are we still on for the visit?"

"Sure. Next Friday, right?"

"Yep. Tell Dad hi for me," he said happily. "Love ya both."

I hung up the phone, frowning. "That was the shortest call in history. What's up with him? He keeps calling to ask the same damn question."

Andy smiled. "Probably checking in to make sure no one forgot."

The doorbell rang, causing Andy and me to look at one another. My house was becoming way too busy.

Andy answered the door while I cleaned up after the pie snack. Frustration mounted as I fought to wash two plates one-handed. Irritation won … I jerked the sling over my head and threw it on the table. I would live with the pain because I couldn't function with one arm.

I heard Andy talking as he made his way back to the kitchen. I recognized the voice and frowned, hoping a new problem hadn't cropped up.

My eyes met Floyd's as he entered the kitchen with Andy. "Hi, Floyd. Is there something wrong?"

He shook his head. "Nope, but I wanted to drop off a few supplies, so I can get started tomorrow. I want the room painted before the carpet is installed."

My eyebrows shot up in surprise. "Wow … thanks."

Floyd glanced toward the den. "Do you still have that guy guarding the den?"

"Yep. Is he a problem for you?"

He shook his head. "Oh, no … gives me someone to talk to while I work. He was great fun when I was taking measurements. Knows some great stories from the old days."

"Really?" I hesitated. "He's never shared much about his work."

"Not work stories, stuff about Atlanta. By the time I finished measuring, I decided I'm going there on my next vacation … sounds like a great city."

"Floyd … Henry was talking about Atlanta in the thirties and forties. I'm sure Atlanta has changed a lot since then."

"Not necessarily. He keeps up with current events. He even told me places I should visit."

I looked at Andy, then back to Floyd. "Henry still visits Atlanta?"

"Sure." Floyd looked surprised. "He still lives there."

"Uh … Floyd. Henry's dead. How can he *live* anywhere?"

Floyd waved a hand. "He lives with his grandson. Sorta keeps an eye on him for his daughter. The kid has no idea though, so don't tell anyone."

I don't know why, but the thought of Henry living with his grandson was a shock. "Does Logan know?"

Floyd shrugged. "I guess so. If Henry was willing to tell me, it stands to reason he'd tell Logan." Floyd's analysis made sense.

I nodded. "It doesn't really matter I suppose."

He looked down at the supplies filling the bucket in his hand. "You mind if I store these in the bedroom? The paint cans are there now, and it will make it easier to have everything in one room."

I nodded. "Sure … no problem. What time did you plan on being here?"

He scratched his chin as he thought about it. "It's not a large room, so with any luck, I could get two coats on by tomorrow night. How about seven-thirty?"

"In the morning?" I tried to keep the annoyance out of my tone. "Pretty early … don't you think?"

He grinned. "I heard all about your three-cup rule. Don't worry, I won't bother you. Your husband can let me in when I get here, and I'll head straight to the bedroom."

I felt a sense of relief—someone who understands my need for coffee.

Andy nodded. "I'll be waiting for you."

"Thanks folks. See ya in the morning." With a quick wave, Floyd turned and walked back toward the door.

"He's such a nice guy." Bob's voice came from the corner.

I turned my attention to him. "Bob, where did you scoot off to?"

Bob turned red. "I decided to check in on Thomas Newman. He's not a nice person at all."

"Nope, he's an arrogant snot. Has Logan and Jack talked to him yet?"

Bob shook his head. "They arrived about the time I left."

I felt a pang of disappointment. "You didn't stay to hear the interview?"

Bob fidgeted a second. "Nah … they'll fill us in later."

I smiled slightly. "It didn't have anything to do with the fact you did a little spying for Jack, did it?"

Bob looked up at me. "It was a good thing I did! There were enough drugs in that cabin to fill a warehouse!"

"Did you find anything else interesting?"

He shrugged. "I could tell someone from our side had been there recently."

"I didn't know you had the ability to sense a spirit's presence once it left an area."

Bob shook his head. "Neither did I."

"What?" I was a little surprised.

"First time I ever experienced anything remotely along those lines … sorta weird."

I plopped into my chair and looked at Andy. "I have a bad feeling about this."

CHAPTER 24

Andy frowned. "What makes you uncomfortable about Bob's experience?"

"Well … for starters … Bob never had the ability before, so what made him 'feel' the spirit? Secondly, if Bob could feel the spirit, it may mean whoever was there was very powerful, or if he or she wasn't then his or her essence wouldn't still be hanging around the area." I shook my head. "Whatever the reason … I have a gut feeling it's not good."

"You are right," Dad interrupted.

I jumped. Dead people don't always announce their arrival, and it tends to startle me sometimes.

Worry creased Andy's face. "What do you mean, Dave?"

Dad looked at Bob. "You've never been able to tell before?"

Bob shook his head, his face full of worry. "You think something's wrong with me?"

Dad smiled. "No … but I also don't think you've developed a new skill, either."

Bob's mouth dropped open. "Really? Are you sure? Dave, I've been working really hard on improving my skills."

Dad nodded his head. "I'm positive. I went by the property myself, and there is no indication of an essence remaining. I'm afraid they were hidden."

Uh-oh … I didn't like the sound of that. "You mean veiled in some way?"

Dad nodded. "Exactly. Bob could feel them, but he couldn't see them. Bob's skills are improving by leaps and bounds, but that particular aptitude is very difficult to achieve. I'd say Logan is one of the few who has the ability. I only have partial talent, and it's taken a great deal of work to accomplish. If someone left behind some aspect of themselves, I should have been able to detect it also. I may not be able to identify the person, but I still would have felt *something.*"

I sighed. "Someone was hiding … not good."

Dad nodded. "Someone from our side, which makes it even worse."

I frowned thoughtfully. "Mendoza people?"

Dad thought a moment before speaking. "Possibly … not definite."

Andy frowned. "Who else could it be? We are under the impression the Mendoza family is behind all the drugs in the area."

"Yes, but who else is involved?" Dad looked at me. "Have you talked to the mayor recently?"

Damn … his tone of voice held a warning of some type.

"You think the mayor is helping the drug dealers?" As much as I disliked the guy, even I couldn't see the mayor being involved with drugs.

"He may not realize he's helping drug lords, he could think he's helping out a big donor."

Jeez … this could get nasty if the mayor was involved on any level. I looked at Dad. "Do we know who else could be behind the drugs?"

He shook his head. "Not yet. We are watching the Mendoza side of things, hoping they will lead us to the partner."

Andy quickly cut in. "How can you be so sure there *is* a partner? Maybe the Mendoza family is running the show all on their own and hiring local criminals to distribute the heroin."

"Sal explained how they've worked in other cities. They are the suppliers, and they always use locals to do the actual work, but this time they are using high school kids. I guess it's their way of keeping in the background and never giving a face to identify." He looked at Andy. "You are correct in the logistics of their operation, but a piece is missing. There is some sort of middleman that we can't seem to identify."

I moaned. "These cases are increasingly dangerous. Give me a local sociopath any day … at least the cast of characters is confined to the township."

Dad nodded. "I agree. Local crime is much easier to manage. International situations compound the danger and the complications."

"Complications? Such as?" Andy pressed.

Dad was silent while he gathered his thoughts. Finally, he started his explanation. "Each country has their own traditions, laws, and unique views of the world around them. Europe views the world through their long history and so does the Middle East." He paused. "North and South America were the last areas to become truly inhabited by other cultures." He waved a hand. "I'm not referring to the natives who resided on these continents for centuries, but the influence of the Western world was tolerated more easily in certain areas."

I frowned, slightly confused. "What are you talking about?"

Dad sighed. "I'm making a mess of this … Logan is better at explaining than I am."

"Dave, tell us the gist of your thoughts." Andy continued to press for answers—I wanted answers as much as he did.

Dad nodded. "We all know the history of North American Indian tribes." He looked at us, hoping we were following his line of reasoning. We were, but what was his point?

Andy smiled encouragingly.

Dad continued. "Mexico, Central America, and South America have a different history. South American Indians existed as far back as 6500 BCE, and the Incan Empire stretched for almost a thousand miles on the western coast of South America."

I was mildly surprised by his history lesson. "I had no idea South America was populated so far back in history."

Dad nodded. "Before Europeans arrived, there were about thirty million people living in South America. North and Central America also had large populations." He shrugged. "We usually think of Aztecs, Incas, and Mayans as the big groups outside of the states, but there were many. Most were highly civilized by anyone's standards. They understood advanced farming, worked copper and gold into jewelry, and used precious stones for adornments. They were not cartoon characters but real, functioning societies."

"Thirty million? Wow." I was in awe.

Dad smiled. "We need to teach in-depth world history."

Andy cut in, obviously determined to understand. "What does the history lesson have to do with the Mendoza family?"

Dad looked out the window for a moment before continuing. "The Spanish conquered those areas much the same way the French and British settled and pushed back the native people in North America. The main difference was that South American Indians were more along the lines of what we would consider empires. Don't misunderstand me, though … the natives in North America were highly cultivated in many ways. However, think about the Incas and Mayans for a moment … they had religious monuments and pyramids that closely resembled those in other parts of the world. Their social and political structures would rival any in Europe because they had very tightly held power and social order."

"So?" Dad's history lecture was starting to bore me to tears.

"Those belief systems and attitudes didn't disappear with the arrival of the Spanish and Catholicism … they merely blended their beliefs with the ideas forced on them. We are talking in some cases where beliefs that existed for thousands of years folded into a new power base."

Dad looked at us as he finished speaking. We looked at one another, then back at Dad.

Andy sighed. "Dave, you've lost us."

"Oh, my God!" Bob's excited voice chimed in.

Jeez … I'd forgotten he was still with us.

Andy frowned. "Bob, what's wrong?"

Bob ignored Andy. His focus was completely on Dad. "You mean the Mendoza family can trace their family lineage back to those early empires … don't you?"

Dad nodded. "Yep. Now you know why Logan is so worried. We're talking about major spiritual power within the family."

I was back to being confused. "But Sal said they are stupid! Stupid and power don't mix well."

"Exactly!" Dad agreed. "While the family, as a whole, has power, they aren't the best businessmen. The living members of the family aren't necessarily our biggest problem."

"They are using spirits from hundreds, maybe thousands of years ago?" Andy sounded as shocked as I felt.

Dad smiled at the fact that we were catching on. "It would explain why Bob could 'feel' an essence, but he doesn't possess the ability to see whoever was at Newman's property."

"This is becoming too theological for me. I want to catch bad guys and call it a day! I don't want to have to worry about thousand-year-old ghosts dealing drugs!" I stomped my foot. Too bad Jack finished the damn pie, I could've used a piece to settle my nerves. Well … maybe not my nerves, but good old-fashioned cream pie would make me feel better.

"Are these ghosts stronger than Logan?" Andy asked. I could see the worry on his face, and I realized how frightened he was by the thought of spirits more powerful than Logan. I didn't blame him one bit.

"I think I'm going to be sick," Bob said. "If Logan is weaker than the Mendoza family ghosts, we're in big trouble."

"Bob, you're dead! Dead people don't puke!" I snapped. I glared at him, but I did have to admit, he looked a little green … holy cow.

Andy pressed on, determined to get to the bottom of things. "You asked about the mayor earlier. Do you think he is more involved than he realizes?"

Dad pursed his lips, thinking. "I think he turns a blind eye to activity he doesn't want to admit could be a problem." Dad shrugged. "Could be something all politicians do when money is involved. Hell … Sal gives huge donations to his campaign and makes deals with him all the time. I admit, Sal is basically a straight shooter, but it does point to the mayor having a history of ignoring a possible problem."

I sighed. "Do you want me to call him?"

Dad shook his head. "A better solution is another meeting. Logan can handle the guy better than you when it comes to shady dealings."

I frowned. "I hold my own damn well with His Highness, in my opinion!"

Dad grinned. "I'm not saying you don't, but Logan might have inside information you are unaware of … information the mayor believes is well hidden."

As much as I hated to admit it, Dad made a good point. Logan had access to all sorts of crap I would never even dream existed. I nodded, keeping my mouth shut.

"I agree with Dave. I believe it is time for another meeting." Logan appeared out of nowhere.

I jumped at the sound of his voice. How long was he listening to our conversation? He was sneaky sometimes. "You want me to call him?"

Logan shook his head. "I would rather have the gathering at his office. However, neither Salvatorio nor Amy is to be involved."

My eyebrows went north when I heard Logan's decision. Sal and Amy weren't invited?

Logan noticed my expression and smiled. "Salvatorio's presence could compromise the mayor in addition to complicating the discussion. Amy needs to be protected by our friend. Therefore, neither is to be included."

I nodded, agreeing with his assessment. The last thing the mayor needed was a known mobster strolling into City Hall for a meeting—tongues would be wagging within minutes.

Andy cleared his throat. "Logan, I have a question." Logan turned to Andy and quietly waited for my sweetie to pose his query. "Dave was explaining the Mendoza family may be descendants of an impressive group of South American Indians. How does their ancestry play into our problem?"

Logan nodded as he listened to Andy. He glanced at Dad, then back at Andy. "I am sure Dave gave you a full explanation of the ancient culture. There are golden years for each culture as their society matures." He paused as he glanced at both of us.

I guess he wanted to make sure we understood his train of thought. I fought a tad of irritation—we weren't morons.

Satisfied with our expressions, he continued. "During a golden age, certain leaders emerged who gained significant power. Many types of power exist—spiritual, political, intellectual, and so forth. The Mendoza family's ancestors were both spiritually and politically powerful for a time." He shook his head. "Power is not always positive, and many in the lineage were what you would consider corrupt. Once the Europeans entered their lives, corruption flourished within their ranks."

I sighed, still confused by all this. "If they were so damn powerful back then, why haven't they become the biggest drug cartel?"

Logan gave me a small smile. "Merely having impressive ancestors is not a guarantee that present-day family members will be extraordinary. What is remarkable, in my opinion, is that they function with any success at all. The Mendoza family is full of greed, which is a weakness. The desire to be successful is hardly the same as greed. If we were facing an enemy who was intelligent, I would have a much stronger ability to thwart their enterprises."

I frowned. "You aren't making sense."

He smiled as if I were a five-year-old, which did nothing to improve my irritation. "Intelligence is based on logic of some sort. Logic allows us to follow a line of reasoning that leads to an understandable conclusion. Greed produces scattered ambitions, which follow no line of logical thought. Therefore, actions are unpredictable."

Andy nodded. "There would be a code to decipher, correct? We could follow it almost like a map."

Logan's smile widened. "Precisely. When there is no map, we do not have the advantage of predicting their next move. My main concern at this point is the spirits using the Mendoza family."

My eyes widened. "You mean your side is using these fools? Not the other way around?"

"Holy cow!" Bob chimed in. "The Mendoza family has no idea they have spiritual help!" He looked at Logan for confirmation, and Logan nodded.

"They're being used by your side?" Andy still sounded confused.

Logan nodded, his face grim. "The family is quite ignorant of their heritage. They have existed for decades on the addictions of others. Greed is another avenue for evil to enter the world. Look back through history, and you will find greed at the root of many wars. Greed for land, power, or money ... evil flows through easily."

I sat back in my chair, thoughts flying through my mind. "Can you do anything to stop the mess on your side? Let's face it ... if you can stop the influence of the Mendoza family, they will ruin themselves with little help from us."

"We have plans in place. For the time being, the burden is on the living to stem as much as possible."

Well hell ... I sighed. "Who was hiding from Bob at Newman's property?"

Logan's expression turned grim. "There is a search in progress. I have little hope of conclusive evidence. Whoever was there is quite powerful."

I raised my eyebrows in surprise. "More powerful than you?"

He hesitated. "Possibly."

I sighed and looked at Andy.

Andy shook his head. "Is the Newman kid involved?"

"Up to his snotty neck!" Bob declared. His statement earned him a glance from Logan. Bob snapped his mouth shut, but his expression remained determined.

"His friend shot me … remember? Somehow those kids got mixed up in something that is way over their stupid, little heads." I turned to Logan. "Greed?"

"They are arrogant young men. They are also foolish. They have very little respect for anyone, including those in positions of authority."

"Jack?" I asked.

Logan nodded. "Precisely."

I thought back to the time when our own boys were teenagers. They were basically good kids, but they could pull some damn stupid stunts. I glanced at Andy and I knew from the look on his face, his thoughts matched my own.

I looked back at Logan. "I know Jack is working hard to get information from the Newman kid. I don't think it's going well, though."

Logan sighed. "Jack has been extremely helpful in this matter. He and I had a meeting earlier, and he is making some progress. Mr. Newman has been made aware of the severity of his grandson's business dealings."

I was surprised they told Newman so much. "Wow … the old guy must be furious."

"Mr. Newman was quite obstinate concerning his grandson. However, Jack was able to produce enough evidence against the boy. His grandfather was understandably stunned." Logan's expression was neutral as he spoke, which I took to mean Newman probably threw a huge fit in Jack's office. I would have to wait to hear the nitty-gritty from Jack.

"Is Tom Newman cooperating now?" Andy asked.

Logan nodded. "Yes, I believe his distaste for the drug influence throughout the area has allowed him to become quite supportive of Jack's efforts."

"Wow … how's Jack taking this new attitude of Newman's?" Personally, I was shocked.

Logan smiled. "Happily."

"I bet," I said sarcastically. "Jack can't stand the man."

Logan shrugged. "Wisdom dictates he accommodates Mr. Newman's personality for the time being. I do not believe it will be a long-term situation."

"I agree. The second the shock wears off, Newman will be furious his grandson is probably facing prison time."

"Possibly." Logan agreed. "However, I have no doubt Jack will handle the situation appropriately."

I shrugged. Jack's temper might get the best of him if Newman started being a pain in the butt. I decided we'd just have to wait and see.

Andy frowned slightly. "What do you want us to do next?"

Logan shifted his gaze to Andy. "The mayor is involved somehow, I am sorry to inform you. It is undetermined at this point how deeply or if he is truly aware. Therefore, I propose a visit this afternoon."

"Are you ready now?" I was ready to get this show on the road.

Logan looked out the window as if the solutions were waiting for him in thin air. After a moment, he turned back to me. "I believe now is an appropriate time. How long would it take you and Andy to arrive?"

"Me?" Andy's tone was wrought with confusion. "Why do you want me to be there?"

Logan cocked his head as he answered. "You are an important part of our team. I would not leave you out of equally meaningful gatherings. I assumed you wanted to be involved."

Andy thought about Logan's response. "I don't necessarily think of myself as part of Peg's investigations. My work is time consuming, and Peg has always handled most of the work with you on her own."

Logan shook his head. "I believe you underestimate our need for you. Personally, I rely on your intuition as much as I do Peg's."

Andy raised an eyebrow, then glanced at me. "Logan, you must understand I have to work. I'm home today only because of recent events."

Logan nodded. "Yes. You do seem to always be available when needed."

Andy sighed. "It does seem that way ... doesn't it?"

Logan only smiled. How many strings was Logan pulling to have Andy present when he wanted him? There was no way to know unless he spilled the beans ... which would never happen in a gazillion years.

Andy slowly stood. "Ok ... I guess we can head downtown." He looked at me, and I looked at Logan.

Logan smiled slightly. "We will meet you at the mayor's office." Bob, Dad, and Logan all began to fade.

"You ready?" I glanced at Andy as I grabbed my purse.

He sighed heavily. "Let's go."

CHAPTER 25

By the time we headed downtown, the evening rush was over, and it was smooth sailing—no traffic to fight and easy parking. We headed toward the mayor's office, marveling at how empty the city felt.

I glanced at Andy. "I hope he's still in his office. I'll be so mad if he's gone for the day."

Andy laughed. "Logan wouldn't let us troop down here for nothing."

"True." He was right … Logan should know.

I faced the dragon in the mayor's office, ready for her usual routine of ignoring me until she absolutely had no other choice. I was surprised when she spoke first, rising from her chair as she did. "The mayor is expecting you."

Andy and I exchanged looks, then followed her to the mayor's door.

She smiled as we went through the door. I almost peed my pants holding back the laughter that threatened to escape my lips. I'd bet money it took all her years of experience to give that smile … tough beans.

Entering the mayor's office, I spotted my three dead guys lined up next to His Honor's desk. Logan didn't bother to dress up for the occasion, so I figured he felt the mayor was ready to cooperate.

Once the door was safely closed, the mayor looked at me. "I swear I have no idea what this Indian is talking about." He was red-faced and already sweating.

I didn't believe him for a second.

Logan looked over at Andy and me. "I have reminded the mayor that he held back vital information before, and behavior of that type will not be tolerated."

Plopping my butt in one of the chairs facing his desk, I looked at the mayor. "Logan has a good point. I advise you to tell us everything."

He glared at me for a moment. "I really don't know any Mendoza people."

I nodded. "We didn't say you did, but you sure as hell know somebody who is connected to those creeps." I pointed to my shoulder. "One of their idiots shot me."

Watching his face pale, I sat back in the chair. I figured I might as well get comfortable.

Andy sat next to me, but he wasn't adding even one word to the conversation.

Logan turned to the mayor. "Sir, while I may believe you are unaware of the Mendoza family, I also believe you have a connection to them. What *type* of connection is what we need to know. I questioned you before on your knowledge of drug influx into your city. You denied knowledge ... that was unwise."

The mayor looked as though Logan punched him in the gut. He quickly glanced back at me. "What exactly do you want?"

"Do you personally know all of your big donors? I'm talking the big money."

He frowned. "Sure ... most of them." He reached down and opened a file drawer, then pulled out a folder. "Who are you looking for?"

"You keep a list?" It never dawned on me he'd have a list so handy.

"Absolutely. Part of campaigning is making sure your biggest donors know you appreciate their money ... Christmas cards, invitations to luncheons, even casual get-togethers ... people want acknowledgment." He shrugged. "It's the way the game is played."

"Along with special building permits, city business for their companies, and any other type of kickback you can give," I snapped.

He scowled. "Sometimes ... nothing illegal."

"That remains to be seen." I held out a hand for the folder.

His eyes widened. "No way! This is private."

I narrowed my eyes. "The only way I will be able to spot something is if I see the list."

The mayor's eyes strayed to Logan's. One look at Logan's face was all we needed. He handed the folder over to me.

I thanked him and started reading. Some of the names I never heard of before. "Who are the Johnsons?"

"George Johnson? They live over in Pittsburg ... big donors for years."

"Pittsburg? Why do you have someone donating money if they live in another state?" I asked confused.

He looked surprised at my question. "We're in the same political party. He owns a trucking company."

I frowned. "Trucking company?" I tapped my finger on the folder. "What do you do in exchange for his extremely large donation?"

The mayor frowned. "Why do you ask?"

"There must be a reason he's donating to you other than political affiliation ... so, what is it?"

His face grew pink. "If you must know, we do business with his company."

"You don't hire truckers from Akron?" Acid dripped off every one of my words.

"Of course, we hire our hometown people! What are you implying?"

I scowled. "You know what I'm saying. What type of trucking company does he own exactly?"

"Big trucks. Akron doesn't have any companies who can handle the jobs we hire him for."

Andy finally spoke up. "Why not?"

The mayor looked surprised. I didn't know if his surprise was because of the actual question or because Andy was the one who asked. "Well ... I don't know."

"Uh-huh ... or you don't allow a company that could match Mr. Johnson's capabilities to receive permits to operate within city limits." Wow ... Andy hit the nail on the head.

The mayor's face looked as though it would explode into tiny pieces.

"Let's move on," I said, gliding a finger down the list. As I read the list, I recognized many names of local business leaders—nothing to be surprised about with those. Turning the page, my mouth dropped open as I spotted a very familiar name.

I looked up at the mayor, shock written all over my face. "Newman? Tom Newman donates to you?"

Logan's eyes zeroed in on the mayor, Dad whistled, and Bob's mouth dropped open.

Andy turned to look at me, but I kept my eyes glued to His Highness.

The mayor frowned. "Sure ... he's donated for years. It's not much."

I ran my finger across the line and shook my head seeing the amount donated. "It's not peanuts."

He scoffed. "Compared to most businessmen, it's small."

"What favors do you give him?" My stomach turned into knots as all the possibilities ran through my head.

The mayor's frown deepened. "We help the township. Our police departments work in tandem, we loan road equipment in emergencies, we rent out snow trucks, a lot of different stuff."

Andy frowned thoughtfully. "Wouldn't you do those things automatically as neighboring communities?"

"Well … maybe. Tom makes sure there are no glitches."

My eyes narrowed. "Glitches? What type of glitches?"

He shrugged. "If Akron rents out equipment, Tom ensures payment is on time. Same for any other help we give."

"You charge for helping us?" I couldn't hide my shock.

"Of course. We carry insurance on every piece of equipment … including the trucks, hell … even the drivers. It's damn expensive. If our police have to travel to the township to give aid or pick up a prisoner, we charge a fee to cover the gas and time. It's common, and every city has to charge. We'd never make the budget otherwise."

Guess I never gave much thought to the expenses before. I was in unfamiliar territory concerning city budgets, but I felt something was off somehow. I sat tapping my finger on the folder. What on earth was I missing? I looked back at the list of names. My vision blurred as I allowed my eyes to lose focus, so my brain could zero in on what was bothering me.

"Any other favors you do for Tom?" I didn't bother lifting my head.

Silence met my question. I allowed my eyes to meet his face … ah ha! "What other favors?"

"Just a few favors. His grandson gets into a few minor scrapes every once in a while."

"Such as?" I could feel the tension from Logan, so I knew I was on the right track.

"Underage drinking in a downtown bar, but it only happened once or twice."

"What else?" I was positive there was more to come.

The mayor shifted in his chair. "I'm not sure Tom would want me to share this information." His tone became pompous.

I glared at him. "Really? You have three dead guys standing next to your desk and you think now is the time to be a pain in the butt?"

He paled slightly but set his jaw. "I should call Tom and run this by him."

"Well … good luck. At the moment, he is helping the police nail his grandson's butt to the wall for dealing heroin," I snapped.

The mayor's mouth dropped open. He stared at me, shocked and speechless—it worked for me.

I continued studying the file on my lap, but no other name jumped at me as a problem. I closed the file, then slid it across his desk. "You need to tell me what other little problems you helped get the kid out of."

He cleared his throat, finally finding his voice. "About a year ago,

Thomas was accused of raping a girl. Tom was convinced the boy was being set up, so we dropped the charges."

"Tom was convinced, was he? Are you an idiot?" I screamed. "So, you drop rape charges because a donor thinks his grandson is innocent. Was a rape kit done? Did the girl have proof? What did you do with the evidence? I'm well aware of how you handle inconvenient evidence." I was on a roll, and I would've never stopped if Logan didn't intercede.

"Excuse me." He turned his gaze to the mayor. "Mayor Hayes, I am deeply disappointed in hearing your complicity in these matters. They are serious, and it leads me to believe the boy is involved in many enterprises that are probably harming not only the township but your own city." Logan shook his head.

"I didn't destroy evidence!" he protested. "I didn't even destroy much when my own son was involved."

I sighed. "You're an idiot."

He began to bluster, but Dad stepped in. "Not now, buster. You've done enough damage … don't add to your problems. I'm sure Logan has his own questions for you to answer."

Logan's expression remained firm. "Why would you help someone avoid accusations of rape? I believe it is a serious charge that carries deep consequences."

"Tom assured me the boy wasn't even in the city the night the girl was raped. I've known Tom a long time … he's never lied to me."

I knew he was beginning to doubt ol' Tom told him the truth. Problem was, I knew Tom also … he wasn't a liar, but his snotty grandson certainly was one.

"Logan, I believe him," I said quietly.

Andy glared at me. "What?"

I shook my head. "Andy, you know Tom Newman as well as I do. Does he strike you as a man who lies easily? No … he doesn't. I don't think the guy has ever knowingly said one untruthful statement in his whole life. He loves rules, regulations, and laws."

Logan listened to my words, his head nodding in agreement. "I concur. However, the mayor's interference allowed a grave crime to remain unpunished." He looked back at the mayor. "Where is the evidence?"

"In the back of the evidence room at the police department." Finally, the fool was giving straight answers.

"I'd advise you to reopen the case," Dad said carefully. "Make the call."

The mayor looked from Dad to Logan. Both men had steel in their eyes, and he knew it was hopeless to argue. He turned to me. "You do believe me … right?"

"Up to a point. I know you play footsies with dangerous people. Just how deeply involved you are with the current heroin situation remains to be seen."

"Never! I would never allow heroin to go unchecked! It kills people," he declared pompously.

I scoffed. "So does your stupidity. Make the call so the girl gets her justice."

"Did the police do DNA samples at the time?" Andy asked.

"I suppose so." Mayor Hayes shrugged. "Don't they usually?" His face was a mass of honest confusion.

"Did you test Newman's grandson?" Andy pressed.

The Mayor hesitated. "No reason to since Tom gave him an alibi." His trust in Tom Newman was obvious.

Jeez Louise ... basic police work muddied again by the idiot sitting across from me. "Make. The. Call." I couldn't decide whether to wring the moron's neck or feel sorry for him.

It was painfully obvious the mayor honestly believed Newman's grandson was innocent simply because Newman himself told him so. While Newman wasn't a natural born liar, it was possible he had a sneaking suspicion his grandson wasn't squeaky clean and tried to protect him.

The mayor reached for the phone, then hesitated. "You're positive the kid is involved with drugs? Absolutely positive?"

I didn't blame him for the question. He and Newman probably had a long history of friendship, and he didn't want to damage their relationship. He also understood the desire to protect your family from their own actions. He did it himself, even though the consequences were horrible for his son in the long run.

"At the very least, he should be ruled out as a suspect," Andy told him. "If he is innocent, a DNA test will prove it. If not, well ..." He left his thought unspoken.

"I'll have to get a warrant for a DNA swab." He punched a button on his phone and asked his secretary to locate Judge Warner. I had no idea who this judge was, and I didn't care. The mayor was finally taking action, and he probably thought a DNA test would prove Thomas innocent. Andy was smart to throw the possibility out there.

Twenty minutes later, the mayor hung up his phone for the gazillionth time and nodded, satisfied. "Everything's in order. The warrant was issued and is being served as we speak. Since Thomas is still in the hospital, the test will be performed tonight." He glanced at his watch. "Nothing will happen until tomorrow when the labs open up, but we set the wheels of justice in motion." He sat back, pleased with himself.

I decided not to mention the tiny fact that if there was blood at the rape scene, Thomas could be in real trouble faster than anyone thought. A blood match is quicker than an actual DNA test, and I had a nasty suspicion the kid was guilty as hell. There was no need to throw any further gasoline on an already burning situation. The mayor took the correct steps, but I knew he wanted to salvage his friendship with Newman. Once the old guy realized his friend, the mayor, was behind the warrant there would be hell to pay.

The mayor looked around his office, smiling at each of us. "Is there anything further you need?"

Dad spoke first. "Sir, how well do you know Thomas?"

"Thomas?" The mayor frowned. "I've never met the boy."

Logan sighed. "You made decisions based on the word of an old friend, who also happens to donate to your campaign fund."

Jeez … I had no idea Logan kept up so well with politics.

The mayor looked confused. "He's also a colleague of sorts. Akron and Bath have many interests."

Logan nodded. "Political? Financial?"

The mayor nodded. "Sure."

"How many people realize Tom Newman donates money to you?" Dad asked.

The mayor's eyes opened wide, and I could see he was surprised by the question. He shook his head. "No idea. I don't discuss donors with many people. Sometimes, it pays not to let too many cats out of the bag."

I saw where Dad's line of questioning was headed, but the idiot across the desk from me was clueless.

"Mayor, Dad is trying to warn you. If it is discovered that Thomas is working for the Mendoza family, and dealing heroin out of his grandfather's cabin, it won't take long for the newspaper to figure out that Mr. Newman is a huge contributor to you." I nodded at the folder on his desk. "The dollar amount may not be much to you, but I'd bet it would be a lot to the voters, especially if the newspaper was against you for any reason. Facts can be colored quite well in newspaper articles. Add in that you've helped cover up a few crimes for the kid, and we're talking big trouble come the next election cycle."

The mayor's face turned snow white as he listened to my words. His mouth opened and shut about ten times before sound finally made it out of there. "You've got to be kidding! I had no idea the kid was involved with any drug stuff!"

I shook my head. How on earth did the man survive in politics for so long, especially while being so blind to his own stupidity?

"With a little luck, we could make this work in your favor," Bob said, rubbing a hand over his face.

"It'll take a hell of a lot more than luck," I snapped.

Bob shook his head. "Not really … give me a second to think."

We all sat quietly waiting for Bob's brain to get into gear. I watched his face, fascinated by his expressions as he worked out the problem. His lips moved silently as he talked himself through whatever steps his mind was moving through.

Finally, he snapped his fingers. "Got it!" He turned to the mayor. "It's simple. You help us solve this case, and the papers will declare you a hero of the city. They'll probably write a lot of mush about your dedication to crime prevention and so forth." Bob hesitated, and the frown appeared again. "How much do you piss off the people at the newspaper?"

Our local paper was located about two miles south of City Hall. It was the sole paper for the area, it was a staple for over a hundred years. While it reports news from around the world, the main focus is on local issues, including surrounding areas. Most stories are in-depth and researched carefully. The mayor needed to realize a nosey reporter could easily uncover damaging dirt if he didn't tread carefully with the Newman mess.

The mayor shrugged off Bob's question. "People don't always agree with every decision I make. A mayor isn't a king. I don't issue orders that are then carried out. Our city is basically a mini version of the federal and state governments. The council and I work together to make decisions that are in the best interest of the city."

I snorted. "Some of those decisions stink to high heaven."

He looked at me, surprised at my irritation. "I can't please everyone, and frankly I don't try to." He rearranged his bulky butt in his chair. "The cost of running a city the size of Akron is massive—schools, buses, road repairs, salaries … it adds up fast. This city, at one time, had a large industrial base. Granted, it wasn't as large as Cleveland or New York City, but for our size, the industrial complex was huge." He shook his head. "Those days are behind us. We are still fortunate to have many different industries here, but it has taken a lot of hard work to make that happen."

I scoffed. "With no thought about how your decisions affect surrounding communities."

He shook his head. "My job is to take care of *this* community. Sure … we make deals with the towns and cities around us … it's common practice. Not everyone is happy with certain arrangements. However, in the long run, most of those deals have compromises for both areas involved and are beneficial for everyone."

Logan cleared his throat. I turned to him, surprised. I never heard him make that particular sound before, but I realized he was trying to bring the conversation back to the case. "As fascinated as I'm sure Peg is with your political discussion, we need to have a plan." He turned to Bob and nodded.

Bob grinned. "You're going to love this!"

CHAPTER 26

Bob quickly outlined his plan. I wasn't totally sold on the chances of success, but Logan was satisfied.

"Admittedly, there is little room for mistakes. However, Bob's idea is basically sound, and it has the possibility of bringing the situation to a close with the least amount of danger for all parties involved." Logan began walking around the mayor's office, peering at family pictures collecting dust on the shelves, and inspecting the few knick-knacks placed around the room. I never saw him so uneasy before, and his uneasiness made my stomach knot.

My shoulder ached, but I decided to ignore it, which proved more difficult the longer I watched Logan mill around the mayor's office. What had gotten into my old Indian? I nudged Andy, and he nodded—Logan was making him nervous too ... not good.

I finally spoke up after a few moments of intense silence. "Bob's plan has enough holes in it to parachute through! Good grief, Logan ... Newman will have to agree to help, which means his grandson goes to prison. You honestly believe he'll go along?"

Logan stopped his meandering and turned to me. "Peg, he will have little choice. The boy involved himself with dangerous people, and Bob's plan offers him a measure of safety."

Bob watched Logan, waiting for the go ahead. Logan nodded, then Bob was gone with a poof.

Bob's sudden departure unsettled the mayor, causing him to look around uneasily. "Um … where did the guy go?" Sweat was beginning to form on the mayor's upper lip again.

I sighed. "You'll get used to it." I hated to admit it but seeing the moron's reaction to Bob's departure gave me a moment of satisfaction. He deserved to be rattled … he aided and abetted a snot-nosed, teenage criminal.

"I believe Peg and Andy have parts to play in the plan." Logan looked at both of us. "Trust things will work." He began fading. I opened my mouth to call him back, but he shook his head as his figure became invisible … jeez.

"You have a few details of your own to perform." I looked at the mayor as I stood to leave.

Andy joined me, and we made our way out of the office with our hands clutched together. I hoped we could trust the mayor would play his part, but it remained to be seen. If he was smart, he would see the advantages in going along with Bob's idea.

Dad accompanied us into the evening sunset, wisely keeping quiet until we reached the car. "Do you two need some time alone, or do you want an old guy to tag along for the ride home?" Even though his voice had a teasing tone, I heard the tension.

Andy spoke up before I could. "Sure, ride along if you want." As we made our way onto Main Street, Andy glanced in the rearview mirror. "Dave, do you think this will work?"

Dad smiled. "Never know till you try. I have to admit, Bob surprised me coming up with a plan … it's not his strong suit."

Andy sighed. "That's exactly why I'm worried. Logan seems to think it will work, though."

"Not necessarily," Dad cautioned. "I think Bob's plan was the only one on the table. Logan has been rather preoccupied lately. I'm not sure what's going on with him."

"Preoccupied? He isn't allowed to be preoccupied!" I snapped. "He better, damn well, get his head in the game because I don't need the next shot taken to actually kill me!" My shoulder was on fire, but I refused to acknowledge it. The last thing I needed was for Andy's focus to be on me rather than catching these creeps.

"Twinkle toes, Logan won't let that happen." I heard the worry in Dad's voice, even though he tried hard to disguise it.

"You should've kept the sling on your arm," Andy said quietly.

I frowned. "How'd you know it was bothering me?"

"Oh, Peg … I'm not stupid." He sighed, turning down our street.

I turned and looked out the window, hoping Andy would change the subject.

He must've taken the hint because the next thing he said had nothing to do with my shoulder. "Um … Peg? I think someone has been in the house again."

"What? How do you know?" My head swiveled around so fast I was surprised whiplash didn't nail me.

There was no need for Andy to answer. Cop cars were parked in the driveway, yard, and even around the back of the house. The lawn would never survive the cases I found myself involved in if the cops didn't learn a few manners.

Jack stood on the porch, barking orders at his officers. Dad skedaddled out of the car the second he saw the horde of cops roaming around our property. He went to stand next to Jack. Even the Indians, who usually resided in the woods in back of the house, were milling around the front yard. Andy and I sat silently, mouths open, watching the circus in front of us.

Finally, Andy looked at me. "What the hell?"

I shook my head as I opened the car door. "Only one way to find out."

I headed straight for Jack, but Bob popped up next to me. "You'll never guess in a million years who's been here?"

My eyebrows knit in confusion. "Who?"

"Guess." Bob's voice was filled with excitement.

My eyes narrowed, and I tasted a snotty remark making its way between my clenched teeth. Bob must've noticed because he quickly spoke. "Your mother!"

My stride faltered, and I stopped walking. As I turned to Bob, I saw Jack heading my way. "Now, Peg, don't get upset."

"Don't get upset? Bob said my mother was here, but her presence wouldn't have the entire police department wandering around our property!" I snapped.

Jack looked around, alarmed. "Your mother?" He was careful to keep his voice a low whisper.

Before I could answer, Sal and Amy came around the corner of the house. He had one arm around her, and she was talking nonstop. They saw me and made a beeline in my direction.

"What is going on?" I asked as soon as they got close enough to hear me.

Sal held up a hand. "It's going to be fine, Peg … I promise."

This was the second time someone told me to stay calm, which meant there was a huge reason to absolutely be upset.

"We've been trying to reach you. Why is your cellphone off?" Amy demanded.

I frowned. "It's not off. I never turn it off." I dug through my purse until I found it hiding in the corner, next to a pack of gum. I pulled the phone out of the dungeon it lived in and showed it to them. "See … it's on."

Andy grabbed the phone, and after a moment of looking through it, he looked at me. "Nine missed calls."

"What! Nine? How on earth could I miss nine calls?" I turned to Andy as I took my phone back. "You were with me the entire time. Did this phone ring?"

Andy shook his head. "Nope … and the ringer is on."

"Why the hell does this keep happening? Every time it's something important, I miss the damn call."

"I believe calls are being blocked from you at crucial times." Logan spoke up … when did he arrive?

"How could someone block a call?" I held out the phone so Logan could see the screen. "See here? The calls got through, but it didn't ring."

Logan studied the phone screen, intrigued. "Hmmm … interesting."

Sal looked at Andy. "Andy, why don't you come around to the back with me, so we can discuss the damage."

"Damage? What now?" I demanded.

"Peg, it really will be fine … eventually." Amy shifted from one foot to the other. I looked at her a moment, then stalked after Sal and Andy.

"Wait, Peg!" Amy called after me. I kept going. Whatever happened must be damn bad given the expressions on the police officers' faces as I passed them.

I turned the corner of the house and came to a halt. Every tree lining the woods was damaged—no wonder my Indian guards were milling around so upset. The small amount of patio furniture we owned was ruined, and pieces and parts were thrown around the yard. I decided I probably wasn't seeing the worst and continued to walk. Turning at the back side of the house, I saw my vegetable garden, well … what used to be my garden. Every tomato plant was pulled up and thrown in the yard. Bell peppers, asparagus, peas, beans … every single plant was pulled up and thrown across the lawn.

Andy stood facing the house. His mouth dropped open, and he was slowly shaking his head.

I made my way through the mess, and as I approached him, I turned to face the house myself. "Son of a bitch!" I yelled.

The entire back of the house had been sprayed with bullets and now sported dozens of bullet holes. Every window was shot out, and the garden hose was turned on full blast.

I turned to Sal. "Who?" It was the only word I could muster.

Sal turned and pointed to where two police officers held a kid, no older than sixteen or seventeen. His face was defiant and almost smug.

Sal grabbed my arm as I started toward the little brat. "Peg, let the cops deal with him."

"Who is he?" My chest was heaving as I fought for control of the tears trying to slide down my cheeks. I lost the battle, and Sal pulled me into a bear hug as I began sobbing. "Andy just had the window repaired … now look at it." I managed to speak between gasps of air. Not only was the new window shot out, but every window on the south side of the house … it was a mess.

"Once the crime scene photographers finish, I'll have my guys nail some plywood over the windows. The bullet holes are an easy fix … trust me. I'll take care of everything." Sal's voice penetrated my muddled emotions.

I nodded as I pulled myself together and made my way to Andy, who was, by this time, sitting on the ground from the sheer shock of the spectacle before us.

I sat next to him, sniffling. "Sal said he'd fix it for us."

Andy nodded but remained mute.

I sighed. "The windows won't be too difficult. We'll use the same guy in Richfield. He'll probably be glad for the business."

Another nod, but again, no words came out of Andy's mouth.

"I bet Sal owns a building company, and they can match the wood for the siding. I don't think a patch job will suffice … do you?" I was trying my hardest to get him to speak.

Andy shook his head, but still … no sound came out.

I looked up at Sal, worried. Andy's silence was beginning to scare the crap out of me. Was he in shock?

Sal cleared his throat. "We haven't been inside yet, but I'm sure any damage will be easy to fix."

I slumped against Andy. The interior was probably as big a mess as the exterior. Tears threatened again.

Andy grabbed my hand. "Peg … you could've been in the house. Those bullets could've ripped through you."

My mouth dropped open. The thought of injury to myself never entered my mind. I gave Andy a quick kiss on the cheek. "I wasn't in there."

Andy's jaw set stubbornly. "You could have been."

I cocked my head and studied his face a moment. He wouldn't meet my eyes, and I knew fear controlled him. I wasn't afraid … I was damn mad. "Yep … I could've been standing in the kitchen. I could've been shot the last time the jerk fired shots at the house. I could've gotten into a wreck on the way home from the grocery store the other day. A plane could fall out of the sky and land on my head."

The last scenario finally grabbed his attention. "A plane?"

I smiled slightly. "It does happen occasionally." I shook my head as I continued. "Andy … I'm not backing down because a snot-nosed teenager hooked up with the Mendoza family and tried to kill me. I'm not quitting my job and living in fear of every bad guy out there. What we do *is* important, and you are well aware of that."

Andy sighed. "I knew you'd say that."

"Tough beans … we're in this together. Adam will be here in a few days, so we have a lot of work to do."

Andy looked surprised. "You're usually the one who ends up crazy about this type of stuff. Why so tough now?"

I surveyed the carnage a few moments. "Because I'm furious. Anger gets my butt in gear, I guess." I looked up at Sal. "How long do you think it will take to fix this mess?"

Sal shook his head. "No idea until I've seen the interior. It probably won't be totally finished by the time Adam and his gal arrive, but it will certainly look better than it does now."

Jack joined the group while I was talking with Andy. I glanced at him. "When are we allowed to go inside?"

"Won't be long now … the guys are almost finished."

I nodded. Standing, I started toward the woods. Might as well see if the trees are damaged beyond help. I noticed my Indian guys found their way back to the woods and stood huddled around Logan, who was earnestly talking with them.

I stopped a few paces away, trying to give them some privacy until Logan finished his speech. I couldn't tell if there was trouble brewing with the guys or if Logan was giving a pep talk.

A few minutes later, Logan stepped away from the group and came to stand next to me. "I am truly sorry about the damage to the house."

I nodded. "Sal's going to help with the exterior. Not sure what needs to be done inside."

Logan winced. "I have inspected the interior. I am sure Salvatorio's men will have ideas."

Have ideas? I must be facing a real catastrophe inside.

I sighed. "Andy's pretty upset."

Logan nodded. "I understand his concern."

I scowled. "I'm pissed."

Another nod from Logan. "I am not surprised."

"I'm not quitting."

Silence from Logan.

"I'm serious."

He sighed. "Thank you."

"This isn't about you." I hesitated before I continued. "Not sure I can explain it very well, but this …" I waved a hand at the house. "… is unacceptable. There's a quote I've heard. 'The only thing for the triumph of evil is for good men to do nothing'."

Logan nodded. "Yes, I am familiar with those words."

I looked down at the ground, then up at Logan's face. "I refuse to do nothing."

Logan stared into my eyes for a moment, then nodded.

I pointed to the woods. "The guys going to be ok? They seemed pretty upset when I first arrived."

"Yes. The trees are important to them. They will work to heal the damage."

"They can fix them?" I was a little shocked.

"Possibly."

"Wow."

"Yes." He smiled.

"Peg!" Jack yelled.

I glanced at Logan, returning his smile. "Talk later?"

"Yes."

I nodded and headed over to Jack. "The guys are finished. You and Andy can enter the house now."

I took a deep breath and smiled. I reached for Andy's hand. "Come on … let's see how much work Sal's men have to do."

As we opened the back door, I closed my eyes. Once I got my nerves under control, I stepped inside and began inspecting the damage. The kitchen was a mess. Glass from the windows was everywhere, and there was a bullet hole in the refrigerator. I inspected every cabinet, then stood back. "No new bullet holes in the cabinets. How'd the little turd manage that?"

Andy walked through to the den, and I followed slowly, my eyes searching for damage. They didn't have to work too hard to find holes, since there were enough to allow the approaching night air to flow freely into the house. Bugs would follow, I thought, slightly annoyed—I hate bugs.

The den was a mess. Andy's favorite chair was shot to smithereens, and glass from the destroyed windows covered the floor. Henry paced through the room like a cat on hot coals.

I forced a smile. "Hey, Henry … you ok?"

"I've been worried sick about ya'll." He looked around the room. "I couldn't stop him. I alerted everyone I could think of but …" His voice trailed off.

"It's not your fault," Andy said as he walked around the room. He shook his head as he ran his hand over his comfy chair.

"It can be replaced," I said gently.

Andy nodded and continued his inspection. "TV's shot."

I nodded. "Yep. Insurance will probably cover most of this mess."

He nodded.

I made my way back to Adam's bedroom. Jeez Louise … what a mess.

"Good thing Floyd didn't start work yet," Henry said from the doorway.

I sighed. "Guess I'd better call and warn him."

"No need, I scooted over and let him know what was facing him. He should be here soon to evaluate the mess."

"Gee, thanks, Henry. I really appreciate your thoughtfulness." The shakes wanted to take hold of me, but I fought them back. The last thing I needed was to fall apart—I had too much to accomplish.

"No problem." He sighed, shaking his head. "About the only way I could actually help."

We hadn't moved the bunk bed out of the room yet, so I sat on the bottom bunk. I leaned my head against the bedpost as my eyes wandered over the room. Glass littered the floor, so I was grateful the carpet was being ripped out soon. It takes a powerful vacuum cleaner to suck up glass shards. I looked over to where the window should've been and shook my head. The night air was pouring in. I grinned at Henry. "At least this room was being torn apart anyway."

He grinned back. "Good attitude."

I shrugged but didn't reply. I slowly stood. "I'm heading back to the kitchen for a cup of coffee." A thought struck fear into my heart. "My coffee machine is still working … isn't it?"

He shook his head. "No idea."

I hurried to the kitchen, and I was relieved to find my lovely coffee maker in fine shape. It seemed to be the only survivor of the slaughter. Thankfully, I brewed myself a cup of my favorite elixir. Brushing glass off my chair, I sat at the kitchen table and pulled a pad of paper out of the rubble—time to start a list.

CHAPTER 27

Pain in my shoulder woke me up the next morning. I snuggled deeper into the comfy bed, deciding more sleep sounded great. I stretched out, realizing the bed wasn't mine. Frowning, I looked around the room slightly confused. The memories flooded back ... we were staying with Sal until our house was cleaned, and the windows were installed. I heard familiar singing in the shower, so I knew my sweetie was in the adjoining bathroom. I wiggled in the bed, enjoying the luxurious feel of a down comforter and pillow-top mattress ... heaven.

Andy walked in from the bathroom. "Hey, sleepy head. It's about time you woke up."

I sighed. "What time is it?"

"Past eight. I'm heading to the office after breakfast."

"You aren't taking the day off?" I asked, eyeing him. "You sure seem better than last night."

Shaking his head, he laughed. "Peg, I can't take off every day to solve your crimes." He stopped and took a deep breath. "I did a lot of thinking and decided you were right. We have to keep fighting the evil, or we are part of the problem and not part of the solution."

I nodded but didn't add anything to his statement. "I have a feeling Logan wants a meeting today."

Andy shrugged. "If he gets here before I leave … fine. Otherwise … I'm headed to work."

Andy tossed me a thick robe I'd never seen before. "Amy brought this up earlier. She knew you forgot yours."

I ran my hand over the robe's thick material. "Wow."

Andy grinned. "All cotton … Amy made sure she pointed that out to me."

I returned his grin and slipped the fabulous robe on, then made my way to the bathroom for my morning routine. Once accomplished, I headed downstairs to the kitchen. I could smell Sal's expensive coffee all the way upstairs and my mouth watered in anticipation.

I heard conversation as I entered the kitchen. I stopped cold in my tracks when I saw Logan standing next to the window. What was it with the Indian that he always needed to be close to a window?

I continued into the kitchen. "I need coffee before any type of meeting."

Logan smiled. "I am aware of your rules."

Sal smiled. "Take your coffee out on the back porch, and I'll bring your breakfast to you."

I nodded. "Sounds good, but don't bother with food … I need coffee first."

"Gotcha. Let me know." He handed me a cup of his special blended coffee.

Once I settled outside, I enjoyed the morning sounds—birds talking, faint conversation from indoors, and somewhere I heard a child's voice. Ah … Caterina must be here, I thought.

"Morning, Peg." Laura came into view. "I heard about the house. I'm sorry."

"Hi, Laura. How've you been?"

She smiled. "Good … peaceful."

I nodded, sipping my coffee. I liked Laura, but not enough to ruin my coffee routine. She continued walking past me, into the house. Someone must've warned her that I'm not nice before my needed amount of caffeine. I rested my head back against the lounge chair and sighed—this was heaven.

I felt a presence next to me and decided to ignore whoever was stupid enough to show up while I was drinking my first cup. I took another sip of coffee, refusing to turn my head. I heard Caterina's laughter as Sal teased her, and I smiled at the sound of her happiness. The girl experienced enough pain in her young life, so I was glad she was now at ease and happy.

Sal made his way toward me with a fresh cup. He placed it in front of me, and silently removed my empty one. He left without uttering one word. I appreciated his kindness. I felt better once the caffeine began to work its magic, and my muscles and bones began to wake—some moaned while others screamed at me. My shoulder ached, but it was much better than yesterday. Maybe the shock of seeing our house partially destroyed eased the pain somehow ... who knew?

I still sensed someone close by, quietly waiting. I knew of only one person who had enough patience to outwait my routine.

"Well, Logan, is the case wrapped up?" I spoke without turning my head.

"Almost. Jack worked all night," he answered quietly.

"He must be exhausted."

"There is much determination in Jack. He kept Mr. Newman up with him. I suspect there is a touch of satisfaction that the gentleman had to survive the night with Jack."

I laughed out loud. "Serves him right for having the mayor cover up for his grandson."

"There is much to be said for your opinion."

We sat a while longer, enjoying the peace and quiet. Sal brought out another cup of steaming coffee, along with a plate of fresh fruit and a blueberry muffin.

I smiled at him. "You'll spoil me."

"They are freshly made muffins. Have all you want." He grinned, nodded to Logan, then left us alone.

I glanced at Logan. "Anything on your mind?"

He sighed. "Your mother."

My stomach knotted. "What about her?"

"She did not escape our hold."

I frowned. "Bob mentioned she showed up at the house."

"Yes. Her *essence* was there but not *her*."

Uh-oh ... this didn't sound good. I wasn't sure what to say, so I kept quiet—might as well let Logan explain in his own time.

A few minutes passed before Logan spoke again. "She has gained more abilities than I was aware she had access to. It is troubling."

"Yes, I agree. The last thing we need is Mom gaining strength."

He nodded. "Correct."

"Can anything be done to diminish her powers?" I was trying to keep calm.

He shook his head. "No."

Nothing like a straight answer. There was no trying to soften the blow at all with Logan.

I took another sip of coffee, then nibbled at the muffin. Gosh ... it was delicious. I focused on eating for a few minutes, and Logan remained quiet.

I popped the last bite of Sal's muffin into my mouth, then turned to Logan. "When you say her 'essence' what do you mean exactly?"

Logan hesitated. "This is difficult to explain, but I will try. We are spiritual beings even while alive."

I nodded … good so far.

"We have our spirit and our soul. While they are woven together in many ways, they are also separate."

I frowned slightly. "Which is our mind associated with?"

His face showed surprise. "You understand my explanation?"

"Yep. I'll let you know when I'm lost." Gosh … I'm not a moron.

"Well, the mind is part of both. It is complicated."

I shrugged. "Just about everything is when you're involved."

He smiled and shook his head. "To continue … we have your mother safely locked away. However, yesterday she was able to send her essence to your house."

I thought about his words a few moments. "How much power does this essence have?"

"Thankfully, very little while away from your mother. Enough to frighten you if you had seen her."

I nodded. "True. I would've assumed it *was* Mom."

"Exactly. Which was her goal."

I drummed my fingers on the rim of my cup. "She wanted to scare me. Why?"

He shook his head. "At this point, an answer would be little more than a guess."

I sighed. "Let's hear your guess."

"Nell enjoys confusing people and situations. It brings her immense joy. This time, I believe her goal was to frighten you to the point that you would not help us any longer."

I scoffed. "Didn't work."

Logan smiled. "No."

I drained my coffee cup and stood. "Let's get on with the meeting. Andy wants to go to work."

He gave a brief nod. "Yes."

We walked into the kitchen together. I went to sit next to Andy, and Logan returned to the window. I noticed Bob and Dad joined our party, and I smiled at them both.

"Thank you for your work concerning the drug case. It has been solved, and I realize you must be interested in hearing the information we discovered."

Everyone nodded.

The back door opened, and Jack slipped in to join us. "Sorry, I'm late." He looked tired, and I swear there was even more gray in his hair than there was a week ago.

Sal began pouring a fresh cup of coffee for Jack, but Jack's eyes found the plate of muffins. Sal laughed and handed them over with the coffee.

"The mayor did as he was asked," Logan started.

I was surprised to hear this. "So, he did call Newman and apply pressure … good for him. I wasn't sure he would follow through."

The only part of Bob's plan that we were able to perform was the mayor's role. He was instructed to place a call to Tom Newman with a mild threat of reopening the rape case if the old guy didn't help nail his grandson on the drug charges. I didn't trust the mayor, but he stayed true to his word. He must be scared spitless of Logan to risk losing Newman's campaign donations.

Logan nodded. "His part was important, and the call had the desired effect. Mr. Newman still does not realize the depth of his grandson's illegal activity, but he will soon become aware of his misplaced faith in the boy."

"He was selling heroin to the kids at the high school! I finally got the little shit's confession," Jack said before he finished off his first muffin.

"Wow … how'd you manage to get him to confess?" I had to admit … I was shocked.

Jack reached for another muffin. "Tom Newman told him about the rape case. So … in a way … the mayor was responsible for that part of the plan working." Jack nodded to Bob who blushed furiously.

Andy shook his head in disbelief. "Doesn't the kid realize he's in big trouble?"

Jack scoffed. "You wouldn't believe the arrogance of this kid. He actually believes he won't be in much trouble."

"Will he be charged with the rape?" Amy spoke for the first time.

Jack shook his head. "Not at this time." Jack sunk his teeth into another muffin.

"What!" Amy was practically shouting. "The poor girl!"

Logan held up a hand to quiet Amy. "I will take care of the girl. She will heal."

Amy nodded, knowing Logan's healing would be better than a trial, which could only be embarrassing and probably cause more pain for the poor girl. Logan could not only heal a body, but he could soothe a soul. I trusted he would be true to his word.

I looked at Logan. "So, the Mendoza family will be caught, and the area will be rid of them?"

Logan looked at Sal, and Sal cleared his throat. "The Mendoza family was only one of the problems. They have kids from every high school in the county working for them. It's a wonder we didn't have dead teenagers all over the area."

I was a little disappointed. "So … we still have to deal with the Mendoza family? Won't they just hire others to peddle the heroin?"

Sal grinned. "The drug cartels hate the family." He shrugged. "It was easy to put the word out that they've been working around here. I doubt there will be much left of the Mendoza family in the coming months. It's not pretty, but it works."

I moaned. "Sal, then the drug cartels will move in … that's not a solution."

Logan stepped in before Sal could speak. "They will wisely back away from this area, for a while at least. They are logical businessmen, and they will want the heroin that is on the streets now to clear out. It will take time, but the heroin will dissipate eventually with the suppliers gone. I trust the large drug cartels will watch and wait. While they are being cautious, I will be working."

"Fine, but I guarantee drugs aren't out of the picture."

Logan smiled at Amy. "True. We do the best we can."

"What type of trouble is Tom Newman in?" Andy asked. "It was his property the drugs were stored on."

Jack shook his head. "Yeah … but he had no clue. I don't like the guy, but he isn't involved with drugs. He was horrified when I showed him his own cabin filled with the stuff. I thought he'd have a heart attack on the spot."

Amy smiled slightly. "Maybe he'll change his attitude toward the police department."

Jack laughed. "Doubt it." He reached for another muffin—the man's waist would never be the same.

Andy frowned slightly. "Who took shots at Peg that day in the kitchen?"

"Same kid who shot up the back of the house." Jack shrugged. "He was bragging about being trained by someone in the Mendoza gang." He shook his head. "I still can't get over the fact that they don't understand how much trouble they are in. His fingerprints, along with Thomas's, are all over the cabin. They honestly think a good lawyer will get them off. Plus, they confessed!"

Andy shook his head. "How have we gotten to this point where kids don't understand the consequences of their actions?"

Logan looked at Andy. "If enough people ignore the evil they see around them, evil prevails. It only takes a few fighting against it for evil to be forced back, if only for a short time. A friend of mine recently reminded me of this." He smiled at me.

Wow … Logan called me a friend. Tears formed, but I blinked them away. I smiled. "Well, I guess this means I can quit gun training."

Sal shook his head. "Nope … if anything, this case convinces me you and Amy need to be trained and armed when working."

Jack choked on his muffin. "Sal!" The shock was evident on his face.

Sal cut him off. "No arguing, Jack. These gals need to protect themselves. I'll have the boys work with them until I'm happy with the results." Sal crossed his arms over his chest.

Jack sighed and nodded.

"I want to thank each of you for your work. I realize Peg and Andy have much damage to their home. Sal assured me it will be taken care of quickly." Logan smiled at us. "I also understand Adam will be home in a few days. Henry will stay until the work is done."

I frowned, slightly confused. "Henry? Why should he stay?"

Logan shrugged. "He told me he did not want anyone to 'steal you blind'. I am not exactly sure what he was referring to, but he was determined. He will be needed elsewhere once your home is back to normal."

I laughed, and Andy grinned.

I stood. "I'm off to get dressed."

Andy also stood. "I've got to get to the office. If Henry's watching the work on the house, I don't need to swing by there before I leave."

Sal scowled. "These are my men we're talking about. They work hard, and they are good at what they do."

"Henry doesn't know you," I said as I sailed past him. "He only knows he doesn't want anyone to slack on the job."

Andy kissed me goodbye, then I headed up the stairs to get dressed.

I was brushing my teeth when I heard a pop behind me. Jeez ... who now?

Turning, I saw Nana smiling as she looked around the bedroom.

"Wow ... this place is really classy." She walked around inspecting the sheets, bedspread, curtains, furniture, and even the carpet. "No expense was spared."

"It is nice. Sal was sweet to let us stay here while his men fix the house."

She nodded. "I went by the house earlier. What a mess! I couldn't believe how many bullet holes there were."

I sighed. "Yep. The kitchen took the brunt for some reason. I felt horrible for Andy ... the den was his pride and joy."

Nana waved her hand dismissively. "He'll get over it once the new furniture is in there. Plus, I think he's secretly thrilled the kitchen is finally getting redone. The fridge took a few bullets, and even your oven is shot to pieces. The kid did a number on it for sure."

"The walls are fine, so the wallpaper stays," I said firmly.

"For Pete's sake, Peg. Get it totally overhauled."

"I like the wallpaper, so it stays." I could be stubborn.

"How's your shoulder?" Nana decided a change of subject was the best course of action.

"Better. I've felt better the past week than I have for ages. I think this menopause crap is finally coming to an end."

She raised an eyebrow. "What on earth makes you think your

menopause is over?"

I watched her, surprised at her question. "Because ... the hot flashes have almost totally disappeared, and the night sweats aren't nearly as bad as they were. It must be the end ... and good riddance."

"Oh, sweetie. You haven't even hit the midpoint yet." Her tone was sympathetic, making me a little uneasy.

I slowly turned to face her. "Nana, what do you mean?"

"Honey, menopause is a *process*. It ebbs and flows. A few months of hell, a few months of not so bad, then a few months of hardly any symptoms. Then the entire process begins again until all the hormones are basically gone."

I put a hand on the wall for support, but it didn't work. I slid to the floor. I sat there for a few minutes, then looked up at her. "You're kidding, right?"

Her laughter filled the room. "Oh, sweetie ... you'll survive."

As I watched her fade, her laughter continued to bounce off the walls ... jeez Louise.

SNEAK PEAK
BOOK 4
(NO TITLE YET)

Chapter 1

Finishing my required third cup of coffee, I surveyed my kitchen. During the last big case I worked for our township police department, the kitchen was shot to pieces by a drug dealing teenager. He, along with a friend of his, was mixed up with a nasty South American mob family by the name of Mendoza. Lucky for him the cops nabbed him before the mobsters got their hands on the little jerk. He made the mistake of bragging to his friend, within earshot of others, about shooting me in the shoulder.

Our kitchen needed a facelift, but I would've rather had time to plan the remodel instead of rushing through the process under those circumstances. I did enjoy our new, updated refrigerator and oven, so I was secretly glad I was finally pushed into making the changes. I was known for dragging my feet when any type of change was involved.

My husband, Andy, and I live in a small township northwest of Akron, Ohio. Once the 'Tire Capital of the World' due to both Firestone and Goodyear Tire Companies being located downtown, Akron is the largest city near us. Cleveland is about thirty-five miles north, and it sits on the southern shore of Lake Erie, one of the Great Lakes. It is home to the Rock and Roll Hall of Fame and the famous Cleveland Clinic. I know the city has a couple of sports teams, but I never bothered to pay attention to them.

Bath, our township, has been around since the late 1700s and at one time, it was home to wildlife and Indians. Some of those same Indians now reside in the woods at the back of our property—my life is complicated.

Our nearest neighbor, Amy Branch, is a retired high school science teacher. Together, we are consultants for the Bath Police Department. Most cases we work are simple and quick to solve. There have been a few that have been problematic, dangerous, and a pain in the butt. Amy uses logic to help with our work, while I usually depend on gut instinct. Deciding which method is more productive is a toss-up. We have agreed the combination of the two techniques is the reason for our impressive success rate. So far, we've batted one hundred percent, but I refuse to become cocky—it only takes one stinker of a case to ruin a perfect batting average.

Our immediate boss is the chief of police, Jack Monroe. The past few cases added gray to his hair and inches to his waistline. He tends to eat pie when the stress level climbs—I should buy stock in pie companies. He and his wife, Lori, along with Andy and I, sweated together through our kids' school years, but now we were safely on the other side of parenting. Andy and I have four boys who live scattered throughout the country. Our oldest, Adam, recently became engaged, and I was still hard at work accepting the fact I would soon become a mother-in-law. I try not to think about it ... much.

"Hey Peg! How's your morning?" Bob asked happily.

Bob ... is ... um ... a dead guy we work with while solving cases. He was actually the first case I worked for the police. He and his horrible wife, Elaine, were murdered in their bed. Turned out the culprit was on the police force, and Jack came close to having a meltdown once the guy was discovered—it wasn't pretty.

A few months ago, for some strange reason—which I blame on menopause—I suddenly acquired the ability to communicate with dead people. My Nana was the first to arrive, followed by Bob and Elaine. Bob, by now, was well aware of my three cup, morning coffee rule and followed it to the best of his ability. While he is irritating as all get out, I have a soft spot for him, but I make sure he remains clueless to the fact.

"Fine. What brings you around so early? Haven't seen you for a few weeks."

"I wanted to see how the kitchen turned out." He inspected the new appliances, nodding. "Looks pretty good. The oven sure is nicer than the old clunker you had." Bob usually looked like he just crawled out of bed. His dark hair was always in need of a haircut, he was disheveled, and wrinkled from head to toe. He'd been working on his appearance lately. My dad had given him a few pointers, which he obviously ignored today.

I narrowed my eyes. "There was nothing wrong with the other oven. A little outdated ... maybe, but it worked fine."

"Yeah, yeah ... you hate change, but even *you* have to admit the kitchen looks tons better." Bob doesn't necessarily understand the concept of 'tact'.

"What have you been doing lately?" I asked mostly out of curiosity. Deadsville was still a mystery to us, and the little bits of information we picked up during cases was fascinating, especially to Andy. He loved hearing tidbits about the other side of life—I was usually irritated by what I heard.

"I joined a few clubs. I'm so excited to finally have a social life," Bob beamed. "Elaine wouldn't allow much socializing even when we were alive. Dead? No way!"

When we learned there were clubs, gatherings, parties, meetings, and jobs to do in the afterlife, I wasn't a happy camper. I wanted peace, quiet, and gold streets. Andy was intrigued and loved to learn as much as possible.

I decided the less I knew, the better. I don't want to *work* or go to *meetings* over there ... I want rest.

The phone rang catching my attention.

Bob smiled smugly. "It's Amy."

His abilities have increased amazingly since we first met. I couldn't decide if it was a good thing or not. He was proud of the fact, and he loved showing me how many new skills he had acquired—some were a tad creepy.

Amy's voice came on the line when I picked up. "Peg? I'm thinking of going to an extra class today. Want to come with me?"

I hesitated, caught off guard by her question. Was she out of her mind? "Um, no ... thanks."

"Now Peg, you know the more we practice the better we'll become."

A few months back, Amy decided we needed self-defense classes. I hated them; she loved them. I still couldn't figure out how an eighty-something-year-old woman could beat the snot out of me each and every class. It took me a while to get comfortable with actually fighting back for fear of hurting her, even though I was the one bruised from head to toe. Even after I started defending myself against her, I lost battles and found myself on the ground staring at the ceiling more often than not. The guys who own the studio, where we take classes, enjoy watching the two of us spar. They get a kick out of Amy while I get kicked *by* Amy.

I glanced at Bob. "I have company."

"Oh ... I'm sorry ... it's so early for you."

"No problem. Maybe next time." I decided to ignore her 'early' comment. This time of the morning would be early for anyone.

She quickly changed the subject. "Bob was by earlier. I think he's a bit bored. I wouldn't be surprised if he shows up at your house soon."

I felt an eyebrow rise as I looked at Bob. "Thanks for the warning. Enjoy your class." I hung up the phone as I continued watching Bob. "You've already been to Amy's this morning? Jeez, Bob ... it's a little early don't you think?"

He waved a hand. "Amy gets up with the birds. Plus, she doesn't have a coffee rule."

My three-cup rule was known by everyone associated with me. It literally takes three full cups of hot coffee to wake up all my pieces and parts—aging sucks.

I shook my head as I rinsed my cup out and put it on the drainer to dry. Andy tried to talk me into a dishwasher while we were updating the kitchen, but I refused. I'd been washing dishes by hand since we moved into this house, and I saw no reason not to continue the practice. There was only the two of us, and it seemed like such a waste of money to install a dishwasher at this stage of our life.

The phone rang again, and I looked at Bob, but his attention was on the woods out back.

"Have you checked on your Indian pals?" Jack's voice boomed at me.

I threw my head back and sighed. "Why?"

"We have trouble."

The group of Indians who resided in my woods had been dead and gone for a long time. They were part of my protection team, so if I could detect them, we were in trouble. Depending on their level of agitation, I could gauge how bad the situation had become. I took a deep breath and turned toward the window. I gritted my teeth when I saw them milling around as they looked at the house—not good.

I turned my attention back to Jack. "What's the problem?"

Jack hesitated before speaking. "So you can see the guys?"

"Yep. They're not too upset, but they're definitely irritated for some reason."

"Damn. I'm coming over."

"Jack! I'm not even dressed yet. Can't this wait?"

He sighed heavily. "I'll give you half an hour to get dressed. Do you have any pie?"

I rolled my eyes … jeez. "You're gaining weight and don't need pie!" I snapped.

"I've lost a pound on the diet Lori stuck me on, and I'm starving." He actually managed to sound hurt.

I sighed. "Fine. I'll see you in a few minutes but give me the entire half hour." I hung up the phone and looked at Bob. "You have any idea what's going on?"

His face creased with worry, but he shook his head. "Nope. I really only came by for a visit. What'd Jack say?"

"Nothing actually. He'll be here soon, so I need to get dressed." I turned and headed for the bedroom.

"I'll keep an eye out," Bob called after me.

Once I was dressed, with teeth brushed and all, I ran my fingers through my stick straight hair, deciding I might need a cut soon. While Amy's gray hair was wildly curly, mine was the opposite. I quickly slapped a little mascara on my lashes, and decided it was enough—a full face of makeup was not needed for a morning meeting with Jack. I stepped back from the mirror and surveyed my image. I stand an inch over five feet tall in stocking feet. I dye my hair because I can't stand the mousy brown it turned years ago. I also have to acknowledge the extra inches around my waistline—four pregnancies didn't help my girlish figure much. I sighed as I gave up the inspection and returned to Bob.

Bob looked over at me as soon as I entered the kitchen. "Do you think I should tell Logan?"

Logan was a dead Indian who happened to be Bob's boss. He lived a long time ago, but since he wouldn't give any information about his life on earth, no one had any idea when or where he lived while he was here. Through the hierarchy on the heavenly side, Logan was given the task of keeping evil at bay on both sides of life. He gave out very little information; usually, only when circumstances became dire and my life was in danger. He played his cards tight to his chest, if he played them at all.

I shook my head. "Let's see what Jack has to say first."

Bob nodded, a look of worry still on his face.

"It's probably local crime and has nothing to do with Logan's 'big picture'." I tried to reassure him, but I wasn't sure how much good it would do.

Logan loved the *big picture*, and I wanted to scream every time he started lecturing about it. Good versus evil was an old story, but Logan had been fighting the good fight for centuries. Amy chewed his butt during our last big case, and I hoped she taught him a thing or two. He hated divulging any type of knowledge for fear of giving the dark side a speck of material to hold over our heads. Logan could be a real pain in the butt.

Jack knocked on the back door before I had a chance to grab the pie out of the fridge. I used to hide the pie, thinking the refrigerator was the perfect spot, but Jack sniffed it out during our first case. I decided it wasn't worth the bother to find a new spot to stash the darn things.

I opened the door. "What's up?" I didn't like his expression, but I kept my thoughts to myself.

"Break-ins … all over the damn township." He plopped his butt at the kitchen table and shook his head. "I usually wouldn't be upset, but the amount of homes being broken into is making me nervous."

I frowned. "Could it be kids? School started a few weeks ago, but I'm sure teenagers can make time for mischief."

He shook his head again. "That's exactly what I thought when it all started. We've been staking out various areas where we think they may strike next, but no luck. A couple of my officers have kept their eyes on the usual troublemakers, but nothing came of it."

I jerked my thumb toward the woods. "Something has the guys upset. Are you sure it's the break-ins?"

Jack shrugged, his frustration evident. "Have you talked to Logan lately?"

"Nope. I haven't seen him since the Mendoza mess was cleaned up."

Jack stared at me in shock. "You're kidding!"

I frowned. "No. Logan doesn't make social calls." I glanced at Bob who had the grace to blush.

Jack turned his attention to Bob. "Have you heard anything at all?" A couple months back, Jack was given the ability to see my dead folks. He was glad to be included in the small circle of people with the capability.

Bob shook his head. "Sorry, Jack … I dropped by to see the new kitchen."

Jack looked around and nodded. "Looking good." He focused on the flooring. "I didn't know you were replacing the floor."

"Andy decided we might as well take care of the floor while we were moving the heavy appliances. I have to admit the old linoleum had seen better days."

Bob snorted. "That's an understatement."

I shot him a glance but kept my mouth shut. It was too early in the morning to start an argument with someone who could fade away if the discussion became too heated.

Jack's eyes strayed in the direction of the fridge, and I laughed. "Don't you think it's a little early for pie?"

He turned his attention back to me. "I haven't had time to eat breakfast, so pie sounds pretty good about now."

Grinning, I grabbed a plate, then retrieved the pie from the refrigerator.

"Make it a good size," Jack instructed. "Last time, you cut a skinny piece."

"Make sure Lori doesn't blame me for the fact that you're cheating to high heaven on your diet."

"Are you kidding? I'm not about to tell her I had pie for breakfast … she'd skin me alive."

I shook my head in amusement as I placed the pie in front of him. "I'll make you some coffee."

One of my cherished small appliances was my one-cup-at-a-time coffee brewer. The little pod thingies could get expensive, but it was worth having a fresh brewed cup each time I wanted my favorite beverage.

After placing the cup next to Jack, I found myself peering toward the woods again. The Indians who lived there guarded the property for Logan and alerted him if there were problems. We had a few mistakes along the way, until Logan made sure they understood any intruders inside or outside were cause to contact him immediately. The arrangement worked pretty well, and I felt more secure knowing they prowled the woods between Amy's and our property.

Jack noticed the direction of my gaze. "Increased activity?"

I shook my head. "I'd feel a lot better if I couldn't see them at all."

Amy saw them all the time; I only saw them when trouble was brewing. Watching them mill around was disconcerting. I decided to take the advice I was given during the last case, so I headed toward the door.

Jack's eyes widened with concern as he swallowed a mouthful of pie. "Whoa! Where are you going?"

"I'll be right back." I made my way across the yard, irritated I forgot to change into sneakers. The morning dew was soaking my feet through my comfy slippers as I approached the small tribe. "What's up guys?"

Startled by my appearance and question, they looked at one another not quite sure what to do.

"I can see you, which tells me there's a problem. Trouble is ... I have no idea what's going on, but maybe you do." My foot started patting the ground as I felt my anxiety growing.

One of the men took a step forward. "You have never approached us before."

"Nope. Decided it was time to take the bull by the horns and discover information for myself."

He looked back at his friends nervously. Maybe they had orders never to talk with me. I might be breaking some sort of code of honor or trust Logan had in them, but I didn't care. If Logan wasn't going to show up and explain why I could see them, then I had every right to question them myself.

The man in front of me hesitated before he made up his mind. "There is a problem in the township. Many structures are being vandalized and items are being stolen."

I nodded. "Jack told me. It doesn't explain why you guys ..." I waved my arm in the direction of the woods. "... are so upset."

He glanced back at his friends, then looked back at me. "There must be a reason we are so unsettled. I believe the problem to be the people who are robbing structures." He paused as he thought a moment. "Whoever is involved is not local."

My eyes widened. "They're not kids from around here?"

He shook his head. "No."

"Where are they from?" I pressed—Jack would be interested to hear this bit of news.

The Indian shook his head. "Someone is behind the activity." He frowned. "We cannot see who ... it is hazy."

"Hazy? What's hazy?" The conversation was becoming confusing to me.

He sighed. "I am sure Logan has explained we do not know everything."

I nodded. I was aware my dead friends didn't have all the facts, but that didn't mean I had to like it.

"There are many times the truth is hidden from our view. Even we did not know your police friend would try to harm you."

Owen had been on the police force and was even the town hero in many aspects. Too bad it turned out he was a sociopath who was murdering people throughout northeast Ohio for over a decade. I learned the truth at the last moment, and I came darn close to being slit open by his knife in my own backyard.

I shook my head, trying to clear it. "Thanks anyway."

The Indian nodded and turned to join his friends.

I trudged back to the house. Bob was nervously pacing back and forth on the back porch.

Jack had joined him, and they were watching my encounter with the Indians.

"Well? Do they know anything?" Jack demanded.

I shook my head. "Nope. Other than the fact that it isn't kids breaking into houses, they have no idea who the culprit is. He said something about it being hazy."

Jack frowned. "Hazy?"

"Yeah. I bet whoever is behind this has some connection to the afterlife."

A look of annoyance flashed across Jack's face. "Shit ... another damn case where the bad guys have as much access to the dead as we do."

"Not necessarily. Remember Mom told me the criminals had no idea the dead were helping them," I reminded him. My mom should know since she was one of the culprits when it came to helping out bad guys.

He ran his hand through his graying hair, then turned to Bob. "How hard would it be for you to nose around and see if you can spot the jerks robbing houses?"

Bob rubbed his chin, deep in thought. "Not sure, but I could give it a go." He glanced at Jack. "You can't tell Logan though. Last time, there was a real stink when I helped you."

Jack held up a hand. "Promise ... I won't let it slip this time."

During our last case, Jack 'borrowed' Bob to do a little spying for him without notifying Logan. Since Bob basically works for Logan, the situation caused some friction between the two men.

I sighed. "Why don't you just tell Logan. He'd understand."

Jack scowled. "Ha! He likes being in charge."

I shook my head as I made my way inside. I didn't want to be a part of their schemes. I knew a headache was just around the corner.

www.ingramcontent.com/pod-product-compliance
Lightning Source LLC
Chambersburg PA
CBHW070448120726
47910CB00003B/976